For
Nancy + Fred ~

Such good friends, five
wonderful years in the making.
Here's to memories of covered bridges,
quaint villages, colorful trees... and whatever
chorus of "Nancy," it was we were supposed
to skip!

Much love,
Your friend,
Mary "C"
The Inn at Weathersfield
Oct. 1999

MW01532148

THE RULING PASSION

Reflections on a Society under Siege

a novel by

MARY J. CARTER

in collaboration with

MICHAEL KAPLAN

THE RULING PASSION

Reflections on a Society under Siege

FONT & CENTER PRESS, INC.
P.O. Box 95
Weston, MA 02493-0005

Published by
Font & Center Press
P.O. Box 95
Weston, Massachusetts 02493-0005

Library of Congress Cataloging-in-Publication Data

Carter, Mary J., 1957—
The ruling passion : reflections on a society under siege /
by Mary J. Carter in collaboration with Michael Kaplan.
p.   cm.
ISBN: 1-883280-13-3
1. Boston (Mass.)—History—Colonial period. ca. 1600–1775—Fiction.
2. Boston (Mass.)—History—Revolution. 1775–1783—Fiction.
3. Boston Tea Party. 1773—Fiction.
I. Kaplan, Michael, 1946– .
II. Title.
PS3553.A78255R85   1998
813'.54—dc21   98-44603
                                        CIP

First Printing 1999
Printed in Canada
10 9 8 7 6 5 4 3 2 1

Dedicated to

Those I Love.

Acknowledgements

The author and collaborator of this story would personally like to acknowledge:

Vincent J-R Kehoe, editor of the extensive and exciting two-volume work *We Were There,* for devoting his valuable time towards creating a constructive review of our Lexington and Concord chapters;

Warren R. Smith, librarian of the Arlington Library in Massachusetts, for his tireless work in verifying some of our more minute, yet important, details;

Kathleen D. Reinig for her sound input and "medical advice";

Ann Grometstein, first editor, who added shape to our stream of consciousness, as well as to Denny Bergman, copyeditor and proofreader, for reining it all it;

Becky Allen Mixter and Gene Ritvo for creating just the right mood for the cover;

And to Ilene Horowitz, publisher, for breathing life into our dream.

We thank you all.

Author's Note

To begin with, the "cap" of author is very new to me. I am your basic, everyday person who was born just outside of Boston and grew up loving colonial American history. During my youth, I devoured every book on the subject. Concord, Massachusetts was, and still is, my favorite town, and many a lazy Sunday was spent walking along the trails of the historic North Bridge. However, life has a way of making us "grow up." I married, had two children, and, together with our good friend Helen, my husband Terry and I purchased a full-service inn in Vermont. Writing became my way of unwinding after a typical fourteen-hour day. The months spent weaving this tale have been a constant joy. I believe it is due to my fascination with revolutionary-war history that no project has ever come easier to me.

However, when one considers publishing their work, a great deal of attention must be paid in assuring that all the historical details are correct—details that were pulled solely from a devoted memory. This task my partner, Michael Kaplan, took on with a dedication I would have never dreamed possible. Not only that, with Michael's interests and knowledge of the American Revolution—being himself an eighteenth-century reenactor—Michael added substance and life to this work. Without him, this little story of mine would have remained stuffed away in a file cabinet. So, above all the many things I could thank Michael for, I would like to begin with blessing the fact that he believed in me.

Our particular account, although fiction, has been set in actual history. Most of our characters are fictitious, and any similarity to any known person is purely coincidental and unintentional. Due to the nature of this novel's subject, some actual personages of history are mentioned, quoted, or "present" in parts of this story. These "visitations" are purely fanciful, and in no way infer an illustration of character.

In some cases we have altered eighteenth-century terminology. For example, you will see mention of a "dressmaker" rather soon in the story, which takes place in the 1770s. The term "dressmaker" was not recognized until twenty-eight years later, in 1803. This is followed up shortly by its actual term of "mantua maker." I merely wanted you, the reader, to enjoy this tale without forever reaching for a dictionary. Verity Lynford's story is from the heart, not from a textbook. Therefore, please forgive these small lapses in art, and simply savor this little tapestry from the past.

Mary J. Carter

21 March, 1776

"CAPTAIN LANDON VALE is a man of great understanding."

How strange that now, at this darkest of all hours, my brain is haunting me with the very first words I ever heard about Landon Vale. It was in this very room, I remember, at one of the Eldredges' typical Thursday evening gatherings, quite some months ago. With a grand flourish of his coattails, the merchant Edmund Platt had seated himself upon the ottoman at Mr. Eldredge's feet. Placing one hand over his heart, which I suppose was a gesture of profound sincerity, Platt leaned towards his host and said with godlike reverence, "Captain Landon Vale is a man of great understanding"—and I paused, a little in awe of what had been said. So many pretentious praises are freely bantered about officers these days. They ride well; shoot well. In some bombastic flair of fashion, they are reckless with money and women, and for that we are to hold such men in high honour. However, this man was different somehow, and I admired him from the first.

But now, death has taken him from us.

Forcing myself to glance about this once familiar room, I am struck with the oddest sense that it is not the safe and comfortable surroundings that has sheltered me these past twenty-two months. Suddenly, it is a rather artificial set upon an imaginary stage, and we are all the actors merely hired to amuse. At this particular performance, the drapes are heavily drawn against a March night dripping with fog, and because of this, the candles have no happy mirror for their dance. Instead, their slim brilliance plays upon the tired and anxious faces of our ensemble. Poor Mary Eldredge, our hostess, nearly ceases to exist. Her ghostly pallor proves that any dreams she once had of returning to her glittering world of London have all too quickly diminished. Her husband, Warren, sits with his head in his hands, staring at the hearth. He also possesses a pallor too easily understood. Having gambled at least twice in life, and losing practically all, his hair has turned to grey nearly overnight. In addition, if one looks closely, they will see that the tips of his fingers tremble ever so slightly as they rest at his temples. Not a one of our company dares speak to him, for he has so very much to say to himself alone.

It is, of course, their only daughter, Lorena, who commands the center of our stage. Dressed demurely in black, her great blue eyes are downcast beneath somber lashes moist with tears. Clutching a small lace handkerchief in her clever little hands, she utters halting half sentences that positively tear at the heart: "Oh, my Landon was so . . ." That is all she has to say in strangled whispers smart with pain, and every young man in the room hastens to her side, soothing her wounded heart with desultory words she most likely does not hear. She is gracious, however. Occasionally, she gifts her attentive audience with a lifted head and a sorrowful smile, and they are gratified. Lorena Eldredge, at a mere nineteen, has been blessed with the ability to make anyone love her, even those she despises. And for that, I hate her.

Dear God, I did not mean that. How cruel of me to revile a young girl so obviously in the throes of despair. It is just perhaps that I feel an utter loss of hope myself, and it does not help to watch Lorena Eldredge receive all the sympathy.

Oh, Landon, you were my dearest friend. Why did you leave me? Of course, to Lorena you were so much more. Her *intended*, as they call you in solemn whispers this very night. Yes, Miss Eldredge deserves this chance to mourn in public. She is, admittedly, a beautiful and admired young girl on the threshold of womanhood. Whereas I, at nearly thirty, can only anticipate the pangs of middle age. Were I dressed as she, I would easily look like a crow caught up in taffeta. I could not manage to cry half as well as Lorena. Her eyes are still handsome, though ensconced in tears; whereas mine would be hideously swollen and red. My voice would not tremor prettily—heavens no! I, Verity Daniels Lynford, would sound more like a sorry mule clamouring for air.

Alas, I am not Lorena. I am no longer nineteen. And as for love, I can only recall the words Landon Vale spoke to me a mere two weeks ago. Private words really, meant only for me to hear. It was the afternoon of the violent storm. We were together for the very last time—only I did not know it then. I wish I had known. However, it is too late for that now. All I am left with are memories mixed with guilt and wonder, and yes, I admit, a sad and desperate longing.

Across the room, Mrs. Ellis is watching me, and her inquisitive, prying stare jolts me sharply out of my reverie. Startled, because my face must have coloured with my thoughts, I nodded, only to have her return one of those odd little smiles people form when they mean to convey sympathy. It is a foolish half smile without a show of teeth; very studied, and very contrite.

Perhaps she knows something. No, the very idea is ridiculous. She cannot possibly. Like so many of the Boston cowards, Mrs. Ellis evacuated just after the clashes at Lexington and Concord. And only now, when General George Washington and his men have reclaimed our abandoned streets, does she come back like an innocent dowager on holiday. Still, her silly expression troubled me, so I pretended to look elsewhere about the hushed and shrouded room.

Jeffrey. Forgive me, but I had nearly forgotten you were here. Of course I would find you drinking port with the less compassionate men in the corner. This entire evening has annoyed you from the start, hasn't it? And soon, I must ask you why, although I believe in my heart that I already know.

Oh, Jeffrey. We are not the same newly married couple who came to Boston almost two years ago for a trial in finer society. You are sadder, even now. There is no light of ambition behind those dark, brooding eyes I fell so deeply in love with. Perhaps, in truth, there never was. And I—I am not the same woman who thought she could conquer your heart in a cousin's borrowed dress. She disappeared, Jeffrey, just sixteen short days ago . . .

For thy sweet love remembered such wealth brings
That then I scorn to change my state with kings.

Shakespeare—*Sonnet XXIX*

∞

*M*Y FATHER was no Harvard scholar, but the lessons he taught me from life proved invaluable.

"Stand tall," Papa had told me. "Face your challenges with a cool head and common sense. And never hide behind the fact you're a woman. Attached to a man's coattails, you are nothing." Assuring me it was only women without gumption who complained it was "a man's world," my father instructed me to always listen, learn, and say no more than was necessary. In time, I was to realise how very right he was.

Justin Daniels, fourth in a line of ten siblings, had come to America from the shabbier side of London when he was but thirteen years of age. Apprenticed to a goldsmith in Boston town, he found the trade little to his liking. So when his time of indenture was through, Justin thanked his master, packed his meager belongings in a cloth tied to a makeshift pole, and headed for the country. I remember Papa telling me his one true desire was to forge into the wilderness and abide amongst the Indians. However, it was when he met Miss Margaret Grayson of Concord, that his wanderings came to a prompt and most satisfactory conclusion.

I never knew much about my mother, save for the fact that her father ran the Crossroads Tavern, and the young Justin Daniels adored her beyond measure. They married in the summer of 1745, and I arrived the following spring. A second daughter, Ruth, came along a short eleven months later. Ruthie was a large baby, and sadly Mother could not survive the struggle of her birth.

I was told Papa was so desperate with grief, he locked himself away in his room for three whole days. He could not even bring himself to attend Mother's burial on the steep hillside in Concord center where timeless rows of grey slate memorials whisper of fine lives long since turned to dust. You see, Mother was afraid of the dark, and Papa could not bear to think of his lovely Margaret forever shrouded from the loving warmth of the sun. In due course, however, Justin came to accept the fate God gave him, and he visited Mother's grave each morning—a tradition he dutifully carries to this day.

Papa never remarried. He said the love of one good woman was all he ever needed. Grandfather Grayson had no other children besides Margaret, so when the proper time came, Justin Daniels took rightful possession of the Crossroads, and brought us girls up as well as a single man with an all-day and all-night occupation could. The patrons of Papa's taproom, who were counted amongst his closest of friends, played quite a part as well. I guess I could safely say that Ruthie and I had a few dozen surrogate fathers in our young lives! Although I certainly cannot recall the event, I was often reminded how I took my first steps across the rough taproom floor, clutching the hem of my skirts in a childish attempt to prevent a tumble. Ruthie's first steps came early, too. From what I was told, she had to get on her feet in order to avoid my bullying!

Once I was older, Martin, the village shopkeep, taught me numbers so well I could add and subtract steep figures in my head. From the farmers, I learned about planting when the soil was right, and how to predict impending weather from the ever volatile signs of nature. Roger Surry, a lovely if not somewhat beleaguered man with five unruly daughters, taught me how to dance. His wife, Elizabeth, it was said, was a favourite in court some twenty years before, and despite the remoteness of colonial Concord, she kept up with anything and everything that was in style.

The delicate old man, Vergne, who lived in lonely solitude on the outskirts of town, taught me French. He claimed to be a tutor to his king, although no one here ever rightly believed him. Doctor Samuels instructed me in basic anatomy, and best of all, Lawyer Allen let me read his law books, which he had purchased at great expense from England. I confess I was fathoms away from ever being called a legal scholar. However, I can vow with certainty that I was leagues ahead of the other young ladies of Concord who swore a true education consisted entirely of knowing how to catch a husband before one was unmercifully cast aside as a thornback.

Ruthie, on the other hand, led a rather sheltered existence. Quiet, gentle, and shy, Ruthie tended to occupy her time in the tavern kitchen where, by the tender age of fifteen, she had become something of an accomplished cook. Ruthie's only flaw was an unhappy talent for overeating. Too often, more bits of food went into her mouth than into the boiling pot.

As children, we were like night and day. Whereas I would climb a tree, Ruthie preferred to daydream beneath its shade. In observing the clouds, I would see dragons and pirate ships and castles. For her part, Ruthie would see teapots and scrub brushes and pails. If caught in a childish prank, I would lie beyond limit to save my hide. Sweet Ruthie would simply tell the truth. I loved to regale my father's patrons with stories—some of them tall tales to be sure, but I had always been an entertainer at heart. Poor Ruthie would break out in hives if she had to so much as deliver a bowl of soup. Yes, we were amusingly different, but also terribly devoted to one another. I could not have been blessed with a better sister and companion than my dearest Ruthie.

When I had turned nineteen, and Ruthie eighteen, our great-grandmother, Effie, came to live with us. She had been quite the beauty in her day, Papa told us. She had also married three times. Her arrival caused great curiosity in the town. The men adored her for her rapid wit, and the women avoided her because of it. I, for one, admired Effie's sense of speaking her mind plain and true, as long as her barbs were not directed specifically at me!

Despite what all the highbred ladies of Boston might believe, tavern life for me was a marvelous existence. Concord, at the time, was home to a rather diverse population, and many of these varied and most industrious men would frequent my father's taproom at the end of a busy day for a bit of libation and some political jabber, or "fling," as Papa termed it. And that is where all these men held one thing in common, for it is a plain fact that New Englanders are never happier than when they are bickering! It is a peculiar trait, to be sure, but a necessary one in a town where every man collects beneath the same roof night after night—excepting the Sabbath, of course—to speak their minds, solve their problems, and cherish sentiments. Papa claimed no Yankee on earth could settle a subject without debating and disputing it to death. It kept the mind sharp. Or so he insisted.

Thus it was, day after day and month after month, the landowners would gather alongside the men who worked for them—rugged, sun-weathered men with boisterous voices and boisterous ways. Add to these, the shopkeepers, the doctors, the farmers, and the lawyers, and you would have one fine mix. Together, they possessed one torch to fan, and that was the goings-on in Boston town. And such goings-on they were!

After years of turmoil—years that resembled a cat scowling too loudly as it chased its own tail—the Liberty Party was finally coming in to its own and being heard. The fabulously rich and powerful merchant, John Hancock, worried a few with his penchant for siding with whichever political party played up to his ego best. However, just when things seemed their darkest, the stalwart and steady Samuel Adams publicly commissioned a portrait of his dearest friend, the Merchant Hancock. Thus, with one sound stroke of the paint brush, Sam Adams secured the greatest purse strings the liberty cause had ever known.

Ignited by such writings as demonstrated by the mysterious Joyce Junior— whom many secretly believed to be none other than Sam Adams, himself—

special Committees of Correspondence sprung up amongst the villages and byways, thus keeping the colonies connected.

From Salem to Savannah, the Tea Rebellion of '73 was all the current speculation. By virtue of a single sentence, Samuel Adams unleashed a hundred and a half eager men upon the tea ships anchored alongside Griffin's Wharf. Within a scant three hours, during which time not a single word was spoken, these men, thinly disguised as Indians, dumped some forty-five tons of dutiable tea into the bay. By this explosive action, Sam Adams was a "Mob Master" turned saint—at least in the eyes of such men as my father.

Yes, it was a confusing time. However, to the young like myself, it was a strangely exciting time all the same. It is not often that one finds themselves perched on the brink of a new era—but there I was. So, if there were any arguments to be had for, or against, this ever changing world, I was right in the middle of it, and Papa was proud.

However, Papa was also concerned about my not being married. I certainly was not. I may have been getting along in my twenties, which for many was considered well beyond marriageable age, but there wasn't a man I wanted until I set eyes on you, Jeffrey.

Oh, the young men of the village were nice enough. Some were even handsome enough. However, the truth be known, I often felt more ambitious and intelligent than many of my suitors. Perhaps that seems a bit pompous for a taverner's daughter to say, but there wasn't a lad for twenty miles that could confess to being impressed by my ability to speak French, cypher mathematics, or discuss politics with some degree of common sense. Oh, Jeffrey—I believed my heart was destined to be a lonely thing, until we met.

How often you had come to Papa's taproom on quieter evenings, just to be alone with your thoughts. You weren't the sort for political babbling, but that was fine. I was content merely to watch you from a corner, your elegant dark eyes adrift in some personal dream . . . How breathtaking you were to behold!

I shall always remember the very first evening I saw you. It was a fine spring twilight, just after a quick flash of rain—and you entered, your fine clothes and golden hair dampened by the storm. It was apparent at once that you were gentle born. Your physique and manner were not those of a labouring man's. Instead, you possessed the skill and grace of a divinely attractive dance master. And such a lovely countenance! I admired at once the strong line of your cheekbones and the aristocratic cleft in your chin. You stayed for hours that first night, conversing little, but what you said was so very charming. I'll wager you do not remember a single word you uttered, however, I certainly do.

The next morning, I asked my dearest friend, Karen, who you were. She laughed at me and held my hand. "Don't you know anything, Verity Daniels?" she exclaimed. "That's Jeffrey Lynford. Jeffrey Francis Lynford, if you please. His grandfather was a nobody who made his fortune in trade. His father works hard at it too, from what I hear. However, your handsome boy, Jeffrey, prefers to play the dandy. Their home is that huge estate on the east side of town. You know, the one on the hill with the multitude of windows that shine in the sun."

So it was that I knew your name, and how you came to be. Many a pleasant afternoon, Karen and I would sit on the back steps of the tavern, peeling vegetables and imagining what it would be like to have you love us, for like friendly foes, we vowed to be happy for whichever one of us turned your head first. Of course, I secretly planned on being the victor. You see, I was hopelessly in love with you in those days. For all my symptoms, it could be nothing else.

Looking back on that beautiful haze of innocent infatuation, I can recall how my hands shook whenever you were near. Why, I couldn't serve you a saucer of coffee without the spoon rattling loud enough to wake the dead. To make matters worse, I often sputtered my words when in your company, or giggled too much. It was downright shameful.

I cannot even begin to count the endless hours I fussed with my hair and my clothes, just to impress you. Imagine then, my frustration when you refused to take notice! Of course, you were coming about Papa's tavern much more often—and it did seem that you came to see me. So many lovely evenings were spent in your company, well after the others had gone, speaking of anything and everything in the world. It was heavenly, really. Heavenly, that is, until I ventured to boast to Karen of it all.

"So you're the best of friends, are you now?" she asked with a cynical smile on her lips. "And has this dearest friend of yours told you all about his relentless passion for Avella Gore?"

Avella Gore! Of all people, Avella Gore? I could not believe it. Do you know, Jeffrey, what most of Concord called her? "Avella Gore, the doctor's whore." Yet, you coveted her, a woman nearly twice your age, and terribly nasty in the bargain. My heart sunk. It just couldn't be true! So, in the fashion of one who has never harboured a subtle bone in her body, I came right out and asked you about Mrs. Gore that very evening. And yes, you readily confessed your strong attraction to her. I suppose I should have admired you for speaking the truth, but my stubborn heart would not allow it. Indeed, I was devastated. Then like the fool I was, I vowed to speak of her no more.

I remember that morning, now nearly two years past, when Karen came running over to the Crossroads with the news. Doctor Gore was dead. She had heard it from Avella's maid, a little slip of a thing named Alice, who cared not a twig for her vulgar mistress. Alice had told Karen how the dear old doctor, who had gently assisted so many others through death's dismal door, had himself passed the long night gasping for air, and clinging to shadows, as it were. He never did ask for Avella. Indeed, he specifically told his manservant to keep her from setting foot in the room. Alice could only guess that the old man knew he was soon to see his first and dearest wife in the beyond, so why should he want to carry the memory of Avella's ruthless sneer along with him? Besides, Avella was not overly concerned with her husband's final sufferings—no, not in the least. While her husband lay dying, Avella occupied her precious time with trying on various costumes of mourning.

The hardest news of all, however, was when Alice confirmed that you, Jeffrey, were the first to appear on the doctor's doorstep. Alice said you had been drinking, and your voice was a trifle overloud. Yes, she and some of the other household servants listened through the library door as you begged Avella to marry you. But Avella turned you down, didn't she? Claiming to have bigger fish to fry, the doctor's widow sent you packing.

I can still recall to this day how I felt, listening to Karen relate the little maid's story. It did not fill me with disgust, as it rightfully should have. After all, how honourable is the man who proposes marriage to a woman whose husband lies not quite cold in the parlour beyond? No, I was younger then, and vanity had taken charge over a great deal of my senses. I should have listened and learned from your words and your actions. Instead, I chose to feel ecstatic over the fact that the woman you worshipped had refused you. How foolish I was to forget all the fine things my father taught me.

I remember going to my room and putting on my very best dress. No, it was not really my dress. It was a lovely thing of rose brocade my cousin in Philadelphia had sent me in hopes that it would "get me somewhere." Well, I vowed that this was the day of days. And yes, you showed up early at the tavern, quite drunk, and terribly despondent. I tried to get you to confess your woes, but you would not. I especially tried to get you to notice me, but alas you would not do that either. Happily, however, a small miracle appeared in the form of Mr. Charles Davenport.

He had come to the Crossroads in search of you, and his fine, distinguished face wore an air of concern. I cannot recall him introducing himself. However, as I brought him a glass of port, his glance took me in from head to foot, as though I were a painting in a gallery, and he said, "What a fine looking girl you are." My ill mood over your lack of interest melted for a moment, and I remember thanking him, my eyes downcast, and a honest blush upon my cheeks.

"Is she not positively divine, Jeffrey?" he went on, and I watched as you merely shrugged under a thick haze of drink.

"If you say so, Charles; then I suppose I must agree."

I did not particularly like the way you had said that. I couldn't be sure whether you were teasing me or your guest. Regardless, I introduced myself to Mr. Davenport, and left you to your discourse. However, I did not go far. If there was one lesson I learned from tavern life, it was that eavesdroppers often heard highly informative things. So, I merely went about the corner and leaned against the cool plaster of the wall where I would not be seen. No, I was not ashamed.

"Now that was a handsome girl, Jeffrey," I heard your visitor say. "Damned handsome."

"So you've mentioned," was your sullen reply.

"Oh, Jeffrey, really—"

"What are you driving at, Davenport?"

Just then, I heard the legs of a chair scraping against the floor. I imagined it was the elegant Mr. Davenport moving closer to you as he lowered his voice.

"She is a diamond in the rough, my boy. A positive jewel. And I was just thinking—if that vision of a lass resided in town, I'd have her in my troupe of actors extraordinaire. Yes, it is for certain I would."

"What makes you think the girl can act?" you laughed in reply.

"Don't be such an idiot, man. Need a woman be trodden with everyday talents when she looks as this one does? Of course not! Why, she could dance like a three-legged dog and sing like a sailor's parrot, and who would notice? Who, in his right mind, would see anything but that rich fell of auburn hair, and those inviting green eyes—not to mention those gracious contours . . ."

I blushed hotly at hearing myself described so, but nothing in the world was going to drag me away from this conversation.

"Good Lord, how you exaggerate, Charles," you replied, and I knew you were steadily drinking your port, for you spoke within your glass. "Verity Daniels is a fine young woman—I'll grant you that. But for all I am terribly fond of her, I just simply cannot envision her gaining acclaim as the next Aphrodite of the stage."

"You have a severe lack of vision, Jeffrey," was the gentleman's calm retort. "Yes, a severe lack of vision in many things."

"And what is that supposed to mean?"

"Straight to the point, that Gore woman," Davenport said, and I heard your drunken sigh of despair. "Yes, Jeffrey, your father told me. And why should he not? What possible future happiness would you have with this older woman who, by proof of three fast marriages, is wooed only by wealth?"

"You don't understand," was your sullen answer. "None of you—no one understands."

The bell at the door sounded. Josiah Pierce entered with two other men; I knew it was him by his voice. I waited for what seemed like an appropriate amount of time, and then walked out into the taproom. The hour was late, and the tavern filled quickly. In due time, your companion took his leave with a graceful kiss of my hand. However, you stayed. And strangely, the more you drank, the more sober you became, or so it seemed. Regardless, it could not escape my notice that you began to watch me with a new fascination.

I will never forget the fact that you were the first to arrive that day, and the last to leave. I remember going about wiping down the ale-splattered tables, secretly grateful that only we two remained, as the twelve bells of midnight thumped and coughed from the depths of the hall beyond. Still, you stayed on, your fawnlike eyes fixed on me while the fire grew cold, and the candles, nearly vanquished, cast strange, wraithlike shadows which danced upon the rough beams overhead.

It was then you asked me to marry you; simple and straightforward. Not at all what I could have imagined, or hoped for. However, at that happy moment, I couldn't fathom what more I possibly could have wished for.

Young girls dream such unrealistic dreams. We imagine the true fabric of life to be woven from the pages of dramatic books. We treasure the prints showing lovers on balconies, lovers in boats, and lovers amidst colourful gardens. Silly images, really, depicting moonlit nights and handsome young gallants dying of love, of nightingales and doves cooing sentiments, and delicate ladies weeping prettily over love letters in rose-shaded arbors. These are the purely innocent and yet strangely intoxicating trappings of romance—an ideal of everlasting emotion that lives and breathes only a short while in the hearts of young women, until one day, perhaps by the feeble light of a single candle struggling against extinction, simple truth prevails.

"Verity," you had said, speaking at last, "have you ever possessed a desire to go to Boston?"

I pretended to pause at my occupation and think.

"Why, yes. Yes, I would. I think it would be terribly exciting."

"Then go with me," you said, and the first glimmer of a smile I had witnessed that entire day began to take over your face.

I laughed, not quite certain what you meant, but ever hopeful.

"Jeffrey Lynford, I'm surprised at you. What would people say?"

"What could they say, if you were my wife."

So that was that. I don't particularly remember how we sealed our agreement. I don't believe you kissed me. In all this time, I cannot remember your ever having kissed me with any true sense of passion.

Thus grief still treads upon the heels of pleasure,
Marry'd in haste, we may repent at leisure.

Congreve—*The Old Bachelor*

☙

APRIL, 1774

URING THE FEW weeks that followed—days during which I should have been experiencing the greatest joys of my life—I can honestly say I remember little. I can, however, strongly recall my stubbornness in wishing to wed at once. Oh, Papa beseeched me to take time to reconsider, and Great-grandmother Effie did her best to insist upon it. But to both, I turned a defiantly deaf ear. I was confident in our love, I had told them. Secretly, I feared that should delay take its sullen course, we would never marry. You see, Jeffrey, I knew it was still Avella who ruled your heart. I simply wished to be your wife before she took over your mind as well.

So it was, on an April morning bright with promise, we took our vows in the front parlour of the Crossroads Tavern. Your father refused to attend, so beyond my immediate family, there were no invited guests. We were going directly to Boston, where we would stay with Charles Davenport until a suitable home could be found, and we wanted to arrive before twilight. I remember how we rushed through breakfast while the carriage waited. Papa attempted at least to be cheerful, Effie was scowling, and my sweet sister was in tears. Yes, even now it is the woebegone look on Ruthie's face that I see whenever I care to recall our wedding day.

I was so fatigued when we arrived in Boston that our surroundings sadly made no impression upon me. My fine sense of bravado had soured to foolish nerves by the time we turned into Garden Court Street. One sight of Charles Davenport's commanding three-storey mansion, and I knew all at once that I had gone above myself. Your father had been right, Jeffrey. I was not of your class. And I had no right to begin pretending so now.

Oh, the confusion of arrival! Charles employed a footman whose face and demeanour was as unyielding as the great stone facade of the house. Stearns was his name, and I remember thinking that never before had anyone's name been so aptly descriptive of character. Charles Davenport was, of course, thoroughly gracious. He tried to put me at my ease at once, and showed me about his lavish place without much pretense. On my part, however, I am sure I made a bad impression by either saying too much or too little. I can recall with horror how I gushed over certain pieces of artwork, or furniture, with youthfully trite and giddy expressions. I could not help it. For certain, I felt like the newly hired washerwoman who was being given her one and only tour above stairs.

Our first evening at Garden Court Street was nothing short of a nightmare for me. I believed we would dine quietly with Charles. Instead, on a lark, Charles had invited several members of his theatrical troupe to join us. Such boisterous people! I could barely keep their names in my head, and their incessant chatter was nothing short of deafening.

Lucy Wellman was the earliest to arrive. I remember her now as we first saw her—just a diminutive thing, with small doe-like eyes and a pallor to her face which suggested this spirited little creature had rarely witnessed the light of day. She was highly animated. I do not believe she ever settled in one place for more than a minute. In any event, she never took the time to converse with us. We were perhaps a bit too inconsequential for her attentions. When Charles informed Miss Wellman we were newly wed, I overheard her to mutter, "Just married? What fools." That, obviously, was the zenith of her initial impressions.

Valentine Hale I remember as a terribly bored woman who had no qualms in letting us know just that. Her bitter stare never seemed to leave Charles Davenport's face the entire night. Rebecca Henley was merely a simpleminded southern girl who loved herself above all others. Of course, Miss Diana Kirby was the most odious of them all. Charles claimed her to be his finest actress. The lofty Miss Kirby took me in from head to foot as though I were inferior merchandise. She then asked my first name, and when I provided it, she uttered with guttural scorn, "Verity? Verity brings to mind the image of a bland and boring nursemaid who tirelessly takes care of nasty little children." If she meant to insult me, she did so with ease.

I must confess that the gentlemen of Charles' theatrical society seemed kinder. It was apparent at once that the young man, known simply as Darcy, was the troupe's comedian. Roscoe Bennett was a rather large man with an exquisite speaking voice. Strangely enough, however, I believe Mr. Bennett spoke the fewest words of all. We then met Sir Alfred Blinn. It was, I admit, a trifle overwhelming to be introduced to a titled actor. But within moments, I found him to be fascinating with his knowledge of English theatre and history—a knowledge he had gathered from fifty-two years upon the public stage. Of all the overblown and foolish conversations we were forced to listen to that first evening, I found Sir Alfred's comments by far the most interesting and informative.

I recall watching you on what was to be our wedding night, Jeffrey. You sat several seats away from me, smiling, laughing, and consuming endless glasses of port. Glancing about the table, I quickly concluded that if this is how married couples in Boston society behave, I would have been better off staying at home in Concord. Sometimes I think of that precise moment now, and I secretly wonder if I had never been more correct. Of course, then I was determined to make things right. I was younger, and perhaps a great deal naive. I had vowed to like your friends, as well as your way of life. Above all, I did not wish to admit to my family that they were accurate in their misgivings.

The next few evenings at Charles Davenport's regrettably seemed to mimic the first. Charles would fill the house with people, and hours later, I would go to our room alone. There, I would sit and sulk while imagining you downstairs, Jeffrey, playing cards and drinking port 'til dawn. However, just when I set my mind to tell you it could no longer be this way, Charles stepped in and assisted us in finding a fit home to lease on Charter Street. Oh, Charles had located larger homes for us to consider, but you were being sensible. You said we would merely buy a house when the current conflict with Great Britain brought the real estate prices down in Boston.

Once we were alone in our little home, the marriage officially began. Of our first true evening together, I have little to say, even now. You see, Jeffrey, you may have been the only man I ever really wanted. However, you were not the first man I ever had.

∞∞∞∞

Five days after we had settled in at Charter Street, you had business to attend to in Salem, and you explained that you would be away overnight. Something of the apprehension I was feeling must have shown in my face, for you added quickly, "Worry not, my fearful wife. I have asked Charles Davenport to send someone over to keep you company, as well as out of mischief."

Within half an hour of your departure, Miss Lucy Wellman came to the door. She was adorned in the most beautiful day dress I had ever seen—blue satin with velvet bows—a wide straw hat, and white gloves raised to the elbows. A black ribbon prettily set about her neck enhanced the porcelain qualities of her skin.

As I ran to the hall, attired in my simple Brunswick dress, I felt more like the scullery maid opening the door to the mistress of the house. Indeed, it appeared the well-dressed little actress did not recognise me, for she said, "Please tell Mrs. Lynford that Miss Wellman has called on her."

Then she proceeded to sit herself down upon the hall chair where she stared at me expectantly.

"I am she," I responded with as much grace as I could muster on such an occasion. I was already regretting the hours that Miss Wellman and I would be forced to spend together.

"My dear Mrs. Lynford—I am so sorry to have mistaken you for—"

"The parlour maid?" I supplied.

"Well, perhaps," she muttered, her face showing surprise, embarrassment, shock, and guilt, all in rapid succession.

"I imagine my upbringing shows at first glance," I admitted with a sad smile. "Especially in the eyes of such a genteel lady as yourself."

"Judas Iscariot!" Lucy gasped in laughter. "I am the furthest from genteel you shall find. I just thought . . . Oh, forgive me, Mrs. Lynford, and please call me Lucy."

I could not help but grin. Perhaps the afternoon was not as ill-fated as I had feared.

"Thank you very much. And please call me Verity. Now, I do apologize for the way I was dressed to receive you. We have only but just moved here from Concord, where I was a taverner's daughter. I have yet to inquire after a dressmaker, and such. However, I should surely do this soon. Judging by your face, my dress is terrible to be seen in."

"Verity, although it pains a female such as me to admit it, you are as lovely to look at as you are to be with. I will take you this instant to Madame Thérèse, the most wonderful dressmaker, and not three blocks from here. As for now, pay no mind to the dress you are in. Why, it is the height of fashion for ladies of station to be put on canvas in dresses just like yours—feeding chickens, and the like. Apparently, my dear, *humble* is very much in style."

We laughed. I felt bad all at once for my foul opinion of Miss Lucy when we first met. She was perhaps the only member of Charles' company who did not place her self-worth on a pinnacle well above all the rest.

We journeyed to Madame Thérèse's shop on Middle Street. I was nearly accosted by her attendants when it was discovered that I was a woman in need of an entire wardrobe. Silks, damasks, satins, brocades, and even cotton prints were rolled out and presented to me over draped arms, at my feet, and even across the body like the togas I had seen in book plate prints at Doctor Samuels'. Three hours in this shop, and I nearly perished with fatigue.

However, as Miss Lucy pointed out, our travels had just begun.

From the milliner's to the wigmaker's, Lucy was like a child leading me from one amusement to another. At one stop, she bade me to purchase a fan from China, and she showed me how to speak with it in gestures that were amorous in nature. I practiced the moves of the hand, and fluttered my fan until Lucy warned me to stop, for we were attracting too much untoward attention on the streets.

The subject of gowns, hair, and hats well managed, we went happily on our way to the Faneuil Hall marketplace in order that I might work towards provisioning our household.

"You will need a good cook, you know," Lucy advised, her small eyes alight as they wandered about the mad confusion of sights and sounds around us. "Especially if you mean to entertain."

"Yes, well—" I said, my gladsome mood diminishing at the thought of us opening our doors to the severely privileged society of Boston. I looked to where I believed Lucy to be, but she was gone. I whirled about, suddenly alarmed at being alone, when I saw her motioning to me from where she stood against the bricked wall of a narrow alley.

Much to my consternation, Miss Lucy produced an oyster, which she had stolen from an oyster cart nearby. She dragged me further into the alley, and removed from her handbag a folding knife.

With the skill of an oysman, she shucked the shell open and gazed at the exposed flesh. Her eyes glowed as she put her lips to the edge of the shell and devoured the white muscle.

"God bless me, but I cannot resist them."

I was made to remember a similar incident when I was young. I was in the company of my good friends, Karen and Ambrose. We had vaulted the fence rails to Mr. Barrett's orchards, and then proceeded to pinch some fine, juicy apples from his carefully pruned trees, which we relished like nefarious criminals a few fields away. Although I had not participated in today's crime, I shared in the pleasure of its sinful accomplishment.

I knew, from that moment forward, that Miss Lucy Wellman and I would be friends.

The ruling passion, be it what it will,
The ruling passion conquers reason still.

Pope—*Moral Essays*

∞

May, 1774

ON THE TENTH OF MAY, His Majesty's vessel, *Lively*, arrived at Boston harbour carrying the proclamation of the town's punishment. Commencing the first day of June, the port of Boston would be closed completely until the tea, which had been destroyed the previous December, was paid for in full. In addition, General Thomas Gage had been commissioned by Lord Dartmouth to insure the ordinance was obeyed to the last letter.

More troops would be sent to the beleaguered Boston, which had been stripped of her title as capital of the colony as well. The town of Salem would now hold that honour, and Plymouth, to the south, would become the seat of customs. Ruination fell like a swift scythe upon the thousands of Bostonians who had always depended on the port for their livelihood.

But for us, Jeffrey, these were golden days. Finally left to our own devices, we were playing the part of divine newlyweds at last. Oblivious to almost everything but each other, these enforced hardships of our *outside* world seemed almost exciting. No personal destruction was to befall us. Unlike so many others, we were actually looking forward to the inaugural reception for our new Governor, General Thomas Gage. For myself, a young woman from the country, the prospect of feting this high ranking officer was, in its own way, the closest I would ever come to being presented to the King.

∞∞∞

The roar of the welcoming cannon rippled across the bay as General Thomas Gage arrived at port from his three day sojourn at the outlying Castle William.

Gage would have set foot on Boston soil sooner, but finding no official committee of greeting, he joined the departing Lieutenant Governor Hutchinson at the island fortress until suitable festivities could be arranged.

At fifty-two years of age, Thomas Gage had been noted for three accomplishments: his viscount father, a peaceable nature, and an utter incompetence at the art of conversation. And for those who looked closely enough, there was yet a fourth distinction, for Thomas Gage bore an uncanny resemblance to the Patriot leader, Samuel Adams.

Rumour had run rampant that Gage meant to arrest every Patriot crusader right down to the last. How curious it was then to see John Hancock leading Gage's escort parade as Commander of the Cadets!

Charles Davenport had told me much about the wealthy bachelor merchant. Born to a poor clergyman who died when John was only seven, he was then adopted by his uncle Thomas Hancock and his formidable wife, Lydia. Thomas had begun his career as a bookbinder, but within the next ten years, Thomas Hancock had become Boston's most remarkable smuggler. His ships carried in all sorts of contraband from South America, and tea from the Dutch West Indies, arriving at Hancock's Wharf in kegs marked as "molasses." Thomas and Lydia remained childless, so when Thomas was struck down by apoplexy in the summer of 1764, nephew John inherited a sum total of seventy thousand pounds and the handsome house on Beacon Street.

True, Hancock preferred lavender suits, and his coaches were always painted yellow. Beyond that, he was somewhat effeminate with his constant headaches, and enormous fits of vanity. Still, he danced divinely, and gave the most elegant parties. Foremost, John Hancock was generous to a fault, supplying the town with a much needed firemen's rig, and financial assistance wherever it was needed; not to mention the work which fed nearly one thousand families. For this, he was known as King Hancock, and he unabashedly thrived on the title. Therefore, this little act of bravado we were now witnessing was very much in character.

"Perhaps Sam Adams will serve the General his bread and butter tonight," mused Jimmy Sloan, an associate of Charles Davenport, who stood very near to us.

"Only if ex-Governor Hutchinson pays the tip," observed the merchant Orrin Blackwell, dryly.

Suddenly, the light of a fanciful recognition burned brightly in the eyes of Virginia Stanwood—one of Charles' older, and more accomplished actresses.

"Tommy Gage—of course! I knew him in London, you see. We met at a wassail party at some sprawling country estate. He caught me under the mistletoe, the naughty boy. Oh, I shall never forget it—even though I was terribly,

terribly young at the time . . ."

I noticed that many in our company exchanged knowing looks at the conclusion of her reverie. It was said Virginia Stanwood possessed a flair for vaunting of a most vigorously romantic youth. I confess at present that I wondered as to why it could not be believed. Even at her mature years, this lovely lady with disarming violet eyes was still exceptionally attractive.

Following a stolid and routine ceremony in which the General was named as Hutchinson's successor, the doors of Faneuil Hall were thrown open wide for a grand reception. I remember entering on your arm, Jeffrey, and I felt at once as though I were being transported into a fairyland.

The hall was heaped to bursting with spring flowers, the scent of which overpowered the airless qualities of a room where the windows had been too long shuttered. The newly polished hardwood floors shone like glass in the warm reflection of the chandeliers above, and the happy sounds of music and laughter did much to dispel any dark suspicions surrounding this General's imminent reign.

"How lovely it looks," exclaimed Charles' niece, Clemence, tugging at her husband's arm emphatically. "Why, I could nearly cry with happiness!"

Her parents, who were invited from Philadelphia by Charles for this special occasion, stood not too far behind. Her mother, Fiona, was surveying the hall with silent appreciation. She was Charles' sister; that was easy to see. Her fine looks were as aristocratic as his. As for her husband, Stanton—why, he was so impassive, he easily appeared to be sleepwalking.

The hall was filling rapidly. The handsome hardwood floors were barely visible now beneath a constant sweep of colourful petticoats and brightly buckled shoes. Glancing about the crowd, I noticed Lucy and a few of the other actresses of Charles' troupe. Clemence and I excused ourselves to join them.

"Halloo!" called out Valentine, waving. "Goodness, but we have been trying to get your attention for the past fifteen minutes. We thought you would never see us!"

I smiled weakly at the dark-eyed Valentine. I was not certain why, but I had disliked her from our first meeting. It was not due to any of the obvious reasons. Valentine Hale was far from beautiful. To be sure, she was well into her thirties, and her attempts to hide that fact only made her look harsh. Miss Hale was also far from gracious. Whatever the cause at first, I was soon to realise I was right in mistrusting her.

"I stopped by your house today," said little Lucy, her happy urchin's face wrapped around a sly, wide grin. "Some teetering old dotard answered the door. I think he mistook me for the milkmaid, for he bade me to go round to the back door."

"Oh, that was Beals," I replied rather sheepishly. "He was a gift from Jeffrey's father. You see, Beals was valet to Jeffrey's grandfather, and simply stayed on. He's a sweet darling, really—despite the fact he is stone deaf, has a mind like a sieve, and boasts not a single recollection since the advent of Queen Anne's War."

Lucy laughed outright, while Clemence looked confused and Valentine gave one of those silly, insincere smiles before looking away with a trite pat to her wig.

"And I suppose as an apt companion for Beals, you have hired a cook who made her start with Hannibal," Lucy went on with a smile.

"Actually, we have no decent cook at the moment," I confessed. "I've been trying to convince my sister to come work in our kitchen for pay, but so far she has declined. It may be best, after all. I do not imagine Ruthie's skills would live up to the entertaining we will have to do in order to reciprocate for all these parties."

"But you don't have to," explained the redheaded Rebecca. "And that's the best part. You see, by being one of Charles' circle, people will want to have you at their parties; however, you are not expected to pay back all the hospitality. The whole thing is terribly foolish, I know, but intensely pleasant all the same. Just like this little soiree."

"I would hardly call this particular soiree *little*, Rebecca."

"There must be a thousand people here," said Lucy with a good measure of awe. "And so many handsome men, too."

"And I had to wear this silly dress," whined Rebecca, who was indeed attired more primly than usual.

"Charles asked that we dress like proper young ladies," explained Val, as I raised a questioning brow.

"Asked us?" interjected Lucy, with an incredulous sneer. "Threatened us, more like. Oh, yes! We have to sit here like a pack of vestal virgins, and pretend to up and faint if any unscrupulous miscreant casts an untoward glance our way."

"Isn't it exciting?" breathed Clemence, like the silly goose she was.

"I would say for all our quaint behaviour, we cannot look half as bad as some of the women in this room," Lucy began, her sharp eyes squinting as she peered about. "Why, look at that one, over there—the dowdy old governess-type in the sack over oblong hoops. Heavens! Did she just wake up and believe it to be 1740? Her hoop is so big, it will take out the buffet. Now look at that insulting one in the brown camlet riding habit, with a wig that looks like a French king's. Gad Zeus, does she want us to think she's a man? Speaking of men—see the old codger over by the punch bowl? There's so much powder flying from his wig, I fear it will rain."

How very amusing Lucy was. True, her outspoken manner had its threatening moments, particularly in certain sets of society. However, the more I was around her, the more I came to like her. She possessed a happy talent for not taking herself so very seriously, and that in itself was extremely refreshing.

Just then, you had come across the room, Jeffrey, to inform us that you were accompanying Charles and Sir Alfred Blinn to a private audience with the General.

"Really?" I said, impressed. "Why so?"

"Charles wants to introduce the notion of theatrical productions here in Boston."

"Does he really feel tonight is the proper time for such a notion? After all, the General has just arrived."

"Oh, Papa Charles does not waste a moment on anything," Lucy replied with a little shrug. "Ice wouldn't melt in his hand for want of something to do."

I watched as you left with Charles and Sir Alfred for one of the antechambers off the hall. I was devilishly proud of you, Jeffrey. You were, by far, one of the handsomest men in the room.

"Do you wish you were going, too?" Lucy asked.

"By that, do you mean would I like to meet a general? Why, I'm not certain. However, I do know for a fact that my father would be overjoyed to have a word or two with him."

"I had no idea your father was a Tory."

"Heavens, no!" I laughed. "Far from it. That is why he would savour such a keen opportunity."

I told the ladies a bit about my father, and of his penchant for holding political court in his taproom, night after night. Lucy then asked about my mother, and I showed her the miniature I had of her, which at this soiree I had secured to my wrist with a cream silk ribbon to match my taffeta lustring gown.

"She is lovely," Lucy sighed, with a glance towards me. "How then did you come to be such a stick?"

Lucy was jesting, of course. At least, she professed to be. It was then that Lucy spoke of her parents. Her mother had been a successful child actress on the London stage. However, that was as far as her talents went, for as an adult she showed no promise. Lucy's father had been married to someone else at the time of her birth. Lucy had met up with him only twice in her life, and on both occasions he demonstrated little to no concern for her well being. I felt a sense of sympathy all at once for her story, but Lucy refused all shows of sentiment. With a mere shrug of her shoulders, Lucy ventured that most girls in her neighbourhood faced the same, or worse, fate than she. So what was there to go on about?

Valentine then confessed that her mother had been a seamstress at the Theatre Royal in Drury Lane. Her own father had never been known to her. Valentine herself sewed costumes as her mother did, but she was soon to discover that catering to the personal needs of egotistical actors created quicker cash. Her confession was a bit shocking, but was told with such simplicity of feeling that I had to accept it. How very sad it all was though.

"Where is Diana Kirby?" I asked in an attempt to lighten our spirits. "I do not believe she was at the ceremony. Certainly, she of all people would not care to miss being seen at such a public event."

"Oh, have you not heard?" gasped Lucy, motioning us all closer. "It's finished with her insipid Sergeant Stedman. Diana's setting her sights on a big one, this time. His name is Lord Sutherland, and from what I hear, he has more money than six generals put together."

"And to think I saw him first!" Rebecca pouted, picking at the stuff of her dress.

"Yes, well, you didn't sharpen your teeth brightly enough, my friend," Lucy said, tapping Rebecca on the cheek with her fan.

"Oh, why bother?" exclaimed Val. "The man is a positive horror to look at."

"Ah, but his money makes him pretty all the same," Lucy replied in a knowing tone.

Lucy then lowered her voice cautiously and began a heated tirade about the seamier side of Lord Sutherland's rather perverse nature. We listened in horror. It was disgusting to hear what amused certain men in the dark corners of their minds. Miss Lucy then went on to enhance our connubial knowledge with the most lascivious lessons on French, Turkish, and even Indian techniques of lovemaking. I was, I confess, both shocked and amazed at it all.

"Oh, do hush!" cried Clemence, her full face colouring like the underside of a peach. "Here come my parents!"

"Clemence, dearest," Fiona murmured coolly. "Your father desires to meet your enchanting new set of friends."

Stanton Parkhurst was a rotund little man with an egg-shaped, balding head which appeared front heavy. Indeed, his forehead seemed to be forever gravitating towards his chin.

"Such wonderful young ladies," he began, sounding more like the headmaster at an academy for well-to-do girls, rather than a father being given casual introductions. He had a noticeably pompous way of speaking, I thought. He conscientiously rounded off each and every spoken word as though he were expelling his very last breath in doing so.

"Ah," he said, turning slowly towards me and showing no more emotion than he would for a display case full of butterflies with pins jabbed through their wings. "My dear Mrs. Lynford. You are indeed charming for so tall a lass. You are not German, perchance?"

"No," I stammered, surprised at his question.

"Then it is of no consequence," came the level response. "Come wife, I hear a brandy calling out my name."

Lucy waited until the Parkhursts were well out of sight.

"Heavens, Clemence. Now I know why you are so damnably strange."

"I am not!" the girl sniffed indignantly.

"Face facts, girl. Your father's full-blown batty."

"He is not! My father asked Mrs. Lynford if she was German merely because he has a true fear of Hessian soldiers. He knows of their reputation as cold-blooded killers, you see. And if we go to war with England, like all these crazy Whigs are threatening, my father says King George is bound to hire these mercenaries, and we'll all be killed in our beds. Yes, killed in our beds for sure!"

"So, there you have it, Verity. You have been likened to a hulking German brute with bloodshed on his mind. Silly girl—you should have left your bayonet at home. Now really, Clemence, does this make sense? For if it does, you are truly as daft as your father."

"Go ahead. Call me crazy now, if you dare, Lucy Wellman. However, you mark my words. Some day soon, this town will be overrun with maniacal soldiers—ill-bred, loathsome creatures who bayonet women before having their way with them."

"If these soldiers bayonet their women first, there cannot be much pleasure in the latter," I commented dryly, as Lucy let out yet another roar of laughter.

"Oh look!" exclaimed Val, pointing. "There's that great peacock, William Collamore, allowing himself to be overshadowed by some toothless old harpy."

"Yes," observed Lucy, "but with that abundance of pearls about her neck, who needs teeth? Oh, men! They can play the game of love at any age, whereas we women . . ."

Lucy did not finish her sentence. Instead, she sat very still, hugging herself tightly.

"Dear God," she whispered at last. "How very cold I feel."

The women did not speak for a time. Amidst the gaiety, the music and the laughter, it seems we were giving thought only toward the winters of our lives.

"Ladies," we heard a voice saying. It was Charles Davenport. "What is this? A wake?"

We answered with guilty laughter and downcast faces.

"Well then, perhaps I should not ask," he went on, studying the perplexed look on my face. "Never mind. Come, Mrs. Lynford. I wish for you to meet His Excellency, the General."

"Me?" I said, dumbfounded. You had just walked up alongside me, Jeffrey, and I looked from you to Charles quizzically. "Why would the General desire to meet me?"

"Mr. Davenport told the General he wished to offer theatrical productions here in Boston," you explained. "In doing so, Charles had to point out to His Excellency that the General Court had passed an ordinance making the presentation of plays prohibited by a fine."

"The General asked at once if we were *any good*," Charles laughed. "He then went on to say that if the amber-headed woman in the cream silk taffeta was included in my troupe, he would surely consider it. And that woman is you, Mrs. Lynford."

I watched as Charles regarded you with a certain look you did not understand. However, I knew what it meant. It was Charles Davenport's moment of triumph going back to that cold March evening when he told you in my father's taproom that he could make an actress out of me. How very long ago that seemed!

Charles would wait no longer. He took my hand through his arm, pressing me forward.

"Come along, my dear," Charles said quietly, although there was a certain intensity in his voice I had never witnessed before. "If ever you wanted to be a great actress, this is the moment."

"I, I don't understand," I managed to say, nervously noticing how everyone so readily cleared a path for us, as we paraded slowly across the length of the softly illuminated hall.

"Don't you?" he returned, kindly. "Then you are not the same innkeeper's daughter I met just a few short months ago—a brave and beautiful young woman who wore her heart on her sleeve. Do not let your dreams die now, Verity Lynford. For there is so much more in life, just waiting for you; I can feel it. And I can make it happen."

"I'm still not quite sure what you mean," I whispered with a little laugh. "I never wanted to be an actress. Why, I never so much as hinted at it."

"You have a way of turning heads, my dear. It's not just your looks. You have a certain command, a very definite something that excites me. And if you will consent to do this one thing for me—my dear woman—I, in turn will do all I can for you."

The force of his words frightened me, but there was no time for riddles now. We had crossed the room, and the General was in sight.

"Your Excellency," I said with all the poise I could muster. Then I bowed very low, sweeping the floor with my skirts. No one about us moved. It seemed as if no one even breathed.

"Mrs. Lynford, I believe," the General responded with a benign smile, taking me up by the hand. As he did so, I lifted my eyes to meet his, and I was no longer afraid.

"Ah," he went on, still holding my hand. "What a ransom I would give to hear the thoughts behind those lovely eyes of yours."

"But your Excellency," I said, with a pretty little blush. "I was only thinking what an honour it is to meet you."

I lied, of course. Most clever women can, and get away with it. The truth of it was, I could bow before this General and smile because all the while I could hear my father's voice in my head, telling this Tommy Gage what a windy little white feather he was! Thank goodness, indeed, for the privacy of thought. Sometimes it is all that we have.

We left for home shortly thereafter. The midnight air still held a measure of chill, but I was quite warm within from thoughts of performing a Turkish turn with you, Jeffrey, this very night.

Sadly, however, my enticing dreams were to go for naught. You proclaimed to be too tired for anything Turkish.

. . . the play's the thing . . .

Shakespeare—*Hamlet Act II, Scene III*

∽

Late May, 1774

"ALL TOGETHER NOW," announced Sir Alfred Blinn to the group gathered about the drawing room. "We are not here merely to sample Mr. Davenport's divine punch, but to create a solid piece of theatrical entertainment containing enough fervor to rouse the soul of any common clerk."

Having achieved silence, Sir Alfred observed each and every person present over the rim of his bifocals, which were perched precariously upon the tip of his rather pointed nose.

"Has anyone amongst you an idea as to how it should begin?"

"With the tea crisis, I believe," opined the vain William Collamore, with great seriousness. "It was a most glorifying bit of theatrical business, to be sure—displaying defiance and verve. Ah, what a notice we could achieve by it. Why, I can just hear the thunderous applause when I, as leader of the bloodthirsty band of mock Indians, give the order to toss the vile and bane weed overboard."

"All the more reason to keep it for the ending then. Would you not agree?" queried Sir Alfred with an imperious little push to his spectacles.

"I have what may seem a silly question," ventured Jimmy Sloan, leaning back in his chair. "Why in heaven's name are we considering scenes praising the liberty party's cause when we have been commissioned by the King's officer to perform?"

"General Gage is not without his sympathies to the grievances of the people," Charles explained simply. "He has even gone so far as to encourage this particular type of production."

"After all, it is the everyday man who will make up the majority of our audience," Sir Alfred pointed out. "At least for the time being. And your typical cordwainer will not fully appreciate the anguishes of Othello."

"Not so, if I were to play it," announced William with a distinguished sniff.

"You couldn't make an earthworm understand dirt," the portly Roscoe Bennett enunciated over his glass.

"These are difficult times for theatrical ventures," Charles said, quieting the crowd. "Mr. Douglass' American Company is failing miserably in Charleston. It appears that tea problems abound everywhere these days. However, my sincere hope is that a play promoting the patriotic gesture will only reap results of success. Now, gentlemen. Have we any other suggestions for material?"

"Yes!" shouted the exuberant Darcy, jumping up from his chair. "The horrific massacre of 1770. And I have it, right here, in my head!"

Darcy circled the table as he spoke, waving his arms enthusiastically with each new thought.

"We begin with the simple setting of the ropewalks. This should require very little scenery, and minimal expense. Now, we open with the foreman, William Green, by name. This role should be played by Mr. Bennett, for he has quite an outstanding line to deliver—a line requiring a voice of tremendous impact and depth."

"Might that not be my role?" inquired William, his voice edged with hurt. "I, too, possess a voice of depth and impact, you know."

"I have other things in mind for you, William," promised Darcy as he paused momentarily at his jaunt about the table, and then, "Back to the scene. We are at the ropewalks, as I had mentioned. A lowly redcoat enters, looking for work. Now this soldier, Walker by name, is a truly despicable sort. And I say Bryce Taggard might play him."

Bryce's beautiful, but empty, eyes went wide, and his mouth popped open. "But I can't act!"

"Precisely!" Darcy went on. "Now, Walker—so excellently portrayed by our Master Bryce as a base, unworthy, bird-witted being of no particular merit—asks our foreman, played by Roscoe Bennett, if there is any work to be had. Then Roscoe replies, 'Yes, soldier. You can go clean out my shithouse.' Hah! Won't that line receive divine approval from the pit clappers?"

"It seems highly unlikely that we can utter the word 'shithouse' upon the public stage and get away with it," remarked Sir Alfred with a lofty tone of concern.

Jimmy Sloan waved his hand.

"Since it was actually said, might we not change it to 'necessary,' or 'little-house'?"

Darcy nearly yelped as a thought came to him.

"No, by Zeus! I've hit on it! Roscoe can say, 'Go muck out my necessary,' and then he shall point upstage to a prop privy which reads over the door, 's-ithouse,' with the board missing where the *h* should be! That ought to be good for a laugh even from the box seats, as I see it."

"We will consider it," mumbled Sir Alfred, with yet another little impatient shove to his bifocals. It was clearly evident that cheap theatrics were well below his personal standards.

Darcy picked up his punch cup and quickly emptied out the contents, ending with a noisy gasp of pleasure.

"On with the bit," he announced, wiping his mouth on the frill of his sleeve, and starting to pace anew. "Our driveling soldier Walker takes a very lame swing at our foreman. But a few of us boys are out there as well, playing ropemakers, and together we make short work of this idiotic Brit."

"Wait just a moment!" cried Bryce with alarm. "I am not sure I like this!"

"Bah!" laughed Darcy. "To be sure, we won't knock all your teeth out. Anyway, Walker then steps forward and informs the audience that he means to have revenge. This rash bit of false bravado will certainly evoke great patriotic zeal from the house. Thus, if Mr. Taggard here suffers a few well aimed raw eggs, it will only mean a speech well done for the sake of art."

Bryce shook his head in despair and reached for the punch bowl ladle. It was obvious that his premiere appearance on the stage was not to prove as glamourous as Bryce might have hoped.

"Could I not beg the audience's forgiveness for what I am about to say?" he ventured meekly.

"What, and sound like a slacker? Heavens, no! You must take your rotten eggs like a man. Now, back to the crux of the story. It is Monday, the fifth of March, 1770. Why, we can even implore our lovely Miss Eve Stanwood to step out, carrying a placard with the date on it. This would be most effective, and the clappers will cease to throw slippery food all over the stage. During this time, we can set the scene to represent King Street on that cold, dark night. To simplify things, we could take the prop privy and turn it round to show the sentry guardhouse. What do you say to that?"

"Who plays the sentry?" William Collamore asked, still somewhat in a huff over his recent slights.

"David Manley, of course," answered Darcy with blunt expression. "For with his superbly handsome looks, he will most assuredly confuse the sympathies of the female members of our audience. Now, as for you, William, you shall play the pompous officer Goldfinch, who is accused by an apprentice on the street of not paying his master, the wigmaker, Piemont."

"I object," sneered William haughtily. "I have no intention of portraying a scoundrel of questionable reputation. Why, it is beneath me."

"Your arse is the only thing I see beneath you. And that's exactly what you will be, if you do not accept this role, for it is the only fancy dress character in the entire piece."

"Fancy dress? Really? My, my, you don't say. Yes, by God, I can see myself now in red stockings and gloves, blue breeches, of course, with a white waist-coat, double breasted and lined with the finest red moiré. This vestment would be of full bastion gold lace, naturally, with blue facings to depict my royal regimental standing. With this in mind, my epaulettes and gorget shall be oversized; the gorget piece adorned with brilliant rosettes. As to my wig, it should be dressed for court, *à l'oiseau royale,* and, due to the nastiness of the weather, I shall carry an oversized bearskin in my gloved hand."

"Whatever, whatever. Now listen, everyone," Darcy went on, "I have a grand scheme for the role of the snub apprentice boy. Let Lucy play it!"

Sir Alfred glared over his bifocals. "I hardly see it as appropriate."

"Oh, not as she is, mind you. Lucy must bind up her hair beneath a cap and wear boy's clothing. Top it all off with a dash of soot on her face, and voilà! The end result will be fabulous. Lucy is a capital candidate for the role of an unruly street urchin."

"I must admit it is an intriguing thought," commented Charles, carefully.

"Now, this apprentice—Garrick, by name—starts up a healthy round of billingsgate directed at the unfortunate officer, Goldfinch. And Sentry White—that's David—serves our little Garrick a blow to the face. This, David can effect nicely, due to his graceful aptitudes; and Lucy, being a female of decidedly practiced wiles, can fall to the floor as if in a dead faint. But then, she bolts right back up and begins hollering at the top of her lungs—another talent Lucy excels at. This attracts a bevy of street people, as well as a company of soldiers. We can utilize our ladies for the crowd scene, as well as whatever extra bodies we can attract by notice. The street people shout all sorts of insults to the soldiers, encouraging the audience to do the same. In the midst of all this emotional turmoil, our little Miss Lucy comes running forward and points at our sentry, screaming, 'This is the blackguard that knocked me down!' Oh, the public will go mad with enthusiasm. Can you not see it?"

Darcy did not wait for an answer. Instead, he quickly gathered up crumbled pieces of paper, and began bombarding the group about the table as he went on wildly, "The snowballs begin to fly at Sentry White, who cries out unmer-cifully for the Main Guard to assist him, all the while ducking shards of ice and snow. The Main Guard appears, led by a certain Captain Preston, who is, we should note, a gentleman above all else."

"Then I wish to portray him," opined William.

"And I say Gordon Russell should do it," Darcy answered sharply. "His emphatic baritone can be heard above the din we shall be effecting upon the stage, whereas your voice, Mr. Collamore, has a distinct bent of the ethereal to it."

There followed an awkward moment when most of the company present attempted to hide their smiles of amusement. Darcy said it true. William did possess a rather light, airy tone to his speech.

"Back to the story, if you please! The scene is now alive with tension as someone from the crowd calls out, 'Damn you sons of bitches, fire!' This remark is carried on by others in the street. Preston claims he will have no bloodshed, and bravely stands before his men. This tender little display should satisfy the General, as well as any other officer who might attend. But then, a soldier is hit by a stick—perhaps this should be Bryce—and he fires into the crowd. He strikes no one, but a marked silence ensues, a grim hush, during which Bryce steps forward with musket raised. Yes, you see! This is the revenge of which he spoke!"

So very proud of himself, Darcy dashed behind Bryce and held him down by the shoulders. He then continued, his voice very low at first, as if to command the utmost silence, "Our boy, Bryce, takes aim at Samuel Gray, one of the ropewalk men, and bang!—he volleys a bullet through his head. This ignites a chain reaction of gunfire, and others fall. However, here is where our only problem presents itself. One of the massacre victims, Crispus Attucks, was six foot two and dark skinned. We have no one to play him. No one, that is, unless we hoist Mr. Collamore up at the heels, and dip his ugly face in tar."

"I will not consider it," spewed William. This was really the last straw for him, and he began to chew upon his fingernails in a loud, snapping way that everyone found so thoroughly annoying.

"So, there you have it. That's the story. There would be much in the way of tears and sympathy for the victims. Why, we could utilize the etching of the five coffins which was executed by the silversmith, Paul Revere—perhaps as large cut outs carried on stage by five somber figures dressed in black. Then we shall move on from there, glorifying each and every breath of the Patriotic movement. Throughout the program, Betsy Sloan could favour the multitudes with a stirring liberty song or two, and Mr. Bennett could recite some patriotic prose. Throw in some tableaux, and then the entire event ties up with a resounding chorus praising the curvaceous—oh, I did mean to say *courageous* virtues of our fair Miss Liberty, so aptly portrayed by the lovely Mrs. Lynford."

With this, all eyes turned to me, seated between you, Jeffrey, and Charles. I am certain that the look upon my face clearly expressed my surprise.

"Mrs. Lynford to portray Liberty?" Jimmy Sloan began, sounding nearly as taken aback as I was. "I believed Diana Kirby was to be presented in the tableau as Lady Liberty."

"So did Diana!" giggled Bryce, until he caught sight of Charles' silencing stare.

"Why is this?" asked Jimmy, holding his head as though it were bursting from too much port the night before. "What has happened?"

"You know Diana," replied Darcy in a matter-of-fact tone. Charles' threatening stare meant nothing to him. "Our determined Miss Kirby would have the role of Liberty, or nothing. Well, General Gage means for our divine Mrs. Lynford to have center stage. So, off goes Diana with nothing. And do I mean that literally! You see, the injured Miss Kirby has convinced her latest conquest, that silly Lord Something-or-Other, to whisk her away to the *beau monde* surroundings of Paris for a season. They left this morning, so I hear."

"I cannot believe it," Jimmy mumbled, his jaw dropping. "I simply cannot believe it."

"Nor can I," laughed Darcy. "For what prestige can there be in strutting about the stage, draped in a diaphanous tunic of virgin white gauze, with your arms and legs bared for all the world to see—not to mention the men dropping at your feet in droves."

The group, myself included, laughed with grand hysterics as Darcy stepped up upon the gleaming mahogany table from his chair and rendered his best imitation of a sultry goddess parading her wares before the men.

"Enough, gentlemen, enough!" said Charles sternly, although he spoke with a smile. "Do remember that we have a lady in our presence. A lady and her husband, who I hope will not believe we mean to portray our model spirit of patriotism in such a way as you have demonstrated, Mr. Darcy."

"Gads, but I thought I did rather well," Darcy pretended to pout, evoking great laughter once again.

Charles turned to us, his face plaintive.

"Please make an honest consideration of our special request, Mr. and Mrs. Lynford. And should you be so gracious as to consent, your costume will be designed to the exact detail you approve."

Not unlike the conceited William Collamore, I let my mind wander for a moment on just what this grand attire of Lady Liberty's would be like. A flowing tunic of shimmering white, the edgings and lacings of which would shine of gold in the brilliant torchlights of the stage. Then I saw myself as I was that very moment, with my brow knit in confusion, and my fingers in my mouth. Such an apt model spirit of patriotism indeed!

"Mrs. Lynford and I promise to talk it over, Charles," you said, standing. "Now, if you will all excuse us, I am expected at my club."

When we got outside in the glistening sunshine, I waited a few steps to speak.

"Jeffrey, what do you make of all this?"

"The story sounds entertaining enough, I suppose," you replied, your gaze aimlessly wandering about the street.

"No, Jeffrey. I meant about me portraying this Liberty character. Do you not think it is rather shocking?"

"Shocking?" you repeated. "Heavens, no. It's just a dull little tableau, meant to end a great deal of nonsense peaceably. I see no scandal in it."

"Is this to say that you do not mind my participation in the piece?"

"No, not really—that is, I possess no opinion."

"None?" I asked, crestfallen. "You haven't a single concern over your wife appearing on the public stage?"

"Why, no, Verity. What I mean to say is, if you do not take the part, they will give it to some plain-as-day dowager, or some young society girl just coming to age. It's good for the neighbourhood, promotes strong receipts, and so on. Good Lord, it's just a momentary thing, and nothing to get excited about. Besides, when it's over and done with, I doubt anyone will even remember your name."

We walked the rest of the way home in silence.

The world's mine oyster,
Which I with sword will open.

Shakespeare—*The Merry Wives of Windsor*
Act II, Scene II

☙

JUNE, 1774

JUST BEFORE seven in the morning, a carriage arrived at our somber little house of tidy brick on Charter Street. And as the horses came to a full stop before the block, a flurry of feminine voices could be heard from the coach through our open windows.

The coachmen dismounted, but even before their brightly buckled shoes touched ground, the doors of the carriage were thrown wide. The girls then climbed out carelessly into the street, a cascade of colours in their billowing gowns and festive petticoats. It was quite a sight to behold with Clemence, in her customary lemon yellow, Rebecca, in apple green, Valentine, in scarlet, and Lucy in a sky-blue attire with a hat so hideously large, she could shade the multitudes beneath its brim.

"I say, my man, are you sure we have it right?" I heard Valentine ask of the coachman, her imperious glance quickly taking in the entirety of our house.

"It's not very big," Rebecca commented flatly. With this, I decided to come out at once for fear the ladies would spy me lolling about by the window, furtively listening to everything they said.

When I made my appearance, the girls rushed forward, greeting me eagerly, praising my hair, my dress, and my tireless look. One would not have guessed we parted company only hours before.

"I've not been to bed yet," Lucy confessed with a wicked little grin. "That useless Merchant Blackwell kept dreeing about his summer estate in Milton—said he wanted me to see it using that sordid tone of voice which means so much more. So, I calmly agreed to see the place. Then, after the seven mile journey—which took centuries, it seemed—I said to his royal fatness, 'There now, I've seen it. So, take me home my impetuous man; I'm late for an out-ing.' Oh, you should have seen his face, my dears. All six chins were warbling with indignation!"

"Is anyone else coming today?" I asked.

"Oh, yes. There's Bryce. He's sulking away in the coach because Clemence here tried to scurry out of the house this morning in a low-cut dress. Naturally, he fears the worst."

"But it is frightfully low," Clemence exclaimed, thrusting out her chest with wide-eyed innocence. "Bryce told me so at least a dozen times."

Lucy made a broad face of impatience.

"Come along, then; come along. We have to take Verity on her tour of Boston, and then get over to the marketplace on time. So for God's sake, Clemence, suck in your chest before you knock someone down with those things."

We ladies marched down the walkway, very businesslike and prim, until we reached the carriage where Lucy swung open the door and addressed Bryce squarely.

"Squeeze up against the wall, my friend. We have to fit six in here, so you and your buxom wife shall have to sit cozy."

Bryce obeyed without hesitation, although his face clearly expressed a fascination as to why his wife insisted on continually traipsing about town with what he considered to be completely worthless females.

"To the Common, please," Lucy instructed with a wave of her lithe, little hand. Thus commanded, the coachmen started off amidst a burst of noisy chatter, as the sun lit a bright path before us. Our outing had officially begun.

"There it is!" shouted Rebecca as she anxiously pointed an arm out the window, nearly filliping Lucy's hat in the process.

"It's the old Frankland place," she went on excitedly. "Someone was telling me about it just the other evening. It's a full storey higher than Papa Charles' place, and it contains a staircase so wide, a supper for twelve can be set on every step! In the old days, when Frankland and his pretty maid, Agnes, resided there, Sir Harry used to ride his pony up and down that magnificent staircase, just for a lark."

"To be so lucky," sighed Valentine, her dark eyes wistful. "Imagine being discovered by a truly wealthy man, and kept in style. Life's a holiday when you're steeped in diamonds and claret, and you never have to worry about a meal when you're ninety."

"*Ninety?*" mimicked Lucy. "Great thunderation, girl! You'd look a fright at ninety. Who then would want you?"

Valentine pursed her thin lips and glowered.

"What would I care? I would have more than enough money to tell everyone else to go to hell. And if you were alive, Lucy Wellman, I'd have the honour of telling you first."

"Don't count on it, Valentine Hale. I, for one, shall never make old bones."

"How old do you think Virginia Stanwood is?" Rebecca asked as she absent-mindedly leaned her chin upon her milk white hand. "Seventy or so?"

"Oh, surely not so much," I ventured. "After all, isn't Eve her daughter? Eve cannot be more than twenty."

"In all probability, Virginia Stanwood gave birth to the first Eve in the Bible," scoffed Lucy. "Aside from all that, my dears, if you want my humble opinion, I would venture that our Mrs. Stanwood has a vigorous appetite for Charlie Davenport. Why, I'd even lay two fingers on the chopping block to say she's bound to get him, too."

Lucy folded her hands sweetly and regarded Valentine with exaggerated innocence.

"Do you not agree, Val?"

"Nonsense," Valentine scowled in return. "Why in heaven's name would Charlie want moldy cheese when he could easily have cream?"

"Are you referring to yourself, pray tell?"

There was a flurry of red and blue petticoats as Valentine leaned over my lap in a concerted effort towards boxing Lucy on the ears.

"Stop it, girls," I warned, putting up a hand to halt the scuttle, for Lucy was becoming quite agitated.

"Oh, for two shillings, I'd dust your back!" Lucy grumbled at Val, sticking out her tongue for good measure.

"Girls, really!" I cautioned, glancing at Rebecca for help. Alas, the red-headed girl from Georgia was not proving to be my ally. Instead, she was feverishly goading little Miss Lucy into battle.

"Oh, it's all so stupid!" hissed Lucy, throwing up her hands in the air. "Valentine Hale is in love with Charles Davenport. Why, it's so bloody obvious to everyone—everyone, that is, except Charlie!"

I saw the abject despair so plainly written on Val's face, and I patted her hand in a tender show of sympathy. Of course, she withdrew at once from my touch. Silly me. I should have remembered these ladies detested sentiment in any form.

We arrived at Boston Common. On this sun-drenched morning, everything looked so lovely. The grass was richly green, the sky so blue, and the only sound to be heard was the gentle ring of cowbells.

After a fashionable stroll about the Common, Lucy insisted on showing us the gallows. We thus proceeded on foot over Frog Lane towards the infamous Liberty Tree, and then down High Street, until we came upon the stark graves of noted criminals and suicides which were marked by crude heaps of stone.

"Isn't it exciting?" breathed Rebecca. "Why, there are probably pirates buried under there!"

"Yes, that could be true," began Lucy. "But from what Papa Charles tells me, there is a small island just off the coast here, called Nix's Mate. This was where captured pirates were set out alive in iron cages and left to starve. In the end, great swarms of hungry seagulls would attack with a vengeance, and peck off their flesh!"

Clemence gasped, Rebecca applauded madly, and Val made a face of bored impatience. Obviously, Valentine Hale did not enjoy walking all about the town, especially just to hear such dubious tales of horror.

It was then that a bright peal of church bells resounded from the distance. Lucy grabbed at my hand anxiously, practically dragging me along as she spoke.

"The market is open! We must hurry!"

We climbed back into the carriage which had ambled ever so slowly behind our promenade on foot. Lucy then called out her orders to proceed at once towards North Square. The high-stepping horses pulled round 'neath the fluttering shadows of the gallows tree; thus heading for the happier sights along Newbury and Marlborough Streets, their hooves clipping smartly atop the cobblestones. Seemingly only moments later, we disembarked once again.

"We have to walk," explained Lucy, reaching for a basket on the floor of the coach. She then led the march, her short legs making rapid strides. "Some of the streets here are so very narrow that even the merchants' carts cannot make it through."

"Oh," was all I could manage, for I was near to breathless from trying to keep up with Lucy's frantic pace. Valentine and Rebecca were meandering quite a distance behind, their ballooning dresses in full sway. Not much further back, Clemence was making quite a nuisance of herself by displaying a keen interest in what went on in other people's kitchens. Poor Bryce was having a time of it. He seemed to be constantly wigging his wife for perching her nose upon unfamiliar windowsills.

Turning the corner, we encountered the marketplace—a virtual hotbed of activity—with vendors situating themselves wherever a stall, cart, or a cluster of baskets could be attractively arranged.

There were vegetables and fruit in abundance, spilling over their containers like massive cornucopias into the street. Game birds hung in such grand profusion that we were forced to hold our hands on our heads, in order to keep our hair and our hats neat. All around displayed, we saw enough fish and shrimp and lobster to sink a schooner—the scents of which mingled with the enticing aroma of sunshine, fresh baked breads, and the salty rush of crisp sea air.

Everywhere, people were shouting over the constant bray of livestock, and the confusing clucking noises of chickens, hens, roosters and pigeons.

The avenues were filled to overflowing with scullery maids and cooks, gentle-men and their footmen, as well as pale-faced housewives chasing after chil-dren who gambolled dangerously amongst the wares. One such child, a muddy little urchin of a boy, had disrupted an assemblage of prudish turkeys, who, having broken free of their hastily strung pen, piled out angrily into the street, warbling away in a most disgruntled chorus.

Small Negro boys, attired in the livery of their masters, stood quietly clutch-ing baskets as their widely curious eyes rolled in the direction of the loose women of Queen Street. Sauntering along in a slovenly pack, these women displayed little concern for their day dresses, which were splotched and soiled at the hem from constant contact with the filth of the streets.

I had never seen a common whore in my life. Strangely, I found myself both amazed and saddened as I observed a rather young female who belonged to the whim of the night, and now faced the day with dark circles beneath her tired, cynical eyes.

We studied one another for a moment—my face alight with curiosity, and the unknown girl's with contempt. Feeling a bit self-conscious, I smiled ever so slightly. In response, the girl ran a rough hand with its broken nails through her matted, unkempt hair before unceremoniously spitting on the ground just to show me what she thought of my pretty dress, my clean hair, and my clear, unspoiled face.

Just then, Lucy came up alongside me and grabbed my arm.

"Whatever are you doing?" she asked with a breathless little laugh.

"That girl—"

"Oh, that," Lucy replied with a certain measure of scorn. "That one's com-mon low, and filthier than dirt, I tell you."

"Do you know her?"

"Heavens no! I am merely referring to her type in general. One would do better to end it all, than to go on like that, groveling in dark alleys for pocket change."

Lucy looked up into my face, and whatever it was that she saw there made her fretful.

"What's all this sickening sentiment?" she cajoled, picking at my sleeve to gain my attention. "Surely it cannot be over the misfortunes of a sorry little strumpet such as that one. You mustn't feel bad for her, truly you mustn't. You see, she's made her choice, and she deserves her lot if she cannot be both-ered to strive for better. Why, look at me. Stand me alongside that trollop, and cleaned up, she'd be voted the prettier trick. However, she clings to the ways of the street, whereas I—well, I have risen above all of that. She could, too. But she won't, Verity. Instead, she shall go on combing the sordid darkness, and putting up with all sorts of dirty dealings from toothless old drunks who have no more than a sou to spare. And she has wallowed in filth for so long, she simply cannot do without it."

I looked at Lucy blankly. Perhaps it was true, but it all seemed so final, so sad.

"Now, let us put an end to this dismal conversation, and go at once to see my oysman," Lucy whispered, the subject of the young whore quite forgotten in her mirth.

"Your what?"

"Oysman. Oysters, silly; and if you behave prettily, and he's agreeable, you can sample a few. Just follow my lead."

Lucy then proceeded to drag me through the crowd, dodging chickens and children and toppling sacks of grain.

"Plump pigeons! Partridges! Robins and quail!" called out a little bow-legged man whose stone-faced wife worked tirelessly by his side. Under their cart, a large black Labrador slept, peacefully huddled in the shade.

"Lobsters! Halfpenny apiece! Lobsters!"

I wrinkled my nose in appreciation. Had I a mere shilling on me, I would have bought out the entire lot, and had myself a monstrous feast that very afternoon.

"West Indies limes, straight from New York harbour!" shouted one man whose voice was nearly drowned out by a vendor hawking fresh bear steaks. Over in another corner, a bevy of children had gathered to gaze upon a prize goose, the grand dimensions of which outweighed any of the little ones who stood in awe of it.

"There he is!" Lucy cried above the din. "Over there, by the fish monger."

We crossed the square carefully towards the oyster cart which stood in the shade of a quaint brick building. I watched as Lucy rambled up to her oysman, a huge brute of a fellow with a sun-weathered face, and a melodic, singsong voice. Pausing just long enough to flash me a knowing wink, Lucy then turned the full force of her vagrant charms upon her robust victim, swaying to and fro like a sly child, and plying him with all sorts of foolish questions in a cleverly helpless tone.

The oysman, however, seemed terribly amused by her efforts, and he smiled broadly, displaying strong white teeth which gleamed sharply against the rough darkness of his skin.

"You were here two weeks ago with the very same questions, were you not, my lass?"

Lucy feigned great deliberation, followed by a smart expression of amazement.

"Why, yes! Yes I was, indeed."

"And I suppose a sample or two would assist you in making up your mind?"

"That it would," cooed Lucy with a studied flutter of her lashes. She was, I had to admit, truly talented at her sport.

I watched on as the man easily shucked the oysters with his large, powerful hands. However, as he held one out for me to try, I noticed the thick rings of black grime under his fingernails, and I refused politely, shaking my head.

"All the more for me, then!" laughed Lucy without shame, taking both oysters greedily into her tiny, waiting hands.

"Well now, Missy," the oysman said. "Will you be buying some of my fine oysters today?"

"I would," Lucy hesitated. "Except that I am not going directly home. Would they spoil in that case?"

"Yes, they would."

"Perhaps then, I could return around two of the clock," she offered in a smooth, lilting tone. "Hopefully you will still be here. I have such a hankering, you see—for oysters."

"I'll be right in this spot until the town clerk rings the closing bell."

The man practically melted under Lucy's artful attentions, as I looked about aimlessly, pretending not to notice.

I saw Clemence at once, for her Botticelli proportions adorned in lemon chintz made her quite simple to spot. Clemence seemed happily engrossed with vexing the fidgety muster of turkeys who had been swiftly gathered up and recommitted to their pen. Clemence strutted about, jerking her head to and fro, imitating their noisy clatter. This she did quite well. It was plainly evident by the glare of exasperation on Bryce's face.

The Misses Rebecca and Valentine were viewing a display of baked goods with plaudits of great appreciation. I watched as Rebecca held up two rather prodigious loaves of round bread.

"What whoppers!" she exclaimed with awe, causing the company around her to snigger at her double-edged remark. Meanwhile, off to the side, I espied the pucker-faced Merchant Platt carefully studying a cod whose countenance closely resembled his own.

It was also at this time that I could not help but notice a rather forward gathering of leather-aproned apprentices, who were openly ogling me with all the brazen bravado of youth.

"Why, they must think me a loose woman!" I surmised with bewilderment. Indeed, I was a solid ten years their senior, so their blatant curiosity could mean little else. I was a bit put off, of course, but after a moment's consideration, I decided I was entitled to a little amusement myself. Therefore, I endeavoured to give my audience what they sought. I lifted my brow coolly and narrowed my green eyes, presenting these boys with a smile so devastating, I succeeded in turning their heads in embarrassment—all that is, except one.

He was not overly tall, but his physique was noticeably powerful. His face had a distinctive air of the street wise—angelically sweet, but shaded by an undeniably devilish charm. The smile he gave me in return was also devastating. I must confess that the devout gaze of his soulful grey-blue eyes caused me to blush exceedingly.

"Let's move on, Lucy," I stammered all at once, still quite captivated by the passionate stare of my admirer. "I believe it's time to go."

But why should girls be learn'd or wise?
Books only serve to spoil their eyes.
The studious eye but faintly twinkles,
And reading paves the way for wrinkles.
In vain may learning fill the head full:
'Tis Beauty that's the one thing needful . . .

Trumbull—*The Progress of Dulness*

∞

LATE JUNE, 1774

MOST EVERY THURSDAY EVENING, the Eldredges entertained associates of the proper society at their home on Cornhill, facing Brattle Square.

It was a dignified little home; neither opulent nor oppressive in style, and respectable enough to reside in the shadow of the newly consecrated Brattle Square Church, which despite its apparent youth, was already the pride of Boston.

An invitation to the Eldredges' was a casual one. No formalities were imposed; the only tradition being that a tea was presented promptly at nine. We arrived somewhat near seven in the evening to find the Eldredges' only daughter, Lorena, holding court in the center of the richly paneled sitting room.

Lorena was a truly beautiful young woman. Her dark hair fell in perfectly smooth ringlets about her shoulders. Her face was divinely heart-shaped, and her hazel eyes alarmingly mature in their expression. Of slender stature, she possessed magnificent poise for one so young. At seventeen, the only insincere mark of her character was her laugh. It had a false and lightly mocking ring to it. Still, I suppose, the men would be driven mad just to witness her smile.

Her circle of friends, on the other hand, were not so fortunately endowed. They were indeed a silly group of girls. Ellen Fuller, whose rather pallid father was the last of a long line of titled English Fullers, was a plump little being of no consequence. It was rumoured that her father had practically exhausted what was left of the Fuller money on gambling alone. You had explained to me that this was a fairly accepted and well practiced "honour." Being a common person, as it were, I failed to see what honour there was in being stupid with one's money.

Pamela Thornton, who was currently under the protection of a maiden aunt, had a strangely severe beauty which might have served her better amongst the lower class. Little Faith Abbot possessed such a delicate countenance, with her flaxen locks and her gentle blue eyes. But she was more than evidently empty-headed about anything that truly mattered. As for Sophie Littlefield—she had a brain, one would suppose—but her heavyset appearance was nothing short of unpleasant. Why, her puffy cheeks were so unsightly, and almost always crammed to bursting with chocolates.

Yes, they were a silly group of girls—silly because they tried to be so serious.

"Oh, Lorena! Wherever did you get that dress?" queried Faith, her sweet eyes bright.

"What, this?" answered Lorena, looking down modestly at her golden gown with its handsome petticoat displaying an array of silk embroidered flowers. "Mrs. Chandler, the mantua maker on Hanover Street, fashioned this from a London design."

"It's charming," said Sophie Littlefield, easily sounding as though she did not mean it. "It would make a nice little day dress for strolling the Mall."

Lorena ducked her pretty head for a moment, and did not respond. Times were such, I am sure, that this attire cost her father plenty. It was terribly rude of Miss Littlefield to say such hurtful things. Why, I imagine Sophie Littlefield happily split the seams of many an expensive gown, and never gave it a second thought.

"It really is a lovely evening," remarked Miss Fuller, sensing the awkward pause. "I'm so looking forward to a carriage ride in the country—if only someone would ask me."

The girls allowed their gaze to travel towards the other side of the somber, poorly lit room, where the men lounged about discussing the Port Bill. Goodness, but if there was ever a topic so miserably boring to young ladies, it was the Port Bill.

"The townspeople are furious," William Abbot was saying, as the room grumbled in agreement. "Not since those dark days of the Massacre, have I seen the rabble so incensed."

"Yes," agreed Merchant Loring. "It was not all that long ago we watched Governor Hutchinson sail away for England. June the first, was it not? Of course, it was the same day the port closed. Ah, how the people despised him. Such a pity, though."

"Oh!" exclaimed the merchant Edmund Platt, clutching at his long, sorry face. "I would have fainted dead away, months ago, if I had been forced to face the trials that blessed man was put through."

"Hutchinson had a fortune sunk in the East India Tea Company," Loring pointed out. "And we all know what happened to that."

The merchant Blackwell screwed up his unhappy face in sarcasm.

"Tisk, tisk, what a pity for the poor old governor. Well, Hutchinson was not the only man to suffer, you know. Plenty of us fine gentlemen will be put to near starvation now!"

Not unlike many of the others in the room, I slyly regarded Merchant Blackwell's tremendous girth. It would be many a day, I gathered, before that man suffered an honest hunger pang.

"It was indeed the first day of June," Mennefer Abbot recalled with a sigh. "The town was in mourning that day. Oh, not for the Governor, as you said, Mr. Loring. The common people had taken enough from him, poor man. But do you remember how the public buildings were draped in black? And the bells tolled with lament all day."

"How deserted the wharves were," ventured Thaddeus Littlefield. "The port shops and the counting houses closed; the auction house shrouded in silence. And in the harbour, not a single topsail, save, of course, the King's warships and transport vessels. Yes, it was a dark day, indeed."

I sat there listening, yet seeing it all in a different way. I did not consider the economic consequences. I imagine we women, as a rule, seldom do. No, I was imagining the bells ringing as the great trade ships anchored in at Long Wharf. I heard the crews shouting and the first mate bellowing out orders, while hordes of seagulls floated overhead, calling out in their shrill tones. Mixed into this din would be the cry of the bo'sun's whistle, and the deafening roar of wooden decks, spars and pulleys lining up to the catch. These were the sounds of the pulse of Boston Harbour. And now—nothing. The wharves were deserted. Even the seagulls had moved on to where a livelihood of people meant a surplus of food.

"Would anyone care for some tea?" Lorena asked, standing; and as she did so, she realised the nonsense of her statement.

"Tea!" she laughed nervously. "How funny!"

"Yes, I quite agree," said Samuel Loring, moving at once to her side. "Tea sounds marvelous, and I should like to assist you, if I may."

The room returned to merry chatter, as I focused my attention on Lorena Eldredge and the merchant, Samuel Loring. What a handsome couple they made. True, Mr. Loring was somewhat older than the vivacious Lorena, but his wistful good looks and worldly manner made nice trappings—not to mention his tidy fortune. I wondered if Lorena's mother was not already thinking the same way. I suppose all mothers of eligible young daughters became readily involved in the hunt. It was only natural.

"Captain Landon Vale is a man of great understanding."

I turned to where I heard the comment. The merchant Edmund Platt had seated himself upon an ottoman at Mr. Eldredge's feet. With a fluttering hand poised to his heart, Mr. Platt had said, "Captain Landon Vale is a man of great understanding," and it was so eloquently put that it gave me pause. I had not heard of this Captain before.

Warren Eldredge was now speaking of the Captain's father. As I was not privy to the conversation, I could not readily gather every word that was being said. I did surmise that the Vale family was of magnificent means, and that Warren Eldredge and the elder Mr. Vale had been inseparable friends. It struck me as odd. If the Vales were so prominently placed in British society, I did not see the fortunes of the Eldredges matching theirs in any way.

"Is it not wonderful!" I heard Lorena's voice just before me, and I was startled. Blushing, because I was most likely caught at eavesdropping, I merely glanced at the tea and lemon cake she was offering.

"Yes, the cake looks wonderful," I murmured with a half smile.

"Oh, no, Mrs. Lynford," she laughed in that silly and rather artificial way of hers. "I meant about Captain Vale coming to Boston. Why, we are all so excited."

"Yes, I can imagine. I've just heard that the Captain's father is a dear friend to your own father."

"Of course," she went on, seating herself firmly at my side. "Ah, it was such a wondrous time, growing up in London. I resided there until I was twelve. Did you know that? I can recall to this day the stately tree-lined squares with their elegant homes of brick, shining in the sun. I had a formidable governess in those days. Miss Pritchum, her name was. How she worked at keeping me from becoming too vain! Such a silly thing, really. But, oh how I was dressed! The crisp, pretty little dresses of white, with sparkling satin sashes and smart buckled shoes. Life was a glorious picnic 'til I was twelve. It was then that something happened to cause Father to lose all his money."

Lorena looked around the room cautiously, and then continued her discourse in a low whisper.

"I never knew the exact truth of it all. And seeing the desperate shame that befell my mother, I never dared to ask. I heard rumours, of course. We all heard rumours; far too ridiculous to repeat. I believed it all to stem from bad business judgments. Poor Father. Well, whatever the cause, we were on board a trade vessel to America within a matter of weeks. It was the only passage

Father could afford."

Lorena sighed and folded her hands, her lovely eyes suddenly somber.

"It all happened so quickly. Gone were the gay dresses, the concerts at Vauxhall, the lush gardens and the walks in the park with Miss Pritchum. Before we knew it, we were off to our new life here in Boston. A life, thankfully, not of poverty, but of great compromise all the same. Father and I have adjusted well. However, poor Mother never really has. In a few short years, I have seen her beauty fade, like tall grass cut down to dry in the sun. Perhaps you did not know this, but my mother was once a woman of great vitality. Everyone in London loved and admired her. Alas, now she moves about this tiny, little shame of a house like a silent, sorry shadow—that is until she heard the news!"

"What news?" I asked politely.

"Captain Landon Vale," she said, taking my arm. "You see, the Captain is coming here to marry me."

"Oh," I replied slowly. "I had not heard that."

"I met him when I was twelve, and he was twenty-five. Oh, Mrs. Lynford, how very, very handsome he is! His face has such strong, serious lines, and his eyes are positively hypnotic. Why, I cannot even begin to tell you what colour they are, for they change instantly with his mood. When he is laughing, they are the brightest blue of a summer day. When he is pensive, they are grey, like a turbulent storm. However, when he is looking at you with longing, ah, then they are hazel with the loveliest touches of gold. And such an attractive physique! Of course, the Captain takes great exercise. He has such a small waist for a man, yet his shoulders are so broad. He looks splendid in uniform, and he dances divinely. Best of all, Mrs. Lynford, is his voice. It would melt your heart, I know it would."

"And in all these five years apart, you are quite certain you love him still?" I asked. It was perhaps foolish of me to pose such a question. I did not really know this young woman until today.

"But why would I not?" she laughed again, and patting my hand, she leaned forward to share yet another confidence.

"Before any of the guests arrived this evening, I sat at my desk penning *Captain and Mrs. Landon Vale*, at least a dozen times. Mother came in to the room, and I crumbled the paper, cleverly dropping it in my lap. She had no idea, of course."

"How nice," I said. What else could I say?

"It is such splendid news that Captain Vale will be here in September. He has been granted leave from his regiment. He is with the Tenth, did you know? How honourable it is to be a Captain of the Tenth."

"Yes," I said, smiling.

"We were all so amazed that he managed leave at this time, what with the conflict here in town, and all. Thus far, the Tenth has not been called to duty in Boston, but just imagine my good fortune if they are!"

"Bring old Miss Thornton some cake, dear," Mary Eldredge was suddenly heard instructing her daughter. "Please, Lorena, before her tea grows cold."

With a little bow to me, Lorena hastened to her duty. I noticed at once she had an aristocratic hold to her head. Lorena Eldredge may not be able to boast of a family fortune any longer, but her bearing had the necessary pretense of it, all the same. Perhaps she would make this esteemed Captain Vale a very apt wife.

"Summer seems to be settling in quite nicely this year," Ellen's mother Ida observed, glancing out the swirling panes of the parlour window.

"Yes, thank heaven for the warmth," her husband Joseph added, scratching his chin. "My old knees turn brittle with the cold."

Thus, the conversation continued in such a vein for quite some time. Weather and health make such safe topics when the threat of tyranny and upheaval spun in a mad, indifferent dance just outside the door.

Darkness was beginning to blot out the fragile wisps of pink and orange light against the sky. The women had grouped tighter together, and were now conversing amongst themselves. The mothers were quite keen on their daughters showing well at an upcoming ball to be held at the Province House. It was said that everyone of note would be in attendance.

"I shall wear my coral pink floral brocaded robe *à l'Anglaise*," announced the snooty Sophie Littlefield. "Mama commissioned Madame Thérèse to make it for me."

"Ooh, Madame Thérèse!" cooed little Faith Abbot with green envy. "Madame Thérèse is the best."

"Not from what I hear," stated old lady Thornton, who had the distinct appearance of a prune. "Oh, she might have been something of a name once. But now she dares to cater to whores!"

This outburst caught the attention of the gentlemen as well. They had been discussing the prospects of autumn weather, but at the word *whore*, each man paused with lifted brows, and mouths agape. On the other side of the room, Lorena's mother and Mrs. Abbot were making a supreme effort to hush the agitated old woman.

"Don't wave your finger at me, Missy," Mrs. Thornton went on with a fierce tap of her cane. "I brought my niece, Pamela, to this so called Madame Thérèse one morning last month. And who do you think we discovered there, but two of those nasty trollops who work for that whoremonger, Charles Davenport!"

I know my face went pale. No one uttered a word. I looked at you, Jeffrey, and you merely shrugged, uncertain as to exactly what should be said. After all, approximately half the men present had been to Charles Davenport's on several occasions, drinking champagne and unabashedly enjoying the company of his "girls."

"Yes, he's a vile creature, to be sure. Oh, his dress is impeccable, and his outward manners beyond reproach. That devil Davenport knows just the right thing to say to anyone. Such a charming fellow. Charming, indeed! Just ask that mushroom where he made his money, and he'll be forced to say it clear. Off of whores, I tell you. A band of greedy, tenacious little serpents in their satins and silks, waiting eagerly to drain the life's blood out of our good and decent men."

It was on the tip of my tongue to say that any man considered good and decent would have no part of whoring, but I kept silent. I did not want my first evening at the Eldredges' to be remembered in such a brash way.

"Mr. Eldredge," his wife called out over the clamourous voice of old Sara Thornton. "It would benefit us all if you escorted the gentlemen to the dining room, where you could happily continue your political conversation over a glass of port." She then looked warningly at Lorena, however she and her silly, wide-eyed friends were not going to budge. Not when a tirade as interesting as this was going on!

The gentlemen gratefully took their departure. And as the last of them crossed the hall, closing the door behind them with a dull thud, Mennefer Abbot was insistent on hearing more about the light ladies who lingered about Charles Davenport's mansion of stone on Garden Court Street.

The clock struck ten. The Eldredges' Negro servants, Tess and Elijah, had come in to clear the tea things as the room faded into a careless sort of darkness. Huge, laughing shadows danced about the walls, as the ladies regaled themselves with tales of sordid women—a subject which has intrigued even the most virtuous of females since the dawn of time—while they demolished what was left of the lemon cake.

That evening, at home, I had a most foolish dream. I was in the marketplace with Lucy, just as I had been two short weeks before. Initially, everything appeared to be the same. All the vendors and hawkers were there with their wares, however, their actions seemed slower, and all the noises about me echoed strangely in my ears. Ever so gradually, I turned my gaze to where the leather aprons had been. But in my dream, they were no longer there. Instead, it was a British officer, and he was gazing at me with eyes that shone handsomely of hazel with magnificent flecks of gold.

In Spite of Rice, in spite of Wheat,
Sent for the Boston-Poor to eat,
In spite of Brandy, one would think,
Sent for the Boston-Poor to drink;
Poor are the Boston-Poor indeed,
And needy, tho' there is no Need:
They cry for Bread; the mighty Ones,
Instead of Bread, give only Stones.

View of a Charlestonian, 1774

∽

BY THE FALL OF 1774, General Gage had commissioned eleven regiments to keep order in Boston. Colonel Leslie's 64th stationed themselves at Castle Island. The 4th, better known as the King's Own, and the 43rd, arrived within two weeks of the Port closing, while the 5th and the 38th appeared soon thereafter.

The Royal Welsh Fusiliers and the Royal Artillery had turned the Common into a campground. Row after row of cloud-coloured tents sprung up like an overcrowded festival, and the air resounded with drill call, gunfire, and lofty laughter. To further complete the picture, the Marines soon landed. With this final stroke, Gage had surrounded himself with over four thousand armed men, representing almost one third of Boston's existing population.

Businesses shut down, and real estate values crashed. Those who could afford to, left. For the distressed and unemployed people who remained behind, there was little to do but watch the prideful soldiers drill in sulky silence. As "Mob Master" Sam Adams put it, such events were an "insult to the feelings of an exasperated people."

Lord North, as well as many other leaders of the House, felt strongly that

Boston, after seven years of riot and confusion, deserved strict punishment. But what Parliament could not see was that by making an example of our Boston, they had only succeeded in casting her as a martyr before the other colonies. In Virginia, the Burgesses declared the first of June a day of fasting and prayer over our enforced port closing. Soon after, food and other provisions came in from all over. Connecticut herded in sheep, and South Carolina sent rice. Virginia shipped corn, and Maryland offered flour, pork, and bread.

Our men of Boston laboured for shares of these bounties. Selectmen saw to it that wharves were righted and streets were repaired. In a town of siege, any work was welcomed. The only jobs not performed well were those commissioned by General Gage himself. Often, his provisions never made it in from the country. Building supplies were either lost or stolen, and stubborn journeymen stood about the General's fortifications, refusing to work. In desperation, Gage sent to Nova Scotia for willing workers. It quickly became apparent to the General that most Bostonians would rather starve than serve him.

However, just when the people of Boston felt they had taken enough, hundreds of Tories flocked in from the countryside, seeking refuge amongst the British stronghold. With the influx of so many diverse people, the town once again became home to rival gangs. Tensions, both verbal and physical, rose to the boiling point with the advent of each new day.

Sam Adams was determined that Great Britain should be made aware that she could not torture Boston in such a way. Penning a plaintive missive to all our sister colonies, he pointed out that we Bostonians were now suffering in the "common cause." He then went on to suggest a gathering of the colonies. Acting as independent yet united states, the mission would be to draft and publish a bill of rights, which would be taken by a representative amongst them to the British court. New York's Committee of Correspondence replied by proposing a general congress meeting of all the colonies. For Adams, such an act of faith was invigorating indeed. In August, our Massachusetts delegates left for what was being called a Continental Congress to be held in Philadelphia. Some townsfolk were skeptical, though. It was highly doubted that a congregation of wealthy planters, merchants, and lawyers could ever properly represent the needs of the people.

On the first of September, General Gage staged a raid on the public stores of gunpowder in Cambridge, commandeering some three hundred barrels of powder. The event was without incident, although a wildly fabricated rumour reached the newly formed Continental Congress that Gage had bombarded Boston, and several citizens had been killed. These same rumours fanned like wildfire throughout the colony of Massachusetts, and in one day's time, thousands of farmers had gathered in Cambridge, ready to march on Boston. It was a dire warning to the General that what Sam Adams had prophesied was true—no insult, no matter how trivial, would be left unanswered. The winds of war blew hot over Boston, and a confrontation of some sort seemed almost inevitable.

But as far as I was concerned, there had never been so much excitement. I must confess it mattered little if families all around us were making supreme sacrifices just to survive. I couldn't have cared less if ports were closed to commerce, or that a meal of spring lamb, fresh beef, or sugar-cured ham was next to impossible to obtain. Why, even the threat of civil war made no visible impression on my happiness.

I felt alive here. And that in itself was rewarding.

∞∞∞

The sultry throes of Indian summer finally gave way to the welcome chill of autumn. The sun, once unmerciful in its punishment, now filtered softly through the thickset foliage, dappling the ground with gentle, soothing patterns of light. Such happy, heavenly days they were.

But then the rains came—steady, grey, and insistent. Yet, for all their dismal magnitude, the habitual downpours could do nothing to shake the masses of scarlet and orange leaves that clung like stubborn children to the benevolent old shade trees of Boston.

It was on one particularly bright and crisp afternoon that some of the members of Charles' troop, myself included, embarked on a stroll about the Common. It had rained the night before, and the air held that comforting smell of cool, dampened earth and the sweet twist of wood smoke, which drifted lazily from cozy kitchen hearths.

We made a handsome entourage in our fashionable fall dress. Clemence, her cheerfully plump face made rosy by the keen autumn air, jaunted merrily on her husband's arm, her full mop of ashen blonde curls pulled back with a strand of black ribbon beneath a lady's three-cornered hat, edged in feathers. Somewhat behind them, at a more somber pace, strolled David Manley and pretty little Eve Stanwood. In their complimentary outfits of the finest violet hue, David and Eve reminded one of a Romney painting depicting young lovers of the prevailing taste.

James and Betsy Sloan were there as well, dressed seemingly for business in their smart outfits of brown. Virginia Stanwood wore a dreamy creation of off-white, while the Merchant Loring appeared very worldly in his suit of grey. Gordon Russell acted as my escort that afternoon. How strong and fine his looks were. I felt such confidence, being seen on his arm.

"I cannot believe it is nearly the first of October," Gordon observed, breathing in deep the bracing, clean air. "How quickly the summer passed."

Jimmy Sloan agreed, "How odd these last few months have been. With no commerce in the port, and the likes of Sam Adams off to his finely engineered Continental Congress, this town has been swept away by a strange, unnerving silence."

"That's not exactly true," ventured Samuel Loring. "The soldiers are still here."

He pointed ahead of us towards the Common where the freshly trampled fields were dotted with red coats.

"That's Percy's Fifth," he added with a knowing tone. "Several hundred fighting men where once only cows dared to graze."

"Lord Percy?" echoed Clemence, her crystal blue eyes bright with mirth as they always were when Clemence had gossip on her mind. "Oh, word has it that Dolly Quincy has her eye on Hugh Earl Percy. And to make matters worse, her Johnny doesn't care!"

Dolly Quincy was the on-again-off-again intended of Merchant John Hancock. He had been courting Dolly for three years, and in '72, he nearly married her. Before Dolly, John had plodded through a ten year courtship with a certain Sally Jackson. However, in the last two years of that relationship, it was rumoured that the merchant spent far more time in the company of a dock-side whore who ran a grog shop near his own wharf.

At thirty-seven years of age, John Hancock was being pressured by his humourless Aunt Lydia to marry. Lydia had even gone as far as to move her likeliest candidate, Dolly Quincy, right into the house, for Dolly was by way a relative. At twenty-seven, the soon to be *thornback* could do worse than to marry the wealthiest bachelor in all of New England.

"Just imagine," sighed Clemence. "All of three years put into a relationship, and la, there's no love."

"It has been known to happen," remarked Betsy Sloan so matter-of-factly that Jimmy regarded her sharply for a moment before nervously shifting his gaze towards the far corners of the Common, his face blanching. It was a reaction which did not go unnoticed by the rest of us.

"Think of the wealth," replied Virginia flatly. "All the foolish folderol that goes with love and tenderness—bah! Where does it get you? A woman should always marry for money. Love fades quickly, but money affords a fine affection for life."

The men were silenced by so calculating an observation. Virginia then strolled up alongside Jimmy and placed one small gloved hand through his arm. With Loring on one side, and Sloan on the other, Virginia rendered a dreamy retelling of one of her adventures from youth.

"It was in London. I was only sixteen at the time; perhaps seventeen, at most. I was strolling in Hyde Park during the fashionable hour with my Aunt Mathilde, when all of a sudden, King George the Second came galloping down the bridle path on a large, russet coloured stallion. What an entourage of handsome young men he had with him as well. We bowed, of course, as he passed. And as the King cantered by, I could feel the heat of his impassioned gaze upon me. Everyone else in the park could sense his immediate awe for me as well, for it was all too definite to be mistaken. Later, at a reception at the Grenville house, I was told in confidence by one of the King's aides that His Royal Highness claimed I had the nicest bustline in all of England."

Virginia smiled wistfully as we regarded one another with smiles of skepticism. Only Eve kept her eyes to the ground.

We crossed onto the Common where acrid wafts of campfire assaulted our nostrils, and the wrenching snap of gunshot could be heard in the distance.

"It's the soldiers taking target practice over at the duck yard," observed David, furrowing his brow in curiosity. "Shall we go at once and take a look?"

We joined a small crowd of artisans already gathered at the scene. Somewhere in the group, a man's voice rang out in gruff laughter. I glanced about, as did Gordon. The laughter came again, and this time more people were noticing. It appeared that the outbreak of mirth occurred with each and every misfire the soldiers made at the target. And this was often, indeed.

"Could you inform me, sir, what amuses you so?"

We turned. A stone-faced officer had located the source of the laughter— a certain, scraggly looking country bumpkin of some considerable years.

"Most assuredly," the man answered, totally unconcerned by the officer's harsh stare. "I respond to the awkwardness of their fire. I could have hit the last ten easily myself."

"Could you now?"

"That I could."

The officer turned on his heel and barked out an order.

"Bring me five of the King's best pieces, and load them for this honest man."

"I don't need so many," the farmer replied evenly. "Any firearm will do. Only, I prefer to load it myself."

Everyone watched in silence as the man prepared his musket.

"Now, where shall I fire?" he asked, nonchalantly.

"To the right of the target," the officer suggested, and the farmer obliged with ease.

"Now where shall I fire?"

"To the left," was the order. It was instantly achieved.

"Where shall I fire now?" the old man questioned in his nasal Yankee tone.

"In the center."

This, too, was accomplished in effortless fashion, and the small crowd in attendance applauded madly.

"Well, now, my abilities don't show for much," said the old man calmly. "But I have a boy at home who can cleanly blast the seeds out of an airborne apple."

The spectators laughed heartily as the disgruntled soldiers prepared to take their leave.

"It will take a great many redcoats to control men like this rustic old patriot," observed Jimmy Sloan with quiet awe. "Perhaps . . ."

He did not finish his sentence. However, those of us who heard him, did so in our own minds.

∽∾∽∾∽∾

We were just about to head towards the Lion and the Lamb Tavern for a bowl of punch, when Clemence suddenly spoke.

"Oh, my! Look!" she breathed with nervous delight. "It's that Eldredge girl. What's her name—Lorena? Yes, that's it. Lorena Eldredge. She's the intended of that celebrated Captain Vale. You know, the one who will be arriving here from Canada in late October. Uncle Charles mentions him incessantly. Vale is a captain in the Tenth Regiment, which is highly regarded, so I am told."

I glanced over towards the entrance of the Common where Lorena Eldredge stood in the company of her four dull-witted friends. Evidently, Lorena noticed me as well, for her brilliant blue eyes stared sharply in return.

"Heavens! They're coming this way," mumbled Clemence, her plump hand to her mouth in horror.

It was inevitable that our two groups should pass. And as we did so, Lorena paused, nodding briefly in my direction as the tapered gold-brown ribbons of her hat fluttered in the autumn breeze.

"Mrs. Lynford," she said coolly, a brazenly defiant look upon her face.

"Miss Eldredge."

Each group moved on. Apparently, however, the females in Lorena's society could not wait a respectable distance before voicing their rather nasty opinions.

"Oh, Lorena! How could you speak to that woman?"

"Better to have ignored her than say anything, my friend."

"It was disgraceful . . ."

"Virtuous young ladies can't even walk the Mall anymore."

"Oh, hush, girls!" replied Lorena with a confident, annoying little laugh. "You're all being quite unfair to the poor woman."

So they considered me no better than a trollop. Worse still, Lorena Eldredge stood up for me in that terribly snide way that insincere women do when they want to appear fine and proper. Oh, it was absolutely maddening to know I had been feebly defended by such a stick!

"She is beautiful," Eve commented quietly when Lorena had passed.

"Yes," replied Virginia carefully, "and perhaps this gallant Captain Vale feels the same. At least for now. But when he finally takes the time to look deeply into her eyes, he shall see exactly what I did—nothing."

We left in silence.

◌◌◌◌

When I got home, you, Jeffrey, were waiting for me.

"Charles has sent round a note asking us to come over at once," you began as I stood in the doorway, scowling at your message. "Something to do with the play, I imagine. He'll be serving tea."

"I would rather have tea in my own sitting room," I said, walking past you in the hall.

"It sounds important, dearest," you said almost feebly, as you poured yourself a glass of port.

"Oh, I know what it's all about," I sighed dourly as I undid my gloves. "That blasted Darcy has come up with some idea for the finale that as I appear as Lady Liberty, fireworks should be going off about my feet. It's absurd."

You regarded me with a comical look.

"Oh, it's all cozy for you," I retorted. "You can sit in the audience as casual as a minute and laugh your head off at my misfortunes. But what of me? How am I to look with my toga caught up in flames?"

"I would venture to say that Charles has managed to neatly combine two of the greatest events in history—the patriot's struggle for unencumbered liberty, and the fiery demise of Joan of Arc."

I laughed heartily. However, as I turned to look at you, your manner was strained, and your laughter nervous.

"What is it, Jeffrey?" I asked. "What is wrong?"

You paused a moment before speaking. And when you finally did, there was such hesitation behind every word.

"Nothing, my dearest—nothing that cannot wait until later, and then—"

"No, not later. Now, Jeffrey. Please. You're frightening me."

"Well, I scarcely meant to. You see, the truth is . . . will you not sit down?"

I shook my head no, even when you said you would prefer it. I could barely bring myself to breathe.

"You see, Verity, the plain truth is, I love Avella still."

My face paled, and my hands went cold. You paused, waiting for me to say something; but in God's name, what were you expecting me to say? Like the glint blade of a callous sword, your words severed my heart. However, my mind had not as yet received the pang of your injury. I was in shock. I almost did not believe you. For certain, I did not wish to.

"We've been writing to one another," you confessed. "Oh, it started out innocently enough, I suppose. However, I soon found myself expressing the truth from my heart, as well as my disappointments as far as—as far as you— well, our marriage was concerned."

"You need not say another word to me," I replied in a voice I did not even recognise as my own. "Just pack your things and go to her."

"Oh, no, Verity! That's not what I meant by all of this."

I made no response. Such rage was flying through my head, but I could not bring the words forward to speak, for fear of crying. I imagine you saw the fury and disbelief in my eyes, for you put down your glass and came to me, putting your arms about my shoulders. Frankly, at that moment, I loathed your touch.

"Please understand, Verity. Things could be better between us. If only you would behave differently; even look differently perhaps, and then—"

"And then what, Jeffrey? Would you be happy?"

"Yes—yes, I believe I would."

I sighed, breaking free from your foolish grasp. I knew by the alarm on your face that you possessed a hurt of some sort which you were desperate for me to understand. However, it was my hurt that mattered to me most at that moment. My hurt was going to be the victor that night, not yours.

"How very nice for you," I said, and I went upstairs.

∽∽∽

I sat at the dressing table in my bedchamber for the longest time. I sat there as still as the grave. I believed I could think things through rationally, but alas I could not. Your jarring words, "I love Avella still," echoed through my brain over and over. "I love Avella still. I love Avella still." A sensible person would have screamed. I, however, could not. I listened to the rebound of your weak-minded proclamation again and again with a coldness which rendered me unable to comprehend anything. After awhile, the sound of your voice faded. Still, I could not ponder your message. Instead, I listened calmly to the noises of life outside my window against the steady drone of the mantle clock. Carriage wheels rolled by, and a small boy called out to his mother. Windows closed, and the town crier called out the hour. The shadows of twilight began to drown out the meager rays of sunlight that clung in a desperate struggle to the polished floorboards of my room. Still, you did not come to speak to me, Jeffrey. I had halfway hoped that you would. I sat there, watching the sun being blotted out by the night, and I wanted you. How silly of me. The shadows grew bolder. The day, now conquered, surrendered all to the obscurity of darkness. There was nothing of warmth left.

I wrote to Charles that very evening, and informed him that for personal reasons, I could no longer portray Lady Liberty in his production. Charles never asked why, but I am sure, in time, he guessed. Valentine Hale proudly inherited my part in the piece. However, once Diana received word in Paris, she was on her way back to Boston with a vengeance. In six short weeks, Miss Hale was forced to abdicate the role to Miss Kirby. It was fascinating how fierce the female heart could be.

If you recall, Jeffrey, we spent most of those next few weeks discussing our differences. Or perhaps I should say, your differences. We came to some sort of resolve, I suppose, but strangely, I cannot recall a word of it now. You see, I had lost my joy in most things. Worse than that, however, I lost my trust in you.

For false diversion, we went often to Charles' soirees. We also spent a great deal of time at the Eldredges. Lorena had forgotten our little meeting at the Mall. Either that, or she was too stupid to know how insulting she had been. Regardless, we continued our Thursday evening visits to her home. Lorena and her parents were greatly disappointed that the Captain was at last unable to obtain King's leave. However, news came that the Tenth had been commissioned to Boston, and as a captain, Vale would be with them. Lorena began gushing about him anew. Whereas once I was amused by her babbling, I now despised it. All lovers are fools.

At least I could take pleasure in knowing that I, and not Lorena, would meet this illustrious officer first. You see, Charles Davenport had invited Captain Vale to dine a full night earlier than the Eldredges, and Charles asked expressly that I be there.

Powder plot is not forgot.
'Twill be observed by many a sot.

Almanac—5 November, 1774

⌒

AT THE FIRST SHADE OF DUSK, the pope's platform rolled out onto the tiny, cramped avenues of Boston, signaling that the Pope's Day celebration had officially begun.

It was a most cumbrous wagon—some thirty feet long, and as wide as the street itself, whereon rode the grotesque effigies of the pope and the devil. The pope was seated at the front, adorned in the ostentatious attire of his station, with a colossal white wig and a ponderous cap of gold lace. On the table before him lay an ominously large book, with playing cards spread all about.

Beyond the pope danced the figure of Nancy Dawson, while behind her, Admiral Byng dangled from his gallows rope. At the far end of the platform perched the devil, covered in thick tar and feathers, and wielding a large pitchfork.

This carriage had as its masters a captain, two lieutenants, and a purser, along with a fine troupe of fiddlers and dancers. A squadron of young boys, hidden beneath a huge paper lantern, worked the strings of the monstrous marionettes who hovered above their heads in a strange and mystical communion.

Throughout the evening, this awe-inspiring vehicle would wind its way from house to house, heralded by whistles and drums. The procession would always pause before the homes of the wealthy, for there the purser would collect donations for food and drink.

The only hero of this parade was to be found in the figure of "Joyce Jr.," who led the wagon astride a donkey, giving a special whistle to his henchmen from beneath his hideous mask. These so-called henchmen were the men and boys of Boston considered worthy enough to join Joyce Jr.'s honourable mob. In history, I was told, it was Cornet Joyce who captured Charles the First and handed him over to the army. Now it was Joyce Jr. who ruled the rabble of Boston and ridiculed a king who reigned over three thousand miles away.

The night would end in a brilliant bonfire, in which all but the wheels of the carriage and the heads of the effigies would be consumed by flame. To this inferno would be added any barrels or tubs and fences the mob might have stolen along the way. It was an evening of innocent fun, and nothing like the Pope's Days of the past when rival gangs from the North and South Ends battled furiously for possession of each other's popes and devils.

However, on this particular night, all the singing, dancing, drums, and conch shell whistles could do very little to enliven my spirits. And try as they might, my friends could do no more to distract me. Before long, I was asking to go home.

"Nonsense," began Lucy in her most determined tone. "You cannot go along now. Besides, if you arrive home before ten, you'll startle Beals, and he may possibly never recover. No, I have it! What do you say to some oysters at the Salutation?"

I could not help but laugh.

"Oh, Lucy! You always seem to be in the mood for oysters, don't you?"

"Why deny it," she murmured slyly. "But then again, there is another motive."

We waited expectantly for her answer.

"The most delectable young men gather at the Salutation," supplied Lucy, as she turned herself about and led us down the darkened cobbled lane, the girls' excited chatter mingling with the clamorous sounds of the festive merrymakers in the avenues beyond.

◌◌◌◌

The Salutation was terribly crowded, and at first the choking smells of spilt beer, curling pipe smoke, and stale sweat nearly overwhelmed me as I paused beneath the inn's sign depicting two well-attired gentlemen bowing to one another.

"Shall we proceed?" Lucy asked brightly as I hesitated just long enough to desperately inhale the last available wafts of fresh sea air before submerging myself in this torrid den of aromas through the ladies' entrance door.

"Somewhat rank, isn't it?" Lucy whispered after observing the pinched look on my face. "But never you mind. You will soon get used to it. These are the true Bostonians, you see. You won't find any fine ladies or pompous popinjays lolling about here."

"I've noticed," I mumbled, peering about the place. No, there certainly wasn't any nobility swilling down rum in this smoky trap. Judging by their sun-weathered faces, and their bowed backs, these were the men who made their day to day living down at the docks. How loud they were! Certainly the farmers and shopkeeps who frequented my father's taproom were far more civilised than this.

Lucy had ambled off in search of the innkeeper, as Valentine, Rebecca, and I had to squeeze up against the wall in order to avoid a collision with a trio of drunken sailors who brazenly argued amongst themselves as they staggered past us. Once all was clear, I glanced at the wall behind me. It was black with smoke stains, as were the beams overhead.

"My dress," I thought miserably. That would teach me to wear my fine brocade to an alehouse.

"It's all settled!" Lucy said, waving her hands triumphantly. "William says we may sit in the back of the main room. He was going to set us up in the ladies' parlour, but I assured him we were not a batch of simpering schoolgirls. After all, if his tavern wenches can take it, so can we. Right, girls?"

We nodded feebly in return.

"Oh!" Lucy exclaimed with great enthusiasm. "How grand it is to be right in the thick of things!"

We followed as Lucy led us across the noisy, overcrowded room to a musty corner table with high-back bench seats. As we paraded through, we could not help but hear a remark or two made our way. Someone had called Rebecca a whopper, which only made her giggle. And one coarse old bibber referred to Valentine as his "light-o'-love."

"How rude!" muttered Val, her nose in the air. "Why, I have never been more insulted in my life!"

"Yes, how true," began Lucy, her voice rich with sarcasm. "Feign your contempt for rascally compliments now, if you wish. But in a few short years, Miss High and Mighty Hale, age will put an end to those whistles of appreciation. And you will be left wondering where it all went. Why, you'll be positively desperate for attention."

"Oh, stuff and nonsense," Val retorted curtly.

"It is a fact, and you know it. Why, with the exception of Rebecca here, we are all of us settled in the summers of our beauty. And it's a short season, ladies. So bask in the heat while you can."

I regarded Lucy with surprised awe. I had never credited the girl with much sense, but this deluge of calm wisdom impressed me.

"Now shut up and drink the rack punch," Lucy concluded. "It's wonderful."

Within moments, a heavyset serving girl with broken nails and a somewhat toothless smile, arrived at our table with a large platter heaped with oysters—enough to feed twelve starving people. As she placed the pewter dish before us, Lucy squealed with delight.

"I'm in heaven!" she said, clapping her hands. "As for the rest of you,

you'd better long-arm it, if you're hungry. I'm feeling rather greedy tonight."

We watched as Lucy slurped down oyster after oyster with glee. Rebecca then lifted one of the slimy morsels to her lips and grimaced before deciding to proceed no further as, across the smoky den, a burly man burst into song, raising his robust voice clearly above the din of the crowd:

> *Have you not heard of Billy Pringle's PIG,*
> *'Twas not very little nor yet very BIG.*
> *When 'twas alive, it lived in Clover,*
> *But now it's dead, and that is all over . . .*
>
> *Billy Pringle—he sat down and cry'd,*
> *Betty Pringle—she lay down and died.*
> *So there was an End of One, Two, Three,*
> *Betty Pringle, Billy Pringle, and PIGGY WIGGEY!*

"Charming," murmured Val, leaning on her elbows with a sigh.

"Tell us, Mrs. Lynford," began Rebecca, squirming casually in her seat. "What has made you so very sad and pensive lately? We all could not help but notice."

I looked up sharply.

"Whatever do you mean?" I asked, my tone clearly edged with suspicion.

"Well, you definitely seem out of sorts lately," Val went on. "Meaning no disrespect, of course."

I paused, frantically wondering just what they really knew—or had guessed. After all, Jeffrey, if it was so easy for you to be open with Avella Gore about our marital state, why not then tell all of Davenport's rapacious company as well?

"I've just been somewhat bored, I imagine. That is all."

"Oh," sighed Lucy philosophically. "Then what you need is a man in your life."

"But Lucy, dear—I'm married."

"And pray tell, what does that have to do with it? Heavens, if there is anyone who deserves romance more, it is a married woman!"

I laughed lightly at the terribly sincere expressions I encountered on the three ladies' faces before me.

"All right, then. If I am to take a lover, just who did you have in mind?"

"Hmm," muttered Lucy, giving it much thought. "We really do not have the cream of society at our doorsteps, now do we, girls?"

"How about Gordon Russell?" offered Rebecca brightly. "He's rather handsome in a roguish sort of way. He reminds me of a romantic highwayman—you know, the sort who would rob a husband blind, but take the man's wife to a private supper, and ply her with champagne and jewels. Oh, I do sound silly, don't I?"

"Yes," replied Lucy flatly. "I say *nay* to Gordon. True, he may have spectacular looks, but he can be more fickle than a woman."

"Lord Sutherland, then. He and Diana will not last beyond the waning of the moon, from what I hear," stated Valentine very matter-of-factly, her nose firmly implanted in her punch cup.

"That pervert!" bellowed Lucy. "Law of Moses, no! He may have money, my friend, but just how much is one willing to put up with to have it? Besides, Verity should choose a lover for romance, not finance. At least, the first time around, that is."

"Not Charlie, I hope," Val ventured in a small voice.

I glanced at her curiously.

"Why do you say that? Is Charles Davenport some sort of moonstruck deviate too?"

"No," moaned Lucy. "It is simply that Val has been making cow eyes at Charlie for close to half a year now. And if she does not say anything about it to him soon, she will never get milked—if you know what I mean."

"Oh!" cried Valentine, her brow furrowing in disgust. "You are nothing but vulgar and crude, Lucy Wellman!"

"Perhaps," Lucy shrugged in return. "But seriously, girl. You will never get anywhere with Charlie Davenport, unless you tell him. What can any female expect when she never lets on to a man that she wants him? Oh, why do some women go about acting so priggish and touch-me-not in front of the men they are so desperate for? It makes no sense to me, whatsoever."

"She is right again," I thought to myself with a start. Yes, how true! Her words prompted me to realise that for all I was married to you, Jeffrey, you never knew how much I really loved you. With all the disappointment you had experienced with Avella Gore, the subject of my genuine devotion lay silenced. I had never revealed my deep and sincere feelings for you. It had all happened so fast. However, here we are, Jeffrey. You have confessed to loving Avella still.

And now, we are miserable and dejected. To be quite honest, I am somewhat afraid to try loving you still, for you will only hurt me again and again. So, what are we to do?

The girls suggested I take a lover. How funny. In Concord, the very hint of it would mean scandal. Here, in Boston, it seems almost second nature—at least within this certain society that Charles Davenport has created. Strangely, I must admit, the idea does not seem so terribly wicked to me. After all, Jeffrey, the conjugal nature of our union has not been exactly what I would call fulfilling. The promise of blissful intimacy has thoroughly faded between us, and now, infrequent as our moments of intimacy have become, you seem only intent on satisfying yourself. Oh, I am fully aware that proper women never discuss finding pleasure in bed. Indeed, most women are not even aware it could exist. But heavens, why would women ever want to fall in love, if it only meant submitting themselves to such repetitious drudgery all the time? It had to be better than this.

Perhaps if I let you know how much I cared, Jeffrey. Perhaps, if you knew, we could attempt to put the pieces of our married life back together again. Despite all the hurt, there still existed a glimmer within my heart that whispered, "try . . . try . . ."

Another three-shilling bowl of punch was called for, as the girls went about constructing a humourous roster of paramours for me to consider in order to ease my boredom. Samuel Loring was a likely gent at first, for he was good looking, in a pallid sort of way. However, his often dreamy referrals to his dearly departed wife did make one feel rather eerie at times. The bungling merchant Edmund Platt would be a sure success, if one had a penchant for dizzy, grandmotherly types. Of course, there was Sir Alfred Blinn. A buzzing skeleton, to be sure. The only benefit a woman would receive from a liaison such as this would be a detailed and precise history of England. And William Collamore—modesty personified! Then why not the great fatty, Merchant Blackwell? He was good for a hearty meal or two out in the local taverns—but his lovemaking was likened to the ill winds of indigestion.

"Perhaps then this newly arrived Captain Vale!" Lucy chirped. "Now there is a real man for you! I have seen him, you know."

"And how is that?" I asked with near indignation. "His regiment has been aboard ship in the harbour for nearly a week now, waiting for proper housing."

"That's the common soldiery, my dear, and not the officers," Lucy explained. "Yes, I tell you, I saw him with my very own eyes! I went to Charlie's on a financial matter—nothing important, really—and that hawk-nosed footman of his, Stearns, made me wait outside the library. Can you believe it? So, I waited. What other choice did I have? But am I glad I did! Within minutes, this terribly handsome officer made his appearance. My dears, how very worldly! That's all I can say. This distinguished Captain Vale has a presence that overwhelms you. It's not just his superb looks. He has an air of confidence that is nothing short of breathtaking. I managed some sort of a greeting, foolish as it was, and he made a reply so proficiently elegant, I forgot every blessed word he said! Now, I know the man would have nothing to do with the likes of me, but good heavens, Verity, it would be worth your while to try!"

"Don't be silly," I said. "The Captain is all but betrothed to Lorena Eldredge.

She told me so."

"Engagements are nothing more than a marked period of time in which each party sets out to discover if there is not someone better in life," Lucy shrugged. "Besides, you should only want to bed him, not wed him. Never, never complicate a good thing, my dear. It doesn't pay. Oh, well. You will see for yourself next Friday at Charlie's supper party, for the elegant Captain Vale will be the guest of honour. However, if you're not interested—"

"How about any of the fine swains in this room?" I ventured instead, surveying the array of mast makers, shipwrights, and caulkers. "Why, with a bounty such as this, we could easily pick out at least ten lubbers apiece."

"Well, since you've mentioned it, I have selected mine already," announced Lucy with a grin. "And, he has been staring at me since the moment we arrived."

"What! Which one is it?" queried Rebecca, for being seated next to Lucy, she possessed the freedom to scan the crowd easily.

"The cute one standing over there by the post. See him? He's the one with the luscious mouth and the terribly brave eyes."

"Where?" breathed Rebecca. "I'm afraid I don't see who you mean."

"First, look at the post, dummy—"

"All right."

"Fine. Now, do you see the tall, pale lad with the poxed face?"

"Yes," Rebecca answered with hesitation.

"Good. Now, look next to him—on his right."

Rebecca's face brightened.

"Oh, my!"

"See! What did I tell you? He's delicious."

"Oh, yes, he is darling. But I don't believe he's looking at you, Lucy."

"Then what is he contemplating, you ninnyhammer? The splinters over my head? No, you are wrong, Rebecca Henley, and I will prove it. Why, I'll wager that it's me he's after—and furthermore, I'll lure that lovely boy over here without so much as a single word."

"'Tis a bet, then. How much do you care to wager?"

"Oh, money bores me," replied Lucy, feigning a trite yawn. "But I'll tell you what. If I win, you can come over to my place in the morning and scrub the front steps."

Rebecca put her hands to her hips at the challenge.

"And if I win, Miss Lucy Wellman, you can come over to my rooms and serve me my breakfast in bed—and clean out my chamber pot, besides!"

"Oh, really?"

"Yes, really!"

"All right then," said Lucy in a singsong voice, as she turned her full attentions on the stranger. "But I warn you. You'll be sorry!"

I could only watch the attempted conquest through Lucy's finely determined face. First, she stared with her sharp, dark eyes as intently and businesslike as though she were viewing bolts of material for a gown. However, this did not last long. Not one minute later, her face softened into a gentle smile, which was followed by a sweet look of confusion. Fluttering lashes and a timid, downcast gaze completed the picture. It was nothing short of fascinating.

"Here he comes," Lucy mumbled under her breath. "Now remember, he's mine."

Feeling an outburst of nervous laughter coming on, I turned my face towards the wall. It was silly how predatory some women could become at times like this.

Lucy's victim was indeed approaching the table, for Rebecca had clasped her chubby little hands to her face, and—much to Lucy's dismay—was now snorting with laughter. When the young man finally did arrive, Lucy countered with her best imitation of a doe-faced virgin. Yes, it was an amazing display of showmanship, and I was truly impressed.

"Oh, I did not mean to . . ." Lucy stammered prettily. "Oh, you could not believe I was . . ."

Sensing it was rude to go on staring at the dusty old Madeira bottles on the rain warped ledge above our table, I turned to address the stranger with what became a smile of curiosity.

"Don't I know you?" I said.

"At the marketplace, nearly six months ago," he volunteered.

I blushed at the memory of that fine morning when I had noticed this boy standing amongst a group of faceless apprentices, ogling me with all the brazen admiration of youth. How flattered I was then. Nearly six months ago—six lingering months that now felt like a lifetime past. That Verity was an entirely different woman. That Verity, who gazed about a common marketplace with innocent awe, had been fond of spring and tenderhearted dreams. That Verity was foolishly hopeful, and sadly naive. Surely, she would have cried with all the misery one could bear over the flimsy confessions of a feeble-hearted husband. However, that was six months ago. Today, this Verity was tired, bitter, and somewhat cynical. Today, this Verity refused to cry.

"Yes, of course," I said at last.

"I'm surprised—and grateful—that you remembered," he said sweetly, as a hint of his special smile returned for my eyes only.

"You cannot possibly mean the market day I took you to, Verity," chimed in little Lucy, gritting her teeth behind what she hoped would pass for a nonchalant smile. "You couldn't possibly, for I would have certainly recalled having met you, young man."

"I did not introduce myself then," he said briefly, never once dismissing his gaze from mine.

"Well, you can make up for it now," stated Lucy, not one to be daunted. "My name is Lucy Wellman. Miss Lucy Wellman. And this is Rebecca Henley, here. And Valentine Hale—oh, and that's Mrs. Jeffrey Lynford."

"A pleasure to meet you, Mrs. Lynford. My name is Perry Talbot."

Lucy slid over, practically grinding Rebecca up against the wall as she grabbed at Perry's arm.

"Please sit down, Perry Talbot. And we'll try not to fight over you. Right, girls?"

We could not help but notice Lucy's very pointed warning.

"Perhaps your friends would like to join us," ventured Rebecca, who obviously did not wish to spend the remainder of the evening with her face pinned to the rough plaster of the wall, while Lucy had all the fun.

"Yes, that is a splendid idea," Perry agreed, standing. "I shall go get them."

"How wonderful!" Lucy exclaimed happily, as he walked away. "That makes two more. Oh, look at them talking! They are dividing us up, you see. Men are like that. It's a pity there's not enough to go around, but you girls can work that out for yourselves. Just remember, Perry Talbot is mine."

I found myself suddenly annoyed. Why, the whole thing was becoming terribly foolish.

"I will make things simple and leave," I announced, standing.

"Don't be such a dolt," Lucy scowled. "Besides, what makes you think you're the odd one out?"

"I seriously do not care. Beyond that, I certainly possess no desire to be bantered about in a little boy's lottery. So, good night girls; and good luck."

"You're not leaving, are you?" I heard Perry Talbot ask anxiously as he came up behind me.

"I was considering it," I answered none too nicely.

"Are you walking? Or do you have a carriage waiting?"

"Walking."

"May I escort you home, Mrs. Lynford?" he asked, his steely blue eyes pleading. "It would be an honour to do so."

I hesitated a moment, not entirely convinced I should say yes—until I caught the poorly disguised glare of jealousy on Lucy's face.

"Certainly," I said at last. "Why not?"

Perry stepped aside, in order that I might gather up my pretty cambric gloves from the bench seat.

"It's all evened up now," I whispered to Lucy with a broad grin. "So have a wonderful night. Only remember—breakfast for Rebecca in the morning. Oh, yes, and don't forget to empty the chamber pot."

"Gardyloo!" Rebecca shouted with glee, punching the dour-faced Lucy in the ribs. "Gardyloo in the morning!"

With a little laugh of triumph, I took Perry Talbot's arm and sauntered through the smoke filled tavern, and out into the darkness of night.

∞∞∞∞

We walked in silence for a minute or two, for as with most strangers, the first words are the most difficult.

The night air was laced with an icy chill, and against the silence of the streets, the not too distant ocean could be heard with its omnipresent churl.

North Square loomed before us, its tidy little border of close-knit homes huddled together like phantoms of wood beneath a dim blanket of stars. All was quiet. The guardhouse and the public marketplace slept peacefully, wrapped in slumberous shadow.

"It must be quite late," I uttered at last.

"I have always loved the night," remarked Perry, looking wistfully towards the unending sky. "It amazes me how many people seem frightened by it."

"Perhaps they mistrust what they cannot see."

He glanced at me with a measure of respect and smiled.

"Yes, I do believe you are right," he admitted, and then lifting his voice to a less serious tone, he went on. "Now, which way must we go in order to safely direct you home, Mrs. Lynford?"

"Charter Street, at the Copps Hill end."

"Oh! You should have said something. We could have gone straight out Salutation Alley."

"Yes," I conceded. "However, you seemed so determined to go by way of the Square."

"I like the Square," he replied. "Oh, I do not live here, of course. But all my most tender memories were born in this square, just the same."

"And where do you live Perry Talbot?"

"On Ann Street, near the warehouse. And as for my trade—which I assume to be your next question—I am a humble blacksmith; servant to all the finest, as well as the most finical horses of Boston, from Beacon Hill to the North Battery."

"I am impressed."

"As well you should be," he teased.

We were before the steps of Christ's Church when I paused to speak.

"And now, Perry Talbot," I began, facing my companion straight on. "Why is it you have sought me out?"

He regarded my face for a moment, and then merely shrugged; the impish smile never leaving his lips.

"Why not?"

Arranging my skirts ever so carefully, I sat down upon the cold stone steps, and indicated with a crook of my finger that Perry should join me.

"Why not?" I echoed slyly. "Because it was clearly my friend, Lucy, who invited you over to our table tonight. Certainly she is more your age and your type."

Perry Talbot scowled in disbelief.

"That eager little mole-eyed wench? My age and type? Most definitely not! Why, that moldy slip of baggage is thirty-five, if she's a day. My age and type, indeed!"

"All right, then. Forgetting Lucy for a moment, I still have a sneaking suspicion that you possess an underlying purpose to all of this. So, just come out with it, young man, and speak the plain truth, please."

"Miss Lorena Eldredge," he sighed all at once.

My face paled with surprise and curiosity as he went on, quite breathless, his conscience now happily unburdened.

"It was just about a year ago, this past summer—I was down at King Street, attending to Captain Richmond's mare, when I saw Miss Eldredge walking along Merchant's Row with that pale and quiet mother of hers.

"Oh, I knew at once she was from a better class than myself, and respectable. But, at that moment, it didn't matter. You really cannot hold much regard for such obstacles when you fall in love at first sight. All I knew was that I was looking at the sweetest and most tenderly beautiful girl in all of Boston.

"I did not speak to her then. How could I? I didn't have any sensible reason to. So, I begged my friend Andrew, who happened to be with me at the time, to follow them home; and he did. Andrew brought back the news that my angel lived over on Cornhill near Brattle Square. He also made some inquiries, and found out that her father had lost his entire fortune due to bad business judgements, or some such thing, and now Mr. Eldredge was here to regain the family honour. It was then that Andrew told me to forget her. He was right. I knew he was right. But somehow, I couldn't force the image of her beautiful face out of my mind. She meant too much to me already.

"So, I kept going around to her house, and I'd show up everywhere that she and her mother, or her friends, went walking. Oh, I would never talk to her. She made me so damned nervous, you see. And the more time that went on, the less I knew what to say. But then, one Market Day, Miss Eldredge came right up to me and said something. I couldn't believe it, but there she stood, saying that she had noticed me on many occasions, and thought I had the nicest smile. Can you beat that? Well, we got to talking, just as natural as could be, even with some old dowager cow named Miss Thornton fussing over her shoulder. And, by the time we finished our introductions, Miss Eldredge invited me to walk the Mall with her and her friends that very next afternoon.

"So, it went on from there. We met almost every day. The only time I wasn't by her side was when it was raining, or snowing too hard. On those days, I would dash across these very streets, and down to the Square, just to be near her. And somehow, Miss Lorena would always know I was out there, and she would wave to me from the front parlour window.

"By February, I told her I was in love with her. And she confessed to being in love with me, too. We made plans, and Miss Lorena promised to talk to her father that very night. I wanted to be the one to tell him, but she would not hear of it. She said it would not be a problem."

He paused for a moment, looking off towards the inky array of rooftops set against a backdrop of velvet night, as I waited anxiously for his next words, my breath caught very still within my throat.

"I never saw her again. Oh, I did see her father. Mr. Warren Eldredge came to my shop demanding to know why I dared court a young woman of means—a girl who was far too innocent, and far too impressionable to know better. He then accused me of wooing his only daughter for the promise of money. And regardless of what I said, or what I vowed to do, Mr. Eldredge stubbornly refused to believe that I truly loved his daughter."

There was a tremor in Perry's voice as he nervously bit at a fingernail, and then stared at his hand for something steady to focus on.

"The unbearable days came and went without a single word from her. I thought, with the spring, I would find her out walking. But her father most likely forbade it, knowing that's how we met. Since that time, I have paced back and forth in front of that silent little house on Cornhill, just praying for the slightest glimpse of her—or a sign. But the shutters are always closed by day. It's as if the master of the house refuses to acknowledge the presence of the sun."

With a sudden movement, Perry Talbot knelt at my feet and gazed imploringly into my eyes.

"Oh, Mrs. Lynford, you've got to help me. You see, I knew it—knew it when I first saw you—that only you can help me through this."

"I—I don't understand," I stammered.

Perry picked up my hand tenderly, and held it as he spoke.

"I was there, in the shadows, on the evening of Gage's reception at Faneuil Hall, last May. I figured with such an event going on, the Eldredges would be there. And I was hoping against hope to see Miss Lorena, or perchance to have her see me. Well, that didn't happen. So, I was about to give up and go home, when all of a sudden, there you were. My goodness, but I certainly took notice of you."

Despite the confusion of thoughts that whirled about in my brain, I ducked my head in modest appreciation of his praise.

"Of course, you know you're lovely. That's why there was such a buzz going round the town about you. Some folks were remarking how terribly fortunate Charles Davenport was to have discovered you. And it got me to thinking.

"You seem so genuinely nice, Mrs. Lynford. I could see that without even making your acquaintance. You're so very different from all those rather false-hearted people in Charles Davenport's society, and it shows. So, if true love holds any weight with you, and I believe that it does, you'll help me to get her back, Mrs. Lynford. Surely you must be friendly enough with Miss Lorena. And if you have a caring heart, which I believe you must, Mrs. Lynford, you'll bring Lorena out somewhere—anywhere that I might talk to her alone. You see, I must find out why she's afraid to keep her promise to me."

His grasp on my hand grew tighter, but I did not feel it. Instead, I was looking far beyond Perry for a wild moment, my mind positively stunned at what it had learned.

How could Lorena Eldredge go on and on about her grand love for the mysterious Captain Landon Vale, having already promised her heart to this fine young man in secret? But then, like a lightening bolt, the answer went through my head. Lorena was not in love with the Captain. She had to pretend to be, for her parent's sake. Perhaps Lorena's most desperate struggle was to find her way back to Perry Talbot once more, but she was being watched and guarded. Suddenly, the entire story sounded so very touching and romantic.

My eyes swelled with tears. How strange that I could cry for the poignant struggles of near strangers, when for myself, I could emotionalize nothing.

"Oh, I am sorry," Perry began, sensing my tearful silence to mean disapproval. "It was wrong of me to hope for so much."

"Whatever do you mean?" I asked slowly, dabbing at my eyes with an embarrassed, little laugh. "Of course I'll help you, Perry Talbot."

This way the king shall come . . .

Shakespeare—*Richard II, Act V, Scene I*

∞

FRIDAY–11 NOVEMBER, 1774

WE WERE INVITED to Charles Davenport's at six in the evening—a full two hours before the rest of the company. This was not uncommon. Charles typically enjoyed having a few guests in for drinks and conversation before the house was full. More often than not, I was the only female asked to these gatherings. I never ventured to question why. I imagined it was because Charles found my discourse and wit amusing. It was really not much more than that.

Charles had brought us together in his favourite room, the west parlour. It was definitely a man's room—dark and virile with its fine red leather chairs and deep wood paneling. The light from the stained glass windows was scarce—the room did better to take its glow from the virile flames of the Dutch tiled fireplace. Above the rippling red and gold border panes of the window, a bold inscription read: "Some Rise by Sin and Some by Virtue Fall." The overbearing merchant, Orrin Blackwell, was studying it with great curiosity.

"*Comedy of Errors*," offered Charles, noting his companion's questioning stare.

"William Shakespeare," he added when the first made no sense. Despite Orrin's fascination with the actresses of Charles' troupe, he obviously possessed little retention for the words they spoke.

"When are the rest expected?" Orrin asked. "I should, perhaps, save them some of this fine port."

"A few of the gentlemen are invited for seven, the ladies at eight. Our guest of honour should arrive shortly after that."

"Good," replied Blackwell, lowering his vast bulk into a chair. "I should like to know from Merchant Platt if his molasses is in yet from the Sugar Islands. Will Loring be here as well?"

"Yes, Samuel promises to be here, as does the Merchant Hancock."

With that, Orrin screwed up his fat, childish face as though a dead fish had just been dangled at his nose.

"You invited that pompous Johnny? Heavens, Charles, if it was not for that blue-eyed boy from Beacon Hill, I could pass myself off as the richest man at your table tonight."

Blackwell meant it, of course. I watched as he removed a laced handkerchief from the cuff of his fine silk waistcoat with an affected flourish and a silly sigh of despair. I hardly imagined him being serious, but then again, he was just the sort who would wish to impress such ladies as were invited to sup at Charles' table this evening—a finical set, really; quicker to judge a man by his purse, rather than by his breeding, manners, or integrity.

The bell at the door sounded, followed by muffled voices. Within moments, two gentlemen descended upon the parlour, quite unannounced by the footman who felt, as familiars, they deserved no formal introduction.

Jimmy Sloan entered first, his languid face a quick cover to his overly relentless nature. I then studied Gordon Russell. Yes, the girls were right in their description of him. He was very good looking, in a rough, sportive kind of way. He was not yet thirty, I imagined, but he had run his life hard. His fine looks would not outlast the decade.

"The twilight is breathtaking tonight," Gordon remarked to no one in particular, as Charles served round more port. "I was saying so to Lucy, just ten minutes ago."

I shot a glance at Orrin Blackwell, noticing that his brow arched ever so slightly at the mention of Lucy's name.

"Oh, Miss Wellman will be here?" he said aloud, casually stifling a yawn. In truth, Orrin Blackwell was just as much an actor as the company around him.

"That she promises," answered Gordon, raising his glass to his lips. "Tim Gorman was with her, badgering her at every turn to move along. Lucy paid no heed, of course. Why, she even received us in her shift, the naughty little trollop."

The bell sounded again, and more voices rang out from the cool white marbled foyer.

"We shall show ourselves in, Stearns," came the deep laughter of men's voices, and two more members of Charles' acting troupe appeared at the parlour door.

"Hallo, Charlie!" This from William Collamore who, as was his typical custom, went straight to the looking glass where he could admire himself while speaking. "Goodness man, but that fool footman of yours is taking his position far too seriously these days. Tisk, tisk. What a Mister High-and-Mighty!"

His companion, Sir Alfred Blinn, said nothing. Refusing port, he sat by the fire, smiling at something in his own thoughts. Amusing as it might be, we did not intrude.

Yet another ring of the bell, and more voices; louder this time. No doubt it was the comical Darcy.

"Greetings and salutations!" boomed Darcy as he burst in upon the scene; kissing my hand with a flourish. Of less than moderate stature, he was definitely a creature of broad gestures and rapid wit. His mind was always whirling with some monstrous plot or prank. At his heel strolled David Manley, quiet and unassuming, despite his fine, youthful looks. David merely nodded in greeting. He had not as yet attained the boisterous bravado expected of an actor.

"You will never believe who I just saw, walking up Garden Court Street!" exclaimed Darcy, his eyes excessively bright with mirth. "Roscoe Bennett! Old Flabby-Boy Bennett must be working off some tonnage in order to seduce the ladies, I'll wager!"

With that, Darcy fell into a fit of laughter. Not a soul joined in, and it seemed like an eternity until Darcy, who was clutching at his sides in an attempt to breathe, realized his faux pas.

"Terribly sorry," he said with studied humility, as the merchant Blackwell stared at the Dutch tiles of the hearth with great disdain, his full face nearly as fiery as the flames.

"Another port, Orrin?" asked Charles, as he threw Darcy a warning glance. The merchant merely nodded and lifted his glass, as the footman, Stearns, thankfully entered and announced Merchant Platt, who hovered behind the stately servant like a shadow of nervous agitation.

"Come in, Edmund," muttered Blackwell as he shuffled his cumbersome weight in the chair. "Stop being such a bore, and come over here at once. I wish to speak to you."

Platt scurried across the room towards his friend as though he were being pursued by scowling geese. Such a flustered fellow, this Edmund Platt! Why, his eyelids twitched interminably, and his mouth was forever twisting about, as if he were constantly on the brink of tears.

The mantle clock chimed the hour of seven. Nearly all the invited gentlemen had gathered in the dimly lit parlour where the ominous words of Shakespeare began to fade slowly into the cloistered shadows.

Roscoe Bennett had finally arrived, flushed and puffing. He sadly did have the vast misfortune to resemble a floundering walrus. But no one could awe an audience with the spoken word the way Roscoe Bennett could. No one.

The merchant Samuel Loring had also made his appearance. Possessed of a most wistful nature, Samuel always seemed to be dreaming of quieter places and gentler times. He was in every way a gentleman, and therefore, in my humble opinion, not much a member of this crowd.

"My myriad of merchants," announced Charles, saluting the group who had gathered about Blackwell's chair. "How gracious of you all to be here tonight!"

"Not all as yet!" shouted Blackwell across the noisy room. "But when King Hancock arrives, we shall certainly be complete. So tell me, when does the dapper duck appear?"

"John told me that if he could not dine with us, he would join us later for brandy and cards."

"Ah, good!" returned Orrin with a sneer. "For then, if the candles go out, we can play by the brilliant light of Hancock's holy aura—an aura he most likely smuggled down from heaven in a keg marked 'salt.' What a business man, that Johnny. Or, should I say, his dearly departed Uncle Thomas. Now, there was a sly dog, indeed!"

It was then that Lucy's animated voice echoed from the hall without, and I watched as a sly smile enveloped each man's face. Now there was a girl who appreciated an audience, and Lucy proved it by entering the parlour, quite breathless with her hand to her heart as if to stop it from pounding wildly out of her chest.

"Goodness, Papa Charles! Am I the first one here? How extraordinary!"

She turned towards Tim Gorman who towered behind her, and promptly punched him in the stomach.

"It's your fault, you great dolt! You swore to me that it had gone past eight a whole hour ago. And I rushed about like a madwoman to get ready. Why, the ordeal of it all has made me positively parched!"

Poor Tim Gorman accepted Lucy's physical attack with little or no resistance. Perhaps he was more than accustomed to it. However, at the sight of Darcy, he scowled. Darcy was the very bane of his existence.

"Master Gorman!" Darcy could not help but begin. "The *première artiste* graces our undeserving group. Naturally, we are humbled." This he concluded with a low, sweeping bow. The rest of us did not know what to make of it all.

"So you are an actor as well, Mister Gorman?" asked Samuel Loring politely; always the diplomat.

"You might call him that," Darcy barged on. "Oh, you should have seen him in his last performance; clad in a cantankerous robe of wilted leaves, and prancing about the stage like an overgrown imp!" At this, Darcy attempted to demonstrate his opinion by bounding about the room in a clumsy and feverish way, imitating Tim's voice in a mocking tone:

> *Through the house give glimmering light,*
> *By the dead and drowsy fire:*
> *Every elf and fairy sprite*
> *Hop as light as bird from brier;*
> *And this ditty, after me,*
> *Sing and dance it trippingly.*

"What in heaven's name was that?" asked Blackwell, quite astounded, as Charles quietly provided the answer.

"A bit from *A Midsummer Night's Dream*. Oberon's speech, actually."

"Oh," replied Blackwell simply, leaning on his beefy hand in boredom, as poor Tim Gorman glared at Darcy from his place by the door. But Darcy was relentless. This time he chose Lucy for his verbal attack.

"Ah, Miss Wellman! Yet another honour. And how lovely you look this evening! Why, your wig has that just-out-of-the-sack tousle to it. Pray tell, how on earth do you manage to dress it with all the appropriate rumples in all the right places?"

Lucy was just about to let go another punch—this time in Darcy's direction—but the bell sounded once again. Thus Darcy, strictly in his element, dashed off to answer to the callers himself. Most of us followed.

"Clemence, you darling thing!" we heard him extol at the top of his lungs. "And Bryce! Why you're especially darling. Did you dress that way just for me?"

Three more ladies had just arrived, their elaborate costumes creating a vivid burst of colour against the stark white formality of the hall. With his typical poise, Charles went out and greeted them handsomely, and the ladies positively cooed under his attentions. It was then I noticed that Valentine Hale had applied a paper and paste British lion to her coiffed hairpiece. She claimed it was a welcoming gesture for our guest. Darcy spoke for the rest of us when he dubbed Miss Hale, the Cat's Paw. Foolish woman that she was, Valentine smiled and thanked him sweetly for "the compliment."

From the dining room beyond, the constant clink of plates and silver hinted at the time. Determined to supervise all that went on, the footman Stearns was nearly beside himself as he dashed about from the front door to the dining room, and then back again. In passing, Stearns overheard Lucy Wellman calling him a nefarious old fart catcher, and he pursed his lips accordingly. Do you remember, Jeffrey, when Stearns strode past us in the foyer, muttering that Lucy was nothing more than a nasty little mort? He also went on to wonder aloud why his master even put up with such "filthy flatbacks," to begin with. Stearns' mumblings were meant for Charles to hear, but alas he paid them no heed. Instead, Charles was glancing at his watch so often now, that the clique of men by the window knew he had become quite anxious over the arrival of this heralded Captain Vale, and they began to whisper amongst themselves in hushed, guarded tones. Where was this officer, anyway? It was terribly rude of him to keep them all waiting like this—as though he was far too important to drink their fine port and French champagne.

The front door opened once again, permitting a chill breeze to cascade over the bare shoulders of the ladies who lolled about nearby. With a trite nod of greeting towards the party who had just arrived, these ladies moved themselves with a languid fluidity across the room, and thus quite nearby the gentlemen who were now forced to abandon their once private post, for fear of being overheard.

Virginia Stanwood stood at the threshold with her angelic offspring, Eve. Virginia, with her stately court wig and beguiling eyes of violet, was emphatically relating to Charles the ghastly time her driver had getting the coach through Garden Court Street. There were spectators outside, she said, and it looked like they were awaiting a king.

The foyer was now a place of gathering—a place where the scents of pipe smoke and perfumes boldly mixed. Glasses clinked and champagne flowed freely. Anxious voices, needing to be heard, grew louder and louder, echoing up in a spiral towards the ceiling where a fresco of delicate little cherubs danced about a skyscape bordered with the inscription: "All that lives must die, passing through nature to eternity."

Still, this Captain Vale did not come. The women were laughing now. It was all too silly, this aggravated anticipation, and a vote went round proclaiming that this glorified officer was definitely not worth the wait.

It had just gone past eight when Celeste Davenport made her appearance upon the stairs, her small, delicate hand resting on the heavily scrolled mahogany railing. Her timid eyes sought out her father, and she did not progress a single step until she found him.

At seventeen, she was nothing short of lovely. Her thick hair had the hue and richness of honey, and her light brown eyes were blessed with a most innocent sheen of gold. Possessed of all the sweet virtues poets and bards had sung to throughout the centuries, Celeste seemed flawless with her fawn-like beauty and gentle grace.

She was evidently not comfortable at these parties involving theatre people. I could see that at once. For certain, acceptable conversation was difficult with such people. One could go on for hours without hearing a single strand of truth. I imagine it was for her father's sake that Celeste endured these soirees with quiet dignity, attempting each and every time to understand these outlandish personalities of the stage a little better.

The clear ring of the bell resounded through the hall, causing chattering voices to fade and anxious eyes to address the door just one last time. Perhaps this was the mysterious officer at last! But, no. It was only Diana Kirby and her entourage.

I watched as the men abandoned their posts, rushing forward to greet her with great shows of enthusiasm. After all, Diana Kirby expected it. She unabashedly thrived on it. Attired in a thin gown of white foulard, done in

Turkish style with a daring red sash, Diana looked radiant as she gave a clever comment here, a wave of her bejeweled hand there, and a smile so artificial, it was nothing short of enchanting. Removing her wide-brimmed hat with its companion ribbon of red, Diana revealed white blonde hair which was dressed unfashionably short, and her sharp grey eyes challenged anyone to criticise her for it.

Behind her, Marlon Reynolds stood in the shadows, scanning the room with dark, disdainful eyes and an elegant sneer of boredom on his lips. His was the face of a gypsy—an arrogant, yet compelling blend of vagabond and gentleman. It was, perhaps, his greatest asset.

The third member of Diana's party was the flagrant dandy known simply as Lord Sutherland. No one knew if he was truly titled, but that did not matter. This Lord Sutherland had more money than Croesus, and he was very willing to spend it in a maddening pursuit of pleasure. Of course, as rumour had it, Diana Kirby was his latest indulgence.

As Diana made her sweep of the room, the other ladies kept their cool distance, watching her with invidious stares. How fortunate was the lady Diana to have snared so opulent a fish. Yes, this Lord Sutherland did look like a silly fish, with his puckered face and his great, bloated eyes. However, by virtue of his purse alone, Lucy christened him a goldfish. By heavens, she was right. The alias was bantered about the group amidst a gale of giggles. A goldfish! It was too droll.

"Ah," said Lucy with a sigh, when she ceased laughing. "They're in the flush of it, you see. No chance of netting that one tonight."

She was referring, of course, to the alleged affair between Lord Sutherland and Diana. It was too fresh; too new, she said, to interfere with. Decidedly, she vowed to wait a month or so. Insatiable men like Sutherland always pursued their prey with relentless obsession, but once they bagged their target, they quickly tired of it. Predictably, Lord Sutherland would soon be showing his white teeth again. Then she would make a play for his pockets.

There was another commotion at the door, but fewer people paid heed this time. I believe they had given up on the Captain altogether. Thus it was that John Hancock's entrance was literally ignored.

A small chit of a servant arrayed in silk stepped boldly into the foyer and chanted, "Mister John Hancock," moments before the harried Stearns could even as much as draw breath. It was an evening for Stearns in which all decorum was lost.

Hancock sauntered by in his suit of lavender, as the ladies made haste to catch a glimpse of his carriage in the shadows of the street. It was quite the thing, really, and they clasped their hands in glee, each imagining what it would be like to be driven about the town like pampered queens.

"Oh, the riches!" murmured Rebecca, as she looked longingly about the room. Indeed, there was a fortune in every corner.

"Dinner is served," announced Stearns in his most official tone, as Charles shook his head, and wearily consulted his watch for the last time. I remember him speaking over his shoulder to you, Jeffrey, and asking you to escort Celeste, as he gallantly offered his arm to me. I was, to say the least, honoured. We led the procession as couples grouped randomly behind us, their voices bright with a merry laughter which turned to awe when the doors to the dining room were opened before us. For there revealed to us was a resplendent glow of a hundred candles, and the gilded mirrors which carried their brilliance into a shimmering eternity of light.

On the table, which was elegantly set for twenty-eight guests, four spiraling stands of sparkling glass held mouthwatering arrays of sweetmeats, jellies, whipped sylabubs, peaches, pears, raisins, and blanched almonds for dessert. The total effect was dazzling.

A lively chatter ensued as people dashed about looking for their place cards, laughing excuses whenever they collided. The troupe was accustomed to Charles' typical seating plan, however tonight it seemed rather at odds. In the confusion, no one noticed Lucy's sleight of hand as she went about making a few clever seating arrangements of her own. No one, that is, except myself, and Charles, in particular.

"No, no, Lucy. You shall sit up here next to the merchant Blackwell. He has expressly requested the pleasure of your company."

I watched with a sense of sympathy as Lucy glanced at the obese man with his greasy face. Resignedly, she shrugged and sighed, approaching the head of the table with an ambling stroll greatly enhanced by champagne. Everyone else was seated and now watched Miss Lucy's sad march. She had the appearance of an errant little parlour maid about to be given the sack.

Charles gave the customary three knocks, and all eyes turned expectantly towards their host. But curiously, Charles did not say anything, an intense look of surprise upon his face. Like the others, I followed the path of his stare to the far end of the table, where, there upon the threshold, an officer appeared, handsomely turned out in regimental uniform. Although I could not see clearly through the well-designed clutter of the table, he seemed regally tall and broad shouldered.

Our host went forward to greet his guest, as a steady murmur of conversation grew from those about the table. The newly arrived Captain was being introduced at the far end of the room. I glanced again, but could not see or hear much save William Collamore's bombastic speech of welcome. I felt strangely nervous, and reached for my wine; not really wanting it, but sensing a need for a calming distraction.

Charles and his guest were rapidly approaching the head of the table. However, as they drew near, Charles passed my seat and instead took the Captain around in order to meet his daughter, Celeste. Even at this close range, I could see only his powerfully set profile. He moved gracefully, and his voice was not overloud or imperious. I knew instinctively he would ride well, play cards with skill, dance and duel divinely. He was everything everyone had said.

I watched intently as he was introduced to you, Jeffrey. Yes, you seemed in awe as well. And awe is a reaction I have never before seen on your face. Your eyes met mine, and we smiled, not really knowing why. And then the acclaimed Captain Vale was introduced to me.

Sadly, I cannot recall the words that passed between us. Brief words, really; typical passages of welcome. But I do remember standing, which was odd, but I did so, meeting the Captain's glance straight on. I vividly recollect him making a pleasant notice of my attire. My gown was a clever creation of golden yellow watered silk, with a pale beige petticoat and garlands of ruffled material bordering the entire dress. These garlands had been fashioned in the finest scarlet lace, and matched the Captain's battalion colours to perfection; just as I intended.

Laughably, of all the persons present, it was solely Charles Davenport who recognised the coy significance of my design. His sly smile of approval was displayed for just a moment—a moment in which I believe Charles had developed a higher sense of respect for my guileful abilities. I had not contrived to have such *abilities*, until the afternoon you scorned me, Jeffrey. My newfound talent was in its formative stages, and therefore fresh and raw in its capacity to excite me. It was, perhaps, most likely due to this inane little triumph of mine, that I forgot my initial conversation with the Captain. It troubles me greatly now. It was something I had hoped to always remember and cherish, like the earliest rose of summer, or a first true kiss.

The Captain was then escorted to the center of the table near Merchant Hancock. I could not see him again without leaning far forward, which I did not intend to do. Therefore, I sat down, reaching for my wine once again; my heart pounding in a peculiar, cold way, while the antics of the room slowly reeled before me, bringing me back to a harsh and strangely false reality.

Sipping my wine, I chose to study my dinner companions at length in order to steady my frenzied nerves. I glanced across the table towards Celeste. Attired in a gown of tender lilac, with a spray of gentle flowers in her honey-coloured hair, she did not seem a simpleminded girl. No, despite her delicate beauty, and her youthful years, Celeste Davenport did not appear to be a silly girl taken with foolish infatuations and giddy behaviour. In truth, her manner and decorum hinted at the vast sense of maturity and quiet charm harboured behind her sedately reflective eyes ringed with gold.

Seated alongside Celeste, and quite in contrast, the merchant Blackwell was attempting to bury his sweaty hand into the folds of Lucy's pale yellow dress. In her agitated state of fatigue, Lucy seemed oblivious to the insult. Hailing a passing footman, she requested a strong saucer of coffee. Perhaps she was praying it would lift her out of this eternal phase of grogginess. Then, she could begin drinking again, and none of this merchant's insulting conduct would matter so very much.

"Strange thing about these footmen," Lucy murmured, as if thinking aloud. "They all look alike."

"Who cares?" replied Blackwell, as he successfully found a resting place for his impulsive hand somewhere above her knee.

"Soups of asparagus, herbal, carrot, or oyster," Stearns called out regally, as footmen approached each end of the table carrying heavily embossed silver tureens. Across the table, Merchant Platt was being asked his preference. And as the question was posed yet a second time, he looked up, stunned.

"Eh, what?" he stammered. So taken was he with the lovely Miss Eve Stanwood who sat beside him, Edmund could hardly fathom a word that was being said in the real world around him. The offerings were indicated to Platt one more time, and he waved his hand in nervous agitation, claiming anything would do. The impassive footman then ladled out a portion of the herbal soup onto Edmund's plate, as the grassy looking concoction was certain to be the least popular selection of the evening.

"Oh, Miss Stanwood," Platt was saying. "You are the most lovely creature—" He could say no more. Unaccustomed to fiery fits of emotion, he was blatantly apoplectic with the heady sensation of it all. Frankly, in my eyes, the man had never looked more foolish.

Eve was truly lovely—an angel personified with her aura of soft golden curls, and her velvety eyes of lilac. Platt must have found her type refreshing amidst this hotbed of brazen women. But there was something about the girl I did not trust. I watched as she grimaced while tasting a liqueur which had been served over flavoured ice, and found her protestation far too practiced. All the same, Edmund Platt was firmly hooked. Eve Stanwood was like a goddess on a pedestal to him within mere minutes.

"How dull," said Lucy flatly as she tasted her soup. For her, the evening was fast becoming a failure, and she did not care to pretend otherwise.

"This carrot soup is divine," claimed Virginia Stanwood to no one in particular. "The only carrot soup I had to rival this was at the castle of a Baron in

France. His name was the Baron d'Var-something-or-other, and he asked for my hand in marriage. But I shook my pretty little head no, and offered him one of my silk handkerchiefs instead. He shot himself over my refusal, the poor dear. They say he put my handkerchief in his breast pocket before firing at his heart."

"Veal in cream, duck á la mode, roasted beef, and quail in orange sauce," chanted Stearns as the soup plates were cleared away noiselessly. The cupbearers also appeared, pouring endless amounts of wine with poised precision. I glanced towards the center of the table, wondering how the Captain viewed his rather lurid surroundings, but I could not see past Rebecca Henley, who was carrying on a rather spirited conversation about herself, in hopes of enthralling the handsomely rich merchant, John Hancock. Meanwhile, behind the talkative guests, the army of footmen continued to refresh the glasses and plates, their faces purely expressionless despite all the shamefully flagrant things they quite easily overheard.

"Don't get me fuddled!" barked Blackwell at the somber attendant reaching for his glass. "Good heavens, man! I believe you are doing it on purpose."

"Yes, it's all too dreadful," Clemence was heard to say. "After all, doesn't *Clemence* mean something like *tempering justice*? How dull! Yes, and how could my mother do this to me?"

"Oh!" exclaimed Valentine with great agitation. "She's vexing us with that again!"

Much to her husband's dismay, Clemence was becoming quite intoxicated. And in the process, she was badgering the now exasperated Merchant Hancock for an alternative name to Clemence. Could he think of any?

"How about Beezaleed?" he offered with grand indifference, before turning his full attention to our elegant guest of honour. Clemence was silent for a moment, and her face was an open field of bafflement.

"Beezaleed?" she repeated stupidly. "Who in the Bible was Beezaleed?" No one answered. No one knew, and no one particularly cared.

At the far end of the table reigned the echelon of the acting troupe, with Diana Kirby as their queen. They boasted amongst themselves most dreadfully until not a single soul could be heard above the din.

"Such lovely hair and vibrant eyes for one so obviously dull-witted," Diana was remarking in a loud, snide voice. And it seemed rather apparent she was looking at me.

The dinner guests were now toying with a selection of salmon trout, terrapin, and oysters. Only the stouthearted displayed any great shows of appetite, and William Collamore, who adored to hear himself speak, was amongst them.

"I love oysters," he exclaimed. "Thrive on 'em. Why, I've had oysters at least twenty-five different ways."

"Pray tell, do any of these particular ways include keeping your fat mouth shut?" asked Diana, drearily.

"I do not find that funny," returned William in a huff, despite the obvious fact that many of his dinner companions were laughing heartily.

Lucy sighed, glancing past the eight waning individuals who blocked her from her paramour. "Poor Timothy," she said. "He has hardly eaten a thing."

"Bah!" sputtered Blackwell at her side. "The man's thinner than a hay rake."

Lucy stared at the merchant's plate, which was heaped higher than a charnel house with quail bones, before throwing him a most contemptible stare.

"Idiot girl," Valentine murmured to Rebecca at her side. "So eager to pass up the pounds," she glanced at Orrin, and then pointedly at Timothy, "for the shilling."

"Some girls just don't know when to lap salt," Rebecca opined in her best Georgian drawl, as Val adjusted the pitiful paper lion atop her head for surely the hundredth time that evening.

"I saw Nancy Hallam perform in Williamsburg a few seasons back," offered Samuel Loring, sensing a lull in polite conversation. "She was exquisite. Such a delicate and womanly countenance. And such study! I witnessed her performance all eleven nights. It was breathtaking."

"I wonder at your presenting anyone to rival her," Orrin bantered imperiously. This was said, of course, to slight Lucy. But Orrin should have guessed that the girl was fully aware of where her talents did, and did not, lie. However, Diana Kirby was visibly annoyed.

"All our actresses are proficiently studied," replied Charles levelly. "As are our actors. We have performed the comedies of Cumberland, as well as the diverse tragedies of Shakespeare. Our own dear Miss Kirby has begun to encroach the success enjoyed by Mrs. Hallam, and our very musical Mrs. Sloan is moving well in a field holding no equal."

The room was silent as Merchant Blackwell bowed his head in response. "Then permit me, kind sir, to inquire how you intend to fair in a town which discourages play acting?"

"True, the town of Boston has had an ordinance against theatrical performances for the past twenty-three years. However, with the ever increasing influx of the King's troops"—this Charles said with a lift of his glass towards the Captain—"the needs of this town are changing, needs that should benefit such worthy gentlemen as are found at this table."

However, the portly merchant would not give up.

"If I may be so bold, do you not feel the British influence will have little or no effect? After all—and please do forgive me, Captain Vale—the British still have no say over specific town laws."

"This is true," Edmund Platt began in a silly voice which I assumed was effected in order to impress little Miss Eve. "Just one short month ago, the First Continental Congress placed a ban on horse racing, cockfighting, gaming, and exhibitions of shows, plays, and 'all other expensive diversions and entertainments.' And General Gage has bowed to the will of our Congress, claiming the time was not right to go about ruffling feathers."

"The old woman," William Collamore grumbled in a huff, as a nervous whisper sprung up about the room. Heavens, but why did he call the General an old woman in front of the Captain?

"Pardon me, Captain," William went on with exaggerated humility. "However, it is a well-known fact that Gage's own soldiers call him an old woman. Why, I imagine even the King, on a good day, calls Gage an old woman."

"It's such a messy thing," remarked Clemence as casually as though she were complaining about rain at a picnic. "These poor little colonial peasants just want to run things their own way without taking orders from some half-crazed king across the ocean."

Bryce had kicked Clemence under the table, but her cry of surprised pain was not heard as the room erupted in opinion. The Captain, I noticed, did not speak, but was actively listening with some interest to the hubbub surrounding him. I believe it amused him. I was not exactly sure how long I sat studying his face through the waving arms and curving shoulders of the crowd, but the Captain must have sensed my curiosity and looked up, holding my gaze for a moment before rendering a polite smile. I remember returning some semblance of a smile—more like a half-witted grin I suppose—and then I turned, pretending great regard for the palladium windows which read: "Come what come may, time and the hour run through the roughest day." I could have stayed quite content, pondering the richly coloured panes of glass, but somehow, through the incessant babble of voices, I heard my name being called. I looked towards Charles, a guilty flush on my face.

"Perhaps you did not hear, Mrs. Lynford. Captain Vale here was wondering how you viewed Boston's open acts of rebellion."

"Why, Captain," I murmured, my eyes downcast, "Only if His Majesty were seated at one end of this table, and the *old woman* at the other, would I be forced to call Boston's heartfelt grievances a rebellion . . . sir."

The room flooded with laughter. I glanced up with a sly grin, bolstered by champagne. Yes, the Captain was laughing too. He was indeed, as Edmund Platt so eloquently put it, a man of great understanding.

"Cream pastries, strawberry souffle, raspberry tarts, and almond cakes," announced Stearns, as the men pushed back their chairs wearily, and the women leaned their elbows upon the table, secretly wishing that the stays beneath their dresses did not feel so very tight.

The subject of politics happily subdued, Charles proposed the customary toast to the health of His Majesty. Sir Alfred seconded with a toast to the Queen. It was then, I believe, that the Captain stood and offered a salute to the ladies. Glasses were raised, and cheers were sounded.

You never noticed, Jeffrey, but Captain Vale was looking solely at me.

☙☙☙☙

The debut of Captain Landon Vale commenced promptly after supper.

Somewhere between the terrapin and the tarts, the guests had fallen to fatigue. The warmth of the room was too great; it emanated from the febrile candlelight, the profusion of dishes, and the vertiginous haze brought on by vast amounts of champagne and wine. The ladies were most lackadaisical now, and they lolled about with little or no concern as to the state of their dress. Soft shoulders and long, white necks were prominently displayed in the golden glow of the chandelier.

Coffee was served, and the dessert trays dismantled; not out of hunger, but from a sheer appreciation for their lofty spires of colourfully tempting fruits. Such a ransom Charles must have paid to have these exotic treats at his table. However, within mere minutes, the glistening glass trays were stripped completely. Even the sly-faced silver cherubs were maliciously robbed of the dew-drenched grapes they bore in their heavenward grasp.

Little by little, the company began to come around again. Coffee had rendered them anxious to resume drinking, as it was discovered that the November night was still young. It had just but gone past midnight.

So it was that Charles and Celeste stood, thus indicating that it was time to adjourn to the drawing room. On evenings such as these, Charles rarely enforced the social policy of the men remaining behind to sip brandy while the women waited in the sitting room beyond. In Charles' society, the ladies drank too, and there seemed no apparent reason to separate his guests as though they were naughty children.

Besides, on this particular evening, the women were eager to meet the Captain. All throughout the ponderous meal, they had watched him through half-veiled eyes, observing the handsome tilt of his head, and the seductive draw of his polite smile every time the likes of William Collamore said something foolish. Yes, the time had come, and the ladies were mad for it.

Charles and Celeste led the procession to the drawing room, a cavernous and foreboding place, where a host of deep cushioned chairs loomed in sensuous shadow. I elected to situate myself in the farthest corner, away from the firelight, the small talk, and the trio of hired musicians. It was my hope that I could sit quietly and observe the fuss. I had thought it would amuse me to watch these women making a show for the Captain. However, the ladies Stanwood, along with Merchant Loring, perched somewhat at my side, thus forcing me into their conversation. They spoke of the Captain, of course. Loring was not personally acquainted with the Vales, however, he knew of people back home in England who were. The father was severe, it was said. He lacked humour, and could not recognise it if it were flung in front of him. The mother, on the other hand, was a delicate beauty, talented in all the true accomplishments of life, and greatly adored.

It was then that Virginia spoke, "The Captain reminds me of a young man I met when I had just turned twenty. This gallant youth was the son of a noted bard. His father was in love with me, of course. However, I did not favour him. Oh, his writings burned with passion, and he wrote many a sonnet in praise of my beauty. But he was old and coarse. His son, quite diversely, possessed the fatal good looks of a god. In time, he was to gain a higher and more majestic fame than even his poetic father."

"And why was that?" Loring asked with gentle intent.

"Because I loved him," Virginia replied simply. And then she said no more, her beautiful eyes fixed near the fireplace where the Captain sat, encompassed by our fellow guests.

I had hoped she would say more. Her story touched me with fascination. However, it was at that moment that Lucy and her persistent suitor, Blackwell, came round behind us, disrupting the romantic tranquillity of our thoughts.

Lucy, having found herself in a most obvious state of migraine, told the merchant Blackwell in no uncertain terms that he bored her to hell. She was finished with him before she had so much as begun, she swore; for men like him were repulsive, monstrous, and uncouth. The heavyset merchant then watched with apparent disdain as Lucy scurried across the room to be near that actor friend of hers, Timothy Gorman, who looked worn to a shadow.

"Bah!" he muttered, the great folds of his face seemingly melting from the heat of frustration. "Good riddance!"

As if in a trance, Mrs. Stanwood stood and silently crossed over to the Captain's circle. Eve merely followed her mother like a patient shadow. Meanwhile, in our corner, the merchant Blackwell sought out other suitable conquests. Scanning the room, his eyes lit on Rebecca. It was easy to read that he felt the vivacious-looking redhead from Savannah might amuse him properly.

"Miss Henley," he said, making his approach carefully. "Would you care to dance?"

Rebecca was enthralled, of course, and accepted prettily, for the promise of glint coin always brought a willing smile to her lips. Lifting her plump little white hand towards Orrin's, she stood demurely and then led him through a merry dance. The merchant grimaced at every step, for he obviously considered dancing an awkward charade. Besides, it put him terribly out of breath.

"Is this not jolly fun?" squealed Rebecca as she executed a most spirited turn.

"Yes—quite," Blackwell gasped through gritted teeth. In truth, he must have been praying for the conclusion of the piece in order that they might retire to some quiet alcove where he could sit calmly and let this anxious girl fawn over him.

Valentine, in a vicious state of intoxication, was desirous of dancing also, and elected that two partners were far superior to one. Calling upon Darcy and David Manley with a frantic laugh, she made quite an exhibition of herself in hopes that our guest of honour would take notice and thus consider her to be unquestionably popular.

But her efforts went for naught. The Captain was surrounded by Charles' best, who regaled him with theatrical stories, many of which had become grander in the retelling. The Captain was indeed courteous. He smiled and laughed when expected to. More often than not, however, he appeared to be unobtrusively glancing about the room.

"Mrs. Lynford," Charles said, coming over to me with his hands out to take mine. "Please join us. The Captain sincerely wishes to speak with you again. You see, you're the first true Whig he has met in Boston town."

We all laughed heartily, even Diana, which surprised me, I must admit. I remember searching for you, Jeffrey, as I crossed the room. At last I found you, heavily immersed in a game of cards with the Merchant Hancock. I gave it little or no thought beyond a quick prayer that you did not plan on losing.

I was given a chair two seats away from the Captain. It was Charles himself who sat between us, however, he pushed his own chair back a bit in what was supposed to be a nonchalant manner. The act seemed rather obtrusive to me; inviting a purpose which I did not quite understand.

Diana was relating yet another reminiscence from her theatre days in London. She attempted to be general in her address, but her eyes kept running up and down the fine physique of the Captain with an insatiable yearning. For his part, curiously, the Captain seemed preoccupied with looking at me.

His regard was neither impolite nor impersonal. I could not bring myself to return his stare. Instead, I was either forcibly devoting my attentions to Diana, or foolishly glancing at my lap. Still, Vale gazed on. I surmised that he could not quite fathom my true place amongst these people. I had not the *amour-propre* of an actress, nor the confidence of a courtesan. But would he want me if I was? What if Charles had offered his guest the pleasure of any one of his ladies' favours? Would this renowned officer desire me? I watched out of the corner of my eye as he glanced across the room towards you, Jeffrey. A flash in his eyes told me that he was just made to remember that I was married. I imagined he went on to guess that we had been married for some time, and not the mere seven months that it truly was. We had that distinct appearance of marital boredom, you and I . . . He was still regarding me with a deep glance as I went on senselessly looking at my lap. I wished he wasn't sitting where he was. I did not like my looks in profile; I was far more pleasing straight on . . . The Captain appeared to be contemplating my role in this ensemble around him. Perhaps he was wondering if I was related to Davenport. No, most likely not. Perhaps all my silly presumptions were well above the facts. Indeed, the Captain could have been just looking beyond me; I was merely in the way. Or worse yet, he could have been observing me with the unquestionable knowledge that I was the most boring person in the room. It would serve me right, for all of my highly capricious illusions.

I decided I could no longer go on studying the design of my dress. I looked up, directly into the eyes of Captain Landon Vale. And when I did, there was a mutual light of recognition that I believe startled us both. It seemed like a small eternity we sat there questioning each other with a glance. But then Charles spoke, and the moment was gone. Charles' latest theatrical venture was being discussed, and I made it a point to watch whoever was speaking. You see, I was rendered nervous in a most strange and exhilarating way. I had not experienced such a mood since the first day you walked into my father's taproom, Jeffrey. And I had never expected to be made to feel that way ever again.

⁕⁕⁕

The ivory clock on the mantle had rung out the hour of two. The dancing had all but ceased, and the music trailed off into somber tones as the cluster I was in began to converse of the past as people are often wont to do when the night grows old and the anxious dawn lays in wait.

Somewhere in the shadows, Lucy and Tim had commenced a pointless round of bickering. Tim was showing signs of true agitation, and it mattered not when the overwrought Miss Wellman took her leave with the sweat plastered Blackwell in tow.

"Serves her right," Timothy grumbled as he made way to join our group. "Serves her right, the little fool."

"Bah!" said Rebecca, having witnessed the same event caustically over her shoulder. "There goes my pin money."

Sir Alfred Blinn was relating a story of his youth, some sixty years prior, when he was a guest on an English estate. He recalled a rather warm afternoon when the ladies, quite toppled by sherry, proceeded to play a game of ninepins, wearing little more than their farthingales. It was just the thing to attract the voracious ears of Lord Sutherland.

"What's this I hear about naughty ladies?" he asked.

Sir Alfred repeated the tale for Sutherland, who licked his lips in unmistakable appreciation, while Diana, quite bored, considered it time to leave. As was typical, Diana's decision to depart dictated the end of the party. We all stood.

The Captain and I exchanged a few pleasantries. I must admit I found him more than charming. I remember him asking if he might have the pleasure of dining with us again at the Eldredges' the following evening. I told him regrettably no; we had not been invited. We then said farewell, although both of us paused as if there was something else to be said. A laugh, and then farewell once more. That was all.

⁂

Throughout the remaining hours of dawn, I slept little. Upon rising, I went downstairs for coffee. Sometime around one in the afternoon, a note from the Eldredges arrived, begging our indulgence; but would we honour them by dining at their home that very evening? The soiree was intended to welcome Captain Vale, and it was their sincere hope we could attend.

I sent our acceptance. If you care to recall, Jeffrey, I did this without consulting you. Then I merrily set about deciding which of my newest gowns to wear, casually humming a tune I had heard the night before.

Thrice toss these oaken ashes in the air;
Thrice sit thou mute in this enchanted chair;
Then thrice three times tie up this true love's knot
And murmur soft: "She will, or she will not."

Thomas Campion—*Thrice Toss These Oaken Ashes in the Air*

MID-NOVEMBER, 1774

"OH! What a precious little doll's house this is!"

Lorena Eldredge entered, tossing her cloak aside with one hand, and taking in all of our quaint abode with her bright, merry eyes. Before I could so much as mutter a single word, Lorena was off, surveying all four of our tiny, first-floor rooms with a clap of her hands and a sigh of delight.

"Charming! Charming!" she exclaimed prettily. "And how nicely romantic, as well. How happy you and Mr. Lynford must be in this cozy, darling home."

"Thank you, Miss Eldredge," I said, my voice rather dubious, but I doubt she truly noticed.

"I grew up in a house that held a dining room large enough to feed thirty-six," Lorena went on to say, as casual as a minute. "Our music room was always cold and drafty. What a chore my lessons were in the winter! Father's library had the most decent hearth, but I could not bring myself to linger in that room very long. You see, Mrs. Lynford, large quantities of books always bore me right to sleep. Oh, my! Now what was I saying? Yes, of course—our house was quite large, but not as large as most. Do you recall the Braithwaites—the lovely older couple we were speaking of at dinner the other evening? They reside somewhat near the Vales, and their manor house is terribly regal indeed."

I smiled and said, "of course," in that special tone of voice that conveyed

I happily recollected every blessed word which had been said about the Braithwaites. In truth, I did not. The Braithwaites were just one of many, many names bantered about the Eldredges' table a few nights past, and just as with Lorena's books, I was well beyond boredom by the time the *regal* Braithwaites were even so much as mentioned.

"How pleased I would be to live in a lovely little house like this," Lorena confessed, practically in a whisper. "But I imagine the Captain and I will reside at Edgecombe Castle. That is the Vale family estate, you know—Edgecombe Castle. How many hundreds of acres and formal gardens it has, I cannot recall, but the tower rooms overlook the sea."

"How grand," I said, my eyes darting towards the back regions of the house where I heard a door open and close, followed by a murmur of voices. Perry Talbot was here; I was sure of it. How ghastly for Perry if he were to overhear Lorena Eldredge boasting of her future marriage plans with Captain Vale.

"So, is there just to be two of us for tea?" Lorena asked, conveniently providing me with the window of opportunity I needed.

"Actually, Lorena, there is another guest who shall join us," I began slyly. "Someone whom you have not seen in awhile, and someone, I believe, you should be very happy to see."

"Really?" asked Lorena, and her manner indicated that she was rather ill at ease with surprises. "Why, I just cannot imagine who it could be."

I called to my maidservant, Adele. Within moments, the gentle, old woman with her sweet, sagging face came to the parlour door. I looked to her expectantly. Adele nodded, and then so did I.

"Yes, Lorena," I went on, with a good measure of nervous trepidation. "I have invited someone so very special; I am sure—"

I did not have to finish my sentence, for Perry Talbot had strode through the door with Adele behind him. I watched as Lorena's face blossomed beautifully at the sight of him. Yes, I was certain at that moment the girl was in love with Talbot. Her facial reaction towards the Captain the other evening at dinner was altogether different. That look was mature, sedate, and plainly confident. However now, for this handsome lad, Lorena's entire expression was one of a tender and youthful longing.

How beautiful is young love in bloom. Such a radiant countenance does not emanate from gazing upon age-old castles with tower rooms that overlook a raging sea. A rose garden which covered a continent could not inspire half so much. This was the visage of love, and no artist, however capable, could ever properly capture the plaintive emotion so clearly defined on this lovely young woman's face.

"Tea is set in the parlour for you both," I said, while neither one of them glanced my way, so engrossed they were in one another. "Adele will be doing some sewing in the sitting room—just across the hall—should you need her, Miss Eldredge. And I will leave the doors open. As for myself, I thought I would take a walk. But only if you are comfortable here without me, Miss Eldredge."

"Oh, yes," she breathed, her eyes never leaving Perry's. "I am very, very happy here."

I believe Perry Talbot thanked me, but I did not wait about for needless conversation. Instead, I went to the front hall, and donned my red wool cape. A grateful pat on Adele's arm, and I was gone.

Outside, the sun was losing a brave struggle against a battalion of menacing grey clouds, and the air was brisk with chill. It was just the sort of day I had always secretly favoured. Since a child, I had always been in awe of swirling, ominous skies. I often vexed Ruthie by warning her that such skies were the result of God "stirring up the pot of vengeance." Why, I had my poor sister so downright frightened once, she spent the entirety of an hour under the kitchen table, waiting for the storm to subside; while I sat laughing by the window, the mist of the rain cooling my face, and the lightning ricocheting off the fields. When she became older and wiser, Ruthie merely claimed that I was silly in the head to admire such depressing weather; but alas, that is how I am. Yes, today was a perfect day, in a sense. Soon, December would be here with its bracing, icy wind that would whistle through the church spires, and whip about the ocean with a churning fury. The promise of this suited me just fine.

I started off at a quick pace down Charter Street. I thought to cross the square and continue on down towards Faneuil Hall and the Battery beyond. But just as I was formulating my plan, a fine figure of a man turned the corner towards me, and I knew with a start that it was Captain Landon Vale.

"Why, Mrs. Lynford!" he exclaimed, heading right for me. "A gracious good afternoon to you."

"Yes," was all I could manage, a huge lump forming in my throat, and my eyes swimming with guilt. Subtlety was an art form lost to me. Great-grandmother Effie had told me so, advising me endlessly to learn it. How I could have used a few easy lessons at this very moment!

"Out walking, Mrs. Lynford?" he asked, to which I could only say "yes" again, like a dull-witted parrot.

"It is such a nice day for a walk," he went on with ease, to which I could only duck my head stupidly; a flush of embarrassed shame on my face. "Perchance might I join you—that is, unless you wished to be alone with your thoughts."

"Oh, heavens no," I managed, looking up at him timidly. "Indeed, it would be nice to have company."

He smiled. What a lovely smile he possessed; it went to my heart immediately. I believed him even better-looking by day, if that were possible. I remember standing there, watching his face for an instant, and realising that I could not envision this handsome officer being raised in a castle. Castles were for kings and their knights; men sitting at long rustic banquet tables, drinking copious amounts of beer and shouting out conversations whilst they threw slabs of meat to large dogs on the floor. A silly thought, really; but it was beyond me as to how modern-day families coped with living in large, stone castles . . . Within moments, the Captain offered me his arm, and we began our stroll. I did not think of castles or knights anymore. The present was much more rewarding.

The streets were not terribly busy. In the Square, weary housewives gathered about the well, all similarly adorned in drab brown petticoats and faded half gowns drawn in about the waist by a cord. Very often, the children or family apprentices were sent for the first few buckets of water at dawn. However, following the breakfast chores, the wives tended to venture out for such a duty. It was the only social time they could look forward to in their busy days.

As we passed, these women ceased their gossip and glanced at the Captain with guarded suspicion. They had a right to, I suppose. Their menfolk were of a breed who were now strongly opposed to scarlet coats and swords.

From kitchen windows floated the enticing aromas of baking breads and pies, of meats simmering and vegetables stewing. Babies cried, dogs barked, while hens and ducks squawked noisily over their daily business of laying eggs. Turning a quiet corner, we were startled by the ominous grunt of an oversized sow. Upon closer inspection, we found her wallowing about in a meager patch of sunshine; the fence bowing precariously against her weight. She was not pleased at our intrusion. Looking away, her sides fluttering with each rapid breath, this indignant miss seemed to be counting the seconds until we would kindly leave her be.

From Paddy's Alley and Mill Creek, a bevy of cows paraded out onto the main road, mooing and lowing their way to the grazing fields of the Common; their tails constantly twitching in disdain of the imp of a lad who believed himself to be herding them on. The Captain and I had quite a laugh for ourselves. These old Besses knew their own way, and they certainly did not need the assistance of this gamboling little hobbledehoy to get to where they had been going faithfully for years.

Crossing through Dock Square, we found it strangely quiet. There was no market today, and no meeting at Faneuil Hall. Only the gulls overhead held any kind of a discourse, wheeling and wailing through the sky, searching for scraps of refuse which might lay hidden about the wooden wharves below.

In Cornhill, there was some activity about the bookbinders' shops, where the sharp smell of ink mingled with the dusty, airless scent of a multitude of books. Along the cobbled streets, we admired the shopkeepers' signs which so easily led the illiterate to their trades—a thimble and needle for a mantua maker, a pair of scissors for a tailor, and a handsome military cocked cap for a hatter. Within this district, several soldiers passed us, but not before saluting the Captain. I found myself rather impressed by the formality of it all.

Turning towards Atkinson Street, the cry of seagulls intensified, becoming sharper and fiercer. Here, the choking smells of hemp, pitch, rotting oysters, and stale salt air would have been nauseating, were it not for the purifying chill of the November day.

There before us was Griffin's Wharf. Only a scant year before, the infamous tea ships had been moored here. It had been all the talk at the Crossroads, in Papa's tavern. How very long ago that seemed!

"So this is your Boston," Captain Vale said, smiling.

"My Boston?" I replied. "Heavens, I should hope not. However, I do enjoy it here very much. But to you, Captain, why it must seem so small and paltry compared to the likes of London."

"Have you ever been to London?" the Captain asked, and I shook my head no. "Frankly, Mrs. Lynford, I rather thought you had. You see, the other night at the Eldredges' dinner party, you seemed so bored with our conversation about London, that I believed you saw the place exactly as I do—filthy, fast-paced, and teeming with danger."

I laughed, as did the Captain. We then strolled about Fort Hill, discussing anything and everything. We spoke of London, and this time I was not at all bored. Today's arrangement was far more agreeable than our evening at the Eldredges'. There, Mary Eldredge had fashioned such an awkward table. I had been seated at the far end with the Abbots, and the irascible old prune, Sara Thornton. Miss Thornton could not hear the conversations at the head of the table, and she kept cupping her ear and shouting "eh?" 'til I thought I would scream in annoyance. Perhaps that was why I did not enjoy my evening. Besides that, I never saw the Captain's face for a single moment that night. All I could watch was Lorena's constant triumphs, and it further piqued me that so young a girl could be so damnably attractive, witty, and smart.

Blissfully, these things did not matter now. The Captain and I were having such a grand time, and all without the supreme benefit of sunshine, or the magic elixirs of evening stars, candlelight, and wine. Together, here on an average afternoon, just the two of us; it all seemed so terribly natural. I could imagine us going to a tavern and continuing our discourse over a pleasant meal while, outside, a stormy sky let loose to the first pretty snowfall of the season. Following that, we would journey home—for in my imagination we were, of course, happily married—delighting in the delicate snowflakes which clung about our cloaks, as we planned for our evening outing to a musical concert at Faneuil Hall.

However, it was then I thought of Lorena. It was a pity to do so, but the Captain and I must have been out for two hours, and surely Lorena and Perry would be wondering where I was at by now. Sadly, I also came to realise that what I was doing was all wrong. How wicked of me to guile the Captain, while his beautiful young intended sat by the fire in my very own parlour, whispering of love to the true captive of her heart. How low of me, and how terribly, terribly demeaning to interfere. Why, if there was ever anybody who deserved to be mistress of a castle, it was Lorena Eldredge. Besides, what if this kindly Captain truly adored her? What right did I possess to change the course of his heart?

"Whatever is wrong?" the Captain asked of me with genuine concern. Certainly my shame was clearly displayed all over my face. Of course, it would not do to confess what I was thinking. Gone were the gentle daydreams of pretty snowflakes and musical concerts. Instead, I saw myself dressed in greasy, shabby clothing. I was walking very fast down Queen Street to where the back alleys lead to despicable little hovels. There, inside a darkened trap that reeked of the filth of base humanity, I would gather with the other gypsies and count my Judas gold.

"How funny you look," Captain Vale went on to say, lightly taking my arm. "What on earth are you thinking?"

"Jeffrey," I said all at once, although I was not truly aware of my intended plan at the start. "Yes, Jeffrey. Goodness, but I promised to be home half an hour ago. How displeased he'll be with me."

So it was that I was able to scurry home without the protocol of inviting the Captain inside. Captain Vale did walk me to the corner, and I was definitely pleased that we avoided seeing Lorena getting into her carriage, or worse yet, waiting for me on the front steps with her arm through Perry's. I remember us making our pleasant farewells at the corner of Charter Street, with a promise to walk together again some fine afternoon in the near future.

When I walked in the front door, Perry was waiting for me, and his face was radiant with joy. Miss Eldredge had left but mere minutes before. Adele prepared tea for us, while Perry gushed on about the happy events of his afternoon. Yes, Lorena confessed to loving him still. However, they had to take heed where her father was concerned. Only time would tell. Then, Lorena promised, she would attempt to speak with him again regarding her true desire, which was to wed Perry. The news made me feel better about my audacious meddling; not much, mind you, but a little.

"Tell me something, Perry," I began carefully, a cup of smuggled tea warming my hands. "Has Miss Eldredge ever mentioned a certain Captain Vale?"

"No," Perry said slowly, his voice edged with suspicion. "Why should she?"

I hesitated a moment, and regarded the young man. What a fine looking lad he was. I would hate myself—and Lorena—if he were being played for a fool.

"Listen to all that I say, Perry, and then make your own judgments. I know from Lorena's family, and from her very own lips, that this officer is expected to be her husband. Now, wait I say! Let me finish. I heard about this intended alliance well before the Captain arrived from Canada a few weeks ago. Miss Eldredge spoke of him with high personal regard, however, I have come to believe that she is doing this only because her mother and father will have it no other way. You see, I know a little more of their family history than perhaps even you do. They were prominent in England, you know. And then something happened that caused Mr. Eldredge to lose all his money. The true shame in all of this is that they will only accept Lorena marrying a man of handsome means. Perhaps they see this step as an act of salvation for them all. Lorena is not to blame for her words, or her actions. And neither is the Captain. Why, he is a most pleasant individual. I have met him. As a matter of fact, by pure coincidence, I have spent the past two hours in his company."

"Who is this blasted Captain?" Perry asked, and a dark jealousy coloured his every word. "Is he young? Is he handsome?"

"His name is Landon Vale, and he is a Captain with the Tenth Regiment. Is he handsome? Yes, very much so, to my way of thinking. But then again, Mr. Talbot, so are you."

I had not intended to humour Perry, but he smiled at my compliment.

"Now, for his being youthful—it depends on your definition of young. You see, the Captain is roughly my age; and I would guess that places him seven or eight years older than you. So answer carefully, Master Talbot: Is that considered young?"

"Oh, yes indeed!" he said, patting my hand, and we laughed agreeably.

We then spoke some more of poor Miss Eldredge and her plight. I promised to chat with her again, as soon as it was humanly possible, and offer my parlour for further meetings with Perry, if that suited her. We imagined it would.

Perry left shortly before you returned from your club, Jeffrey. You were slightly intoxicated, which was your normal course of behaviour, as I had come to learn. We had arrived at a certain truce, you and I. In our revised mode of marriage, courtesy had come to replace compassion. Our conversations politely limited themselves to people and places and things which would never remind us of any pain. We made each other comfortable in those little ways, such as two strangers would do when forced to share a room. At times, a gentle glimmer from our brief and short-lived passion would spark between us. These moments, as uncommon as they were, nonetheless instilled hope in my ever patient heart.

Yes, I remember watching you for quite awhile in silence on that November afternoon, imagining with a bittersweet smile what it would be like for us to trade places with Lorena and Perry, and be truly in love—if only for a little while.

A sweet disorder in the dress
Kindles in clothes a wantonness . . .

Robert Herrick—*Delight in Disorder*

∞

20 NOVEMBER, 1774

ON THIS VERY DAY, Lord Sutherland hosted a luncheon for us ladies in what he termed "the Parisian style," at his elegant set of apartments on Cornhill.

Sutherland's conspicuously garish sense of taste and morally lenient attitude was in great display all about the place—each room harbouring the most lewd and licentious artwork I had ever seen. Portraits of barely clad women hung in mock derision above cool marble mantles where statuettes of lovers frolicked amidst a tangle of loose clothing. Even the furnishings flaunted tawdriness, boasting of low-slung divans of flamboyant red silk sprawling with sinful enticement.

Secretly, I detested the place. However, I was soon to realise that I was terribly alone in my opinion. Lucy and the others were making much of the ostentatious designs with a gleeful clapping of hands, and great gales of shameless laughter. In a frightful fit of admiration, Rebecca extolled upon the beauty of a painting which depicted a maid servant admiring her own reflection in a pond as she bathed. Lucy was plaguing our host as to the origins of the luridly erotic snuffboxes which lolled about the parlours in great abundance. On my part, however, it was beyond me as to how any decent human being could ever admire such outright vulgarity.

A special drink was being passed round—a concoction Lord Sutherland called a "Cranberry Coaxer." At first, I hesitated to drink it, however, Lord Sutherland was insistent.

"It's not lethal, Dearie," he whispered closely in my ear. "Why, it has a touch of sherbet ice in it, brought all the way from Portsmouth for my party. There now. How bad can it be?"

I smiled shyly and ducked my head. It was, perhaps, quite foolish of me to be such a prude. It was all new to me, this newfound social set with their profoundly shocking ways. However, they were not bad people; not really. Why, it was even possible to have fun in their company, if one kept their wits wrapped around them. So, with a deep and determined breath, I took a sip of the mixture, and found it quite good. Why, it did not taste the least bit of alcohol, and I told my host as much.

"Heavens," the silly man exclaimed, placing a fluttering hand to his breast. "Did you think I planned on getting you cup-shot in order to carry you off to my bed? Glory, girl, but that just isn't my style."

With that, I laughed. Somewhere across the room, Diana glared at me as she stood leaning over the back of an overstuffed chair. Why the woman found it necessary to hate me so, I could not be certain. Perhaps it merely amused her to do so. How stupid, really.

Luncheon was a lingering affair of many courses; each accompanied by a specially selected wine or liquor-based drink, for which Sutherland had devised some cleverly naughty name. With the terrapin soup, we had "A Maiden's Kiss"; with the salmon trout, "A Chaste Embrace." I was near dizzy from the effects when yet another beverage appeared—"A Silk Garter," which was an iced mixture of brandied wines, made to enhance the third course of *pâté froid* and *cotelettes de veau*.

Despite the chill of the late November day, the room was becoming unbearably warm. From her station at the center of the table, Rebecca was fanning herself with a gold-rimmed plate, while Lucy, who seemed little affected by the heat, tossed endless berries in the air, attempting with rare success to capture them within her laughing mouth. Val, meanwhile, was making sport by rolling an empty wine bottle to and fro, much to the displeasure of her neighbours.

For the next course, woodcock, served with an elixir Lord Sutherland christened "Virtue Undone." By this point in time, everyone was in high hysterics. Lucy, finally bored with her berries, regaled the group with a flagrant rendition of the most off-colour stories she knew, while foolish Clemence unabashedly pillaged the untouched food from discarded plates nearby.

When the *blancmange* was presented, Diana had promised to favor the table with a song, which she did so very neatly despite the fact she had no accompaniment, as well as Lord Sutherland's hand buried well up her dress.

> *Old Maids shall forget what they wished for in vain,*
> *And young ones, the Rover they cannot regain;*
> *The Rake shall forget how last night he was cloy'd,*
> *And Chloe again be with Passion enjoy'd.*

Obey then the Summons, to Lethe repair,
And drink an Oblivion to Trouble and Care . . .

"Goodness," exclaimed Lucy, her drink-sodden eyes going wide. "It's nearly three! I must run!"

"But dessert hasn't been served yet," Sutherland protested. "You might call it my *pièce de résistance*. And after that, a game of blindman's buff."

"I really haven't time, my good man," returned Lucy as she dashed about in a mad search for her cloak. "Besides, I intend to have oysters for my dessert."

"How utterly pathetic," mumbled Sutherland, his pop eyes taking in the rest of his company at a glance. "Does anyone else plan to abandon my happy little luncheon for other such debase and rudimentary pleasures?"

I panicked. Strangely enough, the thought of Lucy's imminent departure chilled me to the core with unequivocal dread.

"I think I should go along too," I nearly whispered. "I promised Jeffrey I'd be home by half past two."

The greatest fuss was made by all, excepting Diana, of course. I imagine the prospect of my hasty removal thrilled her to no end. It should have. That sordid buffoon, Sutherland, had been studying my contours in great detail every chance he could get.

"La!" Sutherland sighed in defeat. "*Mes beaux yeux.* Ah, well. I shall escort both ladies to their carriages, and soon return, *mes amies.*"

With that, he signaled for dessert to be served with a flamboyant wave of his hand. At once, two stone-faced footmen made their way forward, carrying a large serving platter between them. Adorning this platter were two sculpted gelatin molds, crowned with a cherry apiece, which more than unwittingly resembled a large pair of breasts.

"You are a pervert, Suthie," warned Lucy, as Clemence, who was last to recognise the significance of the art work, let out an ear-piercing scream of surprise.

"Why, thank you, Miss Lucy," answered our unabashed host, as he walked us both towards the door.

Once outside, I was a bit taken aback by the daylight. But I soon realised that the day only seemed bright because I was *birled*, as Great-grandmother Effie so plainly put it. Yes, I was definitely toppled with drink!

"Miss Lucy," began Lord Sutherland, ever so casually. "Perhaps you should take the first carriage, and be on your way. After all, we cannot be sure just how long your oysters are going to hold up, now can we?"

Before I knew what was happening, Lucy had dashed off, and my imperious host was seated in the second coach beside me.

"Lord Sutherland—" I stammered. "Your guests—"

"Oh, hang 'em," he whispered slyly. "It's you I want to be with."

"I'm—I'm not quite sure what you mean, really."

"And in the interest of time, I hope you do," Sutherland crooned, sliding over quite close to me. His breath was horrid; it smelled like an explosion in a grog shop.

"Lord Sutherland!" I protested. But he smiled widely, showing his bad teeth, and kissed me quickly on the cheek.

"There now!" he announced. "We're friends. And as friends, I think you should call me Hector."

"Hector?" I repeated stupidly. "What kind of name is Hector?"

Sutherland sat up straight for a moment. Seemingly quite offended, he immediately attempted to place a look of dignity upon the obscured features of his face.

"It's a very noble name meaning *defender*."

"Oh. I see," I responded carefully. I was, to be sure, near ready to laugh despite my precarious situation. Hector? It reminded me of Davenport's dinner party when Hancock suggested to Clemence that she rename herself Beezaleed. Then I did laugh, in spite of it all.

"So now will you call me Hector?"

"Only if you promise to behave," I answered, facing him as squarely as I could. I seemed to experience great difficulty in focusing. "Now, please return to your lovely luncheon party, and allow me to go home. I've had a most pleasant day, thank you. And I am sure we will see each other again, quite soon."

Having finished my discourse, I extended my hand politely in farewell. But my gesture was completely ignored, as Sutherland rapped on the roof of the coach, instructing the driver to proceed towards Charter Street. And as the carriage lurched forward, I regarded my unwelcome companion with an incredulous stare.

"Whether I behave or not, or whether you call me Hector or not, I shall still see you home," Sutherland explained coolly, settling himself back into the fine leather of the seat, as I merely formed an *o* with my mouth, and stared blindly out the window.

Whatever was I going to do? You were not at home, Jeffrey. In one sense, I was glad, for what a lecture you would give me for my present condition! In the other sense—I shuddered. If a lecher like Lord Sutherland got into our house, there was no telling what might happen to me. Oh, I could have kicked myself for leaving the party like this—ridiculously drunk, and saddled with an immoral maniac besides. What an idiotic fool I was!

Already, Sutherland was grabbing at my knees. The whole thing was despicable. I kept slapping his large paws as though he were a wayward urchin caught at the cookie tin.

"Lord Sutherland, please!" I repeated angrily. But it only incensed him further, as he planted the most repulsive kisses on my throat.

"Stop it!" I demanded, praying with whatever might I could muster that Charter Street would soon come into sight. I contemplated making a jump for it, even though it meant the possibility of a broken neck. Why, anything was better than this!

"Relax, my dearest pet," I heard him murmur against my neck. "You shall come to enjoy it. I know you will."

Suddenly, I laughed. It was all too funny, this bug-eyed man slobbering all over my pretty lace collar, and cupping my breasts as though I were a prize cow. If men only knew how preposterous they looked when acting like this.

"See," he cooed, fired on by my laughter. "You are warming to the sweet fruits of my art. But seriously, my sweet, remark any louder and the coach-man will want to join in."

"Oh, good God," I managed before Sutherland landed his disgustingly wet mouth against mine. I struggled to remain seated, but the slick satin material of my cloak kept propelling me off the leather bench. And Sutherland was not helping any with his clumsy attempts to push aside my petticoats.

"Stop!" I tried to say without opening my mouth enough to permit his impatient tongue. "Stop, damn it!"

Suddenly the coach did stop, and the door was swiftly opened by none other than Captain Landon Vale.

Now, I know I should have been embarrassed. But heavens above, I was never so happy to see an officer of the King in all my born days!

"Mrs. Lynford," the Captain began smoothly. "At last you are home."

Pushing the startled Sutherland away, I glanced out the open door. Yes, by Zeus, we were right there before our tidy, little house of brick. How welcoming it was!

"Yes, Captain Vale. I am home." It was a stupid thing to say; however, echoing short, pat sentences was about all I was good for in my present condition.

"Lord Sutherland," the Captain went on, coolly. "I shall see the lady in from here."

"Yes," Hector murmured, wiping his mouth. "Yes, I'm sure you will."

The coach went off. I stood in the street, my knees shaking, and a horrendous blush overtaking my face.

"How little you must think of me," I confessed quietly. I could tell that the Captain had not taken his eyes from my face.

"What I think is of little consequence, Madam. However, what the neighbours think is another. Now, are you quite all right? Do you think you can make it to the house?"

"Of course," I bragged, taking my first step none too well. "I just had a wee little bit to drink, that's all."

Luckily, the Captain did not challenge my lie. We went inside at once. Beals appeared, stumbling in from the pantry, a silver sugar bowl in one hand and a polishing rag in the other. He regarded me strangely, but I could not mind. Indeed, I must have looked foolish, grabbing for the pie crust table in order to steady myself.

"Beals," the Captain commanded. "Please get Adele downstairs, in order to see to her mistress."

"Very well, Sir," Beals replied. However, the lagging speed with which he left assured that the Captain and I would be stranded in the front hall for days to come.

"Adele," I called up the stairs. "Adele, are you there?"

She appeared at once, and the look on her face made it clear that my afternoon of drinking was as simple to read as Mother Goose.

"Adele," the Captain began, "your mistress is not feeling well. Perhaps you should see her to bed."

"Yes, that sounds nice," I mumbled, trying to set my sights on the stairs in front of me. However was I to conquer them? It was then that I heard the Captain laugh. And I laughed, too.

"Madam," he said, smiling. "You are rather fuddled."

"No, Captain," I replied, taking his arm as he assisted me up the loathsome staircase. "I am most definitely birled. Yes, birled. That's what my great-grandmother calls it, and she should know!"

⊂◌⊃⊂◌⊃⊂◌⊃

Adele had settled me into my bed when a knock sounded at the door. Oh, I feared it was you, Jeffrey, and I tried so very hard to appear straight and sober. However, Adele came back into the room and pulled my dressing screen to the side of my bed. Naturally, I asked her why.

"The Captain wishes to speak to you, Madam."

Oh, heavens, I thought. Now he means to lecture me on what happens to silly women who spend the afternoon swilling rum with lecherous lords named Hector. I supposed I deserved it, but sweet Jesus, must I be reminded so terribly soon?

The Captain was shown into my room. I pulled my coverlet well up to my chin, despite the fact that the screen stood between us, and I bade him to sit.

"Thank you for seeing me, Mrs. Lynford. I would have waited, of course, but time does not permit it."

"You're not leaving Boston, are you?" I asked. In my muddled state, I was finding it rather foolish to be speaking to a Chinese screen.

"Oh, no. Heavens, no. I've come to speak to you regarding the quartering sanction."

"Oh, that," I sighed, shuffling myself beneath the blankets again. "I know all about that. My husband has indicated that due to his constant business travels to Concord, I am very often alone in the house. So that is why we stand exempt."

"Not any longer, Madam," the Captain replied. "Your personal maid and footman serve, in the eyes of the officials, as adequate chaperones. Furthermore, Madam, I have discovered that they mean to plague you with the worst old codger in all of the Royal Navy."

My blurry eyes went wide.

"Oh, no!" I exclaimed, sitting bolt upright in bed. "Who is this man?"

"Lieutenant General Elwood Crawley. A most fearsome old dotard, with a voice that could shatter glass. Horrid appearance—he has only one eye. Lost the other in a tavern brawl. But he sees well enough, I suppose. He killed all three of his wives for cheating on him—or so he says."

"You cannot be serious," I breathed in horror.

"Oh, but I am. And that is not all. Old Crawley demands his breakfast promptly at a quarter past four every morning, and lights out at seven every night. Worse still, I am afraid he shall drink all your rum, and spit on your floors. Navy men are like that, you see."

"Oh, dear God! Oh, dear—Adele!" I practically bellowed. "Get this fool screen out of my way!" This the poor darling did without delay. I think my fit of fear put wings on her heels. The Captain was indeed nonplused, however, at the moment I had absolutely no mind for proprieties.

"Captain Vale, you would not, by chance, be lying to me just now, would you?"

"The only occasion on which I would lie to you, Mrs. Lynford, is when it is strictly for your own good."

"Oh, dear God," I said again, and for a brief instant I thought I saw the Captain trying his very best not to laugh. But in my hazy state of nerves, I could not be sure. "Oh, Captain. You must help me."

"Begging your indulgence, Madam, I already have," he said calmly, clearing his throat. "You see, I had been stationed at Charles Davenport's house. It was all arranged."

"Yes—yes," I returned, clutching the coverlet with my fists. All I could picture was some mean old man with a glass eye hollering for his johnnycakes at the ungodly hour of four in the morning, and spitting on my skirts. The image was, indeed, almost sobering.

"However, I went to Mr. Davenport's this very afternoon, and pleaded with him on your behalf, Madam, to take another officer instead. Happily, Charles agreed. In this way, I could be quartered at the Lynford house—that is, if you both accept."

"We do, we do!" I practically shouted. "Of course, I'll consult Jeffrey," I added for nicety's sake. But as far as I was concerned, the matter was settled. Now our liquor would be spared, and I would not be forced to tiptoe around a silenced house in fear of rattling the nerves of an old, nefarious, three-time wife murderer.

The Captain cleared his throat again. "Of course, I would pay rent to you. It shall, in fact, be a pleasure. And, after your most unfortunate episode of today, I feel it would be my happy duty to offer you my protection, Madam."

"Oh, Captain Vale. How can I ever thank you?"

"Do not give it a second thought," he replied, standing. "And now, Mrs. Lynford, I shall leave you to your rest. I do believe you are going to need it after the rigours of your afternoon."

I blushed. "Of course, Captain."

He went to the door and paused before leaving.

"One last thing, my kind lady. If I might be so bold, I would suggest you let Mr. Lynford know that you have suddenly acquired a tremendous attack of migraine. It will help explain things when you go about the house tomorrow, moaning and crushing your head between your hands."

"It could not possibly be all that bad," I opined with brave confidence.

"Oh, but it will," he answered with a smile. "However, fret not. After completing my early duties at headquarters tomorrow, I shall return to offer a stroll with you at approximately two in the afternoon. That should assist you in clearing your head."

"I cannot thank you enough, Captain," I said as he bowed graciously and left, closing the door behind him.

Somehow I suspected that he lied to me. But more importantly, I did not care.

Music is the only sensual pleasure without vice.

Samuel Johnson—*Apothegms*

☙

THE BEGINNING OF A NEW YEAR, 1775

ON THE EIGHTH OF JANUARY, General Gage's wife gave a ball, to which many of the society ladies of Boston were invited, myself included. I recall being seated at my dressing table, and Adele was putting the finishing touches to my dress, when a bold knock sounded upon the door.

"Jeffrey?" I asked. "Is that you, at last?"

The door opened partially, and the Captain spoke; begging my pardon, but could he see me a moment? I told him to come in, and he did so with great hesitation. I wondered just how many ladies' dressing rooms he had entered in his life. A foolish thought, really, but it amused me to contemplate it.

"Mrs. Lynford," he said, somewhat bashfully. "How lovely you look."

"Thank you, Captain Vale. In truth, you look lovely, too."

"Lovely?" he returned, patting at his impeccably tailored regimental waist-coat. "*Lovely* insinuates I should be in one of those salons where the men dance only with other men."

I laughed, fingering the pearls at my neck.

"All right then," I mused, while Adele fussed with putting my day dress away. "Worldly," I went on, remembering Lucy's description of her first meeting with the Captain two months ago. Yes, she was right. It truly fit him. "Yes, worldly. Is that a better choice?"

"Much," he smiled, ducking his head. How shy for so handsome a man! I watched him in the glass for a moment before speaking again.

"Miss Eldredge will adore being on your arm tonight. How charming you both shall look."

The Captain merely shrugged, and then looked at me. I believe he forgot his reason for visiting. I bade him to sit down, and he did, but not until he was certain Adele was still present, and clearly in sight. The Captain also chose a chair at the far end of the room. I watched all of this in fascination. Frankly, I was not accustomed to such manners.

"You asked to see me, Captain Vale?" I hinted.

"Oh—oh, yes. Forgive me, Madam, but when I see you enveloped in soft candlelight like this—well, you just reminded me of someone I once knew."

"Oh," I said softly, and I looked down at my fingernails for a moment, in order to cover my thoughts. I could not easily imagine the Captain being much attracted to anyone who looked like me. I lacked a certain vitality of character and colouring, I believe, to sway a man whose position can afford him anything or anyone. No, I envisioned this female as regally tall, slender, and blonde with sharp grey eyes. She'd have all the social graces, but tremendous wit and intelligence as well. Nothing like Lorena. This woman of the past would have been slightly older, and her knowledge would have been enticing to a young officer. No, it was only now, when many of life's experiences had been savoured, that a young girl like Lorena would suit a man such as Landon Vale.

"As to the reason for my visit, Madam, I was concerned that Mr. Lynford has not yet returned home, and he was to escort you this evening."

"Yes," I said with a sigh. "I imagine he's still at the Royal Coffee House with Mr. King and Mr. Varney. And he promised me . . . Well, I suppose I shall have to wait."

"If you wish, Madam, I could escort you to the hall first. Then, once you are secure in the proper company, I could go for the Eldredges."

I turned round on my bench and faced him directly.

"How very kind of you," I said, and I meant it. "However, you must not consider it, Captain. If Miss Lorena is late for the festivities, she may never forgive you. I know she shall wish to dance every dance, so please do not give my little predicament another thought. I shall be at the Province House; even if I have to walk there myself."

"You cannot do that, Mrs. Lynford. It simply isn't done."

I smiled. How very much like a gentleman to cite all the grand proprieties in life—proprieties that did not make much sense in a town under military occupation.

"Perhaps I shan't go after all," I said resignedly. "Besides, I always end up being cornered by Charles Davenport's *theatricals*. And amusing as they often are, I do long for some normal everyday conversation now and then."

"I can sympathize with you, Madam. I always find myself *cornered*, as you put it, in the company of the Eldredges and their close-knit circle. And as much as I sincerely do enjoy their society, I also long to converse with others— others such as yourself. What I mean to say is, you and I have so little time for conversation, despite the fact I reside as a tenant under your roof."

"I have it!" I said, clasping my hands together with glee. "If you see me being bored to tears in my particular *corner* this evening, please do come and rescue me. And I, my gallant knight, shall do the same for you."

"Splendid," he replied with a handsome grin. "And now, dear Madam, I should leave. It would not do to have the gallant knight discovered in the lady's bedchamber."

"Correct, Sir," Adele ventured quietly. "For I believe I just heard the front door opened to the master."

"A duel," I chided. "How divine!"

We laughed, took hold of each other's hands for a moment, and promised to meet again within the hour.

⬤⬤⬤⬤

The hall was emblazoned with streams of soft candlelight, and the air was deliciously thick with the scents of bayberry candles, perfumed pomanders, and green, waning pine boughs which adorned every windowsill, bower, and table in the handsome manse known as the Province House, now home to General and Mrs. Gage. Even the chandeliers were dressed with beribboned branches of festive holly, the berries of which glowed a bright waxen red beneath the resplendent rays of light.

By a quarter past six in the evening, the walls resounded with airy, feminine laughter and the ringing boisterous jests of the uniformed men who so gallantly vied for the ladies' attentions. So many military uniforms! The room was a sea of scarlet and blue coats, and dazzling buttons of silver and gold. And so many ladies! Any sister, daughter, cousin, or niece to any man not politically swayed by palsied Whigs or celebrated Liberty Trees, had turned out on this heavenly moonlit night, to dance and flirt, and to fall in love.

Where once this great hall stood silent, startled only by the occasional and dissonant strains of tuning violins, German flutes, and hautbois, there now came a grand confusion of noises. Women exclaimed loudly to one another across the room, as dance cards were called for by bashful and brazen men alike. And then, the orchestra began boldly with a country dance known to all as "Child Grove," the music of which sent a chill of excitement about the place. Yes, it was time to dance, even if the decaying, old matrons clucked their tongues about the "new morality," as they huddled in brightly lit alcoves like babbling buzzards with great wagging chins.

Those caught standing about the dance floor made way as a new throng pervaded it in a blur of swirling satins, brocades, and woolen waistcoats. Then a cheer went round the room, for the festivities had officially begun.

"Forgive me darling," you had said to me above the din, Jeffrey. "However, Merchant King is standing over there with the Varneys, and I must finish a bit of business with them."

"Of course," I replied, not minding in the least. Not minding that was, until I saw Virginia Stanwood spotting me, and tapping Samuel Loring with her fan. Yes, she was pointing at me, and I knew with a sickening drop in my stomach that Virginia was asking Samuel to come fetch me. I turned my back, and pretended great interest in the refreshments table.

"Mrs. Lynford! How radiant you look!" Samuel said when he had made his way across the room.

I turned round again to see the merchant finely attired in a court suit of striped grey silk, edged with appliquéd netting. His formal Cadogan wig with high toupee complimented the very image of elegance.

"As do you, Merchant Loring. That is a divine suit."

"French," he admitted with a grimace. "Imagine that? Imagine wearing French to a British general's soirée?"

"Worse things have happened, I'm sure," I smiled, glancing about the room in search of Captain Vale. "Where is—everybody?"

"Oh, Charles and the others will be here eventually. There was a minor and messy to-do over who was invited, and who was not. You see, Mrs. Gage could not exactly have Miss Wellman and Miss Hale here. Not with the likes of the Littlefields and the Eldredges about. They just don't mix, my dear."

"I suppose you're right," I said, secretly grateful that Lucy and Valentine would not be present. At last, a golden opportunity to spend one evening in the company of a gentler society.

"Speaking of *mix*, were you aware that Charles and Hector were organising some little outing at your father's place in Concord—a duck hunt, I believe, in the spring."

"Yes, I had heard," I responded carefully. It was originally Hector's idea for the party. And when I was so bold as to make note that I had not been consulted, Lord Sutherland caustically replied that it had nothing to do with me. I imagine he was still smarting over the fact that I did not permit him to have his way with me in the carriage, last November.

"The Eldredges have also been invited. Fancy that," Samuel went on to say.

"Yes," I said, a strange, little pang of jealousy nicking at my heart. This meant that the Captain would be compelled to spend the day in Lorena's company, leaving little time for me.

"You and Mr. Lynford have not been round much to the Eldredges'. Is something wrong?"

I know Samuel's question came more from sly curiosity than concern.

Although he was a fine man in many ways, he harboured an almost feminine proclivity for gossip. However, I was not going to give him any satisfaction tonight.

"Heavens, no, Merchant Loring. It's just that we are so often at Mr. Davenport's on Thursday evenings."

Samuel waited for more, but I merely smiled and continued to view the festivities about us. Samuel then asked if I might join him and the ladies Stanwood for awhile. I agreed. We crossed the room, arm in arm. It was then I saw Landon and Lorena dancing. How handsome they were together! Lorena was the vision of perfection in a sapphire blue gown of the finest brocade, with a petticoat trimmed with the most delicate lace. I watched as she glanced about the room with each turn of the dance, her face alight with a most winning smile.

Samuel then led me to an alcove where Virginia and Eve waited in elegant repose. Attired in like outfits of pink satin, they made a pretty tableau, although Virginia was rendered ridiculous by her headdress of oversized, feathery white plumes.

"Mrs. Lynford, my dear," Virginia cooed, her voice and her smile greatly enhanced by champagne. "Come sit next to me, and we shall make a rummage of the men. Samuel, get our Verity a glass of punch, will you? She must be parched."

Virginia watched as Samuel left, her splendid eyes of violet never abandoning his elegant form.

"There's no one to beat my Samuel," she sighed. "No one. Although, he does remind me very much of a man who was terribly taken with me when I was all of fifteen. He was the son of a count, and was ever so charming. He owned a chateau outside of Paris that rivaled Versailles, and his weekend hunt parties were all the rage. Oh, how he adored me! Why, he showered me in diamonds, just to prove it. Alas, I was too young to fully appreciate it all. And when I left him for a wealthier man, he drowned himself in the fountain outside his palatial manse. Such a tragedy!"

"How nice," I mumbled, my full attention caught in a corner of the room where a group of soldiers were paying mock homage to Diana Kirby as the Rebel's Miss Liberty in Charles' play. I watched as the men lifted their glasses in tribute, and Diana answered their praises with pretty blushes and feigned protestations. Frankly, it annoyed me to no end. The role used to be mine.

Loring returned with the punch. Virginia went on about romantic days of old, while I watched Lorena and her Captain dance. To all eyes, they looked so very much in love. But were they?

Secretly I wondered if Perry Talbot was this moment standing outside this festive hall, watching his beloved Lorena from the night shadows. And if he was, could he see the reflection of the Captain in Lorena's beautiful eyes? Of course, Perry and Lorena had to cease their meetings in my home, once the Captain became quartered there. How awkward it would have been for them all to meet in my parlour! I had seen Perry Talbot often since, and he claimed that all was happily moving forward with Miss Eldredge. Then what, pray tell, was this? Tonight, in such magic surroundings, Lorena Eldredge seemed so utterly enraptured with her Captain. Why, I doubted for certain that she would exchange this captivating night for an evening by the fire at Perry's tiny abode on Ann Street, sewing buttons on his shirts.

It was then I realised what I had done. Yes, I knew with a sickening stab of guilt that because of some whirlwind motivation within my foolish heart, some-one was going to be dreadfully hurt.

Of course, the Captain had to adore Lorena. With her style and grace and unquestionable beauty, how could he not? And Perry was in love with her, too. Of that, I could be certain. So now, it was all up to Lorena. The murmur of two men's hearts would beat, waiting for this enchanting young woman to make up her mind. I had not helped with my interference; I had only hindered.

"Oh, heavens," Virginia began, breaking my reverie with a great burst of laughter. "Who is that absolutely homely girl out there?"

I followed her gaze to the dance floor where a rotund young woman with a slipshod wig and dour expression was being partnered by a soldier whose portly dimensions matched her own. I recognised her at once. She was one of Lorena's simple-minded friends, Sophie Littlefield. And of all the couples par-ticipating in the dance, she and her partner were the least suited to the exer-cise. The stocky soldier was sweating profusely, and Miss Littlefield was struggling for breath beneath the confines of her tight silk bodice.

"What a fine pair of piggies," Virginia observed, her eyes moist with the tears of laughter. "Oh, they would bring in a tidy fortune at the butcher's, do you not agree?"

"Be kind," Loring warned under his breath, as an officer approached with the intent of securing a future dance with me.

"I couldn't possibly," I told my hopeful visitor with a sad smile. "My hus-band is not present."

Before I knew it, Captain Vale was at my side. I was astonished at how quickly and quietly he had appeared. I greeted him with enthusiasm, and asked how his evening was progressing.

"The gallant knight is here to rescue you, Madam," he whispered as he bowed over my hand to kiss it.

"And what about the lovely Miss Lorena?" I asked, my eyes darting about the room.

"Miss Eldredge has a rather full dance queue," the Captain mused. "I am yours, Madam, for at least an hour."

"Then let us make the most of it," I whispered back, standing at once. I bid my adieux to the merchant and his ladies, and before Landon Vale could utter another word, I led him to a deserted alcove—deserted because it was brightly lit and definitely too near the disapproving matrons for a proper tryst. Yes, it was certain young lovers would avoid this corner like the plague. But for us, it would serve quite nicely.

"But Madam," the Captain began. "Where is Mr. Lynford?"

I scowled. "Jeffrey pretended to have more business to discuss with the merchants Varney and King. In actuality however, I saw him skulking off to the game room for a round or two of All Fours. We needn't worry about him, really and truly. Indeed, I would adore having a pleasant chat with you, Captain. Why, I've been dreaming about it ever since you left the house."

He smiled and patted my hand. Around us, people were still arriving in droves. It seemed madness to have invited so many guests, for there was precious little spare room to be had. So many voices, so much laughter. By now, the orchestra had to work harder to be heard above the constant din. It was nearly pointless. The crowd seemed driven by the excessive warmth in the room, while overhead, the heat of the chandeliers was only increasing, choking the garlands of green until their scent was all but lost in the stifling qualities of the hall.

We laughed at all we witnessed around us. A woman, rather overdressed in a silver laced court gown and flowered talematongue, lost her towering wig while bending over a tray of fruit tarts. Meanwhile, six young ladies had been locked away in the cloak room by a band of drunken fusiliers. But the most humorous spectacle ensued when four soldiers, lacking dance partners, took to the floor regardless, and were having quite a time of it.

"There, see!" I said in mock seriousness. "All the available men are taken. So I fear, Captain, that you are now forced to spend time with me."

"Do you not enjoy dancing, Mrs. Lynford?" he asked, and I was caught speechless for a moment, for his eyes were so beautiful.

"I love to dance, Captain. But you see, I do not view dancing as mere exercise. It's rather difficult to explain, really. . . ." I was stammering a bit because the Captain's stare was so alluring. Strange that I had not noticed this before. "Dancing is more of an expression between a man and a woman, as I see it. I wouldn't just go about this room, kissing all the men; so, in the same way, I am very particular about who I dance with. Oh, I know this silly little speech of mine does not make much sense. I am sorry."

"It makes perfect sense to me," he said, and his words startled me somewhat. I had not thought anyone else would feel the same way about a mere dance. How lovely.

"So tell me, Madam, how you came to be a part of Mr. Davenport's society. I must admit that is one facet of your life I have great trouble understanding."

I found myself telling the Captain nearly everything about my life. He listened with great interest as I spoke of my father, and of his tender devotion to my dear mother. I recalled all the foolish and funny stories of my youth, and of all my father's friends who helped to raise Ruthie and me. I did not go into great detail about my life with you, Jeffrey. I did not wish to. You see, I was as bitter then as I am now about all that stood between us. And a woman barely married ten months should never admit to emotional defeat. When I was done, I paused, rather breathless, for I had consumed most of our hour with my little history alone.

I thought the Captain would be bored. I believed he would be seeking escape. But instead, he asked me to dance a "Trip to Paris." Without the slightest hesitation, I accepted.

We were selected as first couple, and as such, we were to perform most of the movement in our dance—setting to each other, turning and revolving around one another like swans on a glistening pond. Our smiling eyes never left each other's gaze. We turned again, changed places, and circled four in hand with our neighbours. Oh, how Landon was laughing and smiling! Such a startling change from his typical character, and it pleased me greatly to witness him having so much fun. Perhaps for both of us, it was a moment in which we did not have to take ourselves and the overwhelming world we found ourselves in so very seriously.

The dance had ended. I thanked him with a bow, and proceeded off the floor as the master of the dance announced the next offering, which was "Well Hall." Landon stopped, and with a tender grasp of my hand, attempted to lead me back to the line.

I reminded the Captain that to dance with me, a married woman, twice like this would be scandalous. He merely smiled. The touch of his hand on mine was all the hypnotic lure I needed.

The rhythm of the dance, and the gliding movements of the sets took over the beat of my heart. Calming. Enchanting. I looked to the Captain's face, and his glance was no longer laughing. Instead, the hazel of his eyes led me to his very soul, and the gold that surrounded them shone with brilliance in the candlelight above. And it was in that magical moment that a most amazing transformation occurred. I was no longer the commonplace Verity Daniels, who came to Boston from the country, seeking her dreams in the clouds. I was no longer Verity. For just a few minutes in an oasis bathed with beautiful music, I was Miss Lorena Eldredge. I imagined I had her rich, dark hair and her lovely eyes of blue. A smile came to my lips, and it was her smile, for it radiated from a confident, loving heart within. And I took the message of his eyes into my own, and held it there for the longest time.

The music breathed its last few mystical chords, and slowly, I came back to being. I was Mrs. Jeffrey Lynford once more. Landon escorted me back to where the ladies Stanwood greeted us warmly. I glanced about the room. No, we had not left the mark of scandal with our little moment on the dance floor. Another dance had taken its place, with nameless dancers and nameless faces. Not a minute had passed when Miss Eldredge came to collect the Captain, claiming that her dear mother wished to introduce him to yet another *darling* couple, fresh from the mother country. I allowed my gaze to dart quickly towards where Mrs. Eldredge stood with a pair whose countenances were so dull and waxen, they deserved nothing more than dusty, old frames affixed to their shoulders. Very *darling*, indeed.

I sat next to Virginia, and attempted to hide my triumphant smile. True, I was still the commonplace Mrs. Jeffrey Lynford. However, for one exalted moment, I, like the silver-hearted moon, had risen into a celestial sky, and taken my place in the heavens. I had never, my dear, been happier.

To thee, fair freedom! I retire
From flattery, cards, and dice, and din;
Nor art thou found in mansions higher
Than the low cot, or humble inn.

William Shenstone—*Written at an Inn at Henley*

∞

8 APRIL, 1775

BY NINE IN THE MORNING, a rolling roar of carriage wheels announced the arrival of company.

It was a colourful sight, the six elegant coaches pulled by fine black horses. And the peal of conversation was such that the joyous infusion of voices could be heard well before the turn to Papa's tavern.

Lord Sutherland, dressed as any dandy would be for a day in the country, was in possession of the first coach, accompanied by the Sloans, and none other than Diana Kirby. True, she and Hector had not resumed their sordid alliance; however, the importance of being mistress of the festivities was certainly not beyond Diana's headstrong exigencies. Attired in her customary costume of white, Diana, with her lofty stare, suited the part to perfection.

Betsy Sloan was wearing a nondescript dress of drab brown, which was mocked by an over-large headdress of black feathers. Her husband, James, was strangely talkative. Ever since we passed Watertown, he had been discussing Voltaire like a fiend.

Second in line, I shared a coach with Charles and Landon and Lorena. Mrs. Eldredge had declined to go at the last minute, making the time, I believe, more enticing for Lorena. Within the third carriage, from which there evoked the greatest amount of feminine chatter, Valentine, Lucy, Rebecca, and the forever laughing Clemence rode like queens, crushing Bryce between them. On impulse, Valentine stood while the coach was still in motion, displaying her curious gown of yellow gold, which boasted a grand and foolish confusion of stuffed ornamental birds, held fast by a netting of black silk over her voluminous petticoats. It was a jolly thing, was it not, to bring one's own birds to a duck hunt?

On her part, Lucy was caught up in a feverish state of awe, pointing wildly left and right with passionate exclamations over such commonplace things as fields set to plow and elm trees and geese. It mattered not that Val and Rebecca had voted her silly. Lucy was a child of the city, and quite unaccustomed to wide open spaces, and air that did not reek of chimney soot or the filth of humanity. For her, the heavens opened up on this day, presenting all its glory before her small, eager eyes.

"Oh, look!" she cried happily. "Look at those beautiful horses! And a pond! How lovely. Perhaps we could all go for a swim later. And the geese—look at them! See how that gander chases the slim one about? And just after breakfast, too."

"It's the feed, don't you know," offered Rebecca in her sweetest drawl. "It incites them senseless."

"Bah!" replied Lucy with an upturned nose. "Then Miss Goosey pecked from a different pot. For see? She wants no part of him."

Lucy then leaned over the carriage side, and cupped her voice towards the distant flock.

"Get a copper from him first, my fine feathered gal. Then it won't seem so bad!"

"Oh, hush!" exclaimed Val, dashing Lucy in the ribs with her elbow. "Do you want Verity's father to hear such rubbish? Why, he'd think us most undignified."

In the fourth coach traveled the actors, David Manley, Tim Gorman, Gordon Russell, Marlon Reynolds, and the energetic Darcy, all befitted and painstakingly prepared for this, their best portrayal of gentlemen on a rustic holiday.

Behind them rode more of the assemblage: Roscoe Bennett, William Collamore, Sir Alfred Blinn, and the pouting Orrin Blackwell. Orrin was in a typical fuss because Miss Lucy would not ride with him. Heavens no, she firmly said, pertly adding that she would much rather be dragged along on a rough rope, than be forced to ride the eighteen long miles next to him. Someone had pointed out Orrin's miserable expression to Lucy, but she merely shrugged.

"Bah!" she repeated with a sneer of disdain. "It's too bad for the great gollumpus, now isn't it?"

The first of the remaining coaches carried the merchants Loring and Platt, as well as Virginia Stanwood and her daughter, Eve. With constant and feathery flutterings of her fine lace handkerchief, Virginia appeared to be indicating that the dust from the front carriages offended her great violet eyes, while

Eve sat silent and unmoving beside her.

"What a glorious day!" Merchant Loring called forward, and everyone cheered. Everyone, that is, except the imperious Diana.

Behind the great procession, a large wagon lumbered along, carrying chairs, tables, and linens, as well as food provisions, brandies, and wines. This represented Lord Sutherland's lavish contribution, showing that he was indeed a man who lived solely for pleasure.

The first coach had arrived before the Crossroads' door with a grand flourish, and Sutherland turned round to see if all were met. What ensued was nothing short of confusion—ladies disembarking amidst a myriad of flounces; squealing with delight as the men delivered them down like gracious Galahads. Charles was off at once to inspect the grounds, as Lord Sutherland snapped out orders to the lackeys brought along to officiate over the picnic.

At once, Papa was at the door. It had not occurred to me until that very moment just how much I missed him. And how very handsome he was! Strange to think that I had not noticed as much before this.

"My dear girl, you look wonderful," he said, holding my hands within his very tightly. All at once, I wanted to be ten years old again, and live with my Papa forever.

"Where is your husband?"

I swallowed hard. I had not thought of facing my father with the truth that you, Jeffrey, had little interest in participating in any social event that included me these days. Such strangers we had become, you and I. It was all I could do to convince you to come out to Concord for my best friends' wedding in two weeks' time.

"Oh, Jeffrey could not come today. He wanted to settle some matters before Karen and Ambrose's wedding. He'll be here in just a few short days, Papa." There. The true test was before me. You see, I had sadly become something of an accomplished liar in Boston. What else could I be around all these vain, busybody theatricals? But Papa knew me better than anyone. I looked at his face; he took my sorry stretch for the truth. And I was left with such a pitiful thing to be proud of.

Papa was about to say something more, when it was noticed that one of the basset hounds had gotten loose amongst the ladies, and was barking up a terror at their skirts.

"Annie!" Papa hollered out. "Come!"

But she would not. It took a more commanding tone of my father's voice to bring the basset back with a sad display of drooping head and dejected eyes.

Charles had since returned from the field, and was addressing the retinue of loaders who sat in silence along the stone wall, attending to the gentlemen's fowling pieces. Taking notice of my father, Charles waved in salutation and strode forward to where we stood observing all the hullaballoo.

"Lovely day," Charles exclaimed brightly. "How good of you to have us all here, Mr. Daniels."

After a respectable amount of small talk, Charles announced that it was time to commence with the hunt. Now the only problem was to gather up the company, which had long since scattered about, lured by the area's distractions. The gentlemen found themselves much taken with the grist mill, and had journeyed across the road to watch the mad dash of water against the tireless wheel. As for the ladies, why they were thoroughly entranced by the mountainous sow and her bevy of little ones, who lay in happy squalor by our barn. Lucy pronounced the piglets simply adorable, and urged Valentine to pick up one of the tiny darlings, until Rebecca put an end to the ploy by insisting that the sow would most definitely rip her apart.

"You don't say?" Valentine murmured with a certain measure of fear. "Why, she looks like nothing more than a heap of lard to me."

Lucy laughed. "Oh, yes! She does look a great deal like Merchant Blackwell. Zeus, that's what we'll call her—Orinnella Blackbottom! Go ahead, Val. Jump right in there, and grab up one of Orinnella's fat little bacons. I dare you."

Valentine glanced at the rest, her eyes alert with the challenge.

"Try it then," Rebecca merely shrugged. "See if I care."

"Oh, Papa Charles is waving at us," Lucy observed with a sigh. "It must be time to start harassing the ducks."

Valentine was grateful, although she did not say as much; and the ladies picked up their skirts and started carefully across the drive.

"Come along!" Charles was saying. "Come along! The best part of the morning is fading before our eyes."

Lucy, who was terribly unaccustomed to sunlight, put her white, little hand up beneath the brim of her hat, in order to shade her eyes and peer about the place.

"Where's that simpering Eldredge creature and our oh-so-brave soldier? You cannot possibly begin blasting away at the poor birds until the Captain gives the royal blessing, or whatever it is he's supposed to do at a sacred time such as this."

Charles regarded Lucy sharply, as I volunteered to find the missing couple. I had my suspicions as to where Landon and Lorena might have gone, and following my instincts, I moved somewhat stealthily towards the rose arbour. Of course, I was correct. Seated together on the marble bench, they were a blissful image of contentment, their heads close together in intimate conversation.

I watched as Landon leaned towards Lorena, whispering something in her ear. In return, she laughed lightly and attempted without too great an effort to extract her dainty hands from his gentle grasp. Oh, why did this lovely little slip of a thing have to be so damnably beautiful and feminine? Yes, Lorena was as picturesque as a field of delicate spring flowers, and as sweet as the call of a nightingale. It further tugged at my heart that she could play the coquette so prettily, and with such tender innocence, that she was unquestionably beyond all reproach—even when she led two lovers about on a gossamer string!

Here I was, big as life, and twice as bold. Subtlety was an art completely lost to me. Yes, Lorena belonged in this touching little tableau, and not me. Lorena was as natural to the day as sunlight. The gentle breezes and the cheerful singing of birds were only a backdrop to her charms. Since moving to Boston, and more importantly, into Charles Davenport's circle, I had become a creature of darkness, best suited to smoke-filled rooms where passionate promises faired better by candlelight than before the delicate realities of day.

None the less, I once again found myself imagining that it was I, and not Lorena, who sat alongside the elusive Captain Vale. We would not notice the warmth of the sun, or even be the slightest bit aware of the song birds in the trees. No, this would be a morning created for us alone. Landon would hold my hand gently, and speak to me with tender words of devotion, vowing that I, Verity Daniels, was the most beautiful woman in the world . . .

"Heavens, woman, why are you hiding?" a voice assaulted me all at once. It was Darcy, and he had come up upon me as though propelled by an intense blur of energy, grabbing my shoulders and callously attempting to knock me to the ground.

"Oh, now I see why. You didn't wish to disturb the cooing doves. Zounds, but if you don't, I will. It's repulsive! Hallo there, Captain! Say, my man, do you intend to snub your new friends by playing at Romeo all the blessed day?"

Luckily, I had not been seen, for I would have died of shame if I had. I returned to the group quietly, and with a smile, which I am sure seemed sadly feigned, frozen upon my lips.

∞∞∞∞

We ladies situated ourselves upon a densely shaded bank above the swampy regions of marsh where the men had retreated in order to flush out the ducks.

Well apart from the rest, sat Virginia Stanwood and Diana Kirby, seemingly engrossed in conversation over the recently announced engagement of

Marlon Reynolds and Celeste Davenport, while Eve worked at a bit of embroidery, her still face quite void of emotion. Betsy sat alone, preoccupied with a tangled mess of music sheets, the notes from which she sang occasionally as she flicked at a troublesome bee who hovered about her hideous headdress. Not far away, Clemence was leaning against a shady tree, snoring away with resounding satisfaction.

Darcy, who had no stomach for shooting, was in a gather with Rebecca, Lucy and Val, sprawling in the sunshine; their faces upturned to the welcome warmth. Every few minutes, they would burst into outrageous fits of laughter, which were followed by somber faces of guilt whenever anyone glanced their way.

As for myself, I was content to sit somewhat nearby Betsy and the sputtering Clemence. I had a book of prose with me, which I pretended to read from time to time. However, my mind was adrift with other matters—matters chiefly of the heart.

I had never once in my life felt pity for myself, but now I knew firsthand the bitterness of such a heart-wrenching remorse. Oh, Jeffrey. We were but a year married, yet in so brief a time, things had changed. The love and longing I once carried so vividly for you, had faded into an odd sense of jealousy, then sorrier still, a sad indifference. But how I missed those frenzied feelings, those wild, impassioned desires that once filled the very fiber of my being. Could they truly be dead? It was difficult to say. My heart and my head could find little to agree upon these days.

"And what are we reading this fine morning?"

I looked up, startled. It was Landon, and he was quite alone.

"Herrick," I stammered. "At least, I'm attempting to read Herrick. I fear my mind isn't much on it."

With a polite, questioning gesture, the Captain seated himself beside me, and took the book from my hands; thumbing through the pages, his grand eyes intent.

"Where is Lorena?" I asked. Frankly, I was overjoyed not to have her about, but I knew all the same I should ask.

"Miss Eldredge is lying down with a sick head. A migraine, I believe. Your great-grandmother is seeing to her." This he said with little sense of alarm, which I found rather curious. Moreover, I found it amusing that Great-grandmother Effie had condescended to care for Miss Lorena. Effie vowed that all women who whimpered about headaches should be kicked in the backside and sent to work at something.

"Herrick's prose is often better heard than read," he went on, still in search of something amidst the pages; and then, "Ah, here we have it—

I BURN, I burn; and beg of you
To quench, or coole me with your Dew.
I frie in fire, and so consume,
Although the Pile be all perfume.
Alas! the heat and death's the same;
Whether by choice, or common flame:
To be in Oyle of Roses drown'd,
Or water; where's the comfort found?
Both bring one death; and I die here,
Unless you coole me with a Teare:
Alas! I call, but ah! I see
Ye coole and comfort all, but me."

Landon paused. I heard nothing but the spring wind moaning softly through the pines. I was also finding it terribly difficult to breathe.

"Please read that again," I whispered. He obliged.

It does perhaps sound foolish, but the soothing lull of his voice found a core in me I never knew existed. I was glad Miss Eldredge had taken ill. I hoped she would stay inside, quietly nurturing her sick head for the rest of the day. And, if all went as my greedy imagination fancied, something would burst within Lorena's silly brain, and she would neatly expire, with little or no disruption to our most beautiful day.

Landon completed his reading, and looked into my eyes. I steeled myself into displaying the proper countenance. After all, a woman who sits wishing another woman dead can hardly be deemed truly beautiful.

❧❧❧❧

The tranquil peace of our moment was shattered by an ear piercing scream from Lucy.

"Great Keezer's Ghost!" she warbled. "There's a mammoth snake in my handbag!"

There was quite a to-do, as Lucy stood screeching, and Val nearly fainted. Rebecca, too crippled with fear to stand, rolled a great distance away, displaying a flash of white linen beneath her polonaise gown, while Diana stood with hands on hips, and hollered at the others to "shut the hell up and behave like ladies."

A moment or so of hysteria passed before Landon snatched up Lucy's purse and ceremoniously shook out a garter snake so very small, one should have experienced immediate concern for its being without its mother.

"You call that mammoth?" Betsy smirked. "La! The men must be mad for you, Lucy."

The jest was lost on most, as it was fast noticed that Darcy laughed longer and heartier than the rest.

"Oh!" squalled Lucy, her face colouring bright red. "It was you, my little go by the ground! You put that viper in my purse!"

At once, Lucy began pursuing her foe all over the embankment, pummeling away at Darcy with her embroidered bag. It was quite an education, really. Lucy called after him every foul and vicious name invented to date.

"I'm famished," Valentine announced amidst all the laughter, applauding, and vile bursts of language. Few noticed that through it all, Clemence slept soundly on.

Valentine stood at once and paraded off with a determined face and hoisted petticoats to the swamp, where she would inquire of the men when they might partake of some cold chicken and claret. After all, the company on the high ground had waited long enough.

She found the group deeply engrossed in their sport, and much to her dismay, not a single man acknowledged her presence.

"I say," she whispered hoarsely, cautious not to frighten off any wayward mallards. "You've all been entrenched in the quagmire too long. We're frantic up there, you see, and positively vexed with hunger."

Lord Sutherland hushed her with a wave of his hand. Somewhere out there, a squadron of ducks concealed themselves within a thicket of cattails, and the men were patiently scheming how to best flush them out.

Valentine peered through the bosky mess and frowned.

"Why don't you merely holler, or throw something?" she asked innocently. And just as she spoke, a great rush of movement was heard on the bank.

"What the—?" began Val, until her eyes beheld Annie, our squat little basset, bounding through the clog of last year's leaves, before leaping wildly towards a tuft of bulrushes.

"Stop her!" shouted Orrin Blackwell, waving his musket, as Valentine made a brave attempt at it, only to end up on her backside in the mud.

"Oh!" she uttered in shock. "Oh, you despicable thing!"

However, Annie was already off, vaulting from tuft to tuft, and barking like the idiot she was. Landon and I went at once to assist Valentine, as the men shot dementedly at the frenziedly fleeing ducks.

"Oh!" whined Val. "My dress! My beautiful dress!"

Meanwhile, out in the middle of the swamp, poor Annie had run out of momentum; and she sat upon the most desolate of islets, crying mournfully for help.

"Someone should go get her," sighed Lord Sutherland, clearly indicating that it was quite beneath him to do so himself. Only after a few moment's pause—a pause during which all the men glanced furtively at one another—did Samuel Loring take the initiative to wade in after the bedraggled basset.

"Beastly thing," muttered the merchant Blackwell. Valentine Hale could not agree more.

∽∽∽

It was an odd sight, the long table fully clothed in lace, and decorated with fine silver in the midst of a dew-drenched field. And no one, it seemed, appeared to notice.

The outdoor air prompted healthy appetites in those who rarely ventured beyond their doorsteps before twilight. The company fell hungrily upon the appealing array of fruits and cheeses, cold meats and breads, accompanied by fine wines and brandies, as well as a handsome garnish of boiled lobster for flair.

"I was at a truly elegant picnic social once," sighed Virginia Stanwood, barely audible above the incessant clatter of silver and plate. "It was at Prime Minister Pitt's summer place, quite some time ago. Ah, what a glorious, glorious day! The men were positively mad for me, you know. One elegantly attired man—I believe he was the prince of some such place or the other—went dashing about the lawn, capturing butterflies for me in a net. It was truly charming."

Amidst polite mumblings such as "how nice" and "what a time you must have had," the group glanced at one another with laughing eyes. That Virginia could really weave a fine one when she felt like it.

Miss Eldredge elected not to join us, instead sending a message for us not to worry, although she did hope the Captain would "bring her a little something on a plate for sustenance." The Captain, however, did not hasten to her side. Instead, he secured a place next to me at the table. Silently, I praised God, begged forgiveness for all my evil thoughts against the health of Miss Eldredge, and in exalted fashion, went on to promise the good Lord all sorts of pious behaviour in the very near future.

The men were bantering about the story of Annie and the ducks, which was by this time, greatly exaggerated. By new accounts, Valentine had not merely slipped in the mud, but had been tossed a colossal height in the air. In the same vein, Annie had not alarmed a paltry few birds, but an entire legion of them. It was a grand retelling, to be sure. However, Samuel Loring lent no emphasis to his part in it, whatsoever.

"I merely went in after her," he shrugged. "I didn't encounter any dragons, or secret tunnels to the netherworld, or such. Just a lot of muck."

Everyone began talking at once, as the wine flowed freely about the table. Marlon Reynolds was in his element, making sport of one and all in that elegantly nasty way of his. He chastised Jimmy Sloan for polishing his nails, and plagued poor Valentine about hearing frogs in her bustle. Marlon then went on to regale the entire table with a vivid description of Tim Gorman "fertilizing the ferns," down by the swamp. His admonishments were amusing, perhaps. However, as I listened, I could not help but think what a poor match Marlon Reynolds was for Celeste Davenport. Rather like pairing a preening rooster with a dove.

"Be careful, Miss Lucy," Reynolds warned in conclusion. "Master Gorman may have let his breeches down in a clump of poison oak."

Everyone laughed heartily, and Lucy took no offense in it. Why should she? It was quite apparent that the hapless Tim no longer held any particular charms for her. And it was anyone's guess as to where her bright, fawnlike eyes were set to wandering now.

Bolstered by wine, the men began bragging of past adventures at the hunt, while the women returned pretty phrases of flattery to please them. Captain Vale did not volunteer any stories, and when the tone of the boasts became too ridiculous, he turned his full attentions to me.

"A pleasant outing, is it not?"

"Yes."

"This is where you grew up, I believe?"

"Yes."

"Lovely place; very lovely indeed, Mrs. Lynford."

Oh, why is it we are all so terribly dumbfounded at times such as these? "Yes?" Was that all I could manage? "Yes?" How foolish I must have sounded. Surely, Lorena Eldredge would have possessed more polish at such a moment. She would have smiled in that well-studied way of hers, and agreed. There was never such a pleasant outing, for it was his presence which made it so. This she would have uttered with simple ease. Had Lorena been raised here, she would have amused him with witty little anecdotes about the people here, and their lives, and soon Landon would be smiling in that handsome way of his that makes the tiny lines stand out about his mouth. A lovely place? Indeed. Any place would be lovely, when seated by his side. With that, she would have slipped her arm through his, and looked directly into his eyes with tender love and devotion. Miss Lorena Eldredge would have done all of this as effortlessly as a single breath. She would not have sat on the edge of her chair chanting "yes, yes," like a pale, little scullery maid on interview.

"Landon!" a voice snapped from the other end of the table. It was Diana Kirby. "Landon, my pet. Do wake up and say something. You're boring us."

All conversation came to a halt, and heads turned slowly towards Diana in disbelief. How could she have addressed the Captain so casually, and with such rudeness? When her eyes met mine, Diana challenged me with a glance which plainly said my presence at this party nauseated her. It seemed we regarded one another for a small eternity before Gordon Russell thankfully spoke.

"Good heavens, everyone, look to the high field!" And as we all did so, Darcy was observed in a mad dash towards Farmer Allen's hay barn, with Lucy in hot pursuit, her petticoat flying about wildly above a brazen display of lithe, little legs.

"Dear God, but is Lucy Wellman still smoldering over that tiny mite of a snake?" Betsy Sloan wondered aloud.

"I believe they are on a mission to appreciate the finer points of nature," Roscoe Bennett volunteered in that delightfully droll way of his, and we all met his commentary with a raucous cheer. It was then Landon asked me for the book of prose by Herrick.

"Ah, here it is, just as I expected," he said, and then raising his voice for all to hear, "Everyone! Please pass round some of this unequaled wine, as I read a passage from Robert Herrick in honour of our dear Miss Lucy Wellman, whose health and well-being we shall salute with a toast—

> My Lucia in the deaw did go,
> And prettily bedabbled so,
> Her cloaths held up, she shew'd withall
> Her decent legs, cleane, long and small.
> I follow'd after to descrie
> Part of the nak't sincerity;
> But still the envious Scene between
> Deni'd the Mask I wo'd have seen."

Glasses were lifted on high, and the most politely profane of praises went round regarding little Lucy and the rather unrestrained measures of her infinite passions.

"You know your Herrick well," I complimented Landon, as he returned the book to me.

"Why, thank you. I was enchanted with his writings when quite young."

"And now?" I asked teasingly. Perhaps, for a bold moment, I was speaking as Lorena.

"And now?" he repeated, the light fleeing his eyes for an instant. "Now I find some of it rather vulgar," he concluded simply, and turned his vacant gaze towards the din and the chatter of the table. I was crushed. My spirits dwindled like the smoke of a doused candle. So, I was looked upon as fit company for the likes of Lucy Wellman, and nothing more. She received her cutting bit of poetry, just as I had earlier, and together, we were only worthy of *vulgar* praise. Tears smarted behind my eyes as I wondered just what sort of laud Lorena Eldredge would have been entitled to, had she been seated here beside her adoring Captain. So lost was I in my sullen turn that I was not the least bit startled when a great peal of laughter erupted from the group.

"Look everyone!" Tim Gorman cried out. "Oh, do come and look! It's Clemence Taggard, quite forgotten and fast asleep, with her face seemingly nailed to the tree. Zounds! A shilling says she looks like a pock-faced princod!"

"I thought she was sleeping in the house," Bryce murmured. "Someone told me Clemence was sleeping in the house."

"That was Lorena Eldredge, you fool," retorted Diana. "I was going to ask you where your silly wife was during luncheon. But since you happily did not seem to care, why the devil should I?"

A sudden chill wind came up, and the struggling sun surrendered to a wide expanse of dark clouds. We had seen the best of the day, to be sure; and many of the ladies were now hugging themselves to keep warm as they glanced at Charles expectantly.

"Perhaps it is time to think about going back," Charles said, consulting his gold pocket watch. "And while the footmen are packing up, I shall treat one and all to a tankard in Mister Justin Daniel's fine establishment."

A cheer went round as the company made a hasty departure from the disorderly picnic table for the more welcome regions of the Crossroads' tap-room. I remember pausing, and looking at Landon with great caution. It was then, however, that he smiled brightly and offered me his arm. There was no need to ask him what he meant when he called Herrick's prose vulgar. Perhaps it was nothing. And hopefully, it was nothing to do with me.

ᏣᏣᏣᏣ

"Here's a toast to life!"

"No! To the ladies!"

"Better yet, to the ducks, blast 'em."

To whatever cause, tankards were merrily raised on high by the twenty-some-odd guests who had invaded Papa's taproom with ferocious thirsts. It was indeed a lively group, and Great-grandmother Effie, hearing the happy laughter from her room, made haste to join us.

"So this is the rabble my great-granddaughter got mixed up with," she chortled in the doorway, causing everyone to sit up straight and look sharp. However, within a few short minutes, the old woman impressed her audience by drinking her whiskey neat, and bantering tales that awed even the most uninhibited of minds. Yes, it wasn't long before Effie Daniels was voted quite smart, and I was exceedingly proud of her.

Charles had extended an invitation to Great-grandmother to join us for a Messiah concert to be held at Faneuil Hall in October, but she shook her head and smiled.

"Thank ye, but no. I'm not much for wishy-washy men screeching away like castrated cattle. But I will come and visit my Verity at summer's end. Then you can throw me a great big party with drinking, and dancing, and a bevy of beautiful young men to ogle. That, my dear friends, would suit me just fine."

The group raised their glasses in a toast to Effie. Yes, of course there would be a party, and in her honour, too. Whatever Effie desired. And the men praised her years, and the women marveled at them.

Suddenly, David Manley quieted the crowd.

"Lucy," he uttered with a mock look of concern. "Wherever can our little Lucy be?"

"Darcy, too, don't forget," added Gordon slyly, as Valentine sighed with marked agitation.

"Good Lord, we shall all be here for aeons, just because that inconsiderate slut has an itch for the great outdoors!"

Some members of the company regarded Val pointedly. It did not do to call Lucy such names in front of grey hairs. However, Effie took no offense. In fact, she was rather amused by it.

"We could do a bit of adjusting and leave a carriage for them," suggested William Collamore.

"Or, we could form a search party and hunt the devious duo down," teased Marlon Reynolds, his gypsy eyes bright with mirth. "It's the only civilised thing to do."

At that very moment, as if on cue, Lucy and Darcy made their appearance at the door.

"Goodness gracious," breathed Lucy, acting every inch the innocent. "We had begun to fear you had all left. The field was quite deserted."

"Yes . . . quite," added Darcy, sensing the awkward pause.

"We were walking, you see, when Darcy took an unfortunate tumble in the nastiest mess of thorns you ever did see! Why, it took me nearly forever to pull him out."

"I see," said Sir Alfred calmly, waving off the sarcastic whispers all about the room. "And is that, pray tell, how you got hay stuck in your hair, Miss Wellman?"

"Hay? Really?"

Lucy was astonished, although I was sure she was secretly cursing the old actor's eye for detail.

"How very extraordinary," she added glibly.

"Why don't you admit it, girl?" Effie spoke up. "You've been libbing in the hayloft."

Everyone gasped with a gleeful mixture of horror and delight. Effie was a card, to be sure. As for Lucy, she was just an insatiable little vixen, and no man in the room appeared particularly jealous that Darcy had been her latest victim of lust. Either they had been treated to similar "walks in the woods," or they could happily count on such an adventure in the very near future.

The afternoon having come to a comical close, the company made ready to leave. Lucy raised quite a ruckus by insisting that Darcy ride alongside her in the third carriage. There was already a devilish crush with Bryce sandwiched in between them all. It was not long, however, before a solution was discovered. Valentine, quite sick of the fuss, made straight for Charles' carriage, muttering that bawdy little bunters like Lucy could do better than to lie about with Cheapside actors. Situating herself across from Miss Eldredge, Valentine gave little pause to her opinions. Poor Lorena. Her vexed look of pain grew deeper with every foul word that flowed freely from Valentine's mouth.

I went to each carriage to bid my adieux. Everyone had experienced such a charming time. I made promises left and right for engagements when we returned to Boston after Karen's wedding. Gordon gave me a fond kiss on the cheek, and Rebecca vowed to make note of every rotten thing Diana Kirby said about me while I was out of town, just for humour's sake.

Charles, Lorena, and Valentine occupied the second carriage. Captain Vale, however, was nowhere to be seen. I recall Lorena attempting to smile through her headache. Charles took my hands warmly, and wished me a happy stay with my family. Valentine merely nodded, and the stare she gave me was rather odd. I brushed it off, regardless. I sensed she was still a bit peeved with Lucy.

A spring wind was beginning to rise. The horses were becoming restless, and the coachmen eager to depart. I looked about for Landon one last time in vain.

I remember going back to the inn, and shutting the door with a sigh. I turned, and there before me was the Captain. He startled me just a little. Something in his look conveyed he had been waiting for me.

"I have but a moment, Mrs. Lynford. I did so want to say good-bye."

I thought of all the pretty things I could have said. I could have reminded him of our pleasant day; of the blue skies, and the songbirds, and the omnipresent sun on the golden edge of the earth. I could have thanked him for the poetry, and begged him with my eyes to read me more in the future. But like the silly fool I was, I merely ducked my head and smiled sheepishly.

"Verity," he began, and then paused for a moment. I believe it was the first time he had used my Christian name, and that pleased me. "I wished to assure you that should you find yourself in distress, I will not be far away. I promise you that."

I looked up at him, somewhat confused. There was a near fierceness of emotion in his eyes I could not understand. It almost frightened me.

Landon then took my hand and kissed it gently.

"I have perhaps said too much," he went on, his eyes brightening again with calm sincerity. "It is nothing. I fear for you out here in the country. That is all."

"Oh, Captain, don't be silly. I was born and raised here. This is my home. No harm will come to me here; I am sure of it."

"Indeed no harm shall ever come to you, my dearest friend."

With that, he kissed my hand once more, and left. I watched him through the mullion panes of the window. How handsome was his stride. He lifted himself up into the coach with the ease and elegance of a dancer. Then, he took his place alongside Lorena, and smiled at her as she placed her arm through his.

A rumble of carriage wheels, and they were gone.

I cannot explain it, really, but I was suddenly possessed of a certain sadness I could not understand. True, my friends had departed, but I would see them again. It was not that. I was at the home of my childhood memories, and although it seemed strange to return here a married woman, it was not that either. I thought, and I thought, because the notion of my melancholy bothered me greatly. And then it came to me.

I am not all too sure just why, however, I had the oddest feeling that everything in my world was rapidly about to change.

Worse than war is the fear of war.

Seneca—*Thyestes*

∽

APRIL, 1775

WITHIN THREE DAYS TIME, Ambrose, his mother Eliza, and his sister Hannah arrived from New Haven.

Dressed in a royal blue riding habit and skirt, with a black kerchief about her neck, Hannah appeared at first to have matured nicely in the four years since I had last seen her. However, within moments, it was clearly evident the only thing that had changed about Hannah was her taste in clothing. Beneath her womanly and fashionable attire, Hannah was still the same obnoxious, whining creature she had always been.

"Goodness gracious!" she crabbed, barely out of the coach. "Three whole days cooped up in that dusty old thing with a long-winded Methodist. How much does the good Lord think I can stand?"

Eliza Beckwith then emerged. Small of stature, but always somewhat plump, she was still quite handsome about the face. I watched as her hazel eyes lit up at the sight of Papa. Poor woman. I believe she's been in love with Papa ever since I can remember. Local gossip said that after nagging one husband into the grave, Eliza Beckwith set out to prove to Justin Daniels that she, and she alone, was the soulful twin to my sweet, departed mother. Either Papa was too blind to see, or far too indifferent to care. In any case, Eliza Beckwith had taken to her bed alone these past ten years.

I held out my hands in greeting as Ambrose stepped down from the carriage. Ambrose Beckwith. He was the first love of my life, or at least so I thought at that all-knowing age of seven. How changed he was! I remember how we used to chase after frogs in the pond, and play blindman's buff in the burial ground. As a child, Ambrose's thick blonde hair was forever in a tangle, and his cheeks glowed constantly of a deep, rosy red. Now, he was a fine young man; something of a dandy, even. He held my hands wide for a moment, and looked me up and down with a mock outpouring of appreciation. Within seconds, we were collapsed in laughter.

Papa had come forward to greet the newcomers. He told Eliza how delightful it was to see her after so many years, and she practically melted under the lull of his voice. Papa said he was pleased to have the bridegroom and his family honour his request to stay at the Crossroads, and he hoped their visit would be a most happy and memorable one. The look in Eliza's hazel eyes agreed, although I do not think it was her son's happiness she was contemplating.

You arrived the very next day, Jeffrey. How happy you seemed to see me! Being back in the country was a tonic, you had told me. Compared to the constant entertaining, and the hubbub of Boston, Concord was like a welcome breath of fresh air. I must admit, that gave me pause. I had tried so valiantly to like your in-town friends, Jeffrey, and there you were, saying you could do without them. Regardless of all that has come to pass, I can look back on the spell of these golden days and affirm that we were never more content. And alas, contentment was something I had learnt to settle for.

⊙⊙⊙⊙

During the days and nights that followed, the town of Concord played host to an endless array of parties held in honour of Israel Clarke's only daughter's upcoming marriage. There were picnics and teas, outdoor roasts and suppers, even a formal dance or two, for despite Israel's steadfast conviction that dancing was immoral, the happy father could overlook the notion at such a joyous time as this.

The families of Concord had opened up their homes and their hearts on this glorious occasion; for it was a close-knit community, and everyone was either related through blood or business, or just plain friendship. As for you and I, Jeffrey, the hours merrily spent in the sunshine and fresh air did much to revive our spirits. We rode horseback, ambled on foot through tree-lined country paths, and rowed a canoe along the still, graceful banks of the Concord River.

It may have been only April, but the promise of spring was evident everywhere. The ponds had shed their sludgy blankets of ice, and were now ringed with happy little shoots of green grass eagerly stretching for the sun. Across the fields, the trees echoed with the trill choruses of sparrows, larks, and bluebirds, all heralding the advent of warmer days, spring flowers, and nesting time. Overhead, solemn hawks soared above slowly moving creeks in search of small frogs and mice.

How good the earth smells in spring! A solitary gentle rain has the power to draw out all the perfumes of nature, filling the air with a fragrance so unique, yet so basic and satisfying. And how wondrous are the sounds of Earth's awakenings. Even the slightest hint of a breeze can rustle newborn leaves and budding flowers, grateful for the clear blue skies, and the nurturing radiance of the sun. From the sides of well-traveled roads, sluggish brooks began to trickle freely, skimming last year's withered leaves atop the smoothed rocks and miniature falls which have been fashioned over the roots of venerable old oaks—those timeworn veterans of many a changing season.

Yes, the promise of spring was in the air, and you and I were most happily warming up to it. What appetites we acquired out of doors! The people of Concord are hard workers and healthy eaters, so it was easy to see why each and every social event culminated in a feast fit for Hannibal's army. At outdoor parties, there was roasted venison and pheasant, pork, mutton, and beef. For tea, we had mouth-watering cakes, breads, and candied fruits. And at suppers, one could indulge on rich cheeses, lobster patties, sweetmeats, and vegetables dripping in butter. Perished with hunger, we partook of it all, and without the least compunction. Our newfound thirst for exercise would keep me well within the confines of my small-waisted gowns. Or at least I hoped it would!

Ah, the wonderful hours we passed dashing about the countryside, or dancing 'til dawn. We played at ninepins and shuffleboard like demons. I remember your watching me, and laughing while I attempted to learn a rather raucous new sport called foot ball from the Buttrick boys. Yes, I can easily recall your laughter, as well as the way Eliza Beckwith called me to her side with a most intimidating leer.

"It does not do to represent yourself in such an unladylike fashion," she opined to me, her features hard and stern. "For Ambrose's sake, show some decorum, please. After all, you don't see his sister Hannah running about the lawn with her day dress all akimbo, do you?"

It was on the tip of my tongue to retort that Hannah would run around the yard buck naked, if she thought it would get her somewhere with the men. But I smiled demurely, and said nothing. The last thing I wanted was for everyone to witness Ambrose's mother dragging me in the house by the ear.

So it was that I was forced to spend the remainder of the afternoon sequestered away with a pack of drowsy old matrons. After the thrill of playing at sport, I was nearly reduced to fits of snoring beneath the somnolent rays of the sun. I had to concentrate with all my might to appear intrigued with what all the old hens around me had to say.

"Look at dear Karen," one woman was saying with a voice that warbled with age. "How terribly shy she is."

"Yes," ventured another, as she peered out from beneath a hideous hat.

"See how far apart she stands from Ambrose."

"My daughter was never out much," explained Susannah Clarke in her meek, lilting tone. "Oh, that's not to say there were never any young men wishing to pay court, but Karen rarely showed much interest. But with Ambrose . . ."

As Mrs. Clarke's voice faded away sweetly, I turned sharp eyes towards Karen and Ambrose. The women were right. Something was amiss. All this time I had been home, Karen seemed terribly odd; indifferent to me and to her own wedding plans. I had dismissed her strange mood as the nervous fears all brides go through, yet there was something more to this, something I could not understand. Karen, Ambrose, and I had all grown up together; I should have known her better than this. Perhaps Karen was lamenting that the love she felt for Ambrose was not exactly a romantic one. It was my only notion.

Whatever the reason, it did not promote a torrent of thought in my head. Oh, typically such matters of the heart intrigued me greatly. However, at this moment, all I could contemplate was that I had eaten far too much baked ham to sit about like a useless porcelain vase, and my clothing felt too tight. Worst of all, now I couldn't make room for a plate of strawberries in cream, or some delectable plum cake.

Life wasn't fair! Oh, why wasn't I born a man so I could gambol about to my heart's content, riding horses the proper way, and playing cards for money instead of buttons and pins. If I were a gentleman, I could smoke a pipe, and drink port 'til my eyes popped. But alas, no. Because I was a woman, I was instead forced to sit around with a cluster of old cows, whispering about court-ships, births, and deaths as though no one else in the whole world had ever fallen in love, struggled through a pregnancy, or breathed their last. Oh, how boring it all was!

Not far off across the lawn, you were gathered with the men, Jeffrey, talking about war. How I wished I could join you. I missed those evenings in Papa's taproom much more than I knew.

"Jeffrey, you were there when the King's troops marched on Charlestown and confiscated our powder and cannon, were you not?" Papa was asking. "Surely you have news on that. We hear so little truth out here in the country."

I glanced at Papa and smirked. With his big mouth making mountains out of mole hills, it was no wonder the entire countryside was in such a dizzy confusion.

"Well, yes," you began in return. "Gage's troops were out and back before anyone knew of it, really. By the time the surrounding towns were alerted, and our men had gathered at the scene, rumour was already rooted that Gage had bombarded Boston, and murdered dozens of innocent people."

"Even our delegates in Congress received such a report in Philadelphia," agreed Josiah Pierce, shaking his head.

"But it just wasn't so," you replied carefully. "You must understand that Thomas Gage is a man of rather mixed emotions. Why, he brags openly to the Tories of Boston that his troops could easily crush the colonies in a matter of months. Yet, he urges Parliament to abandon the Intolerable Acts for fear of a local uprising, claiming it would take as many as twenty thousand soldiers to quell Sam Adam's band of liberty boys."

"You see!" Papa blurted out. "Gage is afraid of us!"

"And with good reason," Josiah added. "His September raid on Charlestown proved to him the great number of provincials who are willing and ready to fight. I believe thousands showed up that day. Besides that, they were prepared to come from as far away as Connecticut."

Great-grandmother Effie had walked up to Papa and regarded the company with a glum face.

"Sounds to me like this Tommy Gage is a piddling half-wit," she claimed, matter-of-factly.

"Oh, but he finds your great-granddaughter truly divine," you went on to say, Jeffrey, and my heart was proud to hear you say it.

"Who wouldn't?" Effie merely shrugged. "Now, get me another port, Justin. This war council can hold 'til you return."

"Just one moment, my woman. Did you hear about the incident at Salem Bridge?"

"We baffled those fine boys, didn't we?" Josiah laughed, slapping his knee. I was grateful to you, Jeffrey, for getting up and seeing to Great-grandmother's glass of port. It was apparent Papa wasn't going to not when his favourite topic was being thrashed about—"Oh, they thought they could sneak through Salem and steal our cannon while all our good and pious men were attending church. Those damnable—sorry, Mrs. Daniels—I mean to say those blasted lobsterbacks could have had worse done to them than merely the drawbridge hoisted against their path."

"But would you not say the soldiers behaved like gentlemen when they promised to march only fifty rods and then turn round again—and then did precisely what they vowed?" ventured Phineas McKean.

"Don't be so naive, Phineas," Papa returned. "That idiot, Colonel Leslie, only meant to supply proof for his fool General that he actually entered Salem, despite the obvious dissension of the townspeople."

"Yet Colonel Leslie was sent home across the ocean, all the same," Josiah pointed out.

"Aye," replied Phineas. "And he's a fellow Scotsman too, so help me."

"Well, I never met one who wasn't a fool," ventured Effie as everyone turned slow, questioning stares her way. She merely shrugged once more, and commenced to enjoy her port.

"War," mumbled the silly woman beneath the hideous hat. "As if it's ever going to happen!"

⟡⟡⟡⟡

I heard the tiny bells of the ornate mantle clock thump and cough out the hour of eleven, but still I could not sleep.

Laying awake in a chill path of moonlight, I watched with vacant eyes as the shadow of a lone, gnarled branch danced in the wind that whipped and whistled about the side of the house. Every few minutes or so, a sharp gust would pitch the distorted limb against the glass, creating an eerie scratching noise not unlike that of a large, bony hand demanding admittance. However, it did not frighten me; it couldn't—not with the likes of you, Jeffrey, snoring soundly at my side.

Closing my eyes very tightly, I tried to talk myself into slumber. However, I was troubled by the frenzied jumble of images which flew through my mind. First, I saw myself, Karen, and Ambrose, when we were all around eight years old. I saw us sitting together on the banks of the river, watching for fish. Ambrose leaned over and whispered in my ear that he would love me forever. Karen must have heard, for she promptly pushed me in the drink. Then I saw us grown up some. Ambrose's father had died, and his pompous mother moved them to New Haven—but not until after a long trial of trying to win my father's love. Then there was you, Jeffrey. Why was it that Karen and I had a habit of falling in love with the same men!? Oh, the sight of your handsome good looks impressed me greatly. How I had struggled to win you over. I imagined you to be a means to an end. However, now that the end to all I ever wanted had come and gone, there was a sad, empty cavern in my heart. So difficult to explain, really, especially when I loved you so very dearly.

I rolled over on my side, and blinked back the tears. More images were coming now, fast and furious, and far too blurred to be distinctive. I saw the marketplace in Boston with all its confusion. Perry Talbot was there, and he wanted to speak with me. Faneuil Hall, in a vast array of flowers; the fragrance of which overpowered the air. General Thomas Gage had just arrived from England, and thousands had gathered to pay tribute. Then, on opulent Garden Court Street, Charles Davenport was escorting me to his dinner table on that beautiful starlit night back in November. Lucy Wellman draining glass after glass of champagne. Then the invitations—mountains of them, fluttering through my mind's eye like snowflakes on a blustery winter day. The dancing, the small talk, the music, and the laughter. Captain Landon Vale, so aloof, so resplendent in his regimental coats, trimmed in silver, and scarlet red, like freshly spilt blood.

Sleep was coming at last, as a soothing rhythm took hold of my mind—ta-da-dum, ta-da-dum, over and over again, luring me into the shadow of dreams—when suddenly, the rhythm became louder, jarring, incessant and almost cruel, where only moments before, it had been so pleasing.

I opened my eyes with a start, and scrambled out of bed towards the window. A rider was approaching. I could see his phantom-like form at the crest of the drive. He then called out "hallo!" before even so much as dismounting. I tried to make out his face, but could not, despite the fact the moon was so bright, the lawn appeared to be covered in snow.

The front door was opened, and I could hear the voices of my father and Josiah Pierce, rushed, excited; running over one another. Who was here? What could it be that agitated them so? I reasoned at once, with a nervous shrug, that perhaps a neighbour's house had caught fire.

"Daughter!" Papa called up from the foyer below. "Daughter, are you awake?"

I reached over to the trunk at the foot of the bed, and grabbed my wrapper, pulling it tightly about myself. Still, you did not stir, Jeffrey. Most likely it was all that brandy you consumed at the Buttricks' picnic earlier.

"Yes, Papa," I answered, scurrying to the top of the stairs, and peering down with eyes which were unaccustomed to the sudden lamp light below. "What is it?"

I heard you moving about in the bedchamber behind me, Jeffrey. However, I did not call out to you, for the sight of my father's anxious face had unnerved me completely.

"Daughter," he began, and his voice was edged with a certain intensity I had never witnessed before. "An acquaintance of yours from Boston comes to us with some very grave news indeed."

A horrid suspicion dashed through my brain as I stood paralysed. Landon was dead, and someone was here to tell me so. What else could it be?

"Mrs. Lynford?" I heard, and then I knew exactly who it was.

"Perry!" I cried out. "Perry Talbot, is that you?"

"Yes, Ma'am," he said, coming forward to where I could see him. His hair was wild about his head, and his face was drenched in sweat and dirt.

"I'm—I'm not dressed," I stammered, as you came up alongside me, Jeffrey, in the cloistered shadows of the landing.

"I'm sure we've all seen a woman in her dressing gown before," Papa said, gently coaxing me to come down. "Now please join us. And you too, Jeffrey."

Resting one trembling hand on the rail, and holding my wrapper close with the other, I descended the stairs. I remember that my hair was loose about my shoulders, and my eyes were wide with fear. Below, in the foyer, Ambrose was the only one who appeared calm. Perhaps too calm, in fact, for he looked almost bored.

Papa ushered us all into the front parlour. Perry was still breathing hard from his urgent ride. His face was flushed, and his expression taut. My father nearly had to propel his every step.

"Tell us again, boy; from the beginning."

"The British regulars have marched from Boston, and they are on their way here."

"Here?" I said, startled. "Here to this tavern?"

"No, to Concord town, Mrs. Lynford. General Gage got wind that there is a vast supply of military stores to be found in this village, and he has sent out grenadiers and light infantry to capture them."

"When did they set out?" Papa asked, and his eyes were fervently aglow.

"Two hours ago, maybe. But it's no surprise, really. Doctor Warren's special committee sighted the maneuver as far back as four days ago. And the silversmith, Paul Revere, heard of it through three of his spies."

"Yes, I know," said Josiah Pierce, moving towards the mantle, and taking down five clay pipes—one for each man present. "Revere himself rode out here to warn us, last Sunday. He told us it seemed certain the troops would be carrying orders to arrest our Whig leaders, Hancock and Adams. They're in Lexington, you see, stopping over after the Provincial Congress meeting, which was held here in Concord."

I recall sitting down suddenly, and hugging myself against my own foolish shivering. The men had lit their pipes, the embers of which shimmered against the dim shadows of the room. For all the insanity that was happening, I found myself strangely fascinated with the wraithlike patterns of smoke which drifted lazily above my head, while Perry went on with his story:

"The Liberty Boys have been waiting for the next move. Then it happened. Just after midnight, on Sunday last, the British set their boats back in the water. They had been hauled up for repairs, you see, and that was suspicious enough. Then yesterday, Captain Havershall brought his horse to me—oh, I'm a blacksmith, gentlemen, on King Street—and he gave me explicit instructions to have her shoes good and tight; as if for country riding. Well, I pretended to be real good and busy, and I grumbled a bit, and asked him how long I had to get the job done. So, the Captain replied he'd need his mare ready for the road by Tuesday—meaning today—by two of the clock, and no later. There must have been something in the look of my face, because the Captain made some excuse about an invitation to dine out west of Cambridge."

Eliza Beckwith appeared at the doorway, her face pale and deathly curious, as she tugged at the end of her long, white-blonde braid with nervous fingers.

"What is this?" she asked, and her eyes darted savagely from my father to Ambrose. "What's wrong?"

"Eliza, this is Perry Talbot, an acquaintance of Verity and Jeffrey's, from Boston. Master Talbot, this is Mrs. Beckwith."

As tired as he was, Perry stood and nodded his head with respectful courtesy.

"Eliza, Master Talbot has come to us with news of the British army's advance. They are headed for Concord."

"Why?" she asked, taking hold of the chair beside me for support. "Why? What have we done?"

"General Gage is after the stores of ammunition we have stashed here in Concord."

"How far away are they?" she mumbled, as if in a haze.

"Hours yet, Ma'am," answered Perry. "They hadn't so much as gathered at the Common until eight of the clock, this evening. And it was a full hour, at least, after that before they got moving."

"So how did you get here so fast?" asked Ambrose, gnawing on the clay tip of his pipe. His face had a lofty sneer of suspicion I did not like.

"After the Captain collected his horse today—somewhere around half past one—I went to my friend, Andrew, who goes out fishing for the British officers. You can't get in or out of Boston these days without a pass, you see. And I knew I'd never manage to get one, especially today. So, I asked Andrew to row me out a ways, and then I swam over to Charlestown. I know a family there by the name of Underwood. It was from their house I watched the troops being rowed across the Charles. Then I borrowed a horse to ride out here."

Then you spoke, Jeffrey, leaning towards Perry; your manner intent.

"How many troops set out? How many men? Could you tell?"

"Five hundred, anyway."

Five hundred, I thought, the panic rising in my throat. Surely I had seen as many as five hundred soldiers about the streets of Boston. But not all at once. And definitely not under these circumstances. These were five hundred soldiers carrying muskets. Five hundred determined men of war, with orders to kill anyone who got in their way.

". . . There are dispatchers out, spreading the alarm," Perry was saying. "Maybe Lexington has gotten word by now. But it might be awhile before Concord knows. There are advance soldiers out here, already. I had to hide behind a thicket of oak trees when I saw six redcoats riding towards Lexington."

Josiah Pierce stood at once, moving in a straight line towards the foyer where he took his hat and his cloak from a peg on the wall. The passive look had long since left his grey-blue eyes, and the lines of his face were suddenly as hard set and determined as his voice.

"I must go and tell the others. I'm aware that four of the cannon were transported to Groton this morning, but there will undoubtedly be more ammunition to hide. If the troops are on foot, as you say, they've got twenty miles ahead of them in the dark. My guess is that they won't be here until dawn, at least."

"I am going with you," Papa announced, but I protested at once. He couldn't leave us now!

"Don't be silly, Daughter. A man must help where he can. Come, Ambrose. You are going with us."

"No, Justin," said Eliza, and her voice wavered with pain. "Not Ambrose, please!"

Papa's eyes fairly snapped as he turned on her.

"Have sense, woman. Think it through. Your son will have his hand in history, and never once will he be in harm's way. Why, I promise you, by the saints above, we will all be back under this roof well before a single soldier sets foot on Concord soil."

Eliza sunk back in the chair, and bit her lip.

"All right, then. If you promise," she answered quietly, while across the room, Ambrose made a face of disdain. It was purely apparent he had no desire to be a part of "history," as Papa put it. No, Ambrose Beckwith merely saw it as being forced to skulk about the countryside sinking cannonballs into the swamp by moonlight.

"I shall go with you, too," you had offered, Jeffrey, looking towards my face for a reaction. What could I say?

"Count me in," said Perry, as the men nodded at him, and made for the door.

"I'm going to get dressed," I announced, hopping up from my chair in a complete jumble of nerves.

"Oh, no!" warned Eliza. "You're not going, too!"

"Sweet Jesus, of course I'm not!"

I probably would have rambled on foolishly, except for the fact that Great-grandmother Effie suddenly appeared in the doorway.

"What's all this fuss?" she asked plainly, her liquid blue eyes not yet in focus. Papa then came forward and took her by the hands.

"The British army is marching on Concord this very moment."

"Is it war?" she asked calmly.

"They say it is to seize the military stores."

"Then it will end up in war. Come, Verity. We must get dressed."

"That's what I was just saying," I replied, throwing my hands up in the air. Perhaps I looked like a lunatic, but at that moment, I could not possibly care. For this was madness, and in madness, no rules of propriety need apply. At least great grandmother was showing signs of sense, for she took immediate charge of the situation.

"With your permission, Mrs. Beckwith, we shall arouse Hannah, and begin work. We've got to start some coffee and soup, hide the livestock and the silver, pull up as much cold water as we can from the well for drinking, and boil some more for emergencies. We should also collect some blankets, and roll some linen for bandages, just in case—"

"Then let's get dressed!" I practically shouted. "Land of Goshen! The last thing I want is to be shot dead in my bed gown!"

cⱭcⱭcⱭcⱭ

When I returned to the front parlour, Perry Talbot was still there.

"Your father and the others decided to let me stay behind, and rest up a bit from my ride," he explained. "There will be plenty to do in the morning, so at least one of us has to be bright-eyed and able."

He paused, probably noticing the anxious look on my face, and smiling, he stood and took my hands in his.

"Your blue Brunswick is lovely, but I much preferred you in your night-dress. At least your hair is untouched. I like it that way."

"My hands shook too much to do anything with it," I confessed, feeling rather sheepish.

"Here," Perry said, pouring a glass of brandy and handing it to me. "Drink this. You'll feel better."

I thanked him, taking the glass with both hands, and lifting it to my lips. The first sip of the thick, sweet liquid made me shiver as it cascaded down the depths of my throat.

"More," Perry instructed. "Take another sip."

"You're not trying to get me drunk, are you?" I asked with a little laugh. Indeed, the second sip was better. The brandy warmed my veins, lulling my entire being.

"Get you drunk? Don't you think I'd pick a better time and place than this?"

"That is true," I smiled over my glass.

"All the ladies are hard at work, I see," Perry went on, pouring himself a drink. "How admirable."

I laughed and leaned back into my chair.

"Oh, not all the ladies! Miss Hannah Beckwith is still asleep. That little snipe could sleep through the advent of the apocalypse."

"That kindly old woman there. Is she your grandmother?"

"Effie is my great-grandmother. And for God's sake, don't let her hear you calling her *kindly*. She'll curry your hide."

"Oh, I see. Did she raise you?"

"No. Great-grandmother has lived with us since I was eighteen or nineteen," I said, shuddering with gratitude from yet another long sip of brandy. "Maybe older. I really don't remember." I paused, my eyes constantly darting towards the dark panes of the window.

"Relax," Perry smiled sweetly. "The regulars won't be here for hours yet. Besides, what do you have to worry about? Back in Boston, you were singing liberty songs by day, and supping with gold-laced Generals by night. So, who on God's green earth do you have to be frightened of?"

We laughed, and toasted one another. And for one shining, brief moment, the threat of war was very far away.

⌾⌾⌾

Somewhere around three in the morning, the men returned with a wagon load of ammunition.

An hour or so before that, Perry Talbot had fallen asleep, sprawled out across the intricately embroidered couch in the parlour. However, I could not sleep. My brandy had rendered me far from tired. Instead, I sat bolt upright in my chair, watching the shadow of the clock's pendulum. It was a curious apparition. At first, it soothed me with its gentle, easy sway. But then, the pendulum seemed to take on a strong, canting rock, which frightened me. It reminded me of marching—of troops marching—and they were coming to get me.

When I heard the cart in the drive, I ran outside to make sure it was really our menfolk approaching. It was perhaps a perilous move, but I felt comforted with the presence of Effie and Perry in the house.

As I stepped out onto the porch, the chill, moist night air assaulted my nostrils. I felt dirty and unkempt, as though nervous sweat was pouring down my sides. It was not unlike a bad dream, the dewy air and the unreal light of the quiet hour only added to my unnatural feeling of confusion and exhaustion.

"Daughter! Come see what we have!"

I peered into the back of the wagon. There were kegs of powder and numerous stacks of cannonballs carefully hidden under mountainous clumps of hay.

"Why ever do we need this?" I asked, running a nervous hand through my hair.

"As soon as daylight comes, we are going to bury it all in the cornfield."

"But that may be too late!" I exclaimed. "Why, the regulars could come around and bayonet us all for stashing these things."

"Relax, daughter," laughed Papa, draping his cloak about my shoulders. I did not appreciate his laughter, nor did I want the cloak about me. The heavy garment of wool felt clammier than the night air.

"Let us go inside," said Mr. Pierce. "We have a good hour or so before there is enough daylight to work by."

Slowly, we moved as a group towards the door. And as we did so, the church bells of Concord began to ring.

"What is it?" I asked. "What does it mean?"

"The British troops were in Menotomy not too long ago," Papa answered, wiping the sweat from his brow. "An express rider came through Concord just after one. And now—"

He paused, listening to the solemn toll of the bell.

"And now, everyone knows."

I put my arm through his, and we went inside the house.

They are able because they think they are able.

Vergil—*Aeneid*

∽

19 April, 1775

I SLEPT. Somehow, through all the dark fear and trepidation, after all the nightmarish and headlong preparations against the unknown, I managed to lay myself down upon the high-backed sofa in the sitting room, and close my tired eyes in sleep.

Since the men's return, I had worked alongside the others in a frantic effort to hide anything of value from the scrutiny of the King's troops. The silver plate, china-handled knives and forks, and gold-based candlesticks all made their way into bed pillows and beneath fluffed up counterpanes; while stuffed wallets, shiny coin, and pieces of heirloom jewelry were promptly planted under stouthearted flower beds.

Hannah had finally been summoned from her bed, and ordered to work in the kitchen along with her mother, Effie, and Papa's new cook—a gentle, humorous old African woman named Beulah. Beulah, a freed slave, had worked in Doctor Gore's kitchen for pay for the past fifteen years. But when the good doctor passed away, and his vicious widow decided to pick up and move to Connecticut, poor Beulah had nowhere to go. Or so she thought. Papa heard of her plight, and hired Beulah to assist Ruthie in the kitchen. And now, with Ruthie away visiting family in Philadelphia, Beulah's services were never needed more.

So it was that Hannah peeled and chopped onions by lamplight, her fumbling fingers close to extinction every time Effie spoke of the army's impending approach. As for Beulah, she kept rolling her large, bright eyes heavenward and exclaiming "Lordy! Lordy!" with every mention of looting, rape, and bayonets. It may have been all the brandy I consumed, but I found it almost funny. But Hannah was near collapse with apprehension. I imagine she saw herself as a terribly popular victim of the bloodthirsty redcoats. It was just her luck to be, as she saw it, the only attractive female available in a town under siege.

Perry Talbot had arrived at the thought that should there be a skirmish, the troops may think to steal as many horses and conveyances as they could find, in order to transport the officers and the wounded. So when the men returned with the ammunition, a concerted effort was made to herd the best of the village's stallions and brood mares into the furthest fields, while chaises and other light carriages were hidden carefully behind outbuildings beneath heaping mounds of hay.

How strange it was to see the homes of Concord alive with light and activity at such an early hour! Indeed, by daybreak, the townspeople had accomplished the nearly impossible task of preparing for invasion. Cannon were plowed under furrowed cornfields, kegs of powder were piled about the confines of the courthouse, and roughly five hundred pounds of musket ball had been tossed into the shallow depths of the millpond for safe keeping.

Other supplies had been concealed as well. The church's communion silver was buried deep within a soft soap barrel. One neighbour hid approximately fifty-five barrels of beef, and nearly two thousand pounds of salt fish in his cellar; while others, like the Clarkes, stashed what they could about their homes and barns.

And so, by the time the sky was showing pink and orange against the awaited dawn, what could be done, was done. However, when the first word came that the column was indeed approaching Concord, I did not hear it. Instead, I lay fast asleep in a dreamless exhaustion, quite unaware of what was happening beyond the tightly shuttered windows of our sitting room.

ಯಿಯಿಯಿ

A loud noise, sounding like the snap of nearby musket fire, shook me from my slumber. But as I sat up, dazed and confused, I was to discover that the sharp, cracking noise had come from the front door opening and closing quickly.

"The regulars are here!" I heard Perry calling out, his anxious voice like a haunting echo in my ears. "They're on the drive! The regulars are here!"

I swung my legs around to the floor, suddenly conscious of how heavy they felt. Peering across the shadowy room towards the stately quarter chime clock, I could faintly make out the time as being twenty minutes to eight. This meant I had slept only less than an hour.

Then Perry's words sunk in. The regulars were here! I rushed out to the foyer where the others had gathered, and focused my attention towards the foot of the drive. Yes, there they were—dozens of them, their muddied common shoes scuffling along the smooth path of gravel, as they approached our tavern beneath the broad shade of Papa's treasured oak trees.

Yes, there they were—closer now—their polished buttons glistening like beacons in the stark passages of sunlight that filtered through the foliage. Before the foot soldiers rode a boisterous officer, his unruly coal-black stallion kicking up clouds of dust and prancing carelessly upon our lawn. At the rear of the line, two additional officers rode in on elegant little sorrel pacers, seemingly less interested in making the show their front runner was.

"Oh, my God!" moaned Hannah, clutching her stomach with great dramatic flair. "They're here to raid the place! And if these brutes find anything, they'll point a bayonet at my chest, and demand to have their way with me—I know it!"

"I don't think that's exactly why they'd be pointing at your chest, Hannah," I said, with a cool tone of sarcasm. You see, Hannah was so very flat chested, and I said it to break the tension. However, I guess my words accomplished far from that, for Hannah retorted with the loudest screech I ever heard.

"Oh hush, Hannah!" Papa snapped. "Everyone calm down, and go do something. Yes, be seen doing something, for it will not do to be found standing about with guilty looks on our faces."

"Ambrose!" cried Eliza. "Where is my Ambrose?"

"He's in the back pantry packing down the great big breakfast Beulah made for him," replied Effie, dourly. "So you needn't worry about him. Why, your bloated boy's eaten so much, the entire army couldn't carry him off if they tried."

"Oh, my God!" Hannah whined for the second time, prompting Effie to reach out and unceremoniously grab her by the ear.

"Come along, you silly little flibbertigibbet. I imagine these newly arrived guests of ours will be demanding breakfast, and you're going to help us prepare it."

"I will do my embroidery," Eliza announced to no one in particular. "It will look proper for me to be at ease as your house guest."

"Come, daughter," Papa said, placing his hands gently on my shoulders. "Sit in the parlour with Eliza and Jeffrey, and steady yourself with a mite of sewing."

"Steady myself?" I laughed, glancing out the swirling, mullion panes of glass. "Why, I am so unnatural with needle and thread that the British are bound to—" I paused, my words freezing in my throat.

"What is it?" Papa asked, alarmed at my sudden reaction.

"Oh, my God," I said simply. "It's Edmund."

"Who's that?"

"Do you remember Captain Landon Vale, Papa? He was here with the others from Boston, a few weeks back?"

"Yes," Papa mumbled suspiciously, coming closer to the window.

"Well, that isn't him, Papa. This man is Captain Vale's archrival, for lack of a better term. His name is Edmund Thayer Ferrol. Captain Edmund Thayer Ferrol."

"Do you know him?" Papa asked.

"Yes."

"Do you like him?" Papa hissed.

"Not in the least," I replied, standing up straight and brushing my skirts in place. "So, you had better let me handle this at first, Papa."

I did not wait for a response, instead lightly pushing my father away from the door, as I stepped outside, drawing in a deep breath as I did so.

"Captain Ferrol," I exclaimed, effecting what I hoped to be my prettiest smile, as I walked towards him on legs that shook. Thank heavens for long skirts! "You really didn't come all this way just to see me!"

Upon hearing my voice, Ferrol turned and regarded me incredulously, his bold smile in fine company with his dark, rakish eyes.

"My dear Mrs. Lynford! On the contrary, Madam, one would think you have come all this way to see me. My, my, but news travels fast."

"What news?" I asked coyly. His response was a glance which plainly indicated Edmund did not swallow one blessed bit of my dubious words or behaviour.

"I am here for a wedding," I went on smoothly, choosing to ignore his stupid, mocking stare. "Remember? I told you all about it at Charles Davenport's party, last month. My dear friend Ambrose Beckwith is marrying my best friend, Karen Clarke. Goodness, I've been here almost two weeks now, and—"

"Is your father at home, Verity?" he interrupted bluntly.

"Well, I should hope so," I answered slowly, pretending to glance about the place. In truth, I was hiding my anger. I did not like this rude man addressing me by my Christian name. He had no right.

"I am here on official business, Verity. As you are probably well aware, your father is a known Whig sympathizer."

I laughed. It was not all that difficult, really, for I believed my nerves were becoming completely unhinged.

"My father—Justin Daniels—a Whig sympathizer? Oh, Captain Ferrol, you simply must be joking!"

I paused, feigning to glance slyly over my shoulder, before addressing the priggish Edmund in a whisper.

"Don't let my father hear you calling him that. It will go to his head, you see, and we will never hear the end of it."

"Nonetheless, I shall have words with him," Ferrol replied, making a sudden move towards the front steps. "So, if you will first be so kind as to introduce me. Secondly, please have word sent to your kitchen that there are officers of the crown here, desiring to be fed."

His attitude was nothing short of supercilious. I watched as he held the door open for me with an over-gracious air. Why, the arrogant little coxcomb was mocking me still!

"Everyone," I announced with marked indifference, leading Ferrol to our parlour. "This is Captain Edmund Ferrol. He is here to see you, Papa. The Captain claims you are a Whig sympathizer, and he must have words with you. Then we are to hop to it, and happily serve breakfast to him and his fellow officers."

"Jeffrey," Ferrol acknowledged through clenched teeth. I remember your nodding to him in return as though he were no better than a tradesman come to collect for his wares. It was truly brilliant, Jeffrey.

"Mr. Justin Daniels, I believe?" Edmund went on, turning to Papa. "Then I state my purpose for being here. By order of General Gage, I have been sent to this community of Concord to seek out and destroy all artillery, ammunition, provisions, tents, arms, and all military stores, which have been raised to support a rebellion against His Majesty, King George."

"You don't say?" Papa replied with grand nonchalance. I was terribly proud of him. "Search as you like, then. But I assure you, there is nothing of that sort to be found here."

"Regardless, I shall commence with my inspection of the house. Perhaps, Mrs. Lynford, you would be so kind as to accompany me. When we are through, I will take breakfast in the taproom."

We ascended the stairs without a word. When we arrived at the second floor landing, Ferrol observed the array of closed doors at a quick glance.

"What is in this first room?" he asked.

"Oh, that's my great-grandmother's bedchamber," I said, opening wide the door. "But she won't be—"

I paused, my eyes going wide, for there in her bed was Effie, the counterpane pulled smack up to her chin, and the most wanton of smiles on her wrinkled face.

"Great-grandmother," I stammered, terribly confused, for Effie was supposed to be in the kitchen. "What are you doing here?"

"What does it look like, you silly goose?" she retorted with a wide grin. "I'm having myself a little lie down. Oh, halloo!" she went on, eyeing Edmund. "And who are you, you handsome thing?"

"This is Captain Edmund Ferrol, Great-grandmother. Captain Ferrol, this is Effie Daniels." I stumbled over my introduction slightly, for it had suddenly come to my attention that Effie was stowing away the family silver in her bed. I could make out the outline of a candlestick base by her foot. Thankfully though, Captain Ferrol did not seem to notice.

"A pleasure, Ma'am."

"Indeed it is, Captain," Effie replied. "Now tell me—have you come here to drag my great-granddaughter back to Boston?"

"Sorry to say, but no, dear mother."

"Now that be a shame; a true shame. But then again, I suppose you've tired of her."

"Great-grandmother!" I protested, wondering all the while where Effie got such a ridiculous notion in her head.

"If you will pardon me, Mrs. Daniels, I am here on official business."

"Whatever you say, Captain," Effie cooed over the edge of her blanket. "Please don't let me keep you. After all, women keeping men is rather unnatural; not to mention most unfortunate. Do you not agree, Captain?"

"Emphatically, dear mother," he laughed, saluting Effie as I closed the door, standing dumbfounded in the hall.

"Sometimes Great-grandmother can be so incorrigible," I mumbled, as if thinking aloud.

"Yes," Ferrol replied casually. "Now I see where you come by it."

I was about to make a fine retort when the Captain opened yet another door and peered in.

"That's my bedroom," I stated matter-of-factly, as Edmund sauntered in and glanced about. "Mine and Jeffrey's."

"Ah, so you've permitted the browbeaten husband into your sacred adytum. How monumentally gracious of you."

I wasn't terribly sure what an adytum was, but I could easily detect that Edmund Ferrol was still the same old pompous jackass I knew in Boston. Still, his presence was oddly comforting. After all, a strange officer could have been alongside me this very moment, pulling bureau drawers apart, and ripping into mattresses. Therefore, I decided to relax a bit and play his game.

"Why wouldn't I sleep with Jeffrey?" I chided, leaning against the door. "After all, he is my husband."

"Why?" he murmured, moving towards me. "I'll show you why."

Instantly, he was up against me, pulling me tight to his chest as his lips struggled to find mine. I was, as I look back at this, neither shocked or bewildered, but altogether disgusted. I fought for release, but he pressed on me harder, hemming me in between the door and the abruptly painful contact of his sword hilt. What a fool I was to gamble my way into this!

Then suddenly, he stopped as quickly as he began. Taking a step back, Ferrol wiped the side of his mouth, and regarded me with a lofty sneer.

"My, my! Landon Vale told me you weren't the least bit fun, like Charlie's other light ladies. But I simply refused to believe him. You see, all this time, I had a notion you were secretly treating my good friend Vale to a flourish or two in the rose garden. Well, well. Landon was correct after all, my dear woman. Your commodity is solid ice."

"Captain Vale said no such thing."

"Ah! What is this? Do I detect the venom of unrequited love in your querulous voice? Then I do pity you, Mrs. Lynford. For if you are fool enough to think that a man such as Captain Vale could hold even so much as an ounce of personal regard for you, then you deserve all the sympathy the world has to offer. In England, there were ladies of every virtue ready to fall at his feet. And right here in Boston, there is the lovely Lorena Eldredge. Dare you think to compete with her? She is beautiful. She is young. And she is, how shall I say, delightfully fresh for the taking."

"You are a vile, despicable creature," I managed to utter while struggling for breath. "Yes, horribly, despicably vile, and—"

He put a finger to silence my lips, which I immediately slapped away.

"Hush, Madam," he replied, removing me from my stance at the door with one gently insistent tug on my arms. "There is positively no need to nag. And now, might we inspect the remainder of the house?"

I glared after him incredulously.

"Don't you think you owe me an explanation? After all—"

"After all what?" he laughed lightly. "Oh, why is it you so-called decent women want to discuss everything to death?"

With that, he walked out of the room, the sound of his laughter taunting me as it echoed down the hall.

◌◌◌◌

Having inspected the second floor and finding nothing, the Captain proceeded down the service staircase towards the back regions of the tavern. I followed, as I remember, rather sullenly, a few paces behind.

"What's the matter?" Ferrol called out to me over his shoulder. "Cat got your tongue?"

Although he was not looking directly at me, I proved I still had my tongue by childishly sticking it out at him. Oh, why wouldn't this vain idiot just hurry through this charade of an intrusion, and then get out of my life forever?

It was at that moment, and without warning, that the Captain stopped suddenly in his tracks. Afraid he had discovered something he should not, I peered cautiously over his shoulder from the staircase. What I saw brought my hand to my mouth, and tears of laughter to my eyes. For there before us, sprawled luxuriously in a tub of soapy water, was Perry Talbot, his toes clutched over the edge, and a lit clay pipe in his mouth.

"Heavens!" exclaimed Perry in his finest imitation of a languid, insufferable fop. "Company, and here I am completely unprepared. La! Could you ever find it in your teeny, tiny hearts to forgive me?"

Edmund bridled visibly at the boy's blatant impertinence. He knew who Perry was, and probably rightfully guessed it was he who ran the news of the army's advance all the way from Boston the night before. Good, I thought. It served him right.

"What are you concealing in that tub, young man?" the Captain demanded imperiously.

Without a moment's hesitation, Perry Talbot stood before us, naked as the day he was born, and a snide grin from ear to ear. And as Edmund glared, I could not help but surrender to great gales of laughter.

"I have nothing to hide from the King's officers," said Perry, turning slowly about. "Either before, or after, the fact."

Highly insulted, the Captain marched out of the room at once, shouting angrily for me to follow him.

"You cannot order me about like this, you know," I observed, sauntering across the room at a snail's pace; my hands leisurely locked behind my back. "I'm not one of your lackeys. And I am certainly not one of your light ladies."

Turning the corner, I encountered the Captain in the hall.

"Shall we go to the kitchen?" I asked, poorly attempting to hide a smile of triumph. "Our cook, Beulah, is there. And from what I hear tell, she can bake up a devilishly good cannonball pie. And, you can wash it down with a stiff gunpowder and gin, if you'd like. Or would you prefer to give up, and go home?"

"Really, Verity," he began, and his voice was a trifle more caustic than usual. "Are things so desperate in your weary little life, that you've resorted to bedding boys?"

At first, I could not fathom what I was hearing. Glancing quickly at Edmund's face, I saw a thinly disguised veil to his dark eyes, and it pleased me. Why, he was jealous! It was true after all. Edmund Thayer Ferrol was burning over what appeared to be a liaison between me and that young scamp, Perry Talbot. How delightful! I really could not believe my luck.

"Well," the Captain said impatiently. "Don't you have an answer for me?"

"An answer for what?" I sighed with great exaggeration. "Oh, why is it you so-called decent officers have to discuss everything to death?"

He turned on his heel at once, and stormed towards the front of the house. I followed him, of course, praying that every footstep would carry him further and further away. And as we passed the parlour, my father could be heard reciting from the Bible, as he sat in elegant repose, his tiny rimmed spectacles perched precariously on the tip of his nose.

"'I would that they were even cut off which trouble you, for brethren, ye have been called unto liberty . . .'"

"Thank God this is your family, and not mine," Edmund observed, his hand on the door, as I stood watching him from the cool shadows of the hall.

"This is, perhaps, the last time I shall ever see you," he remarked, and his voice was strangely distant. "Good-bye, Mrs. Lynford, and good luck!"

With that, he was gone. Rushing towards the door, I watched as the Captain furiously motioned his platoon on with a wave of his hand. Never before had I witnessed a face so dark, so hard, and so very cold with emotion.

"You've done it, my girl!" cried Papa, coming up behind me and grabbing me about the waist. "The stinkin' redbacks are leaving, without rummaging the fields or the barns. Yes, you've done it, my girl!"

Everyone else had hastened to the hallway in order to triumph over the departure of the soldiers. While we watched the file of red coats marching down the drive, each person present gave their own account of the martial inspection, until they were all rambling at once, like a flapping pack of crows. Only I stood apart in stony silence—tired, annoyed, and terribly close to tears.

∞∞∞∞

Not a quarter of an hour had passed, when the rapid pounding of horses' hooves was heard once again upon the drive.

Looking at one another in panic, naturally we feared the worst. With blanched faces, we women dashed towards the window as Papa went to the door, opening it wide.

"Relax, everyone!" he shouted over his shoulder. "It's Amos Noble."

We gathered about the doorway and watched as Amos, a man most assuredly in his fifties, sprung off his horse as easily as though he were a lad of nineteen.

"Justin!" he called out, quite breathless. "Mrs. Daniels," he addressed Great-grandmother, merely nodding at the rest of us, for his news was far too important for formalities. "I've come to tell you. There was gunfire on Lexington green. A dozen of our men were killed, they say; maybe more, maybe less.

And the British officers have sent back to Boston for more troops—" Amos paused momentarily, drawing much needed breath. "And now—now the advance guard is here in Concord!"

"We know," Papa replied calmly, leading Amos to the parlour. "Some were here, camped out on my lawn, and eating a big breakfast of meat and potatoes, while others were out raiding the village."

"Aye," said Amos. "Unfortunately, they found the twenty-four pounder cannon we stashed in the jail yard. I imagine in all the confusion, we forgot to hide it properly."

"Did they find anything else?" you had asked, Jeffrey, while Papa went about pouring port for all the men present.

"No, thank the good Lord above. They searched a few farms, and then nearly set fire to the courthouse. However, old Mrs. Moulton put a stop to that notion."

"Bless her grey hairs," Papa laughed. Perry had a questioning look on his face, so Papa ventured to explain.

"Mrs. Moulton is a dear little mite of a woman. And all of eighty, to boot! She resides next to our courthouse."

"And if she had not bullied the British into putting out the fire they had started, we would have all been blown clear to Saint Peter's gate with the grand amount of gunpowder we had laid up in there!"

"Oh, dear God," whispered Eliza, clutching at her heart, as Effie made so bold as to begin pouring glasses of port for the ladies as well. After all, were we not struggling through this sordid hell too? No one, however, seemed to mind.

Amos put down his glass and cleared his throat.

"Now, what I have come to tell you, Justin, is that a skirmish of some sort is expected at the North Bridge. The light infantry are there now—perhaps only a platoon, at present—but they're watching our men with war in their eyes."

"Our men? What do you mean? How many are there?"

"Nigh on four hundred, so I hear. Companies from Lincoln, Acton, and Groton arrived at dawn. Why, did you know that our men bravely led the British troops into town this morning, headed by none other than Major John Buttrick? We met them on the road, you see, coming in from Lexington. I even hear tell our musicians outplayed their namby-pamby fifes and drums."

"It's settled then," Papa announced. "I am going to join them at the bridge."

"But Papa! You mustn't!"

He merely stared at me for a cool instant, his face inexplicably sad and determined, all at the same time.

"It is my duty to go," he said quietly.

"I should go instead," offered Perry, swallowing hard. "I have no family to speak of, so—"

"It is because of my family that I go," Papa went on. "And I will take no argument save my own."

Eliza stumbled towards Ambrose, her voice choking with frightened tears.

"You will not take Ambrose! You will not take my baby boy!" She clutched him close to her breast, daring the others with her eyes to dictate differently.

"I will go," you said so very quietly, Jeffrey, and I knew not to fight you.

It was all like a nightmare, every moment of it. Yes, it was a terrible and frightening dream that I was watching from the outside. I was no more than a casual observer, and I could do nothing to alter its headstrong course. This could not be happening to me. My father, my husband, and one of my dearest friends could not be going off to war. What was war anyway? I had never known it. Yes, this was merely a horrible dream that I was struggling to shake myself from. And soon, I would wake up safe and snug beneath the cool, crisp sheets of my four-poster bed. Outside, the whippoorwill would be singing, and the warm April sun would be painting pretty patterns of light on my bedroom floor. Yawning and stretching, I would try to recall my dream, but would not be able to. Casting it off, I would smile, and instead trifle my brain over which dress to wear to the Allen's picnic to be held this very afternoon.

You had come to my side, Jeffrey, placing your hand gently beneath my chin.

"I will come back, you know," I heard you whisper.

I remember sitting on the couch and staring at you blankly, as though it were for the last time. From the hallway, Papa's voice could be heard calling out for you to hurry. The air about my head seemed foggy, and all your voices so very far away. I tried to smile, foolish thing that I was. I felt like an actress upon the stage who, in front of hundreds of people, has forgotten her most critical lines.

"You won't take him!" Eliza shouted, long after the front door had closed with an ominous thud. "You won't take my baby away from me!"

Sinking back on the couch, I held my head in my hands, and closed my eyes wearily. It would have been so easy to scream; so easy to go mad.

Effie refilled the ladies' glasses, humming an oddly discordant tune.

∽◌∽◌∽

Only the ticking of the quarter chime clock could be heard, as we women sat in the parlour like silent statues of stone.

Ambrose had left to get some water from the well. And as if in a hypnotic trance, Eliza watched as the hands of the clock whirled slowly by. After ten long minutes had passed, she raised a handkerchief to her dampened, puffy eyes.

"My son has joined them," she said quietly, as a fresh flow of tears overtook her face.

"Oh, I don't believe that," I scowled, standing. "He may be staying outside, just to avoid us. Why, it's like the aftermath of a wake in this room."

I began to walk towards the door like a dumb thing, wanting escape, but not entirely sure how to obtain it. Over in a corner of the room, Hannah lounged in a chair, her legs dangling over the arm, as she sighed unmercifully over and over and over. Yes, I needed to get out of this house. If I stayed, I would surely go mad.

"You're not going out!" Eliza called after me. As she spoke, I noticed a hurriedly scrawled note in the hall. It was from Ambrose; the thought had occurred to him that Karen and her mother might be quite alone, and he went to make sure they were safe and secure.

I told Eliza of the note, and she agreed that she and I should go to the Clarke farm at once. Hannah then expressed immediate concern at being left alone, however, Effie quelled any notion of that.

"Don't you worry," she said. "If the redbacks return to this tavern, Miss Beckwith, you can step outside and show them your scrawny legs. That ought to scare them straight back to Boston town!"

I went to the door, closing it behind me. How wonderful it was to be in the fresh air! I took a deep breath with gratitude, pulling and fussing with the sleeves of my gown which I had, by this time, been attired in for nearly twelve hours.

The sun seemed so very bright after the stifling darkness of our parlour. Screening my tired, aching eyes with my hand, I glanced about me, uncertain as to whether or not it was safe to venture across the fields. There was an eerie silence, punctuated only by the sound of a distant fife.

How could the threat of war be hatching on a day such as this? The sky was a handsome shade of blue, with just the slightest hint of clouds. How good the earth smelled—all fresh and green and new. It was difficult to imagine this newborn haven of grass defiled with murdered blood.

Oh, why did men fight? What glory was there in it? How could everyday men march off to face certain death, and be proud of it? Was there not more greatness, more pride, in building a home, and finding a good wife, and watching one's children grow? How could pain and suffering and anguish ever equal up to all of that? No, I would never, never understand the so-called glories of battle; not if I lived to be a hundred.

"Oh, Landon," I whispered without the least bit of wonder as to why I was thinking about him specifically at that moment.

Eliza appeared on the doorstep. Obviously, she had had words with Effie regarding the slight against her daughter, for her round face was flushed with indignation. We started off for the Clarkes' in silence. There was not a soul on the streets. And when we got to the house, no one answered our knock. Eliza went round to the garden to see if the women were there. It was my guess to search for Ambrose by the barn. I doubted he would have ambled off much further than that.

My suspicions were correct. I found Ambrose Beckwith seated on a bale of hay, his stare fixed sulkingly on a broken window, where I imagine he really saw nothing at all.

"Ambrose," I said quietly. "Everyone back at the Crossroads has been terribly worried about you, especially your poor mother. It wasn't very smart to wander off like this."

"I am ashamed," he mumbled, without turning his head.

"Why?"

"My silly mother won't allow me to grow up and act like a man, that's why."

I walked around to face him.

"Is running off and getting yourself killed acting like a man? If so, Ambrose, I see that as a foolish bit of reasoning."

"Karen must think me a coward. Don't you see? I'm the only man who didn't go."

I knelt before him and took his hands.

"I don't think you're right, Ambrose. Why, I'll wager Karen is thanking the good Lord above that you'll be safe, and married on Saturday."

"But I'm going to miss the entire war, Verity! Why, it's probably over, even as we speak."

"Over for whom? For the British? Can you honestly tell me that the mighty empire that rules us would send their soldiers to take a few aimless shots at us, and then call them home for good; giving us all that we ask? Or, might it be over for our patriots? Do you suppose if we are knocked down today, it's back to the fields and 'God bless the King?'"

I peered into his despondent face and continued.

"No, Ambrose. If this is a war—and I suppose now it is—it will go on for a very long time before it is through."

I paused at the truth of my own words. I had never known hatred. I had never witnessed anything of blind killing and despair. However, now, the magnitude of its horrible truth frightened me deeply.

"Let us go in the house, and see if Karen and her mother are there," I said, taking my hands from his, for they were shaking. "There is no sense in having everyone worry about us."

Ambrose agreed. And as we stood, a sudden snapping noise outside the window distracted us.

"What is it?" I whispered frantically, as Ambrose put his hand over my mouth to silence me.

Someone was outside, for a shadow scampered across the broken glass like a wavering spectre. We threw ourselves against the wall, so as not to be seen, but I was petrified that the incessant pounding of my heart would surely give us away.

Suddenly, the figure of a British soldier passed the open barn door. He was very young; perhaps not even twenty years of age. He was also, I noticed, unarmed.

I closed my eyes for a moment, in a desperate attempt to steady my breathing. But it was only for a moment. An abrupt movement caused me to open my eyes in fear that the youthful soldier was about to attack.

However, it was not the motion of the solitary boy I had sensed. It was Ambrose, charging at him with a pitchfork, which was raised over his head. Relentlessly, he brought it down on the unsuspecting intruder, easily knocking him to the ground.

"Ambrose!" I shouted, as he swung at the unconscious lad time and time again, like a mad, vicious thing.

"Ambrose!" I shrieked, my nerves snapping. "For God's sake, stop! He's dead. Sweet Jesus, he has got to be dead by now!"

I rushed towards the boy on legs that would not support me, and sunk to my knees as if in a faint. Ambrose had quit his violence, standing over me as his breath came in demented, rasping gulps.

However, for this lad, breath would no longer come. His once golden hair was thickly matted with warm, oozing blood. Slowly, I put out a trembling hand to turn him over, but froze at the thought of witnessing a dead boy's gaze.

Instead, I looked up blankly at Ambrose. His eyes were blazing in a wild way, as he shivered from head to foot. But it was not fear that possessed him. It was the intoxication of murder, and I was facing its ugly visage for the very first time.

At once, Susannah Clarke and Eliza were running towards us, like something out of a dream.

"My God!" Eliza panted as she drew near. "What has happened?"

"He killed him," I said, and my voice was startling cold, and clearly not my own. "He was probably just some poor boy trying to desert—just searching for a place to hide—and Ambrose killed him."

"He would have killed us!" Ambrose retorted, on the verge of hysterics. "He would have killed us all, you know, if I had not stopped him!"

I ran my hands through my hair, my face incredulous at his words.

"How can you say that? He was not even armed!"

"He's a British soldier!" Ambrose screamed back. "What else could you expect?"

I could have told him. Yes, I could have told all of them, but they would not have believed me.

"Hush," Susannah Clarke said, and her voice was amazingly calm. "Hush, or Karen will surely hear you. Now, we have to think."

"No," I said, standing because the boy's profusion of blood had drenched the hem of my dress. "We have to go and find an officer and tell him, and—"

"Are you really such a fool?" Eliza snapped, grabbing my arm. "If we go to the British, they will hang us all. No, we have to bury this boy. And we cannot tell anyone—not even Karen, you hear?"

And so, Eliza, Ambrose, and Mrs. Clarke buried him under a new bank of lilacs where the ground was still soft. They worked steadily, and without a single word spoken. How resilient these women were. I had known them both all my life. They were well-bred women, whose hands were meant for nothing more strenuous than to bathe a babe, or thread an embroidery needle. I was not like these women. I could not face murder with an iron jaw and a pickax. For myself, I could only stand by the site of this freshly dug grave, holding the soiled hem of my dress away from me, as though it were a living reminder of the sin I had just witnessed. Perhaps in truth, it was.

I could not stay. I ran through the fields, and across the lane to the Crossroads, careful to avoid the parlour where Effie sat in a chair, snoring contentedly in a deep sleep. It did not concern me as to where the others were. Nothing would ever matter again.

I went straight to my room, and ripped my dress from my shoulders in long, tearing rents. I never wanted to see it, or the Clarkes' farm, or the visual memory of this horrid day, ever again.

Outside, the scuffling sound of soldiers on the march resounded from the street. I could not watch; instead, I cowered in a corner of my room, and wept uncontrollably.

◌◌◌◌

You must have thought it odd, Jeffrey, to discover me propped up with pillows in our bed; a book of prose in my hands. Yes, you surely must have considered me a most callous wife. But then again, you had distractions of your own.

"I must tell you, Verity," you had said, sitting on the bed, and reaching for my hand. "I must tell you what it was like on the hill."

I said nothing. In truth, I was not certain I could take hearing it.

"Israel Clarke and your father introduced your young friend, Talbot, to as many of the men as they could. It was not, perhaps, a time for social proprieties, but the Company saluted him heartily, commending the boy for his brave decision to fight."

I merely nodded. I saw nothing brave about killing, but I nodded all the same.

"Oh, the heat, Verity! The sun seemed already at its zenith, and the sky was filled with smoke. We were all horrified, thinking that the King's troops had burned the entire town. Were you aware of what was set afire, aside from the courthouse?"

"No," I whispered hoarsely. I did not remember smoke. Why, it seemed a lifetime ago, I stepped outside these doors with Eliza Beckwith, and praised the breathtaking blue of the sky. Yes, it was another lifetime; another person.

"Regardless, the men were incensed. They felt certain their women and children were now homeless, you see. One man shouted, *Will you let them burn down the town?*, and soon several voices, raised in anger, rang through the air. Enough time had been wasted, they said. Enough concession had been paid in allowing the redbacks to hold the bridge. It was time to move. Many cried out that it was time to avenge the deaths of our gallant souls in Lexington."

You stood and ran your hands through your hair, gazing at the braided rug on the floor, as though it represented the very scene you envisioned from the hill.

"The order was given to move out. I was still with your father, and your friend, the Talbot boy. Israel Clarke and Josiah Pierce were with us as well. I remember how we all regarded one another before we loaded our muskets—each man, I am sure, thinking his own final thoughts, while the church bells of Concord chimed plaintively. How solemn were those bells! Their unearthly echo reverberated long after, through the fields."

I could not recall the bells ringing, but I watched as you paced back and forth, back and forth, your voice becoming smaller and tighter with fear.

"I must confess to you, Verity, I could not manage to load my musket. Good Lord, I had not used a musket since I was a boy. But your friend, Perry Talbot, he helped me."

You ceased your relentless pacing, and placed your hands on the mantle, watching me in the glass which hung above.

"Without a word, Perry took the musket from me. I watched as he braced the butt of it on his hip, and tore apart the paper cartridge with his teeth, then primed and poured the contents into the muzzle. I felt foolish, you see; foolish about so many things. And that is when I asked him about you, dearest."

You came and sat on the bed very close to me, and took my hands, your eyes intent. I imagine you thought I would speak at this time—however, I did not. I was thinking about the boy—the boy we buried. His hair was the same colour as yours, Jeffrey . . .

"Perry was still working my musket, and I said to him, 'Mr. Talbot, last evening, you were introduced as being a friend of ours from Boston. But for the life of me, son, I cannot place you.' 'It's true we were never introduced,' he had said to me, dropping the ball inside, and keeping his eyes pretty much to his task. 'I was somewhat infatuated with a young lady of your wife's acquaintance, you see, and your lovely wife did her best to assist my cause.' I hadn't known that, Verity."

"Yes," I said simply. In truth, I wished you would stand and walk away, Jeffrey, for your clothes smelled abominably. They held a strong odor of stale perspiration and acrid gun smoke.

"How relieved I was, dear wife. I must confess, I believed your young friend to be in love with you. Why, I even asked him. And do you know what he said?"

I shook my head no. I did not really care.

"He said he was in love with you, a little. I thought that was rather touching."

Yes. Perhaps one day I would call such a notion "touching." However, at this very moment, "touching" seemed so very trivial.

"Anyway, your father had joined us once again," you went on, thankfully standing, and returning to the mantle. "He told me I should not feel compelled to fight. But I told him I must. I told him you would be ashamed of me."

How little you know me, Jeffrey. How very little.

"The drums droned out a march beat," you went on, and your voice quivered with tension once more. "Your father seemed triumphant. It was like a tonic to him, I suppose, after all these years of talk, and all these months of hope. Yes, Verity, your father was more than ready to fight. And as we approached, we saw the British regulars far below, like little stick figures of red, wrenching up the wide planks of the bridge. Our leaders knew the time was never better. There were a hundred or so of them, and over four hundred of us. And they had their backs to the river. Nothing could be better."

Nothing could be better? What an odd thing for a gentleman brought up on fine books and brandy to say.

"We were, perhaps, a half mile away. The day was so hot. It was more like the depths of summer than a gentle morning in spring. All around us, tender white cherry buds seemed near ready to blossom. And the birds were singing, imagine that."

I could not.

"Drums were beating—constantly beating. Major Buttrick shouted out to the redcoats to halt their destruction of the bridge. Behind him, a fifer pushed out the tune of "The White Cockade." We were close now—so close, that only the steady pulse of the river separated us. The redcoat captain called his men at once into street formation. Then it happened. A warning volley went off. Then another, and yet another. A frantic moment of searching proved the King's men had indeed fired first. You see, there was some confusion at Lexington as to who fired first, but here, at the bridge, it was decidedly different."

Did it matter, Jeffrey? Did it really, truly matter?

"That was all the men needed to know. 'Fire!' Major Buttrick shouted with triumph in his voice, 'Fire, fellow soldiers, for God's sake, fire!' The smell of musket smoke filled the air. Somewhere quite near me, that brave little fifer from Acton was silenced as he fell to the ground, pale and wounded. And when I saw that happen, I—I could not move. I raised my musket slowly, and attempted to pull the trigger, but nothing happened. My finger was seemingly paralysed with fear. I heard your father shouting to me above the constant explosion of muskets. He was telling me to fire, for Christ's sake! I turned to where I had heard your father's voice, but the ground was so thick with smoke, I could see no one. Despite the deafening madness all around me, I had never felt so terribly alone."

You said no more. I was waiting for you to tell me that Papa was dead.

"I am so ashamed, Verity. I stood there, not knowing what to do, and I—I retreated. I was a coward, and now I am afraid to face the others. Your father, and Perry, and a few others are downstairs in the taproom. However, I can not join them. I feel like a fool."

"Don't," I said simply. And then I slept. Yes, somehow through all the fear and trepidation . . .

ೲೲೲ

The wedding went on as planned the following Saturday. Karen was an oddly detached bride; seemingly unwilling and sad. Eliza and Susannah plainly attributed Karen's deathlike trance to the unfortunate events of the past few days, and were merely grateful that no one from the families or the invitation list had been lost in the battle at North Bridge.

At the reception, subdued, of course, by the dark sorrows and somber heartaches of war, there was nothing but endless whispers about the horrendous events at Lexington and Concord. From my stance at the window, I overheard two gentlemen discussing the case of a British soldier who was wounded, and left behind at the bridge. Apparently, some young boy of Concord was frightened to find the soldier still alive, and bludgeoned him to death with an ax.

I put down my wine glass, and found you at once, Jeffrey. It was definitely time to go back to Boston.

An hour later, as we rode out, we passed the peaceful bank of lilacs which grew in great profusion by the Clarkes' barn. Staring at the freshly turned earth, I offered my first sincere prayers to God. Somehow, it eased the madness that had taken root in my brain.

A gentle rain had begun to fall, like sad, tiny tears from heaven, while a chill breeze cried through the air. Spring was gone. Like a murdered innocent, it would never come back again.

Marriage, at best, is but a vow,
Which all men either break or bow.

Samuel Butler—*The Lady's Answer to the Knight*

∞

SPRING, 1775

MARLON REYNOLDS AND CELESTE DAVENPORT were married on the morning of Saturday, the 27th of May, at the Hollis Street Church. It was a small ceremony. Charles felt that Celeste, being altogether shy and nervous by nature, would prefer it that way. The Reverend Mather Byles performed the sparsely attended service in double quick time, for he was anxious to get to the reception and sample the rum punch and roasted goose.

A little more than one hundred and fifty guests greeted the bridal party before the house of pearly white granite on Garden Court Street. It truly was a charming day. The oblique rays of midmorning sun danced about the gleaming brass appointments on the spotless blue landau, as the bride and groom, and their smiling attendants, disembarked amidst shouts and cheers of joy. Clemence, as bridesmaid, was radiant in a gown of satiny peach, while Gordon Russell, as groomsman, was profoundly elegant in a waistcoat of azure blue, the colour of which matched Celeste's bridal gown to perfection.

Charles traveled in the second coach with his sisters, Vera and Fiona, as well as Fiona's rather torpid husband, Stanton. In their fine attire, Charles and Fiona were indeed stately and handsome. How different from the plump, babbling Vera! At three years Fiona's junior, Vera Davenport had never married. Her life was a sheltered one. For nearly two decades now, she had resided with Fiona and Stanton. Rumour now had it, she would be spending the next two with Charles.

The guests pushed forward, crowding into the street. I watched as Celeste stood in sweet confusion, against a pretty shield of sunlight. She was an exquisite bride, this was true. However, it was even more apparent that she was a reluctant one.

Stepping inside the broad front door, bridal party and guests alike were heard to exclaim over the sights which greeted them. Once stark and formal, the cool, white foyer beckoned us warmly with a legion of floral arrangements. On every table, and in every available niche, jasmine, buttercups, and narcissus overflowed like delicate knolls of perfumed color. Carnations mingled with meadow lilies, while nearby, lithe yellow lady's slippers drooped daintily amidst the maiden pinks and goldthreads. And on the buffet table, handsome clusters of peonies bordered the regal array of dishes. On each guest table, glowing azaleas floated in shimmering crystal bowls, surrounded by freshly cut sweetbrier roses.

"It's like the Garden of Eden," sighed Virginia Stanwood, as she pressed her slender, little hands sheltered in their prim, white lace gloves to her lips. The years seemed to fade from her face, as Virginia silently recalled gentle springs from years past—those gentle, pretty days, spent idly in long forgotten rose arbors.

Neatly tucked away under the wide expanse of stairs, a most congenial orchestra broke into the sprightly strains of a minuet. The footman, Stearns, was going out of his head, for he had charge of the hired help this day. Bewigged and aloof servants, adorned in impeccable silks and glistening shoe buckles, lurked about the reception hall; announcing in lilting tones the particular wines and champagnes they carried aloft their polished trays of silver. It was a pointless gesture. Party guests never fussed over what was in their glass, as long as it was free. Well, no guest that is, save little Miss Lucy Wellman.

"Judas!" she exclaimed, making a guttural sound of disfavor. "This sack posset tastes like something drained out of a day-old chamber pot."

The group about her burst into amused laughter, as Lucy leaned forward and tapped the fidgety Edmund Platt on the shoulder with her fan.

"You there! Yes, you with the great goggly eyes. Go get me a decent glass of wine. This stuff's only good for pickling beef."

Lucy watched a moment with the others, as Edmund scurried across the hall towards the refreshments table like a yellow chicken with a hungry fox hot on its tail.

"What a silly man," she mumbled. Then turning, she addressed me.

"So, I hear you are leaving us."

"Yes," I answered dryly, "at the end of next month."

I can still look back on this very moment with the same pain and bewilderment that twisted my heart even then. How sorry life had become for us at that time. We had returned from a once tranquil and peaceful haven in the country, our past home of Concord, where such a foreign and grievous concept as war was lamentably introduced. On the road back to Boston, people had passed us in droves. They were leaving Boston, they said. The British meant to have it, and so it would be. That decided me as well. I wanted to go back to Concord. I wanted to be with my father and my sister and my great-grandmother, and perhaps repair the broken pieces of my marriage in quieter surroundings. You had said you did not wish to return to Concord, Jeffrey. Our first week back in Boston was so maddening for us both. But then, the scavengers began to appear—those so-called fine and fancy folks who wanted to reside, and wreak havoc, in the shadow of their beloved British. That decided us both. The town of Boston had become hospice to the lowest of the low, and it was definitely time for us to leave.

"That is such a pity," Lucy went on to say. "And just when things were starting to happen in this town. Yes, what a shame. For I've come to like you, Verity Lynford—yes, like you, despite the fact you're leagues more beautiful than myself. And you stole that pretty boy away from me at the Salutation, last November. Remember? Now, what was his name?"

"Oh, I don't recall, really."

"Bah! It doesn't matter now. What does matter is that I shall miss you very much. Only do not tell anyone. I shall be forever scoffed at for being maudlin, if you do."

Thus, Lucy and I became fast friends for the remainder of the afternoon. What had promised to be an occasion of drudgery, instead became a most jovial and high-spirited time. Separating ourselves from the others as best possible, we two launched our new careers as the wedding's worst critics. No one escaped our venomous insults, as we huddled together in the window seat, consuming vast amounts of Lisbon wine, and laughing at anything that seemed the least bit sentimental. Drink had magically transformed pessimism into chaotic nonchalance. And so it went on for hours.

We refused to dance, and turned up our noses at every plate offered to us. Inebriation had rendered us superiour to anything, and anyone, who crossed our path. It was perhaps only when Charles approached us, that we two made any attempt to behave soberly.

"Ladies!" he exclaimed, his arms stretched wide. "Why sit here all alone and sulking?"

"Sulking?" Lucy echoed, her cheeks colouring brightly. "Who, us?"

Charles seated himself between us on the plush window seat with its cushions of deep vermilion-red velour. He watched the festivities for a moment in contented silence. I remember thinking he had the profile of a Roman god.

"Now, my dear Mrs. Lynford, what is this I hear about you leaving us?"

"I had thought to tell you," I answered plainly. "But at the time, it seemed so inconsequential."

"Never, never. Why, that's utter nonsense. You see, you cannot leave us just now, my pet. We need you."

It was such an odd statement, but I felt too befuddled by drink to ask exactly what he meant. To be certain, I could see no plausible reason why anyone—above all, Charles Davenport—should ever need me. I was considered unworthy of performing on the stage. I was no longer Charles' primary hostess; indeed Diana Kirby had resumed that role with complete certitude. In your eyes, Jeffrey, I was not the proper kind of wife. And to wholly finish the picture, I was not even capable of conforming to murder. Yes, just who then on this insane earth could need me now?

"In case you are wondering where your husband is, Mrs. Lynford, I have invited him to join a few of my new friends—gentlemen, really—at the gaming table. And, when I left him, just five short minutes ago, he was doing quite nicely."

I said nothing for a moment; merely nodding for lack of anything proper to say.

"And now, if you'll excuse me." Charles stood and bowed, disappearing at once into the noisy throng of guests.

"So, Papa Charles is helping your fine man out," Lucy observed with a knowing tone. "How positively divine. Perhaps then, we should not say any more wicked and horrible things about his silly guests. Oh, heavens! Look over there—there near the man with a girth as big and round as the rings of Saturn. It's that overbearing Eldredge girl with our Captain Vale!"

I peered across the crowded room, and saw them at once. One could not help but notice Lorena Eldredge. Dressed in a robe à la francaise of the palest lemon silk, she was nothing but striking. The folds of her dress only emphasized her reedlike slenderness. The delicate pearls at her throat were well complimented by her alabaster skin and her handsome wig, which was done in the style of Madame du Barry.

"How disgusting," I mumbled, utterly impressed.

"Miss Eldredge's mother is the grand-niece of the daughter of the Marquis of something-or-other," Lucy reported with thinly disguised awe. "But then, the poor girl's ruined by the sins of the father. So what's it all for?"

I shrugged. I really did not care. You see, the girl outright annoyed me with her penchant for playing Perry against Landon, and vice versa. She had a right to feel popular, I suppose, however, it had gone far enough.

"I had thought that you and the Captain would have been something together," Lucy said slyly.

"That's rather doubtful, Lucy," I nearly whispered.

Landon had not spoken to me since our return from Concord, and that was now over a month past. Indeed, he had gone out of his way to stay elsewhere than under our roof. I had seen him, of course, at Charles', and occasionally at the Eldredges'. Strangely though, he had done his best to avoid me. My head reasoned that an officer's first duty was always to his King, and certainly those days were now upon us. However, my heart insisted that regardless of war, something in Landon's friendship for me had changed completely. And that change was not pleasing.

"You know, Verity, Diana Kirby cannot manage to snare the Captain, try as she might. It's Lorena, you see, and Diana is having a dickens of a time trying to horn her out of the pen. But you—you could do it."

"I have no interest in the subject," I answered flatly.

"Poor Verity," Lucy sighed, patting my hand in an abstract way. "All of twelve months in Boston, and still no suitable conquest. But then, who is there, really? Oh heavens, look! There's that insolent ass, Marlon Reynolds. He thinks he's the cock of the golden walk, now that he's gone and married himself a theatre company."

"I never thought of it that way," I admitted, stunned and astonished once again at Lucy's remarkable insight.

"Great Caesar's ghost!" came the laughing reply. "Why else on earth did you think he did it? For love? Bah! Be sensible, Verity. With a naive girl like Celeste, it simply doesn't exist."

⌘⌘⌘

The shadows of evening had long since fallen when the first of the guests began to take their leave. Coaches were called for, and sleeping children were carefully lifted from their beds, grumpily rubbing their heavy eyes while insistently asking where they were.

The heartier of the revelers kept dancing, as the hall resounded with hornpipes and endless country dances, minuets, and jigs. Hundreds of virgin white candles had been lit, and the dancers continued in a frenzied state of exhaustion. From my place by the window, I watched mesmerized, as the same couples swayed rhythmically about the room in a repetitious blur of sweeping skirts and waistcoats, like frantic moths about a flame. Landon and Lorena danced endlessly as well; their eyes never leaving each other's heavenly gaze. It was, I must admit, intensely enviable.

The night wore on. No one danced anymore. You had finally emerged from the billiards room, Jeffrey, your weary face searching the crowd. And when you saw me, you appeared astonished, as well as a bit concerned, to find me still seated where you had left me.

"Verity, my dear," you exclaimed, breathlessly. "I've just won a little over two hundred pounds at cards. Is that not splendid?"

"Positively," I murmured, surprised at how difficult it was to focus on your face.

"Listen, dearest, Charles has interested me in an idea on investing in his next theatrical production, and I thought—"

"I thought we were going home to Concord, Jeffrey."

"So we were, however, it bears consideration to—ah, but you look absolutely withered. We should, perhaps, discuss this splendid prospect at another time."

"Perhaps," I sighed, like an insolent child.

"Verity, are you all right?"

"Never better," I claimed, lifting my wine glass unsteadily to my lips.

"Where is Miss Wellman? I believed her to be here with you."

"She went home with—" I began, and then stopped myself. "She left."

"You still do not look well. I think it best if I take you home."

I glanced about the wide expanse of cool marble towards the entrance foyer where Marlon and Celeste were bidding farewell to their guests. Amidst the confusion of overloud voices, and crumpling embraces, Celeste was flagging. Her face had a pinched, unnatural strain to it; as though she were trying terribly hard not to scream. As for Marlon—he was basking in the praise and adulation like a leading actor upon the stage—and not like a genteel groom at all. At this moment, he was speaking with Landon and Lorena. Landon listened politely, while Lorena picked at the sleeve of his regimental coat aimlessly in that trite little way that demonstrates possession.

"Yes, let us go home," I agreed at once. "There is nothing to keep us here."

I stood somewhat awkwardly, looping my arm through yours for support. All around us, a bevy of tireless footmen scurried about, picking up the endless debris of glasses and plates; many of which were still laden with stale and wasted food and drink. From their berth beneath the stairs, somber and sweat-drenched musicians silently packed up their cases, fanning themselves in noiseless unison with their various pages of musical notes.

We stepped up to the end of the receiving line, and as we did so, I took one last glance about the hall. All of the guests had departed. Only the staff remained behind, their livery crumpled and stained; their white wigs tossed haphazardly about the scattered chairs and sideboards. Scanning the first-floor rooms for any additional refuse, these hired hands were easily heard muttering under their breath about the inappropriate behaviour of many of the so-called ladies and gentlemen who had entered this home as guests.

The receiving line progressed. I clung to your arm, Jeffrey, allowing you to do all the talking. That was best, you see; for in truth, I had nothing to say.

In the shadowy depths beyond, footmen rushed about, extinguishing the half spent candles; filling the air with eerie, dense pools of smoke—the pungent smell of which mingled with the unpalatable and dull scent of dying flowers.

CANCANCAN

We were just about to withdraw in our carriage, when you had remembered a certain piece of correspondence you wished to leave with Charles. I decided to wait for you in the coach, and it seemed but moments when Captain Vale appeared at the door.

"Madam," he began, rather formally. "I wished to inquire as to how you were."

"And why should you?" I returned pertly. Oh, for certain, it was the drink talking, but I did not care. And I made sure not to address him as Captain. "Yes, why should you, when your terribly frigid opinion of me was made quite clear through your dearest friend, Ferrol."

"Ferrol? What has Ferrol said to you?"

"Perhaps it would be best, sir, if we kept our conversation to such safe topics as the weather."

"Verity, don't," he said, and the tone of his voice melted my resistance. I turned to him.

"Verity, please, for God's sake, tell me what the man said to you."

"It is, perhaps, more what he did to me—that is to say, he was not a gentleman."

Landon practically leapt forward to my side.

"Did he hurt you, Verity? Did that beast hurt you in any way?"

"No," I said quietly. "For he's a slight little weasel, and easy to topple."

There was a momentary pause. Then Landon sighed, and our hands touched in a quick, tender embrace.

"We will talk," the Captain promised quickly, for you were just returning from the house, Jeffrey.

"Yes," I murmured, a most joyous smile overtaking my lips. "We will talk."

You passed a few pleasantries with the Captain. I remember, for you were most cordial. I believe for the first time since I had known you, Jeffrey, I was a trifle more intoxicated than you were.

The door closed, and the coach disembarked in a heavenly stream of moonlight.

Man alone at the very moment of his birth,
cast naked upon the naked earth, does she
abandon to cries and lamentations.

Pliny the Elder—*Natural History*

❦

16 AND 17 JUNE, 1775

THE DAY was very hot.

Stretched out on the divan, in little more than my chemise, I lay desperately still, attempting to commit to memory the prose of Titania.

"'These are the forgeries of jealousy,'" I sighed as if in one breath, while gently resting one hand over my tired eyes. "'And never, since the middle summer's spring, Met we on hill, in dale, forest or mead, By paved fountain or by rushy brook, . . .'"

I glanced wearily at my book and held it aside, sighing once more. Oh, why was I doing this? I did not wish to understudy Virginia Stanwood in *A Midsummer Night's Dream*. I was not capable. I was not interested. So why, Jeffrey, were you so insistent on my doing so? Yes, yes, you were financially vested in this production. Besides, you had told me, it would be fun; just a lark. Indeed, you even committed to attending rehearsals with me. Oh, I had my suspicions about your curious enthusiasm, even then. However, I could not bring myself to believe what I know to be truth now.

"'Or in the beached margent of the sea, to dance our ringlets to the whistling wind,'" I recited aloud, dully. "'But with thy brawls thou hast disturbed our sport—'"

"Madam," I heard Beals' voice at the door. Lifting my hand from my forehead, I opened one questioning eye.

"There is a Sergeant Stone here to see you, Madam."

I sat up, feeling momentarily dizzy from the heat, and I stared at Beals for an instant.

"To see me? Are you sure?"

"Mmm . . . that is what the gentleman says, Madam. Shall I ask him again?"

"No," I sighed, and standing a trifle unsteadily, I crossed the room to the looking glass with its gold oval frame, and hastily checked my appearance in the shadows of the shuttered room.

"Show the Sergeant in, Beals," I said at last, straightening the lines of my flimsy dress. How pale I was! Certainly as a rule, I had more colour than this.

Sergeant Stone entered the room, looking effortlessly cool in his scarlet coat and meticulously white breeches.

"Thomas," I smiled, holding out my hand. "How kind of you to call."

"The pleasure, Madam, is all mine," he replied; bowing elegantly over my offered hand, which he held ever so lightly within his own. "However, I do come to you on the request of Captain Vale."

My eyes widened.

"What? Has the Captain taken ill?"

"Oh, no, Madam. I assure you, Captain Vale is in excellent health. His concern, however, lies in the fact that Mr. Lynford is still away in the country. With that in mind, the Captain has asked that I escort you directly to the home of Merchant Loring."

"Why? What has happened?"

"Nothing; nothing at all—that is—No, Mrs. Lynford, you should not suffer a single care. Simply, the merchant Loring is hosting an evening party, and the Captain thought you might enjoy attending."

"Do not mislead me, Sergeant Stone. I have heard the rumours. They speak in my kitchen, and on the streets; the Cambridge army is plotting to attack Boston, and it is going to be tonight. It's true then; isn't it?"

"Oh please do not panic, Veri—, I mean Mrs. Lynford. The Rebels have not moved from camp. And even if they dared, they could never destroy us. Why, there is not a chance in Hades of that happening."

My look of anguish turned rapidly to one of near sarcasm, as I remembered the events of Lexington and Concord. However, there was no time for comparisons now. Land of Goshen, it was going to happen again. I did not care what false securities the Sergeant had to offer. It was going to happen again—war and death and pain and—oh, Jeffrey! Why did you have to be away on business at a time like this—at a time when I needed you so.

"Please, Mrs. Lynford. Do not fear. I am here, and I am going to take you to Captain Vale. So rest assured, Madam. There is not going to be any fighting."

"Wait here while I go change my dress," I said, rushing towards the door. "Help yourself to the port, Sergeant. I shall not be long."

I nearly vaulted the stairs, the stifling heat increasing like an inferno with every step. Dashing into my room, I threw my wardrobe wide and donned the first brocaded corset I could find, tugging at it with fingers that trembled. Next, a belt, which in my nervous state I cinched far too tightly.

Sitting at my dressing table, I rummaged frantically through my hairpins, wishing desperately that Adele had not been called away to attend to a dying sister. If Adele were here, I would know what to do. If Adele were here, I would be calm.

The clock ticked away towards the hour of six, but by the heat in my room, it felt more like noon. On the wall sconce beside my bed, one of the candles had melted to the point of nearly bowing to the floor, as if spent in exhausted defeat.

"I've got to get out of here!" I mumbled through clenched teeth. "I've got to get out of here!"

Then, like the flash of a lightening bolt, a thought seared through my brain.

"Vera!" I said aloud, almost forgetting my guest chaperone. "Oh, my God, Vera."

Scattering my hairpins upon the dresser, I jumped up and ran down the hall towards the bedchamber, where the old woman had been napping since four of the clock.

"Miss Davenport!" I called out, knocking vigorously upon the door. "Miss Davenport, get up! The war—it's started!"

I opened the door to find Vera Davenport sitting up in bed, stunned; her rouged face ridiculous against a riot of false blonde curls.

"War?" she warbled. "Oh, good heavens, Verity! What does it mean?"

"It means war, Miss Davenport. Now, get up!"

Never before had the old woman moved faster. I helped her on with her cumbersome corset, for in bowing to that preening goddess known as vanity, Vera would not go without one. Grunting and groaning, her face now brighter than the powder she plied on it, Vera then struggled to secure her fat, little feet into her too-small shoes.

"Come along!" I urged. "Come along! Sweet Jesus, we haven't got all night!"

Downstairs, we found the Sergeant waiting in the foyer. His face seemed anxious, although I may have been reading into it. Regardless, I grabbed the railing at the sight of him.

"Are we ready, ladies?"

"Law of Moses, yes," I said, reaching for my straw brimmed hat from a peg near the door, and tying the ribbons under my chin none too successfully.

"Where are we going?" Vera quavered, her mouth screwed up as if she were going to cry.

"To the redoubts," I snapped, my hand on the front door. "I thought we'd load some muskets while we sipped our tea."

Opening the door, I ushered the others out ahead of me into the sweltering heat of the night.

∞∞∞∞

I was surprised to see so many people at Merchant Loring's house.

Jimmy Sloan had opened the door to us, a chilled glass of champagne in his hand, and a smile of intoxication on his lips.

"Halloo!" he exclaimed in a singsong voice. "How good of you to come to our little soiree!"

I glared at Jimmy skeptically, as he swung the door wider to reveal what appeared to be a festive party. Why, there were scores of people inside, all talking, laughing, shouting. In the center of the hall, Valentine Hale had ingratiated herself amongst a dashing conflux of officers, while, amidst wild shrieks of hysterical giggling, Lucy was allowing herself to be tackled to the floor by the dynamic Darcy.

"What is going on here?" I asked in disbelief.

"Oh," replied James with a bored, little laugh. "I believe Lucy has snaked an anchovy down Darcy's breeches, or some such place."

"No, I meant with the war," I returned flatly.

"War? Oh, it isn't really war—not yet, anyway. From what I hear, the Rebels are threatening to barge their way back into Boston because they've run out of decent liquor, or some such thing. But if you truly must know what is going on, ask Captain Vale. He's in the formal dining room."

I walked past Jimmy in a huff, nodding vaguely to those I knew, as I made my way through the throng to the back of the house. Somewhere before reaching the dining room, a footman offered me a glass of champagne from a brightly polished tray which he held in his white-gloved hand. I refused, shaking my head. My nerves were far too volcanic to even consider holding a glass just yet.

I found Landon, along with some other officers, standing by the filtering light of the floor-to-ceiling dining room windows, which clearly overlooked the bay. Despite my feverish feeling of dread, I could not help but pause to admire this awe-inspiring room with its walls of rich golden leather, and the sixteenth century tapestries depicting scenes of delicate virgins and magnificent unicorns, which reigned over the great mahogany sideboards at the far ends of the room. The table beneath the glistening chandelier boasted seating for thirty; each chair heavily scrolled and deeply upholstered, balancing on gleaming, majestic lion claws.

"Madam!" Landon smiled, coming forward and taking my hands. "You got here quickly enough."

"Your Sergeant had the sense to scare me into it," I answered, attempting a weak smile in return.

"What is this? What did he say to you?"

"It was what he did not say that frightened me," I confessed, staring out the handsome bank of windows into the seemingly calm lull of twilight. "So Captain, please tell me the truth. What is going on here?"

Landon looked about, and taking my arm through his, he walked me away from the others to a quieter spot where we would not be overheard.

"A few days back, the Connecticut Rebel, Israel Putnam, marched two thousand of his men over to Breed's and Bunker Hills—directly across the river, there. They gave one war whoop, and that was all. We believe this was done because the Rebels got word that General Gage planned to strike on the eighteenth, this Sunday, at Roxbury."

"And does he?"

The Captain glanced over his shoulder before speaking.

"Good heavens, the man should have struck two months ago! He was advised to. We had received word, you see, following the events at Lexington and Concord that the Rebels meant to secure the Charlestown hills. However, the General procrastinated. In truth, Thomas Gage is always putting off 'til tomorrow that which should have been done ages ago."

I said nothing, intent on watching Landon's troubled face. He was confessing to me perhaps more than he should have regarding his General. However, I was proud. It demonstrated that he had trust in me.

"So what does General Gage do instead? He has Johnny Burgoyne pen an idiotic proclamation, that comes off more like a speech Moses might have made against the heathen of Egypt. And for what purpose? It only incensed the Rebels even further."

"Do you blame them?"

"No," Landon replied after a pause. "No, I suppose I cannot, really."

"So what is it they intend to do in Charlestown?"

"Again, Verity, please believe me when I tell you that there is no definite report on the Rebels' activity. True, it was noted by our spies that many meetings have taken place recently at their headquarters in Cambridge. Their men were idle today, which indicates some sense of action is at hand. Also, a great deal of rum has been commissioned for their troops. In other words, it is believed that at some point in the very near future, the provincials will secure fortifications around Breed's and Bunker Hills. This will prevent our easily getting out of Boston through Charlestown and Dorchester."

"And how will the King's army react to this, should it happen?"

"We would propose to occupy the hills before the Rebel Army can act, and be ready to meet them on the high ground."

I took a deep breath, and looked out once more over the tranquil waters of the bay. With its gentle beacon of light, Charlestown seemed so peaceful and serene; yet so unaware of its imminent destruction.

"Perry," I sighed in despair. "Perry will be with them."

"Who is this?"

"A friend. A boy. A young boy who does not deserve to die."

A momentary panic raced through my brain. If Lorena Eldredge had made so bold as to mention any competition for her heart, Captain Vale surely would have recognised the name of Perry Talbot. How insensitive I would be then, to remind him of it.

"You must care for this young man a great deal," Landon said sweetly, and his tone showed not a hint of acknowledgment. Obviously, Lorena had never said a word. Of course, it was not her self-satisfying needs I cared about at that moment. No, it was Perry I was thinking of—Perry and all the other young men who would come to die for this cause they believed in—an endeavour for a freedom they may never live to know.

"What is going to happen now?" I asked instead. "What are we going to do?"

"Nothing much, at the moment. We must wait. General Clinton has his suspicions, and the Rebel camp will be watched. And when the King's troops make their move, tomorrow, you will be able to witness it all from these very windows. It ought to be quite a show."

"Will you be here?"

"Most likely not, Madam. You see, I have been temporarily appointed Clinton's aide."

"Oh, Landon! Do you have to go, too?"

He watched my face for a moment, his eyes searching mine with a strangely anxious intensity that I could not comprehend. But then, a shadow crossed this mood and, as quickly as it had appeared, the keen flicker in his eyes vanished, and a jovial light took its place.

"Could this possibly mean you might miss me?"

"Captain—" I mumbled, staring at the floor.

"A man about to be blown to bits by a stray cannonball needs to know these things."

"Stop teasing me."

"Madam, I am not."

His reply was made so seriously, that it caused me to glance up sharply at his face. I saw no persiflage there; no mocking. Instead, he had the disquieted countenance of a troubled child, and the sight of this went to my heart at once.

The twilight was fading fast, and the room seemed to be choking in night. The feeble glimmer of one solitary candle was not enough to defeat the darkness.

"Oh, Landon," I whispered, my cheeks colouring. "You know I—"

I lifted my eyes to meet his. And for one blissfully sweet instant, we were not surrounded by the anguishes of war. No, for a brief but tender moment, it was a moonlight night from an imaginary spring—a mystical night that erased all the pain of adult realities, and rendered me a young girl again, with a heart so eager for love.

"Vale, my man!" Major Bassett bellowed out from the doorway, causing us to part at once. "Cease your illicit conversations in the shadows, and bring the lady in here for some of this splendiferous champagne. The revelers are commencing to toast me, and I need everyone to hear it. So, come along, then, you two. Come along!"

Slowly, we followed the Major out of the sanctuary of our shadows, and into the harsh, artificial light of the parlours beyond. And it wasn't until I looked back upon the moment, that I realized how tightly we held on to each other's hand.

⚭⚭⚭

The night wore on.

Most of the ladies, as well as those gentlemen not particularly intrigued by battle marches, drills, and redoubts, lounged about the common rooms pacified by huge amounts of port and victuals from the buffet, while discussing their latest theatrical efforts at length. Lucy, for her part, was greatly aghast that David Manley had been chosen above all others to play Lysander.

"The boy is a positive stick," she announced with a lofty lift of her head before draining her glass of champagne in one fell swoop.

"Yes," agreed Diana. "But he is a handsome stick, all the same."

"Still, neither of us shall have a good time of it with the likes of him."

"Have you seen our fairy costumes?" Clemence breathed with great awe. "They are delightfully sheer! Why, mine is this little puff of a thing, with yellow skirts way up to here—" she paused to indicate a spot half way up her thigh—"And Rebecca's is white, with tiny little seams of brown for Moth—"

"Zeus!" Lucy interrupted. "Where is Rebecca, anyway?"

"Who knows?" snapped Clemence, anxious to continue. "As I was saying—now, Val's dress is by far the naughtiest. It's not unlike a little see-through fishing net for her character of Cobweb. But Eve's, I must admit, is indeed the loveliest. For Peaseblossom, she has this darling little green gown with sprigs of lily of the valley all over it."

Samuel Loring, who was seated alongside Eve, placed a gentle hand atop hers, as Eve smiled back in sweet confusion. Nestled at his other side, Virginia viewed this tender scene with a blanket of troubled envy behind her great violet eyes.

"I, for one, find the costumes quite hideous," sniffed Val, as everyone glanced towards Diana stealthily. Val's hurt was easily understood. The role of Helena would have been hers, until Diana selfishly demanded it back.

There was a knock at the front door, and we women glanced about wondering just who it might be. Within moments, Loring's footman came in to announce that a messenger had arrived from the home of Charles Davenport, seeking Marlon Reynolds. He was bade to come home at once.

"His dear little wife must miss him," Samuel exclaimed, clasping his hands together in glee. "So, where is that fortunate boy? Oh, I know! He was terribly engrossed in a battle over the billiards table, when I saw him last. You must search him out there."

"Oh, Stanton," Fiona was breathing in her low, handsome voice. "You've gone and made a glutton of yourself again."

Stanton and Roscoe had just returned from the buffet, their plates piled near to collapse with stewed venison and curried chicken.

"Ah, yes," Stanton responded in his typically slow and drawn-out manner. "But as the Good Book says, Let us eat and drink, for tomorrow we shall die."

"Where is Hector?" Diana sighed in a petulant huff. "I am becoming quite bored."

"He's with the grown-ups in the dining room, playing war," Roscoe replied, attacking his tankard of rum noisily with his slick, greasy lips.

"How very tiresome," Diana said, rising to her feet and straightening out the folds of her delicate white gown. "Well, I'm off. Suthie can stay here all night, if he wants to. However, I have no great desire to sit about in blessed anticipation of the clang of distant pickaxes and shovels."

"Oh, Miss Kirby! May I escort you home?" Jimmy Sloan offered anxiously— almost too anxiously, I believe, for many of us turned and took notice. "After all, the streets may be none too safe."

Diana answered him with little enthusiasm.

"If you wish. I seriously do not care. Now, if someone would be so good as to inform Hector . . ."

"I will let him know," said Samuel, as he walked them to the front door. "Good night, dear Madam. And above all, be careful."

Betsy stood and silently watched as they left. We all ducked our heads, embarrassed for her. The poor woman. How could Jimmy be so blatantly cruel?

"Mrs. Sloan," David Manley began softly, his eyes nervous with intent. "Perhaps you would like to take a stroll in the garden? It's really rather close in here."

"Yes," she answered with a smile, and her warm response surprised me. "Yes, that would be lovely."

Slowly, they walked out towards the garden terrace, the smooth stones of which were bathed in tender moonlight, and the air rendered heavy with the sweet perfume of summer roses.

"Well, well, now. Take a look at that one," Lucy said, and drawing myself and Val closer with a wave of her hand, she went on, her voice barely above the slightest whisper. "I saw that jackanapes Jimmy out with Diana Kirby just last week."

"No!" breathed Valentine in mock horror.

"Yes," Lucy nodded. "They were leaning in the dark alcove at Diana's doorway. Oh, they did not know I was anywhere nearby, or they never would have said or done the highly indecent things I witnessed."

"What? What?" Val hissed.

"Well, Jimmy Sloan was going on and on to Diana how much he loved her—that vain and vaunting piece of work! Anyway, after simpering and mumbling like an idiot for five minutes, our boy Jimmy asks to be invited inside. Miss High and Mighty Kirby then says, 'I don't know, Jimmy. That all depends.' Then the simpleton finally realizes that Diana means to be paid for her efforts, so he produces a fistful of four-pound notes. Well, that puts the gleam in Diana's eyes at last, and she slides her hand over his until all the crisp bills are now wrapped around her fingers. Then she says, 'You may kiss me now, you silly man,' and of course, Jimmy goes at her like a sailor on shore leave. Diana pushes him back a moment and says, 'Don't hurry at it, fool. Spend your money, like your time, wisely. And above all, Jimmy, don't bore me this time.'"

"How terrible," I said, as Val merely laughed, holding her face with her hands, and stomping on the floor with her feet.

"What is so amusing?" Samuel Loring asked, as we all turned with great looks of guilt upon our faces.

"Lucy was just telling us a very humourous tale about a drunken sailor," I lied smoothly.

"I don't think so, dearie," Samuel laughed, followed by everyone else in the room.

"I had a pirate in love with me once," Virginia Stanwood began dreamily, as we all pretended to listen. "I was, perhaps, only thirteen at the time, but I was so very worldly. This pirate risked life and limb to bring me trinkets and treasures from all over the world. My poor father bade him to cease. We were running out of room to store it all, you see."

"Who is she?" Major Bassett grumbled in Orrin Blackwell's ear.

'That's Virginia Stanwood," the merchant replied drolly. "She has survived all the great plagues of Europe, only to become a greater plague herself."

Bassett rolled back his head in laughter, nearly upsetting the entire contents of his champagne glass all over his scarlet coat, just as Captain Vale entered the room hurriedly. He whispered something to the Major, and stood in attention as the Major merely regarded us all with wide eyes.

"Ah," he said at last. "It seems Sir Henry has just issued news that the Rebels have commenced activity on the hills above Charlestown."

Not another word was necessary, as everyone rushed towards the dining room windows, eager for the closest sight of organised warfare they had ever witnessed. Why, it was the moment they had all been secretly waiting for.

"How dark it is," Lucy exclaimed breathlessly, as the distant church bells began to toll twelve, droning ominously in the still, muggy air. "Why, I can't see a thing."

"Did you expect the Rebels to volley a few torches, and send out invitations to their midnight carnival?" laughed Gordon Russell, at her side. "Oh, Lucy! Don't be such a goose."

"It does seem darker, perhaps, because all the homes in Charlestown have been evacuated," offered Samuel Loring, always the diplomat.

"There, you see!" whined Lucy, sticking out her tongue at Gordon, just as an outrageous hiccough rang sharply above the mumbled conversations about the room.

"Who the hell was that?" asked Val, stifling a giggle.

"It's my wife," moaned Bryce, just as Clemence let loose yet another spasmodic and noisy gulp.

Only the officers, and a few of the interested gentlemen, remained behind in the dining room to peer off towards the hills, while the rest rushed Clemence towards the parlour in order that her peculiar gasping sounds did not frighten off the Rebels across the bay. It was then that the most delightful comedy ensued, for each and every person present set about to rid Clemence of her most awkward and unfortunate complaint.

Gordon vowed that sucking on sugar cubes would arrest the problem posthaste. However, the moment Clemence managed to cram her mouth full of the stuff, the very sight of everyone waiting in apt silence only caused the silly girl to burst into gales of giggles, and thus spew the entire contents of her mouth onto a dainty pie crust table at her side.

Samuel Loring voted that Clemence should down a full glass of brandy without pausing for breath. However, this gave her no relief, save perhaps the desire to have another spot of the grand elixir.

Lucy then spoke up with a solution she had witnessed at a social once, where a gentleman was cured of the horrid convulsions by jumping up and down fifty times. Deeming it a neat trick, Clemence enthusiastically began her gymnastics to a count chanted by the company. However, Bryce was forced to halt her early in her numbers, for Clemence was dangerously close to popping out of her low-cut gown.

It was then that Darcy, not announcing his intentions, tiptoed up behind the girl, and screamed loudly enough to frighten Clemence out of her malady. But the end result was that Clemence only sloshed her second glass of brandy all over her pale linen petticoat.

The group was near to admitting defeat when Clemence's mother arrived with an empty wineskin, instructing her daughter to breathe deeply and slowly into it. However, Clemence quickly pronounced it foul smelling, and opted to gulp down another glass of brandy instead. The warm liquor, which tasted faintly of sweet apples, might not have been producing the trick; however, Clemence was definitely feeling less anxious about her calamity.

Captain Vale then stepped up to the task. He bade Clemence to sit, and gently, he pushed her forward from the shoulders, until her head was well below her knees. A few nervous giggles were witnessed about the room, and then, silence—a silence which held long enough to prove that Clemence's hiccoughing fit had indeed vanished.

A loud cheer went round as Clemence slowly sat up. Sporting a vague smile for an instant, Clemence then suddenly turned quite green in the face, before scrambling off to become ill in private.

"Miss Davenport," Loring's footman called out, his stance erect and his jaw stern despite the dubious glint in his eye as he observed Clemence's rather hasty retreat. "Miss Vera Davenport."

"Yes, here." mumbled Vera, her plump face blanching white.

"Your brother, Mister Charles Davenport, has sent the coachman to retrieve yourself and Mrs. Parkhurst. Mistress Celeste, he fears, is not faring well."

A hushed and heavy silence fell upon the room as everyone stared at Loring's impassive footman with questioning stares. What was this? Why, what could it be? Little Celeste, barely married, and now ill? It was then that David Manley entered the room, his face exceedingly troubled. He had just heard from the coachman that Celeste had ingested a rather lethal amount of laudanum.

Celeste was dying. Here we all were, laughing and joking about Clemence's silly and extremely inconsequential hiccoughs, when, just a few streets away,

Celeste Davenport Reynolds lay dying. I sat at once, hugging myself, as a queer, cold feeling of dread overcame me.

"Laudanum?" Lucy echoed, after the women hurriedly left. "Zeus! And here I thought we were the overly dramatic ones!"

"I feel so helpless," I mumbled to no one in particular. "What can be done?"

"Greetings, one and all!" exclaimed Jimmy Sloan, bounding in from the front door with a sickening smile of deceit—a smile which promptly vanished when he encountered the woebegone looks on everyone's faces.

"Why, what is it?" he asked curiously; noticing at once, I suppose, that his wife was not included in the present company.

"The damned Rebels are digging up Charlestown," Roscoe Bennett answered calmly over his perennial tankard of rum. "And Reynolds' pretty little wife is dying."

Jimmy paused, stunned.

"Where is Betsy? Where is my wife?"

"Betsy?" Stanton Parkhurst extolled, looking stupid. "Ah, yes, I remember now. That comely beau ideal, David Manley, proposed a quiet stroll to your ever-patient wife. And she, of course, accepted prettily."

"Where did they go, Mr. Parkhurst? Did they say where they were going?"

Stanton glanced up casually at Jimmy before answering.

"To the garden of the Hesperides, I believe, in order to savour the golden apples."

"I'm—I'm going to look for them," Jimmy stammered, turning himself clumsily about and heading for the door. And when he was gone, the two rotund men regarded one another with somber looks.

"Such a disgruntled cuckold," Stanton said with a weary shake of his head.

"Perhaps he has not heard that imitation is one of the most revengeful forms of flattery," remarked Roscoe, his watery eyes affixed on nothing at all.

My nerves, however, were on edge. I had to leave this room, and all the foolish people within it. Yes, I had to leave, and go to Celeste. No, I did not know her any better than the rest of this company, but somehow I felt I could help her. She was so young, so helpless, and so unhappy. This I had known from the start.

I located the Captain at once, and confessed my headstrong plan. Landon was on his way to headquarters, however he agreed to escort me to Davenport's door. I took his arm gratefully, and we strode out into the bedewed darkness of night, our shadows looming large before us in the sparse light of the silent and waning moon.

From the street below, we could hear Celeste's anguished screams.

Landon took his leave as soon as the door was opened to us by Stearns. Poor Stearns. His face was wracked with worry. It seems he was human after all.

"What's the word, Stearns?" I asked quietly.

"Not good, Madam. Miss Celeste—I mean to say, Mrs. Reynolds, is not . . . cannot . . . We are much distressed, Madam."

"Is a doctor with her?" I questioned, and Stearns nodded. "Fine. I would like to see Mrs. Reynolds a moment, if I may. That is, should Mr. Davenport permit it, of course."

"Mr. Davenport is in the west parlour with his sister, Madam. I will bring you directly."

I remember entering the foyer and finding it brightly lit with a legion of candles; yet all the adjoining rooms lay in mournful darkness, appearing like mystical caves leading to nowhere.

From the silent domain of the west parlour, the light of a single candle quivered and danced in fiery torment. I walked slowly towards Charles and paused, frightened by the sight of his empty gaze.

"She is not—" I stammered. "Oh, she can't be—"

"She's delirious," Charles whispered. "My poor baby girl does not even know who I am."

Vera, who had been cowering in her chair, began to sob aloud, while Marlon Reynolds sat quite apart from the others, his eyes burning with an odd, cold fear. However, it was Charles who surprised me the most. Charles Davenport, the master of all he chose to control, seemed at this very moment to be no more than the crusting shell of a little old man who has found himself powerless; just when he needed power the most.

"I'm going up to see Miss Celeste," I said quietly. I decided not to ask permission. There was not a rational person in that room who could grant it to me.

I walked out of the parlour, the heels of my shoes echoing dully on the cool, white marble floor. Lifting my head, I glanced about the empty and overbright foyer. How barren it was, yet somehow deceptively alive with all those candles. The room had the appearance of a stage setting, silently awaiting the arrival of the players.

Feeling like I had not one ounce of strength left in my body, I grasped at the heavy mahogany stair rail as though it were a lifeline, and propelled myself up the wide and seemingly endless staircase. Far above my head, a fresco of angels laughed down at me; a painted border about their delicate wings, which prophetically read: "All that lives must die, passing through nature to eternity."

The door to Celeste's room was closed. I knocked, and as the door was opened to me, a waft of stale, damp sweat assaulted my nostrils.

"Come in, Mrs. Lynford," Fiona Parkhurst whispered, looking up at me from where she sat on the edge of Celeste's bed. Then turning her gaze, Fiona took her niece's hand, and spoke to the seemingly unconscious girl in a bright but artificial tone.

"Celeste, dear. Look who is here. Your dear friend, Verity Lynford."

However, Celeste made no response. Mournfully stretched out on her rumpled, water-splotched bed, the poor girl was completely unrecognisable. There were dark, heavy circles about her eyes, and her lips were crusted white with dryness. It was as if her once lovely face had shrunken somehow. And her small hands were gnarled and twisted, as if from some internal pain. Every few moments, she would grasp at the bed sheets, mumbling something we could not understand in a faint and tortured voice.

"Oh, dear God," I muttered, as the doctor, a slender, dark-eyed gentleman in his early thirties, glanced pointedly at me and shook his head.

"Despite appearances, Mrs. Reynolds can hear every word that is said," he whispered in a kind but cautionary tone.

"What is to be done, Doctor?" I asked, watching as Fiona folded a cold, damp cloth, and placed it gently over Celeste's feverish brow. "Mrs. Reynolds will pull through this, won't she?"

"Mrs. Reynolds has, in actuality, not ingested an overly dangerous amount of the poison. And, if she did not fight our attempts to keep her alert and walking, Mrs. Reynolds would have easily passed through the crisis by now. However, that is not what troubles me."

I looked at the doctor quizzically.

"Mrs. Reynolds has continuously called out things of a highly personal nature, which leads me only to the sorry conclusion that this poor young woman will, in any event, force her own demise."

"If I might ask, what was Miss Celeste saying?"

Fiona quietly provided the answer.

"Doctor Olney has told me that my niece repeatedly asks for a person named Perry. She claims, quite emphatically, that she cannot live without him."

My face paled instantly. The doctor, therefore, had no problem in noticing the flash of recognition upon my face.

"I take it, Madam, that you know this person of whom Mrs. Reynolds speaks."

"Yes," I answered slowly, glancing from the doctor to Mrs. Parkhurst. "Perhaps . . . But how can it be? How would Mrs. Reynolds be acquainted with Perry Talbot?"

"Talbot! Indeed that is the young man, for she spoke his whole name," Fiona replied.

"I do not understand it," I went on, as if thinking aloud. "Perry Talbot? But how? You see, he is a blacksmith. I met him through—friends. But as to how Miss Celeste has come to know him, I cannot even begin to guess."

"She is in love with him," Fiona whispered, pressing the cloth to Celeste's forehead. "Of that, we are certain."

"Oh," I said, attempting to disguise my troubled mood. In love with Perry? Oh, good Lord, how could this have happened? And did Perry love Celeste in return? To have the beautiful Lorena Eldredge so easily shaken from Perry's heart did not seem possible. And if it were so, why had he not told me? Of course, when we were together in Concord, there were far more important things to discuss, such as impending war. However, in some madness of fate, this girl now claimed Perry Talbot to be the sole possessor of her love. It was all too bewildering to comprehend.

I walked across the room like a sleepwalker, and sat by the open window, leaning my head wearily against the sash. There was such a strange silence without, and not a single, solitary, cooling breeze. The delicate curtains had not so much as shimmered an inch.

"My poor little lamb," Fiona cooed, resting Celeste's lifeless hand against the side of her face. "Only the young believe it is necessary to love in order to live."

The room fell to silence. Only the clock on the mantle could be heard against the unsettling stillness of the night.

☙ ☙ ☙

My face nearly buried in the stiff white curtains, I was startled suddenly by a dull, echoing explosion which rattled the very glass over my head.

"What was that?" I stammered, unaware at that moment that I had fallen asleep, as I focused my blurry eyes on the doctor and Mrs. Parkhurst.

"Most likely there has been activity in the bay," the doctor replied as he stood over Celeste, his expression furrowed with concern.

"Oh, dear God," I breathed, jumping up quickly from my cramped position at the window. "What time is it?"

"Going on five, I believe," the doctor replied.

I pushed aside the curtains, and peered out into the strange half light of day. Five in the morning! My dress felt heavy and damp, and my face was oily and slick with sweat.

A subtle knock sounded at the door. It was Stearns, and he had brought a tray of tea things. Beside him stood Betsy Sloan.

"Mister Charles thought you might need this," Stearns said softly, casting a solemn glance towards the fretful Celeste. "How is my young mistress faring?"

"Her spells of delirium should subside soon enough. You can inform her father of that."

"Very good, sir."

Betsy stepped forward and began to pour the tea. Stearns was commencing to take his leave just as Celeste clenched her tiny fists and rolled her head from side to side in desperate anguish.

"Perry," she moaned through parched, dried lips. "I want Perry . . ."

"That will be all, my man," said Dr. Olney, closing the door before Stearns' startled face.

"Yes, my beloved," Celeste murmured, relaxing her tensed hands and smiling suddenly, like a sweet, seraphic angel. "We will go to Charleston in the spring . . ."

Charleston. Then Celeste was at least acquainted with Perry, for he had mentioned having a wealthy uncle residing in Charleston who possessed a rather magnificent rice plantation. Perry had thought to impress Lorena with the possibility of moving to Charleston and assisting his uncle with the management of the place. Perry's uncle had no sons, so perhaps one day . . .

"My darling, Perry . . . you promised . . ." Celeste whimpered.

I walked towards the bed slowly, wincing at Celeste's heart-wrenching words, while outside the window, another ominous rumble of cannon fire crackled through the air.

"Oh, Perry," Celeste sighed. "Come in from the storm. My father is not here. He will not know."

There came a knock on the door. This time it was Charles. Fiona quickly took Celeste's hand in a binding grasp, and tenderly whispered to her to hush.

"Stearns says my daughter—"

"Should come through, I believe," Dr. Olney answered gruffly. "But we must not be disturbed."

"I see," said Charles, wearily. He appeared to be twenty years older than when I last saw him. "I just wanted my little girl to know that all her friends are downstairs, waiting to hear that she is quite well, and fully recovered."

"Who is here?" asked Fiona, looking up sharply.

"Miss Wellman, and Miss Hale—as well as your daughter, and Bryce. Oh, but Darcy has been holding vigil the longest. Young David Manley is transporting the battle news to and from Merchant Loring's. The cannonade has just started, as you've probably heard, and our men are firing on the Rebels from the bay."

"Yes, my love, in the spring," Celeste murmured, and Fiona pretended to wipe Celeste's mouth in an attempt to muffle her dangerous words.

"What is my poor girl saying?"

"It is only the delirium produced by dreams," the doctor answered evenly. "And now, Mr. Davenport, I must ask that you leave. There is work to be done."

"Yes, yes—of course," Charles sighed, closing the heavy door quietly behind him.

CASCASCAS

I believed I would never survive the morning.

With each quarter hour, the temperature seemed to rise with such leaps and bounds that by noon, Celeste's flouncy and frilly white bedroom was a sweltering inferno. I remember closing the venetian blinds against the dazing sun; causing the room to be thrown into a stuffy, shadowy gloom. The only light to be had in the stifling, damp chamber came from the chinks and gaps in the blinds which bored like hot pin holes onto the shining floorboards beneath.

Celeste faded in and out of consciousness. Sometimes she sobbed gently, and at other times, she screamed. Most of her words were unintelligible now, as she spasmodically wrenched her body encased in its clinging, sweat sodden nightdress.

Fiona and I had perched ourselves on either side of the rumpled bed, trying to lift Celeste to a standing position whenever she wrestled herself about. The doctor suggested that walking Celeste would assist her body in pushing through the remaining effects of the laudanum, as well as calm her. He was, by this time, terribly concerned by her frantic behaviour. However, Celeste fought us at every turn, crying out for Perry, and promising to meet him by the wharf at midnight. I was astonished at her feverish strength, for my knuckles were cramped and tender from contact with Celeste's clawing stronghold.

News came upstairs to us about the war. Every twenty minutes or so, a solemn knock would sound on the door, and Betsy would venture outside to hear from David Manley what was happening. English warships were firing. Then, the cannon ceased momentarily, only to start up with even more fury from the four British transports with their numerous guns. It was such a sight, David said, to see the cannonballs blazing through the air, and churning up great clumps of tall grass in the meadows across the bay. The regulars were now staging a direct assault against the Rebels' poorly constructed fortress atop the Charlestown hill. It was said that the foolish provincials had neglected to cut holes for their artillery. And the rear of their line seemed sadly defended. Sir Henry Clinton had noted all of this, and was now urging that his men march along the Mystic River, and force an attack on the Rebels from there. But a frontal assault would instead prove the profound bravery of the King's troops, and so it was decided.

I did not wish to hear anymore. The oppressive warmth, and the rank smell of sweat nearly overwhelmed me. I was glad my stomach was empty, for it certainly would have revolted under the stress and strain, and the putrid air in that room.

The pendulum clock ticked on, sometimes in rhythm with Celeste's nervous breathing, and sometimes so slowly, I thought the heat had rendered it powerless against time. It was after two in the afternoon when Betsy returned with grave news. Charlestown was in flames. General Gage wanted to prevent the Rebel army from hiding out in the town's deserted homes and buildings, picking off his soldiers with musket shot, as they had done on the return from Lexington and Concord. Heated cannonballs and "carcasses," hollow shells filled with burning pitch, had been hurled onto rooftops and lawns. And now, the once elegant Charlestown was burning like the rages of hell.

"Charleston . . . in the spring . . . Perry!" Celeste called out with a mournful wail, as Doctor Olney moved swiftly about her. Wiping the sweat from his forehead with the sleeve of his elegant, frilled shirt, the tireless doctor now assisted me in raising Celeste to her feet. The laudanum, he sensed, had worn off completely. We got her to a sitting position, and as we did so, Celeste's pale face fell on my shoulder, and her long, perspiration-sodden hair dragged across my face.

"Celeste," I whispered. "Celeste, pull through this, and I will bring you to Perry Talbot. I promise you."

Celeste began fighting us and babbling incoherently again. It was as if she were standing alongside Perry in Charlestown. Of course, her images stemmed from all that Betsy had been relating to us. However, in Celeste's deranged mind, the entire holocaust was occurring right before her eyes. She shouted to Perry to escape the flames. She pleaded to him through hysterical tears to run, to hide, to do anything to avoid being hurt. Otherwise, she sobbed, they would not be together in the spring. If he were to die, she did not wish to live. It was maddening—the heat, the stench, the pain—and every time Celeste screamed, I was frightfully tempted to do the same.

Betsy then appeared with news that the official attack had begun. From Merchant Loring's window, David had watched with the others as, across the bay, the regulars swarmed the hill like little red ants in the distance. Higher and higher they climbed; higher and higher against a hellish horizon of flame. They appeared invincible. But then, provincial marksmen hiding behind rail fences began systematically gunning them down as if they were merely standing targets. Soon, the beach was thick with British dead, the waves lapping red with their blood.

Despite my dull, aching desire to sleep, my mind raced with a confusion of flashing images. Charlestown was in flames. Perhaps now those flames were spreading wildly towards other unsuspecting towns and outlying stretches of woods and fields. At least Boston would be safe, hemmed in by water. Fighting. There was fighting. Exhausted men were struggling under this fierce, hot sun for something they called freedom. And Landon. Perhaps Landon was out there somewhere in this ungodly heat, facing death. Or maybe he was already dead; lying mournfully still on a sun-parched shoreline, his tender, beautiful face covered with cold, wet sand.

"Oh, hurry!" I cried aloud, not caring what the others thought. With a sympathetic look of concern, Betsy gently removed me from my place at Celeste's bed, and quietly took over my chore.

"Perry—" the girl murmured feverishly. "You must bring me to Perry . . ."

"Might Mr. Talbot be downstairs with the other visitors?" Fiona whispered to me.

"Perry Talbot?" I replied with a tense little laugh. "Perry Talbot would never set foot in a house like this."

Oh, why did I say that? Why was I so needlessly cruel? I walked towards the shuttered window, every muscle in my body trembling with fatigue. Pulling my sweat-drenched skirts away from my legs, I knelt at the windowsill and buried my face in my hands with a weary sob, trying in vain to drown out the doctor's countless instructions, and Celeste's insistent cries for a young boy who was probably out there in a pit with countless dead. What sense did it make? It was madness; all of it.

"Oh, dear Father in Heaven," I prayed silently in a frantic blur. "Please bring Celeste through this, and Perry, and Landon—"

I paused suddenly, as a startling cold wave of loneliness overwhelmed me. No, God was not going to listen to me. Not now. Not on this staggering day of prayer. There were so many wives and mothers and daughters with needs more important than mine. But did they have to be? Landon Vale was my truest and dearest friend. I loved him as I would a brother. Could I not care as well? Could I not bow my head in hopes that this singular man, my friend, could somehow have the hand of the Almighty hover over him, too? Or was he just to end up slaughtered under a brutal and merciless sun, because it was God's will? Suddenly, at that profound moment, I had a great difficulty understanding the fairness of it all.

"Come here, Mrs. Lynford!" the doctor shouted. "Come over here right away!"

Scurrying to the bed, I took Betsy's place at Celeste's side. And as I did so, my knee brushed up against a crumpled piece of paper beneath the pillow. Perry's name was signed to it. Stealthily, I pushed the note off the bed. It landed by my foot.

"Did you mean what you said?" Celeste murmured. "Will you bring me to him? Will you bring me to Perry?"

"Yes," I answered firmly. "Yes, you know I will."

Celeste sighed, and fell asleep.

"The crisis is over," the doctor said gently. "And now, I shall go and speak with her father."

"What are you going to tell him?" Fiona asked cautiously.

"Only what I have to," he replied, and we women knew at once that Celeste's secret was safe within the confines of this now silent room.

"Thank you—Sir," I mumbled skyward. "Wherever you are."

∽∾∽∾∽

Betsy, being the only one with any vivacity, rushed downstairs to share the news of Celeste's recovery with the others. As Fiona was well-occupied with watching over her niece, I took myself quietly over towards the window, where I read Perry's letter against the vague passages of stifling hot light.

Miss Davenport,

I wish only to inform you that I have left Boston, and joined the fight for independence. This is for the sake of my future happiness. May you always be content in the life you have chosen.

Perry Talbot

"How strange," I thought, returning the letter to its place under Celeste's pillow when Fiona's back was turned. Then the door opened, and Betsy appeared, her face dour and troubled.

"Verity, Sergeant Stone is here to see you. It's important."

I lifted my head and stared at Betsy for a dark, frightened moment. But then, a sudden sense of calm came over me, rendering my mind unable to whirl its vicious thoughts all about, and I walked resolutely towards the door.

It was cooler in the hall. I closed the door to Celeste's room behind me, and breathed in the fresh, clean air gratefully, before moving oh so very slowly towards the stairs.

Sergeant Stone was standing in the foyer below. He was alone. But I knew the others were watching from the west parlour. People always possess a morbid fascination for the pain and suffering of others.

Down the steps I went, one at a time, my sweaty hand sliding on the banister beside me. With every motion of descent, the air seemed less heavy; less oppressive. Keeping my eyes on the Sergeant, I managed a vague, weak smile. He did not smile back. I hardly expected that he would. How dark and tired his eyes were. And how very solemn he seemed.

I paused near the last step. I could not move another inch until I knew.

"It's the Captain, isn't it?" I asked in a voice that spoke with deathlike composure.

The Sergeant nodded. And the sorry look on his wearied face was the last thing I remembered, before the air went black about my eyes, and my mind screamed out in pain.

Drink to me only with thine eyes,
And I will pledge with mine . . .

Ben Jonson—*To Celia*

SUMMER, 1775

☙

WAS SEATED at the side of a very still lake. My dress was unfamiliar to me. It was a gown of some light material—a silken gauze, perhaps—and it glowed with the radiance of the sun. The air around me was delightfully cool, and yet this charming effect was accomplished without the slightest hint of a breeze. The leaves on the statuesque trees hovered with nary a rustle. How at peace I felt. I had not known tranquility like this for months; perhaps never.

Then, I heard Landon calling to me from the other side of the lake. I could not see him, and his voice possessed an unearthly reflection to it. However, I knew it was his voice, and that he was calling to me from a great distance away. I became instantly troubled.

I attempted to stand, but could not. I leaned forward and touched the water. It had a strange resistance to it, as though it were a lake of tufted cotton. In my frustration, I called to Landon to please wait for me; that I would try once again to come to him. Not surprisingly, my own voice reverberated like an echo from the depths of an ominous cave.

Then I could hear Adele calling to me from somewhere above. I looked to the trees, and I peered towards the cloudless sky, but I could not find her. Suddenly, all that was around me filtered gray, like the coming of a rampant storm. I tried with all my might to stand again, but was not able. Completely defeated, I began to cry.

"Madam," I heard. "Madam, please open your eyes."

I attempted to do as the voice asked of me, but my eyelids were so very heavy. Then, I found myself blinking a few times; and at last, I opened my eyes to see Adele's wonderful, sagging, old face above my own. I must have been dreaming, I suppose. However, it all seemed so real.

"Madam," Adele smiled, as tears formed at the corners of her great, sad eyes. "Madam, we were all so concerned. But at last, you are back."

"Adele," I whispered, and my throat was so very dry. "Oh, what a terrible and strange dream I had. At least, I think it was a dream."

I glanced slowly about the safe haven of my room.

"Yes, I imagine it was a dream, because for one frantic moment, I believed I had died."

"Died, Madam? Heavens, no. However, you fainted at Mr. Davenport's, and struck your head on the stairs. Mr. Davenport was nearly beside himself; especially with all that happened to Miss Celeste. And poor Sergeant Stone. Ah, he blames himself, you see—"

And then I remembered the reason why I had fainted, and the tears now flowed freely down my face.

"Oh, Adele," I managed to whisper through my pain. "It would have been better if I had died. Better indeed, for my Landon is gone."

"Madam," Adele began, taking my hand in hers at once, and stroking the hair from my face with the other. "You do not know. You had no way of knowing. The Captain is not dead."

"Not dead?" I echoed, my heart commencing to pound away loudly in my chest. "Not dead? How can that be?"

"Sergeant Stone told us that when he went to see you at the Davenports', you knew somehow that Captain Vale was the reason for his mission. It shocked him, you must understand; and for a moment, he could say nothing. However, what you did not know was that the Captain was merely wounded."

"Wounded?" I exclaimed, sitting bolt upright. I meant to get out of my bed at once, but curious dark spots were dancing madly before my eyes, making me dizzy. "How badly? Where is he?"

"You must lie down, Madam," Adele returned quickly. "Perhaps you cannot realize it, but you fainted nearly a day and a half ago. You are weak."

"I do not care about myself, Adele. I want to know about the Captain!"

"He is here, Madam; asleep in his own room. But he waited outside your door for the longest time on the evening of your accident. The doctor was so angry with him. However, the Captain refused to leave your door until he knew you were all right."

"He did?" I ventured meekly.

"Yes. The poor man had not slept in over a day, due to the horrid battle. He was wounded when a musketball creased his head. In all the confusion, Sergeant Stone was led to believe that he was mortally wounded. But he is not. As I said, he waited just outside your door for hours. Sergeant Stone was here, too. We were all insisting that the Captain rest. The poor Sergeant was suffering such guilt over it all. Regardless, it was not until this morning that Captain Vale finally took to his bed."

"I must see him," I said, standing slowly. The blurry waves of darkness were still plaguing my vision. And I realized how empty my stomach was. But I seriously did not care. I had to see Landon. I had to know for myself that he was really and truly alive. I moved cautiously across my room towards my wardrobe, clutching at tables and chairs along the way for support.

"Yes, Adele, I will see him. Send Beals to the Captain's room at once. Have Beals prepare the Captain that I am coming to see him; that I must see him. Do you understand?"

Although her expression was anxious, Adele merely nodded, and went about her errand. While she was in search of Beals, I found a suitable dressing gown to wear. I went to the looking glass in order to fix my hair, but then abandoned the project. I did not wish to wait any longer.

Adele returned. She insisted on brushing my hair for me, and she pulled it back with a ribbon. I did not want her to fuss anymore. I needed Landon. I grabbed her hand in thanks and went to the door.

"There's just one thing I thought you should know, Madam. We sent a courier to Mr. Lynford, to inform him of your unfortunate accident. Captain Vale arranged for it, you see. We are expecting Mr. Lynford at any time."

I thanked Adele, and closed the door. Then I went down the hall, my arms hugging my sides as my heart pounded wildly in my chest. Yes, I could hear Beals in the Captain's room. But I could not wait. I knocked on the door, and told Landon that I was there to see him. He bade me to come in at once, which I did. I surprised even myself by going straight to Landon's bed and throwing my arms about him. We laughed, and we nearly cried, and I think I even kissed him on the cheek, but I cannot truly recall it.

What I do remember is the apoplectic look on Beals' face. I believe it was the most emotion the poor old man had ever displayed in all his many days. I also recall vowing to Landon that I was going to restore him to health, and then look after his well-being from this moment through forever and a day. He took my hands, smiling, and shyly agreed. I do not believe any woman had ever fawned over him so; perhaps not even his own dear mother. And no, I had not given a single thought to Lorena's future place in his life when I made my promise. I imagine I should have, but at that moment, we were the only two people in a very joyous world.

Adele came into the room and insisted that I go back to my own bed for rest. I obeyed her. I was too happy to argue.

Somewhere around six in the evening, you came home, Jeffrey. You displayed tender and true concern for my mishap, but then you turned around and journeyed back to Concord within a day or two. Your actions only went a step further in proving to me just how far apart we sadly had grown.

For the next ten days, I hovered over the Captain like a nervous mother hen. I made sure he took all his meals, and prepared most of them myself. We ventured out for an occasional walk in the warmth of the day, but for the most part, we stayed inside and read or conversed. And despite the daily threat of continued war, we were most content.

Miss Eldredge came by to see the Captain every day, initially. During these visits, I would excuse myself from the room, in order to give them privacy. However, by Lorena's third afternoon call, they both pleaded with me to stay with them. I remember that occasion quite well. Landon spoke, at last, of the day on Breed's Hill. I had brought my embroidery with me, so that Lorena would sense that I did not consider myself an equal to their company. However, within moments, Landon's words took over my every sense.

He spoke at first of the naval attack on Charlestown. Like so many others, Landon had watched with awe, as the gallant array of British warships fired upon the slipshod fortress across the scant third mile of water that separated Boston from the fighting provincials. It was a sight, he told us, that gave one tremendous pause—a sight that truly defined the twisted splendour and overwhelming wonder that is war. Over fifteen-hundred infantrymen were set upon Charlestown land—a boggy meadow, really, with sea grass grown to an average man's waist, and filled with sinkholes and stones. It was when the troops began to traverse the fence rails that the provincials returned strong fire. General Howe was not hit, but Landon recalled seeing him surrounded by scores of wounded and dead. The troops' return of fire was reckless and ill-planned—most of the rounds sailed over the provincials' heads.

In the horrid confusion, the King's wounded were being ferried back to Boston. But there were so many. Cries of agony rose from the tall grass everywhere, and it was suggested by Howe's remaining officers that he not attack again. Brigadier General Pigot's line was completely collapsed. But Howe pushed on a second time, and a third. Howe was, by this time, practically without aides or staff, and at last he ordered that his men could remove their ponderous packs. The powder smoke hovered low, but the sun was strong and high; the heat overbearing. At last, the troops broke through the provincial's stronghold. That hastily dug redoubt had quickly become a pit of death. There was only one exit, and the provincials were scrambling through the dust and black smoke to find it. Landon spoke of the cries of death, and I could hear them too. It was a brave fight on both sides, he confessed, however, the cost of lives—or, "the butcher's bill" as Landon had termed it—was too dear.

And then he ceased to speak. There was more to say, I am sure, but I imagine Landon felt that as ladies, we had heard enough. He finished his story, and I remember ducking my head in order that my tears would not disturb him.

Miss Eldredge, however, was not similarly effected. Whether it was because she sensed a lull in conversation or not, Lorena chirped on with great enthusiasm about the romantic friendships forming between her female friends and the soldiery. It was mildly amusing, I suppose, to witness so young an opinion on the subject of love. But the truth be known, I doubted that Landon heard a single word that she said.

By the fifth day, Lorena did not call again.

No man loveth his fetters, be they made of gold.

John Heywood—*Proverbs*

∽

30 JUNE, 1775
CAMP AT CAMBRIDGE, MASSACHUSETTS

SHADED MY EYES against the brutal rays of the sun, and peered across the vast and crowded field in despair.

"Excuse me, sir," I said, halting a passing soldier who reeked badly of dried sweat and rum. "I need to find—my brother."

"What's his company?" the man snarled between the dark, toothless gaps in his mouth.

"Company?" I asked, dumbfounded. "Why, I do not know."

"Where's he from?"

"Do you mean originally?"

"No, lady—now," the gruff man sighed, a great deal short on patience.

"Boston," I supplied with a nervous smile. "My brother, Perry Talbot, is from Boston."

He raised one arm, the sleeve of which lay in near tatters about his shoulder, elbow, and wrist, and pointed vaguely off to his right.

"Try over there—over there by those fool, hoity-toity tents belonging to those wretched Rhode Islanders."

With that, he turned his head and spit something foul. Wrinkling my nose in poorly concealed disgust, I daintily picked up my rose-coloured petticoat, and hopped over a puddle I prayed consisted merely of rain.

Glancing about, I easily located what the crusty old man had referred to as "hoity-toity" tents. How splendid they were—done in the proper English style, I suppose, and standing at odd variance with the myriad of diverse structures set up all around them in the cluttered field. Some tents were made of sailcloth, while others were built precariously of stone and loose board. In addition, not too far off, there were a few structures made of such a strange conglomeration of materials, I was afraid to inspect them on a closer basis and witness just what went into their making.

Some tents were set up like permanent homes, with windows and doors done up with decorative wreaths and withes. Others were thrown together so hastily, I secretly wondered if these imitation lean-tos would indeed stand up to anything more vigorous than a sweltering summer breeze.

Everywhere around me, soldiers lolled about, laughing, drinking, sleeping in the sun. None of these men appeared to be attired in any distinctive uniform. Therefore, it was difficult to distinguish one company from another. Besides, what many of these men wore seemed to be rotting on their backs from lack of washing.

"Perry!" I cried out, spotting him over by a stack of barrels, writing something in a ledger book. "Perry Talbot, at last!"

At the sound of my voice, Perry turned his handsome young head incredulously in my direction. Almost at once, he handed over his journal to a nearby comrade and unashamedly ran towards me, giving me a warm and friendly embrace.

"Have caution, Perry," I laughed. "For I told one man you were my brother. We must therefore keep it believable."

"How good of you to come all this way to see me," he murmured, smiling. "At least I hope it was me you came to see. Regardless, come meet my new friends."

Perry brought me over and promptly introduced me to his three companions. Timothy Straw was a tall, lanky youth from New Hampshire. He and his contingent had been camped in Cambridge ever since the twenty-first of April, when they had marched a full fifty-five miles in eighteen hours, following the news of Lexington and Concord. Standing beside him, dark-eyed and silent, was Enoch Webster of Falmouth. Enoch descended from a long line of sea captains, Perry explained, and now longed to be in the navy; if only one were planned. The third boy, Benjamin Hall, was a gentle-faced lad with the kindest eyes I had ever seen.

"Well, gentlemen," I began with a cheery grin. "You know, we folk in Boston are so very proud of you all. Why, we speak of nothing else."

It was not true—not in my particular set, anyway—but I felt the lie harmed no one. Besides, I was troubled by a vision burning in my brain of any one of these fine boys, if not all four of them, lying in a moldy ditch somewhere, silenced by death.

Nearby, a group of high-spirited men were gathered about a campfire, roasting a plump, savoury chicken over the bright, orange flames, as one man sang in a pleasant, if not nasal voice:

Father and I went down to camp,
Along with Captain Gooding,
There we see the men and boys
As thick as hasty pudding.

Yankee doodle, keep it up,
Yankee doodle, dandy;
Mind the music and the step,
And with the girls be handy . . .

"It sounds familiar," I said. "What is it?"

"It's the old English nursery rhyme, turned into a march tune. But we've stolen it now. Why, we're even having a broadside printed up next month."

"Perry," I whispered, once polite conversation had run thin. "Might I speak privately with you for a few minutes? I really haven't much time."

"Oh, of course," Perry replied, dismissing the others at once, as I watched on with a smile of curious surprise.

"Perry, they called you 'sir'!"

"Well, my dear friend, I am a Quartermaster Sergeant."

"No! Really?"

"Yes," he returned with bashful pride. "However, I suspect the only reason they made me one is because I can read and write."

I glanced about for a quiet minute, watching as a small group of men washed clothes by the river's edge, slapping their laundry against the rocks in order to dry it. Over in a distant part of the field, two men were wrestling each other to the ground, as several onlookers shouted and chanted for the opponent of their choice, while, not too far from where we stood, two men were having a terrible harangue over whose army fought better—the Virginians, or, as one of the men put it, "that drunken, filthy, canting mob from Massachusetts."

"Oh, Perry," I sighed. "This is a horrid place."

He paused a moment, observing my troubled face.

"Why, I've rather come to like it."

I turned and looked at him through disbelieving eyes.

"No, it's true," he laughed. "Things may seem a little haphazard to you, right now. We've got men here from several colonies, so there's bound to be some rivalries and what not. And without women around, well, we've all gotten a bit lazy about things . . . Speaking of which, I should warn you about something. The soldiers tend to bathe naked in the Charles River, by the bridge. So, I would avoid that area if I were you, Mrs. Lynford."

"Having witnessed you in my father's tub, Perry Talbot, I can honestly say

I am somewhat prepared for such a spectacle."

Perry ducked his head and chuckled.

"Aside from our current distresses, things are going well. Why, Congress has advised us to set up a temporary government, and they've voted in a Commander in Chief. Rumour had it for the longest time that John Hancock was to receive the title. But I guess the southerners won, and a certain Colonel of theirs, named George Washington, got the honours."

I made a "how very nice" face, as Perry continued proudly, "And I'm in charge of taking inventories of supplies. The neighbouring towns have been truly good and kind to us, Mrs. Lynford. Every day, wagonloads of food, cider, rum, and other needed provisions come rolling in. Why, just look at it all!"

I peered about the piles with a jovial shrug.

"All I see here is rum, Perry."

"But the men like rum, dearest *sister*."

"Do you suppose, Perry Talbot, our future generations will be instructed that their forefathers' dreams of independence were nurtured on endless quantities of rum?"

"I suppose you could be right," he said, and then remembering something, "Oh, Mrs. Lynford. Even your father sent us some supplies. Look—see that fine hay over there?"

"Did he really? Oh, Perry, were you able to speak with him?"

"Yes, as a matter of fact, I did. Everyone is well, he insists, and coping. The inn is busier than ever, it seems. Your father looks wonderful, you should know. He's been happily at work in his fields, raising crops for the army. Your sister is home from Philadelphia, and quite changed, so your father says. He's left it up to Beulah to set her straight. And as for your great-grandmother, well, all is normal on that score. She seems to be running the inn operation with tireless self-possession."

"I miss them so," I confessed sadly.

"Yes, that reminds me! Your father mentioned the desire to send a letter off to you. However, he is concerned with the fact that all correspondence is getting intercepted at Boston Neck. I then suggested that he write to you through the attention of Captain Vale. Was I right in doing that? I only hope I have not made too forward an implication."

I blushed and shook my head. Oh, why did I have to blush? In an instant, Perry was kneeling at my side.

"No, you did right in suggesting so. In fact, it was Captain Vale who secured me a pass to come here and see you today."

"You didn't come here alone, did you?"

"No, there are—others with me."

"That is good, Mrs. Lynford. For otherwise, I would have real cause to fret. Now tell me, please, how are things in Boston?"

"Well, Jeffrey is producing a play with Charles Davenport. It is Shakespeare's *A Midsummer Night's Dream*, and I am understudying the role of Titania."

"What does 'understudying' mean?"

"I only go on stage if Mrs. Stanwood becomes ill, or some such thing."

"Guessing at actresses' egos, that seems highly unlikely. And I suppose you'll be performing for the King's officers?"

"Who else is there in town?" I responded with innocent guile.

"Oh, all right then. I imagine I can try to live up to the fact that while I huddle alone in my tent, and eat meager rations of rice, my beloved and dear *sister* shall dine on veal and drink champagne with the King's own Generals."

Seeing that Perry was laughing, I smiled and took both his hands within my own.

"They are such little men, you know," I confessed with a wicked giggle. "Oh, they present themselves fairly high and mighty. However, beneath their grand uniforms and polished gold trimmings, they truly are lowly fools. General William Howe, 'Gentleman Johnny Burgoyne,' and Sir Henry Clinton—what a trio of dogs. Yes, dogs you see, for everyone remarks on how these three generals arrived last May, aboard the Cerebus. And Cerebus, in Greek mythology, is the three-headed dog who guards the gates to Hades. How fitting, do you not agree?"

"Very."

"It's a mammoth task just to find respect for them. Burgoyne is a playwright, you understand, and he talks like one. It's all adjectives with him, and so far, no objectives. William Howe is a self-adoring peacock with very bad teeth, and Sir Henry is nothing more than a scowling, little squab with not an ounce of brains. How these three are to win a war is beyond me."

"What about dawdling Tommy Gage? Is he still in Boston?"

"Oh, yes—and still managing to wash both his faces."

Perry smiled, as did I. The moment struck me as being very pleasant between us.

"Such an insight you have on the war, Mrs. Lynford. Perhaps we should have made you Commander in Chief."

"No," I answered slowly. "For I would most certainly faint at the sight of blood. But worse than that, I am sure to detest the uniforms. However, I will impart one fine piece of advice. Once your new commander arrives, he should call upon General Howe to settle matters over a game of cards. The man has a mania for gambling, and from what I hear, he isn't very good. Why, they say he was sent here to pay off his gambling debts. So what's one more little, insignificant game, after all?"

"You don't say. My, my, Mrs. Lynford, you certainly have quite a knowledge of the British aristocracy."

"What a poor little talent to possess," I sighed, thinking sadly of my true mission in being here today.

"Seriously now, Perry. How did you fare on the hill? It seemed such a senseless battle to all of us," I said instead.

He sat on the ground at my feet and glanced away.

"I'm here in one piece. That makes me luckier than most, I guess. No, Mrs. Lynford, it was not so spectacular a time. Why I'm in this war, I cannot really say. There's something in my brain that tells me I should be a man and fight. But there's another message from my heart, and it holds no gumption for the task. I'm not saying I'm a coward. Why, I fought to the end. But the end was hell, begging your pardon, Mrs. Lynford. You see, we repelled the King's soldiers twice; and we were proud. But the third time—oh, they got us bad, Mrs. Lynford. I stayed in that miserable pit and fought as long as I could. It got to the point though, that we couldn't see through the choking smoke, or hear through the cries of pain and death. The regulars were actually rather decent, in a way. They didn't use their bayonets as much, or as often, as you would have thought. Maybe it was for the reason that in all the confusion, they could not be quite sure just who they were hitting."

The cries of pain and death—Landon had mentioned the same thing. Why, he had used practically the very same words. How very odd, and how terribly sad that here were both sides of this foolish war, recognising the very same conclusion. It just did not make any sense. Would the world always be this way? I wondered. Or would there come a day when men realised that it did not have to come to *the cries of pain and death* to resolve such simple problems.

I drew a deep breath. I really did not care to mention Celeste Davenport, but time was running hard, and I had no choice.

"I had a rather rough time of it too, Perry. For you see, I spent the entire time of the battle, attending to Miss Celeste Davenport."

He looked up at me sharply.

"Why? What happened?"

"It seems, Perry Talbot, that she ingested a near fatal dosage of laudanum because of you."

He looked at the ground again and sighed.

"What you must think of me," he murmured, and taking a small stick, he outlined circles in the dirt aimlessly.

"What I think may be of no consequence. Perhaps, it is not my business as well, but it does seem to me that it would prove rather tricky to divide one's heart in two. What of Miss Eldredge? Is it finished between you two?"

"Absolutely not!" Perry replied, and he knelt again at my feet. "Listen to me, Mrs. Lynford. I know you most likely will not believe what I am about to say, but I will say it all the same. Miss Celeste Davenport has been following me about ever since she met me at your house."

"At my house? When could that have happened?"

"Oh, last winter. I went to your house around three in the afternoon one day. I had hopes of finding you there, for I wanted to speak to you about Miss Eldredge. But you were not home. Adele said you were out walking. So, I paced about the street for a bit, on the possibility you might come round the corner. Then Miss Davenport arrived. She was looking for you, she said; something to do with a present she wanted to make for her father. Well, we talked in the street for awhile. I remember it was snowing. Now, don't get me wrong, Mrs. Lynford. Miss Celeste is a lovely girl. But she started to show up everywhere I went! I must have told her in conversation where I worked, for she appeared there the very next day."

I thought of demure little Celeste Davenport—the shy child who never said a word unless spoken to. It did not seem possible.

"What then?" I asked cautiously.

"She began to bring me gifts, and ask me to take her on walks—things like that. I tried to refuse all the presents she gave me. But I knew that if I returned them to Garden Court Street, her father would be extremely angry with her. So I did nothing. What a fool I was!"

"But Celeste was getting married. Why, she married Marlon Reynolds only last May."

"What difference did that make? She told me she did not love him. Miss Celeste said her father was forcing her into it. So, I guess I became her way out. You see, Miss Davenport wanted me to marry her. Why, she had this whole, harebrained scheme laid out where we would elope the night before her marriage to Reynolds. Yes, she maniacally insisted on it. To be honest, Mrs. Lynford, she frightened me to death."

"Miss Celeste Davenport did and said all these things you are telling me? I'm sorry, Perry, but I am having a most difficult time believing this."

"But you must, Mrs. Lynford, for I am telling you the truth."

"And you never once gave this unfortunate girl the least hope that you were in love with her?"

"Of course not! Why, I even told her about Lorena! But that didn't stop her. Now, Mrs. Lynford, I can say with all sincerity that I am sorry Miss Davenport attempted to take her own life. But I am not to blame, truly I'm not. You do not see her for what she is, Mrs. Lynford, but I will tell you right now; for your own good. Miss Davenport will look upon you with the gentle grace of one of the Lord's finest angels, and you might feel blessed indeed. But her words are driven through her lips by the Devil himself."

I believed him. I am not sure exactly why, but I did believe him.

"Oh, dear God," I said at last, for I realised the folly I had just walked the two of us into.

"Perry," I went on, swallowing hard. "You must promise me two things."

"Yes, anything," he said.

"First, please call me Verity. For all we have been through, together, I believe it is time to end such needless formalities."

"I'm—I'm not quite sure I can do that, Mrs. Lynford."

"Wait, Perry, for I have good reason. And that is favour number two . . ."

I paused, and Perry watched my face intently. I took a deep breath and began again.

"Favour number two—You must come and speak to Miss Davenport, for she is in my carriage, even as we speak."

"Verity!" he exclaimed. "How could you do this?"

"It is just another fine example of my poor little talents," I shrugged.

Perry agreed to talk with Celeste briefly on the road. I remember promising to him that I would assist in making the conversation short. It would not be so very difficult, I had said, for Betsy Sloan and David Manley were with us. Then I hugged his arm, and we walked in silence as the fiery sun sweltered on the blue, rippled horizon.

. . . Love is not love

Which alters when it alteration finds,

Or bends with the remover to remove.

O, no! it is an ever-fixèd mark

That looks on tempests and is never shaken; . . .

William Shakespeare—*Let Me Not to the Marriage of True Minds*

∞

MID JULY, 1775

IT WAS AN ARDENT and airless afternoon. The cobbled streets before our house seemed to be baking in the heat of the constant sun, like tidy little rows of fresh bread. At least there was a hint of rain overhead in the tumultuous skies.

I had seated myself on the back steps of our porch, facing the gardens. Leaning against a post where a shady roping of fragrant honeysuckle grew, I removed from my pocket a letter I had just received from my father, as promised and delivered, through the Captain. I settled myself and read his flowing lines, my brow furrowed, and my lips moving along with the words.

7 July, 1775

My Dearest Daughter,

*I write this to you between mending the fences and raking hay—
the two great events of this hazy and horribly humid Friday afternoon.
Everyone is fine. I assure you of this fact. Perhaps the only*

calamity to report is that Ruthie scorched a thatched-house pie this morning. Her latest expression is "droopin' pantaloons," and she says it quite often. Too often, in fact, for I am near out of my head with hearing it. Only the Good Lord knows where she picked it up, but I imagine it was while visiting with your cousins in Philadelphia.

Effie has not changed a wink. And she says she does not intend to, either. But that's your great-grandmother. One of our lodgers a while back was suffering from a most horrendous toothache, and our Effie told him it was due to the fact that he had not carried the tooth of a murdered pirate around in his pocket to ward off the pain. If we are not all hauled in for witchcraft, I shall be truly surprised!

Josiah Pierce is raising horses—far more than you would ever believe possible. At present, they have more than four paddocks full of healthy little colts and fillies. This, as you may have guessed, is his wife's doing. Mrs. Pierce has convinced her husband that there is a strong market for prime stock, what with the threat of full-blown war and all. But so far, the kindly woman has shown no enthusiasm for parting with a single one of her "precious little darlings."

I, too, am well. The increasing demands on the farm are constantly hammering at me, and the tavern continues to prosper. This is due, in part, to the fact that countless numbers of Boston families have migrated to the country when the port was shut down. So many men are looking for work here, that I can just imagine what it is like in town where you are. How is Jeffrey managing through all this? In whatever sense, rest secured, we are all fine. Why, with all I have on my hands, I can still find the time to rant and rave about the bloodthirsty British in my taproom every night. So all is normal on that score.

We all miss you terribly. Why, Effie still goes on, endlessly bragging about you portraying the goddess Liberty in the Boston pageants. But my concern lies in the costume she describes. Now, daughter, I realise it was ages ago, but did you really wear a sleeveless tunic with absolutely no petticoat, or chemise on underneath?

There was more, but I did not read it. Instead, I let the coarse, bulky pages drop to my lap as I closed my tired eyes and sighed.

I truly despised any reference to those early days here in Boston. Yes, I loathed to be reminded of when things seemed fine and beautiful between us, Jeffrey. Admittedly, it hurt to the point of tears to remember that afternoon you confessed to me that you loved Avella still.

Worse yet, I now know why you are taking all these lengthy trips to Concord, Jeffrey. It is not for business. You are there seeing Avella Gore. Avella moved back from Connecticut, disheartened at the lack of eligible bachelors with fine wealth. Lucy told me all about it. How Lucy Wellman hears of everything is beyond me. But at least she told me, Jeffrey. You have not.

So now I understand why we have not moved back home to Concord. Oh, yes I was well aware of your claim that Charles Davenport had engaged you to look after his shipping interests, or some such thing. However, the truth be known, I believe you were merely attempting to keep me and that Gore creature as far apart as possible for your own selfish pleasure. How could anyone be so callous and cruel?

"Your . . . lemonade, Madam," announced Beals, as he made an awkward appearance from the dark, cool regions of the back hall.

"Thank you, Beals," I mumbled, as the tray was set down rather precariously on the porch table.

"It appears the wrath of summer will be with us for a very long time to come, Madam."

"Hmm?" I replied. "Oh, yes—it has been a long, relentless summer, hasn't it?"

Beals began to take his leave when I stopped him.

"Beals—"

"Yes, Madam?"

"Take these things away, and bring me an ale, instead."

Thus it was that I spent the afternoon contemplating what my life could have been without you, Jeffrey, watching with tear-swept eyes as the shadows of twilight swallowed up the day.

"How very far away you are."

Startled, I glanced up, and focusing my eyes against the murky, dark grey air, I saw Landon Vale standing before me, a mischievously curious smile adorning his handsome face.

"Oh, it's you," I stammered, attempting with little success to hide my ale beneath the folds of my dress.

"Such a heartfelt greeting," he laughed. "Perhaps I should turn around and try my entrance again."

"Oh, Captain. I am so sorry. I was just thinking."

"I know," he replied, folding his arms and leaning against the honeysuckle-wrapped post. "I have been watching you for the last quarter of an hour, and you haven't so much as blinked an eye."

"Really?"

"Yes, really. Now tell your friend Landon what is wrong."

"Not a thing—why?"

"Come now, Mrs. Lynford. No woman sits alone, drinking ale on her back steps in front of all the neighbours' servants, when nothing is wrong."

"Oh, all right. Scold me, if you must. It's just that I received a letter from home, and I miss my family. That is all."

"I see," said Landon, seating himself at my invitation on the step above me, and thus submerging half his face in shadow. "However, I would wager that you are troubled by much more than mere melancholy. It shows in your eyes."

I simply shrugged in response and glanced to the ground, a guilty flush overtaking my face.

"Very well. I understand now that I should not intrude. So, I shall leave you to your much needed solitude, if you wish. You only have to say the word. However, I do prefer to stay."

"Please stay, Captain. And have an ale with me. At least it would give all the silly old babblers something worthwhile to tittle-tattle about after church on Sunday."

He laughed heartily, which provoked me to do the same. And then, all seemed right with the world again.

Adele was called for, as more ale was needed. However, when she appeared, she regretfully reminded me of a social obligation I had committed to at Merchant Platt's, that very evening.

"Oh, heavens!" I scowled. "I had all but forgotten. I cannot consider going there now. Edmund Platt has arranged for some old relic to entertain on harpsichord; and for the life of me, I could not possibly sit through the entire ordeal without running for the pot every five minutes, considering all the ale I've consumed."

I know the Captain hid his face in embarrassment over my words. But this was me, and he would just have to get used to it.

"Adele," I began coyly. "Please send round a note to Merchant Platt's, offering some kind of quaint and feasible excuse. Tell him anything you'd like. Or better yet, tell Platt that I am in the company of my dearest friend, Captain Vale, tonight; and I do not care to be shaken from my comfortable roost for any ill-clattering of keyboards."

"Perhaps I could mention a sick headache," Adele suggested calmly. "However, before doing so, I shall send you and the Captain another ale."

"Perfect, Adele," I smiled. "Nothing could be better."

I leaned back against the step behind me, which nearly placed me at Landon's knees, and sighed happily as Adele made her way to the pantry, humming an old nursery ballad; reminiscent of her days as a governess in Paris. I was content at last.

There passed a long time during which Landon and I did not speak. However, between good friends, words are not always necessary. Then, from the depths of my mind, which was whirling all about with sad thoughts of you, Jeffrey, I ventured a silly belief I had just established out of the clear blue.

"Love is a strange thing, Captain. It seems we foolish humans make the most of it when it is gone. Yes, it is as if there is an entire world out there, thriving on misery. But not me. I cannot be bothered to waste my time being miserable."

"What makes me think you're lying?" he replied quietly, just as a great blaze of light transversed across the sky, and the air blew cool for an instant with the sweet promise of rain.

"Lightning," Landon said, as Adele made her appearance with a pitcher of ale and some glasses. "We are in for quite a storm."

"Then Madam should consider coming inside," Adele opined, her worrisome eyes fixed upon the sky.

"Oh, no, Adele," I murmured, far too pleased with the moment to let it slip away so soon. "Why don't you sit down with us, and have an ale. It is so nice out here by the garden. And the storm, I believe, is still some distance away."

Adele smiled at the offer.

"Well, if you insist, Madam," she said, settling herself within the oversized wicker cane chair on the porch, while the Captain poured her a glass.

"I insist as well," Landon said, slyly. "For perhaps you can resolve a debate for us, Adele. You see, your mistress here is rather cynical about love. She claims that people adore making themselves ill over it. I happen to disagree."

"There is some truth in what my mistress says," Adele began carefully. "No man and woman love one another equally. There is always one who loves a little more than the other, it seems. And, if that one is jilted, they tend to—how shall I say it—immortalize the one who left them; even when another might come along who treats them with an even greater love and respect. Yes, in that case, some do cling to the memory of their first love, blind to the betterment of all the rest."

"What a dismal way to be," Landon replied quietly.

"But that is life!" Adele answered kindly. "Dismal one day, and full of promise the next. You see, love is as imperfect as we are. Perhaps that is why we cherish it so."

Silently, we watched the vivid horizon for awhile, saying nothing, thinking much. In due course, Adele excused herself to go to bed. She was too sleepy, she said, to stay up and watch God's fireworks until all hours of the night. With that, she left us.

"Do you believe in God?" I asked Landon suddenly, my gaze fixed on the sky.

"Occasionally I have difficulty understanding a supreme being who permits starvation, and poverty, and wars."

I turned and looked at him sharply.

"You are a military man. Yet you despise war, Captain?"

"Perhaps," he answered cautiously. I watched his face, for the turbulent sky was now alive with light. How foolish I was. I believe I had offended him.

"Oh, please, Landon," I said quickly. "I meant no disrespect. Indeed, I would like to know why you chose a military life. It has always intrigued me as to why men of a certain standing would actively seek a career in the business of war."

"That—" he began, moving closer to me until I was now indeed resting against him. "That is a very long story; one which I shall divulge to you some day, I promise. However, tonight, I want to learn all there is to know about you."

I was going to remark that there was precious little of interest in my life, when a deep roll of thunder sounded from the hills beyond; the echo of which shook the house, and rattled the very panes of glass in their frail casings. Such a loud disturbance! It frightened me to the point that I cowered between Landon's knees. Why, I practically had my back to his chest.

I turned around to face Landon, and mumbled some feeble apology for being such a fearful idiot. Then I laughed. However, he did not laugh with me. Instead, he took my face in his hands as I knelt before him. And he spoke softly to me, so very gently, and with, I confess, more power of seduction than any man has ever spoken to me before, or since.

"If I had the power of a god, I would turn back the years with a wave of my mystical hand. Yes, I would erase all that has happened within the past five years. And I would be the man I am now, but oh my dearest, God willing, I would be with you."

I replied nothing, instead gazing headlong into his beautiful eyes. I was overwhelmed. In truth, I was not even positive I had properly heard what had just been said.

"If this were an evening for just us two, Verity . . . If you and I were in Concord, and there was no Jeffrey Lynford in your life—"

"Please," I whispered, placing my fingers to his lips. "I beg you, do not speak of Jeffrey. As you have promised to tell me one day of your life, I shall speak of him another. But not tonight. Not when I am with you."

He took my fingers gently and kissed them.

"So be it, Verity Daniels. Then I shall inquire instead: If this were an evening for just us two alone, and we were in Concord, what would that wondrous night be like?"

"Ah, indeed it is wonderful there. For in Concord, the skies above are deeper, richer. The stars hold more majesty. You would see that at once, Landon. I know you would."

It had begun to rain. Softly, at first, almost timid, like my words. But the rain grew in strength behind us, and we did not mind.

"If we were in Concord, I would choose an evening towards summer's end. And you and I would walk quietly amongst the scenery of the night. Across the hay field, two twisted maples would show scarlet against the coming dawn. Just beyond, in the orchards, apple trees would hold tightly to their fruit, like gnomish sentinels in the shadows. With the light would come the pestering crows, prancing about the limbs with their awkward, large feet, in hopes that the ripest of the branches' bounty might tumble. But now, as we are together, only a contented silence. Nearer to the split-rail fences, we will see berry bushes, their leafy limbs bowed heavily with dew. Beneath them, sleeping rabbits are nestled in their hutches, quietly confident that an outburst from our family dogs is still hours away."

The rain shed more heavily now. But we did not take notice.

"As our wonderful evening draws to a close, an unseen owl will begin her rhythmic call. And soon, the whippoorwill will answer, in a happy chant. We would lean against the pasture rails, listening, and taking in the towering shadows of a distant grove of pines which bow before the greater power of the wind. This is my home. There, we do not hasten to the false notes of champagne and laughter. There, you and I would be happiest just waiting for the whippoorwill."

I looked into his eyes. I believed at once he saw it all as easily as I could.

"Perchance," Landon began, his voice so very tender. "while we waited—

might this humble servant entreat the honour of a kiss?"

"Yes," I whispered, without the least hesitation. "Oh, yes."

The rain was coming hard. It vented upon the earth like a fury, releasing with it a cool wind which blew a delicate mist upon us both. But we were unaware. We did not pay heed.

He knelt fully against me. The touch of his body to mine sent a shiver of pleasure through my entire being. So very slowly, Landon slid his hands up my arms, and we moved even closer to one another; closer, and closer still. I was breathless with a desire, the likes of which I have never known.

Just then, the door opened behind us, and you appeared, Jeffrey, standing in the streaming mist. Landon and I parted quickly. I was never really sure just how much you witnessed, or even how much you sensed. Your words proved nothing.

"Such silly children you are, sitting out here in the rain," you laughed, and your laughter did not seem artificial, or forced. "Come. Come inside, and have a glass of port with me."

We stood and kept our gazes to the ground with all the guilt we deserved to bear. We then went into the house behind you, Jeffrey, and we never spoke of the episode again.

Looking back, I wish to God we had.

And what have you got now for all your designin',
But a town without vittles to sit down and dine in,
And stare at the floor and scratch at your noodles,
And sing how the Yankees have beaten the Doodles.
I'm sure if you're wise, you'll make peace for a dinner,
For fighting and fasting will soon make you thinner.

The Irishman's Epistle

LATE SUMMER THROUGH FALL, 1775

ALTHOUGH the King's army could claim victory at Bunker Hill, it was a grievous one, for with nearly one third of their forces cut down by provincial muskets, their losses were appalling.

There was a new and dangerously restless spirit to the town of Boston these days—an ominous mood which, like a vicious, hell-born sprite, cast turmoil and confusion wherever it flew.

Nearly fourteen thousand people had abandoned their properties to the British, leaving so very much of the town open to the whims of the soldiery. Homes and stores were recklessly plundered during this mad, new caprice, whether they belonged to Whig or Loyalist. Every new day that dawned brought exposed threats of fire or bombardment. For those who had holdings to guard, or simply nowhere to go, these were days and nights consumed with the constant dread of attack.

But we did not suffer. With Captain Vale as our quartered officer, we possessed clear access to most all the luxuries available. Beef in the market was eight pence per pound, and a three-pound lamb brought in the astronomical price of a dollar. However, when other folks were barely surviving on fatty pork and beans, our guests dined on elegant victuals night after night.

All around the colonies, preparations went in full force towards war. Ladies from all levels of society were doing their patriotic part by wearing home-spun. In Virginia, it was even considered smart. However, in certain parts of Boston, a disparate society prevailed. The women of Charles Davenport's company would accept nothing less than the garish finery from France and England, which arrived monthly aboard royal blockade vessels.

With the secured blessings of Generals Howe and Burgoyne, Charles had happily begun the task of remodeling Faneuil Hall into an adequate theatre in which to entertain the troops and their officers. The much delayed *A Midsummer Night's Dream*, would commence the season sometime in late August or early September. During this lull, Gordon Russell was assuming Marlon Reynolds' role of Demetrius during rehearsals. Reynolds, it seems, had made a rather hasty departure for New York. Charles claimed the benefits in two reasons. Firstly, Celeste needed rest and solitude. Secondly, there was a mysterious need to investigate the theatres there. Lucy added her bit of intrigue by claiming to know that Celeste Davenport Reynolds was stealthily sending off rather bulky epistles to a common soldier at Cambridge camp. On my part, I merely maintained polite curiosity at it all. I believe Betsy Sloan and David Manley reacted the same. It was best, I had convinced myself, to remain well outside the cyclone we all now recognised as the Davenport nature.

In gratitude of his appointment, Charles made sure to it that his "Gentlemen Generals," as well as many of the other privileged officers, were kept smartly amused with splendid socials and supper parties at his home. For Valentine, Lucy, and Rebecca, the personal rewards and pretended romances were never better.

So it was that we whiled away languid evenings listening to heavenly chamber music, while outside, countless funeral dirges passed without even so much as the proper and respectful tolling of church bells, the ringing of which had been forbidden under royal rule. While Charles Davenport toasted his company with champagne, homes and barns were being destroyed by fire, and properties and livestock seized. For every dance, a cannon roared, and with each song, another provincial imprisoned. And with each mouthful of elegant food we ladies swore we could not manage another bite of, some-where only a few doors away, plain and fancy folk alike were reduced to eating rats.

Yes, despite the hardships that surrounded us, we saw survival as an easy trick. It was as though the hostilities of war had never existed. For myself, I must confess, my "society under siege" was made all that much nicer by the ever constant presence of Captain Landon Vale.

Somehow, during those insane days of disorder, Landon Vale had become something of a romantic hero in the town of Boston. And his reputation, as mysteriously fabricated as it was, gained higher plains of notoriety due to his "unsavoury association" with the company in that gleaming house of stone on Garden Court Street.

For the simple fact that no one really knew very much about him, grandiose stories were frantically woven about his life. Within weeks, even the lowliest kitchen wench fancied she recognised the Captain as the disinherited son of a dismal, old Earl. There were rumours of his incessant lust for gambling, and debts of outlandish proportions were bantered about the taverns daily—ridiculous sums, over which the Captain had supposedly killed a man. Of course, his highly illustrious past was riddled with beautiful women—ladies of wealth, and of royalty; not to mention countless courtesans of the fashionable persuasion. How the Captain ever had time for all these women, no one could really say. And how Lorena Eldredge viewed this adverse publicity was yet another thing. Regardless, the Captain's popularity had skyrocketed, especially in the eyes of the young ladies of Boston. It was, to a degree, almost comical.

Hearing these stories, most often from Lucy, amused me greatly. I would then find great pleasure in repeating them to Landon over breakfast. It was a golden opportunity to chide him relentlessly.

"At least they got one thing right about you," I had said with a sly grin. "They guessed you were from England."

Yes, the tales were nothing short of ridiculous. However, I was discovering for myself that the man behind the myth was more real, and more curiously wonderful, than I ever could have imagined.

Landon had fully resumed his residence at our fusty, little house on Charter Street. Why, he was about nearly every moment he was not required at headquarters. Being witness to the terribly tense and anxious atmosphere around Boston, I was frankly glad for his company. With moral opinion in mind, Vera Davenport was retained as a permanent house guest; for your continual absence, Jeffrey, was often commented upon in the streets. Although it is wicked to say so, I found that bit of information rather humorous, too.

For a soldier who could evoke such fear and trepidation on the battlefield, Landon Vale was a man who could pamper and spoil a woman to distraction. Oh, his attentions to me never again hinted of sexual desire, although there were times I would catch him looking at me in a certain, covetous fashion. However, when I would ask him what he was thinking, Landon always had a quick, plausible response. It was delightful, and maddening, all at once, for Landon lavished the beauties of his heart on me like I was a queen. In the mornings, he most often made it a point to return from headquarters and take breakfast with me. Such delightful chats we would have. And in the afternoons, he would break away from his official duties in order to walk the mall with me, or take me to dinner at any one of our favourite taverns. In impoverished times such as these, this grand gesture of his was overwhelming; not to mention further fuel to the fire of his fame. At one point, I told Landon that he need not treat me to so many expensive meals out, but he merely laughed.

"What with all the supposed fabulously wealthy fathers I have, buying off my silence, this is a pittance, my dear—a mere pittance."

He confessed to admiring my mind, when I wasn't being foolish, and I admitted to preferring his company over that of any of the "pretentious prigs," as I called them, to be found at Garden Court Street. Landon taught me how to play whist and all-fours, as well as how to shoot billiards and toss dice. Draughts and chess were attempted as well, but I found them tedious—especially chess. You see, I had always found it difficult to remain silent for long periods of time, pretending to be steeped in the utmost of concentration.

In retaliation, I taught him Hustle Cap, and Nine-Men's Morris. On one occasion, I even got him to sit down to a round of Goose. However, Landon pronounced it a silly waste of time. At least he was smiling. Why, if the truth be known, Landon Vale was smiling a great deal these days.

Yes, our compatibility was astounding. And it could have been even more so, had we each not expended so much mental energy trying to deny it.

⊙⊙⊙⊙

It was a late August evening, as I remember it. You were home from Concord, Jeffrey, and we were invited to Charles Davenport's for yet another "royal" social. Just moments before we were due to leave, you had knocked on my door, requesting to see your "beloved wife." Frankly, your words surprised me. I had not considered myself "beloved," indeed not even your "wife," for months now.

You stood behind me, and placed your hands on my shoulders. I glanced up at you in the glass and smiled—rather curiously I am sure—however your actions seemed strangely new to me.

"What is it, Jeffrey?' I asked.

Your answer was to sit upon my bed, and catching my eye, you patted the counterpane with a mischievous grin.

"Let us not go out, tonight. Let us instead amuse ourselves right here, right now."

"Oh, Jeffrey—" I stammered. I hardly knew what to say. You see, I wanted to go to Charles' party. Landon was going to meet me there with a brand new book of poetry he had just received from England. Besides, Jeffrey, our moments of "amusing" intimacy were just a flicker of a memory within my mind. By this point in time, I am sorry to say, I found myself greatly disinterested in your playfully coy offer.

"Jeffrey," I tried again. "We promised Charles—"

"All right then," you sighed with a smile. "However, my dearest wife, might your husband be granted just the smallest of interviews with you sometime during the course of this most agreeable evening? There are things, Verity, most pleasant things, that I wish to discuss with you."

"I—I do not understand," I returned, nervously.

"Heavens, woman! Are you going to make me say it now?"

"I'd rather you would."

You stood and returned to me, placing your hands on my shoulders once again, and leaning down so that your face was clearly visible in the sheen of my looking glass.

"My darling wife. I have, I must admit, been amiss in this marriage. For months now, I have been racking my brains to understand why. The plain truth, Verity, is that—and now, hear me out, if you will—the plain truth is that I do not love you as you love me."

"And how am I to respond to such a statement?" I asked, and my voice was neither imperious, nor incriminating. That in itself was a shame. It meant I cared little.

"What I am trying to tell you, Verity, is that I am willing to try. I want to try. So, come now; smile. I believe this is exactly what you have wanted to hear for a very long time."

It was. You have no idea, Jeffrey, how many evenings I had cried myself to sleep over your lack of love for me. I would have given the world, just mere months ago, to have you utter the words I heard tonight. However, that was then. What my mood was now, I could not be certain of.

I looked up at your face. It was such a handsome, well-born face. Then I recalled, once more, that glorious afternoon when I first saw you. Could that overwhelming and beautifully innocent need ever return to my heart? Perhaps. Hope was not so bad an ambition.

I rested my hands atop yours and smiled. A compromise was then made. First, Charles' party; then the amusement.

Not a soul was permitted out of Boston these days, for the Generals feared that with the last patriot gone, the provincials would maliciously set fire to the town. So with that in mind, William Howe ordered every suspicious character he could get his hands on thrown into jail. Better they were rotting behind bars than hanging out warning lanterns, or sending secretly coded messages across the bay.

A certain Mr. Carpenter was arrested for just that. Apprehended by the night patrol, Carpenter was sentenced to death simply for swimming to Dorchester and back. He was dressed for execution, and had even been made to stand before his own coffin in the gaol yard, before his sentence was pardoned.

The printer, John Gill, was imprisoned for reasons of treason, inciting rebellion, and printing sedition. The learned navigator, John Leach, was also put behind bars for the vague accusation of "being a spy, and suspected of taking plans."

On the provincial side, Doctor Benjamin Church had been tried and convicted as a British spy. This revelation was a great blow to Sam Adams and the Liberty Boys, for Doctor Church had worked alongside them in their cause for an entire decade now. A charter member of the Long Room Club, Church had assisted in penning a vast array of scorching criticisms of Parliament, as well some admonishing words for our English-paid governors and judges. He had spoken at the third anniversary of the dreadful Boston Massacre, and had even so much as volunteered to risk his life by going into Boston for medicine, after the battles at Lexington and Concord.

Sadly, it was now discovered just why Church vowed to chance life and limb. The sly doctor journeyed into Boston with the sole intention of reporting to General Gage all he had heard from the provincials' Committee of Safety, which had been meeting in Cambridge. Church might have been able to persist in his sordid dealings, had it not been for his pregnant mistress. She was run in for attempting to deliver a coded message of Church's to a certain British Major.

At Church's trial, even the galleries of the Old Meeting House were packed to overflowing. Never before had such a sensational scandal presented itself in stodgy, archaic Boston, and the townspeople were hungry for it. Surprisingly though, the accused spy—who had, much to everyone's embarrassment, just been appointed surgeon general to the American army—was merely condemned to a Norwich, Connecticut gaol, and denied paper and pen.

Zealously, I had attended the doctor's trial, with Lucy and Rebecca in tow. Landon voiced a strong opinion against my going. He felt the rabble would be greatly incensed at the sight of the turncoat Church, and create riot. I thanked

Landon for his interest in my well-being, but assured him that no better protection existed for me than little Lucy Wellman. For surely, she would fillip anyone who got in our way. Landon merely laughed before extracting a promise that I would meet him at the Lion and the Lamb the moment the trial had concluded. It was a promise I was more than happy to make. We were, at that precious time in our lives, practically inseparable. And if Landon were anything less than an officer of the King, I would have adored his company at the trial.

". . . Seriously, Captain," I remember saying as we sat over a meal at the Lion and the Lamb—a meal I could not manage to eat because of my silly little rantings and ravings—"Hanging is not good enough for that odious traitor, I tell you. Not half good enough!"

"But my dear lady," replied Landon evenly. "Surely you do not expect your beloved Whigs to advertise their shame, do you? After all, how would it sound to the rest of the waiting world, if America's first convicted spy was also one of their premiere and trusted patriots?"

"Besides," he added with a sly grin. "Spies are becoming so passé. What, with every Loyalist willing to gab all they know, just to hear themselves talk—who needs to pay anyone for the privilege?"

I sat silently before him, an ill-humored frown on my lips.

"Does this mean then, Captain, that I could not be awarded an occupation as a spy?"

Landon threw back his head in laughter.

"You? A spy? Oh, heavens, do be serious."

"I would wager this very moment that if Miss Lorena Eldredge asked to be employed as a spy, you'd permit her."

How strange to me now that I had even so much as mentioned Miss Eldredge's name. During these past few months, Landon and I had come to a sort of relationship that I could only describe as flirtatious. In all this time, we had never discussed her. But now, I had just brought her to both our attentions, and the realisation of this made me watch Landon's manner of response very carefully.

"Miss Eldredge is too much a lady to even consider so foolish a question."

"And that means I am?"

"Are what, Verity? A lady, or foolish? Given a choice, I would most definitely vote on the latter."

I am sure he found my glower of wrath amusing.

"Oh, come now, Verity. The only reason you are enchanted with becoming a spy is because you have attended a spy's trial. And now, you have molded some completely ridiculous notion that espionage is somehow altogether glamourous."

Oh, I know Landon was being lighthearted about it all, but none the less I responded with a flippant jerk of my chin.

"The real truth about spies, is that if they are caught, they are always tortured. In addition, they are very often put to death for not revealing their mission. However, I imagine we have little to fear about that with you. You, my dearest friend, would blab away at the first threat of missing a meal."

He was teasing me, of course. How fun it was to banter with him!

"Would not!" I pretended to pout.

"Would too," he grinned.

"Would not!" I retorted, this time tossing my tattered piece of bread at his tailored waistcoat.

We laughed wholeheartedly. All around the room, people were putting their heads together about what a grand time the gambling, womanizing Captain Vale was having with Jeffrey Lynford's wife. Oh, what a petty little society they were to gossip so!

Secretly though, I adored every minute of it.

I will now begin to sigh, read poets, look pale,

go neatly, and be most apparently in love.

Marston

∞

16 December 1775

SINCE NINE of the clock this morning, I had been shifting pieces of furniture about our front parlours in a desperate hope that the small, stuffy rooms would come to accommodate some fifty or so party guests later in the evening for Landon's surprise birthday party.

"Oh!" I exclaimed in frustration at my third attempt to create a dance floor within the confines of our pallid little music room. "We cannot so much as offer lap tea for ten in here."

Clemence, who had come offering assistance, but had thus far only succeeded in making a nuisance of herself, stood by with a typically troubled expression on her face.

"Perhaps we could put some of the larger and unnecessary bits of furniture out in the back yard, and cover them with blankets," she ventured meekly.

"And how are we to do that, pray tell?" I retorted, blowing back a loose lock of hair from my face. "Abracadabra, sideboard, you are now outside? Really, Clemence. I cannot manage it by myself. As for you, well, I am sure you have never lifted a finger in your life. Why, you couldn't even carry out the cat."

Too foolish to take offense, Clemence put her hands on her hips, and surveyed the room critically.

"There must be something we can do here . . ."

Just then, Beals shuffled into the room, and cleared his throat.

"Madam. The . . . mm . . . Captain has returned, and wishes to see you."

Clemence and I regarded one another with looks of undisguised horror. So many people had assured me they would keep the Captain busy until late in the day. How could this have happened?

"Landon," I gasped, staring headlong into Beals' impassive face. "Just tell him—"

"My dear Mrs. Lynford," Landon began cheerfully, letting himself in the room without the benefit of butler, and reaching out both hands in greeting to me. "How . . . disheveled you look."

I tried to laugh it off as I wiped my hands on my apron, and patted my hair back into place as best possible.

"Mrs. Taggard! How very nice to see you here."

"Oh," Clemence warbled, blushing brightly. "It is nothing out of the ordinary—I can assure you of that!"

"Would you take tea, Captain?" I asked, secretly wanting to strangle the dimwitted Clemence for her severe lack of subtlety. "Perhaps some breakfast?"

"I took my breakfast with Hugh Earl Percy, thank you. No, my dear lady, I actually came by to see if you wanted a spot of dinner at the Red Lion."

"Did not Charles—?" I began, and then stopped myself with an awkward pause. Here I was thinking Clemence Taggard a dolt, when I myself had just this moment blundered so badly!

"What I meant to say was, had I not heard Charles Davenport asking you, just last Sunday, to dine with him today at the Royal Coffee House?"

"No. I do not recall his having asked."

Landon was right. Charles had not asked him last Sunday, but was planning to. Obviously, Charles had not managed to get a card sent round to the Captain in time.

"Hmm," I murmured, covering my thoughts. "I must have imagined it then. Strange thing though, for I plainly remember the Royal Coffee House being mentioned for its superb plover pie and the Whistle Belly Vengeance."

Clemence's eyebrows shot up so fast that the ringlets on her forehead reverberated.

"Whistle Belly what?" she asked, mystified.

"Whistle Belly Vengeance," Landon offered in response. "It is a sordid concoction of sour beer and rum. And I cannot think for the life of me why Charles Davenport would extol the least bit of praise for such a witches' brew."

It was a prank on my part, of course. You see, Landon Vale was consistently attempting to raise my standards, just as I was forever endeavouring to knock down his. Who else but a tavernkeeper's daughter would be aware of one of the most ignoble beverages available to mankind?

"Oh, well," I shrugged with a poorly disguised smile. "It is not for me to say."

"Then say you will have dinner with me. I am ravenous, you see. I watched the dawn come up over the card table."

"Yes, I see," I muttered with a little laugh. "But the problem is, Captain, I am right in the midst of rearranging my furniture."

Landon glanced about the room, a droll smirk of disapproval on his face.

"You are doing a poor job of it, then."

Before I could utter a single protest, Landon began deftly moving the crow-foot chairs and the heavy mahogany drawing table back towards the center of the room in a most amiable fashion.

"There is far too much against the walls, Mrs. Lynford," he explained as he worked. "You've got the place looking like an assembly hall—or, in your case, an assembly closet."

I watched in despair as my efforts of the past two hours were so easily blighted.

"There now. What do you think?" he asked, glancing about his handiwork with pride.

"Words fail me," I answered glumly.

Beals teetered in once again, a most stupefied expression fixed upon his sagging face at our latest remodeling of the music room.

"Er, Mr. Charles Davenport, and Mr. Marlon Reynolds, to see the Captain, Madam."

"Show them in at once, Beals."

"Very good, Madam," he mumbled, and turning himself around carefully, he muddled his way towards the hall, where he paused a moment, his brow furrowed in deep deliberation.

"If you'd care to hear my opinion, Madam, the room looked best the first time around."

I was about to throw my hands up in despair when Charles and Marlon sauntered happily into the room.

"My dear Mrs. Lynford!" Charles said brightly. "And Landon! You naughty fellow. Where have you been hiding yourself all morning?"

"I was losing at cribbage most abominably."

"I see. Had you forgotten? You promised to dine with me this afternoon."

Landon glanced at me, to which my only response was an "I told you so" smile.

"I suppose I had forgotten after all. Oh, well. It is of no consequence now. So ladies, gentlemen, shall we all go, and make a grand party of it?"

"Oh, I couldn't really," I mumbled, grasping at excuses. "My hair is disgraceful."

"Shove it up under a hat," Landon replied. "And change your sweet little ragamuffin dress in order that we might start off at once. I am positively famished."

"No, no," I insisted. "I have so very much to do before we go to Lord Sutherland's this evening. Besides, I am not exceptionally hungry."

"And I am on my way to Henry Knox's book shop to purchase a copy of Goldsmith's *The Vicar of Wakefield*," offered Marlon, casually brushing a fleck of lint from his coat sleeve.

Clemence's lips began to tremble nervously as she felt all eyes upon her.

"And I am, I am so very busy, too—at something, or the other . . ."

"There you have it, Captain," laughed Charles, with a pat on Landon's back. "It appears to be just you and I, I'm afraid. Now, let us move along, before the riffraff retrieve all the best tables."

I walked them to the door. Outside, the skies hovered low with dismal clouds of grey, and the cobbled streets were greasy with rain.

"Not a terribly nice day for a birthday," Landon commented offhandedly.

"Oh, is this your birthday?" asked Charles with ease. "Then I shall buy the dinner. How does that sound? Now, come along, come along."

"I will be with you directly," Landon said, pausing by my side as Charles proceeded down the walk with Marlon. I really wished the Captain would leave. I had to look a fright in my simple curaco jacket and brown cloth petticoat and apron.

Blushing, I glanced up at Landon. I saw at once the intense energy which seemed to wholly possess him. The blue of his eyes fairly burned against the fascinating contours of his face.

"What is it?" I asked shyly. "What is wrong?"

"Have you ever been on the verge of something truly wonderful?" he began breathlessly. "Have you ever stood at the precipice of your future, and were totally unafraid to jump?"

I stared at him blankly, silently cursing myself for not comprehending just what he meant. He moved closer to me—so close I could almost feel the warmth of his breath on my cheek, as he gazed into my eyes intently.

"Today, I have beheld the path of my direction in life," he was saying, his voice low and alluringly determined. "I was unsure—even yesterday—so aimless and naive. I had questions. I possessed doubts. However, as of this very day, I have seen through the veil of my future, and it pleases me greatly."

For a wild moment, Landon's words whirled around in my brain. Did all this talk of the future, and of change, and of knowing this day just what it was he wanted from life, refer to the dangerously wonderful conclusion that Landon had found himself in love with me? No. This could not be true. Moreover, I would be a complete and utter fool for imagining it.

"All this over cards at daybreak?" I instead offered meekly.

"My sweetest pet," he laughed lightly. "You really do not understand, do you?"

I shook my head no, still staring headlong into his eyes; hoping beyond hope to see an answer there.

"Verity!" I heard Clemence warbling from the sitting room beyond. "Verity, what should I be doing now?"

I sighed, secretly wishing the floor would suddenly open up and swallow Clemence Taggard whole.

"Do something useful," I called out. "Go count the punch glasses in the pantry."

"All of them?" Clemence questioned, dubiously.

"Now what do you think?" I replied, rather flustered as Clemence made her way noisily towards the back of the house, mumbling something about requiring paper and ink for such a project.

"Landon!" Charles chanted from the walk. "Do hurry, my man. It's beginning to rain."

"Just a moment," he said, and there was a sense of frustration in his voice as well.

"I hope you did not mind what I said earlier about your hair and gown," Landon said, turning to me. "I never meant to embarrass you, and heaven scorn me if that is what I have done. The truth, my dear, is that you look lovely with your hair loose. So very beautiful, and bewitchingly wanton."

He brushed the loose tendrils of hair from my face. And as he did so, I closed my eyes and shivered ever so slightly at the tender touch of his hand.

"Oh please, Landon," I said, taking his hands. "Please make me understand. You and I, we have conversed often. I feel closer to you than almost anyone. Yet, I cannot fathom what you were just telling me now. I feel so foolish."

"You need not resolve my words so carefully," Landon said, and the tone of his voice seemed to be begging me to grasp his meaning all the same. "Verity, just look straight into my eyes and tell me what you see there."

The unmistakable creak of the pantry door swinging on its hinges was heard, and Clemence appeared in the hall.

"Forty-seven!" she announced proudly, waving her plump, little hands. "There are forty-seven punch cups in the pantry. Oh, greetings, Captain! Heavens, but are you still here?"

"I was just on my way out, Mrs. Taggard," he replied, his tone resigned. However, he waited for Clemence to wander off, before picking up a slender book from the side table. I had not seen the book before this.

"Here, Verity," he said softly, handing the book to me. "I want you to have this. It would mean a great deal to me if you would read from this, and think of me, a little."

I watched as he took his leave to join Charles at the far end of the walk. And as the gentlemen disappeared into the shrouded mist of the day, I opened the book, which consisted of prose, and noticed at once the inscription written on the title page in a bold, dark hand:

To Mistress Verity—with Fondest Thoughts of Springs and Fountains.

Landon 16 December, 1775

"Thank goodness!" Clemence exclaimed, as I closed the door. "Why, we nearly all but gave ourselves away, now didn't we? Well, that is done with, and it is getting late. Shouldn't we now call for Beals, and get this furniture rearranged once again?"

I ambled slowly towards the music room. Outside, the brief rush of rain had ceased, and little, light beads of water dripped like liquid diamonds from the rooftops and the shivering trees.

⟲⟳⟲⟳

As usual, Lucy Wellman was the first to arrive.

"The downstairs is magnificent!" Lucy announced as she burst into my dressing room, a little before six in the evening. "All ablaze with candles, and silver—"

She paused abruptly, her little face paling at the sight of my dress.

"Gad Zeus! You're not going to wear that, are you?"

"But of course I am," I replied with a snide twist of a smile, as I stood to reveal my gossamer-thin white gown of delicate foulard. Its accompanying tapered black ribbon was quite divine, for it reduced my waist to nothingness. "Why should I not wear it?"

"For the simple reason that Diana Kirby is the only woman who expects to be noticed in foulard in the winter—that's why!"

I sat down before my looking glass, and patted the lovely assemblage of pearls which adorned my thick, auburn hair like a cluster of lucid stars.

"Surely you do not believe I should cower before the likes of Diana Kirby. Certainly not you of all people, Lucy."

Lucy's dark eyes flashed with laughter.

"Yes, I suppose you're right," she admitted with abandoned modesty. "But then again, I do not go about dressed liked a cunning vestal virgin, either. My, my, but won't Lady K be spitting fourpenny nails when she sees you in this little frock."

"Oh, I seriously do not care," I replied with studied nonchalance, frankly more intent on the vibrant reflection of my green eyes in the glass. Something in my mood had rendered them most luminous on this very magical evening. "Why, I couldn't care in the least."

"Oh, don't you, my fine friend? Then why bother to copy one of Diana's gowns right down to the ribbon?"

"I beg to differ, however, you are wrong, Lucy. This is not the exact duplicate you believe it to be. You see, Miss Kirby typically wears a red ribbon, whereas I have selected black. Red can be so tawdry; do you not agree?"

"You are such a sly fox, Verity Lynford. And I positively cannot wait to witness the battle of the hen baskets!"

I laughed at the sudden image of myself and Diana clawing each other's eyes out in a fitful tangle of hoops and petticoats.

"So, who did you come with, Lucy?"

"Edmund Platt, of all things," she moaned, sitting down upon the divan with a dejected thud. "Judas, but he is such a milksop!"

"Then why particularly him?" I asked, moving my candle closer to the looking glass for light.

Lucy shrugged.

"Who else, at the moment? There's not a man in our immediate circle with more than sixpence in his pocket. Actors, bah! What a bad lot. They are a great deal like soldiers, you know. Do not endeavour to get yourself involved with either, if you can help it."

I said nothing, covering my awkward blush with a quick study of my fingernails.

"Oh, dear God," Lucy whispered. "Now I know what this is all about. Diana Kirby has sharpened her fangs for the elegant Captain Vale, and you mean for her not to have him."

"That is nonsense," I said, my voice not at all forceful. Thankfully, a knock sounded at the door, and I bade the caller to come in.

The door opened a mite, and the voice of Charles Davenport called out softly.

"Perchance, might we bend the rules of decorum, and permit a strange and unannounced gentleman into the sanctity of your boudoir?"

"Most definitely," I laughed, and standing, I extended my hands to Charles. "The stranger the better, I say."

"Miss Wellman," he exclaimed, stepping shyly into my room. "How nice to see you. And Mrs. Lynford. What a lovely gown. And no formal wig. Indeed, your own hair is so very beautiful. I have always attested to that."

"Thank you. Why, you look quite dapper yourself, sir."

In fact he did. Charles Davenport employed the same tailor in London that Governor Hutchinson once did, and his exquisite suits of silk were styled in the height of European fashion.

"And thank you, Madam," Charles replied with an elegant little bow. "Now, my dearest ladies, are we prepared to give our celebrated Captain Vale the surprise of his life?"

"I should like to see him surprised," I confessed with a laugh. "Why, I do believe the most emotional outburst I ever saw the Captain display was the rise of one sole eyebrow—just like this—"

I pursed my lips like an old dowager sniffing a three-day-old fish, and cocked one brow, ever so superciliously, over a cold stare. Of course, I was greatly exaggerating, but it was quite amusing all the same.

"How's that?" I asked, holding my incriminating pose.

"Perfect," Charles agreed with a grin.

"Speaking of which, Charles, how was your outing today with Captain Impeccable?"

"Oh, interesting, to say the least. He spoke a great deal of Miss Eldredge. I am not well acquainted with the young lady, for all that she attended the duck hunt with us. Quiet little thing. What was her first name?"

"Lorena," I said slowly. "And she is quite lovely." It was an admission my heart was very sorry to make.

"So I hear," Charles went on smoothly. "And although I should not be gossiping behind closed doors, it seems that her father, Warren Eldredge, is looking for a declaration from our gallant Captain. It was, frankly, a surprise to me. I was not aware things were so defined between Landon and this certain young Miss."

Something went cold inside me as Landon's words of this morning floated through my mind, mockingly. He spoke of experiencing the verge of something wonderful—something he had not known until this very day—and of the precipice he was not afraid to forge. Oh, what a ridiculous dolt I was to dare believe it had anything to do with me!

"Lorena Eldredge," Lucy laughed, stretching out on the couch like a lazy cat. "I heard her old man went broke. They say he ripped through all his family's fine money on pleasures and bad investments back home in London. Then, here in Boston, it is said he embezzled funds from the Cornhill bank where he was an associate, and squandered it all on a Queen Street whore."

"Wherever do you hear such things, Lucy?" Charles asked with tremendous curiosity. Indeed, even I had not heard as much.

"In the taverns, just like everyone else," she shrugged. "And for the record, I never felt for a second that the Captain held an ounce of regard for that sniveling stick of a girl, for all she possesses beauty. No, it is our Verity he really cares for."

"You're crazy," I scoffed, my brain all a blur, and my face showing far too much in the way of frustration.

"Oh, am I? All right, then. But you just study the way he looks upon you with his melting eyes, my silly ninnyhammer. Lorena Eldredge, indeed!"

"Shall we go downstairs?" Charles asked, fanning the lace frills of his cuffs. I was sure his true purpose was to put an end to the current topic, and I was glad of it. "Our guests should be arriving any moment."

Charles went out the door at once, but the indolent Lucy lingered on the couch.

"Did you know about the Captain having to face up to things with the Eldredge girl?" she asked casually.

"No, I did not."

"And did you invite this supposed and simpering intended of Captain Vale's to this very elegant soiree in his honour?"

"No, I did not."

"Ah," Lucy replied thoughtfully. "Now I understand the dress."

Despite my troubles, I had to laugh. Then, taking Lucy's hand, we went together down the steps.

∞∞∞∞

For a frantic fifteen minutes, it seemed as though people arrived in droves. Earlier in the day, I had finally felt satisfied that all these bodies would fit comfortably within the confines of our little "doll's house." Now I frenziedly wondered where they all would fit!

The merchants Blackwell and Loring appeared with the ladies Stanwood. Virginia seemed ecstatic over something; it showed in the vivacious manner of her greeting. Even the reticent Eve showed signs of being gladsome. If one peered closely enough, they would witness a slightly upwards curve to her soft lips, resulting in the tiniest hint of a dimple on her chin. Within the violet depths of her eyes, there shone a most curious light.

Clemence and Bryce were the next to arrive. They had been walking the Common earlier, they said, in order to provoke a proper appetite for the evening's festivities. Clemence then made her way about the room, taking credit for all the decoration with great sighs of self-pride.

Val and Rebecca came in, closely followed by a group of officers from the various regiments. They were a vibrant pack of men; lean, anxious, and terribly mysterious. As for the girls, they were in a haze of excitement. Never before had there been so many handsome young men to gape at.

The Sloans appeared with the merchants Varney and King. The tension between James and Betsy, which had been but vaguely noticeable in months past, was now blatantly evident. They were barely in the foyer when the two parted company.

The door was opened to yet another group of merchants—a languid lot, with their smart silk suits and their costly white wigs. Social events had merely become an excuse to banter politics, and this gathering was no exception. Like a portly pack of ganders, these men of business huddled about the sideboard, squawking loudly about the news of the day, and their latest woes.

"The Captain should be here soon," cautioned Charles, just as a hullabaloo was heard from the hall. Darcy and Gordon had burst in upon the scene, announcing the arrival of Bacchus. Then, just as quickly as they had entered, they dashed out again, leaving a trail of raucous laughter in their wake.

"Well, they are obviously in their altitudes," hissed one of the merchants' wives, as all eyes turned towards the foyer.

Within moments, the men returned, carrying Lord Sutherland on a litter atop their shoulders. He was attired in a conglomeration of sheets, drapery cords, and winter greens; representing the Greek god of wine. The rotund Roscoe Bennett solemnly led the procession, chanting away at some contrived and bombastic speech praising the drunken deity.

"My lovely lady," began our Bacchus, as the litter was brought to a halt before me. "I present to you the mystical potions and aromatic elixirs of the gods."

Indeed he had. The makeshift litter on which he rode was piled high with an array of bottles boasting seemingly every intoxicating spirit known to mankind. Lord Sutherland then snapped his fingers, and in strolled William Collamore, David Manley, and Timothy Gorman, all bearing trays of cheeses, fruit, and biscuits.

"For those who wish to debauch their wine by shoveling food on it," our Bacchus cited grimly.

"Lord Sutherland," I cooed appreciatively. "How very kind of you!"

Those who stood about the tiny foyer, as well as anyone who could see from the crowded parlours beyond, madly applauded Sutherland's spectacle of charity.

"Thank you, one and all!" Hector proclaimed, taking a most majestic bow and basking in the glory. "Zounds, but this costume is a bit breezy. I was torn between this, or appearing as an Indian in commemoration of the tea party incident, which occurred but two years ago this very night."

"Indians?" Betsy Sloan said, shivering. "I have never seen one, nor do I care to!"

"My great-grandmother, Comfort Winslow, saw the Sudbury Massacre of

1676," one woman was saying. "The savages came through at dawn, and there was no chance of getting to the garrison house on time. Comfort was only eight years old then. In order to save herself, she climbed out her bedroom window onto the massive oak that shaded the house. From there, she watched in horror as her family was murdered off, one by one—brutally scalped before her very eyes. Her mother, her father, and her three brothers, all gone. She had to watch, she said. She was afraid to close her eyes—afraid to, because if she did, she could hear the wings of painted demons beating overhead."

There was a deathly nervous still about the house. Even the ladies' fans had stopped pulsating to and fro.

"Zeus!" exclaimed Lucy, breaking the silence at last. "We never had that sort of thing in Liverpool."

"Everyone, please!" broke in Charles, as another tumult of anxious conversation took wave. "Our guest of honour should be here at any moment. Perhaps we should all get on with the business of hiding, or the surprise will be on us!"

There was a fluster of excitement, and the fear of Indian attack was all but forgotten as the guests dashed about the house, searching for places to hide. The rakish group of officers had settled themselves under the staircase, while Lucy managed to wriggle under the punch bowl table with a little laugh of triumph.

"Not everyone is here yet," I said, taking hold of Charles' arm. "Where are Marlon and Celeste? And for God's sake, where is Jeffrey?"

"I sent your husband round to my place to retrieve some champagne, for a toast later," Charles said. "He will return soon enough. As for my daughter, I regret to say that she is not feeling well. She and Marlon may not make it here."

I was about to say that I was sorry to hear Celeste was unwell, when Darcy came bounding in the door.

"He is here! The Captain has just turned the corner. He's here!"

There was a frantic effort amongst the younger crowd to make sure no one's coattail or dress hem was visible beneath the parlour chairs and curtains, as the less adventurous of the guests ambled towards the back regions of the house to drink claret and wait out the nonsense. There was a general order to remain silent, which was observed only seconds before Lucy was heard giggling beneath the white lace table skirting.

"Oh, for heaven's sake, Lucy," hissed Tim, who was hovering behind the Chinese screen. "What are you on about now?"

"I need the pot," she confessed with a frightful fit of laughter.

"Good evening, Beals. I believe Mrs. Lynford is waiting for me."

Beals peered forward into the shadowy night, and blinked a few times before speaking.

"Mm, I should hope so, sir."

There was a momentary pause. Beals had not budged so much as an inch.

"Might I come in?" Landon asked curiously. "Or is there something wrong?"

"Come in, Captain," I called out rather nervously. "I am here in the front parlour."

I listened anxiously as Landon's footsteps approached, and then lingered in the doorway. All was quiet as he entered the room, his shadow engulfing the far wall, and looming large in the meager light.

"What is going on here?" he asked, his voice a near whisper. "First, I arrive to find Beals acting as if his wig is on too tight, and here you are daydreaming in the dark. Now what, pray tell, does all of this mean?"

Initially, I could not utter a word. It amazed me how Landon dwarfed the room with his presence, and at that moment it was all I could think of.

"I wanted to speak with you—Captain," I said finally, clearing my throat. "I wished to tell you something before we left."

Landon said nothing at first, though he was intently studying my face.

"I just wanted to say—" I stopped. He was watching my every expression like a hawk, and it was making me terribly nervous. I sat down on the sofa at once, for my knees were shaking.

"Just speak to me," Landon said, soothingly. "Tell me what it is you need to say. I do so wish to hear it."

I blushed hotly as he knelt before me, taking my hands; his darting eyes expectant. This was not the reaction I was counting on. No, I had anticipated a witty remark, a clever gesture merely for fun. For this was the way we had always been together, he and I. However, now, things were entirely different. From just this morning, we had changed. Yes, the news Charles brought of Lorena Eldredge had confused me. But no longer. We had changed, Landon and I. I knew this in my heart now. And I was, I must admit, so very glad.

"I read the poem," I stammered at last. And in that blissful moment, Landon and I were the only two people alive in the total universe. "Yes, I read the poem—the one you meant for me."

He replied nothing, but his eyes were asking me a million things. I bowed my head, and recited the verse in a low, tremulous whisper:

I heard ye co'd coole heat; and came
With hope you would allay the same:
Thrice I have washt, but feel no cold,
Nor find that true, which was foretold.
Me thinks like mine, your pulses beat;
And labour with unequall heat:
Cure, cure your selves, for I discrie,
Ye boil with Love, as well as I.

There was a small passage of time in which neither of us spoke. My breath was coming in short, irregular spurts, and I felt near to fainting.

"Landon, I—" I stopped suddenly. What was I trying to do—confess the secrets of my heart in front of some fifty or so guests all stashed away in various parts of the house? Why, for a wild but wonderful instant, I had forgotten all about them!

Landon's response was to lift my hand to where it rested against the side of his face. And when I looked into his eyes, I saw his very soul speaking to me.

"Landon, I—"

"Shh," he whispered. "Do not speak."

He turned the palm of my hand to his lips. Something inside me went hot and cold all at the same time, as my breath stopped short in my throat, and my entire being began to tremble.

"Landon—" I murmured, my voice rendered weak with the overwhelming power of his touch. It was maddening to be made to feel this way—all frightened, and flustered, and giddy. Yes, delightfully maddening. I had never experienced such a confusion of pleasure in my life.

"Landon!" I protested somewhat with fear, for the arduous warmth of his mouth on my wrist was more than I could bear.

"Can all this fidgeting mean my attentions excite you?" he asked slowly, his eyes alight. "Or could you possibly be embarrassed to have Miss Wellman peering out at us from under the punch bowl?"

"Oh!" I cried out, pulling back my hand as indignation coloured my face. "You knew! Oh, you are the vilest, most ill-bred thing. You knew, and yet you let me go on like this!"

There was an awkward pause before everyone emerged from their hiding places with muddled greetings and laughter. I am sure most of our guests were frightfully bewildered by what they had just witnessed.

As for myself, I backed off as several people crowded Landon. I attempted to smile and laugh like the rest, but I could not. The Captain was graciously receiving his guests, however his eyes often returned to me with a gaze filled with wonderment and turmoil.

I had to speak. I had to tell him that I had uttered all those horrid things out of sheer chagrin. I did my best to allow a dozen or so people to surround Landon, telling him this and that and whatever, before boldly making my way to his side.

"I did not mean it," I nearly had to shout, but no one heard us, I am sure. "I did not mean to say you were vile or ill-bred, you know. Oh, Landon, you do believe me, don't you?"

"Yes," he sighed, smiling, but his smile was cautious. "However, Verity, I must be assured of one thing. Did you mean everything you said before that?"

I could have been a lady, and reserved my truth. I could have been coy, and made him guess. However, I haphazardly chose not to be any of those things.

"Oh, yes, Landon. I meant *every word of it.*"

His eyes and his smile brightened. He took my hand quickly and squeezed it. Then, like happy, prattling children who must part at eventide, we were carried off by our separate groups demanding conversation. For myself, I was secretly anticipating the very next moment the Captain and I could be together, alone.

☙☙☙☙

"Tea?" laughed William Collamore, raising his wine glass on high. "Why, every-one knows that tea causes fits."

The gentlemen lounging about the parlour regarded one another with curi-ous expressions, while, from the adjoining room, Valentine Hale chimed away brightly, if not perhaps a trifle harshly, into song:

> *A Soldier and a Sailor,*
> *A Tinker and a Tailor*
> *Had once a doubtful Strife, Sir,*
> *To make a Maid a Wife, Sir,*
> *Whose name was Buxom Joan . . .*

"I believe it was Doctor Thomas Young, who wrote in the *Boston Gazette* that tea brings on the most frightful consequences, such as melancholy, hypo-chondria, and despair; not to mention the fact that it performs a nasty turn on the stomach lining," said Merchant Loring as he reached for a clay pipe.

"You don't say," Edmund Platt mumbled over Val's singing, like a nervous old hen. "My, my!"

For now the time is ended,
When she no more intended
To lick her chops at Men, Sir,
And gnaw the sheets in vain, Sir,
And lie o' nights a-lone,
And lie o' nights a-lone . . .

Roscoe Bennett grimaced as if to indicate that Val's voice was rather offensive, as he ventured to speak.

"Doctor Warren, God rest his soul, went a few steps further by stating that tea promotes spasms, vapors, nervous fevers, and in some cases, cancer."

"Cancer?" quavered Platt, nearly disrupting the entire contents of his glass. "Heavens!"

"What did I tell you?" offered William with an elegant toss of his head. "Fits!"

"Fits?" I exclaimed prettily. "What fun!"

The gentlemen laughed at my lighthearted jest, as did I. Ah, they could have been speaking of rain-water barrels for all I cared. Landon was at my side, and it was all I could do to keep from wrapping my arm through his, and resting my head against him just to know he was really and truly there. Why, even Val's vocalising was close to tolerable at such a happy time.

The Soldier swore like Thunder,
He lov'd her more than Plunder,
And show'd her many a Scar, Sir,
That he had brought from far, Sir,
With fighting for her sake . . .

I glanced in the direction of the music room, and what I saw dismayed me. You were there, Jeffrey, alongside Valentine. She appeared to be dedicating all her energies towards you. Worse still, you were most obviously enjoying her attentions.

"Oh, gentlemen," I stammered above the din, my countenance a trifle unsettled, I am sure. "Please tell me more about the tea incident of two years past. I was in Concord at the time. All we heard was potentially exaggerated gossip—especially when my own dear father rendered it."

"Yes, please; I would like to know as well," Landon was saying, as he took my hand through his arm, and patted it. He had, of course, seen exactly what I had witnessed between you and Valentine, and most likely meant to comfort me. "You see, gentlemen, I was stationed in Niagara at the time."

I tried to concentrate as Charles attempted to relate the history of Boston's tea problems over the hubbub of noise all around us. It had begun in the years following the brutal Massacre of 1770, when Parliament abolished all duties on tea shipped to the colonies. By this action, the small tax on British tea still made it less costly than smuggled tea from Holland.

The Tailor thought to please her,
With offering her his Measure,
The Tinker, too, with Mettle,
Said he would mend her Kettle,
And stop up ev'ry Leak . . .

There was an outburst of coarse language from you and the others in the neighbouring parlour, as Charles raised his voice in order to continue:

"The Whigs attempted to establish a boycott on English tea, but it failed miserably."

"Really?" I asked, glancing towards the next room where Valentine was dancing before you, Jeffrey, holding a silk scarf about your neck as you laughingly undertook to drain your glass of port. The entire episode was despicable.

"That's because their chief buffoon, Johnny Hancock, set a fine example for the rest by dragging in shiploads of the stuff from Liverpool; true Patriot that he was," cited Orrin Blackwell, as he savoured a pinch of snuff.

But while these three were prating,
The Sailor slyly waiting,
Thought if it came about, Sir,
That they shou'd all fall out, Sir,
He then might play his part . . .

"The Tories saw the suggested boycott as an excuse designed by the Whigs in order to have us all swilling rum," laughed Samuel Loring.

"It's a damned sight better than tea," mumbled Roscoe Bennett, dourly. "Why, everyone knows that a healthy splash of rum at breakfast gets the heart pumping. Tea? Bah! Drinking those cursed Chinese leaves makes your eyes go slanty."

"Fits!" interjected William Collamore. "What did I tell you? Fits!"

Our gathering was suddenly startled by the sight of little Lucy tearing through the room as though demons were pursuing her. Squealing hysterically, with her sky-blue petticoat billowing behind her, Lucy was soon shadowed by an obviously intoxicated Tim Gorman. Within mere seconds, they had raced on through to the adjoining room.

"'Tis the season and all," ventured Orrin rather offhandedly, as we regarded him with blank expressions.

"Christmas," he explained with a yawn. "Miss Wellman most likely has some mistletoe pinned to her fanny pad."

> To Loggershead they went, Sir,
> And then he let fly at her,
> A shot 'twixt Wind and Water,
> That won this fair Maid's heart . . .

"Do you care to hear more on the vexing tea situation, Mrs. Lynford?" asked Landon with a sly smile, "Or would you care to take a jaunt around the house?"

"On, no," I replied as demurely as I could manage. "Tea first. Then perhaps a quick run later for exercise."

We had always jested this way before, Landon and I. However, this time, it had a dangerously sweet curve to it—a heated, deeper meaning which, I must admit, I found vastly enticing.

Charles went on to explain the problems of the East India Tea Company, and I interjected an occasional "is that so?" and a "how very interesting" or two, just to show that I was pretending to listen. I was, in part, but I was also rather disturbed by the fact that once Valentine finished with her tawdry song, she took to trying to lick the port from your lips, Jeffrey. Had I any doubts regarding my own behaviour, they were overshadowed by your repugnant actions, my friend. Rebecca had now taken Valentine's place by the pianoforte, and was butchering *A Fox May Steal Your Hens, Sir*, in her best Georgian drawl.

The men in my company were complaining about the tea consignees, who were actually comprised of Governor Hutchinson himself, his two sons, and a son-in-law, to boot. With odds stacked so, there had been no measure of fairness to the other merchants, such as Mr. Blackwell, and Mr. Loring.

I saw the dim glimmer of a coach light filtering through the windows. Moments later, I watched as three mist-shrouded figures floated through the chill shadows, and up our front steps.

"Miss Diana Kirby," began Beals, positioning himself in the doorway where he might be heard to full advantage. "Mr. and Mrs. Marlon Reynolds."

Diana was so very agitated. Her face blazed white with rage; her lips were pursed in anger. The gentlemen were nonplused. Obviously, they had missed something.

However, William Collamore did not. One look at my attire, and then at Diana's, and he could not help but roar with laughter.

"Everything is so beautiful!" sighed Rebecca, wrinkling her nose in appreciation of the fresh pine boughs, bayberry candles, and the vast array of dishes simmering in rich wines and gravies. "Just remember, Papa Charles, my birthday is next month. The third of next month, to be precise."

"I shall try to remember, my dear," he answered with a smile, and I watched as he turned to Diana, who stood as silent as a stone pillar at his side.

"Lovely party, is it not?"

"Hmm?" she murmured, feigning not to hear.

"I said, lovely party, don't you agree?"

"I've experienced better," came the snide reply.

"Diana, really..." Charles began. However, sensing the blatant annoyance so clearly written on her face, he ceased abruptly. It was pointless to go on when Diana was in such a state. Charles Davenport knew, as did nearly everyone else present, that Diana Kirby thrived on animosity.

"What is it, my girl?" he ventured instead. "Surely it cannot have anything to do with finally losing old Hector, now can it?"

Diana laughed aloud.

"What? Remorse over that oily fish? Never! Why, I've thrown him back, you see. And he's all the worse for wear, I can assure you of that."

"Come now, dear. Don't be bitter. Enjoy the dancing instead. It's quite delightful."

It was then that Diana turned and faced me. It was clearly written all over her face what little regard she held for me. I suppose in her mind, I was downright intolerable. To her way of thinking, I had taken away everything that had ever mattered to her—her roles, her audience, and, in a way I had never intended, her men. And now I, a common, lowly barmaid, possessed the insufferable nerve to copy her clothes.

"Diana—"

She veered round sharply to discover Jimmy Sloan staring at her like a lovesick cow.

"What?" she returned callously.

"Oh, nothing really. I just wanted to say hello."

"Then hello and good-bye. I am busy."

With that, Diana took herself past me with such a swift look of derision, my head nearly spun. I watched as she headed straight for Gordon Russell, and they put their heads together, whispering. How childish it all was. Yes, and how childish I had acted when I chose to wear this dress. Why, the purpose did not seem so very important any longer.

"Verity!" I heard Lucy say breathlessly, as she ran up to me, taking my hand. She glanced about furtively, and then went on, her voice a near whisper:

"You must go to Adele at once!"

"Why? Whatever has happened?" I asked, expecting the worst.

"Just go, Verity. Now."

I raced up the stairs, my heart pounding. I had visions of poor old Adele ill; perhaps dying. My brain was echoing things the gentlemen had mentioned earlier . . . spasms, vapors, nervous fevers, fits. It was foolish, really. I had left Adele only a few hours before, and she was just fine.

With my face quite ashen, I am sure, I opened my bedroom door to find Adele hovering over Perry Talbot, as he sat in a chair, a blood soaked towel pressed to his head.

"Adele? Perry? What in God's name is happening here?"

"You might say I've had a little run in with three redbacks," Perry said, grimacing while Adele dabbed at the wounds on his face.

"There's a great deal more than three of them beneath this very roof," I warned, coming over to his side. I put my hand over Adele's, and gently pulled the cloth away. One entire side of Perry's face appeared to have been dragged through a jagged pile of broken glass.

"Who did this to you?" I asked, frowning. "And above all, how did you get here from the Cambridge camp? Do you not realise how dangerous it is?"

"I had permission," he began defensively. Perhaps I was sounding too much like a mother to him. "Besides, not much was going on at camp. Most of the men were sitting around, talking about what it was like to participate in the destruction of the tea, two years ago. You know, in truth, there were around a hundred and fifty men who actually tossed the stuff overboard. But by the number of buffoons bragging about it tonight, you would have to say there was at least a thousand who pretended to be right there in the thick of it."

How strange. We had been discussing the events of two years past in my very parlour. And somewhere across the river, hundreds of men huddled about campfires, doing the same. Only, I suppose they were not drinking champagne, as we were.

"Anyway, I got written permission to slip over here for just one night. I wanted to say good-bye to you."

"Good-bye?" I echoed, grasping his hand. "But where are you going?"

"To war, silly. You don't think General Washington is going to let the Brits continue to hold their grand party here in Boston, when all the truly genteel folks are starving, do you?"

I glanced away, my face colouring with shame. He was right, of course. All around me, decent people were dying from hunger every day. And here was I, a certain nobody, wearing fine clothes and drinking wine with not a single concern for the 'morrow. Yes, what a fine person I was. Just imagine how proud my Papa would be . . .

"I am sorry," Perry said, patting my hand. "I didn't exactly mean you."

"Oh, really?" I returned, looking at Perry's poor, battered face. "Then tell me, who else in this very room did you mean?"

He said nothing. Of course, Perry would not. I took the towel from Adele, and placed it gently against his temple.

"So who did this to you?" I asked. "No lies now; just tell me straight."

"Well," he answered slowly, the hint of a smile coming to his lips. "Back when I lived here in Boston, there was a certain pock-faced Corporal who has been a bit of a foe of mine ever since I cleverly tripped his big butt into the stinkin' mud—accidentally, of course."

"Yes, of course," I chided.

"So now, he's had nothing but vengeance in his empty head, y'understand. And when he just so happened to see me tonight, his foul madness came back on him. That kind of thing comes easily to a Brit. He and two of his less-intelligent companions decided to drag my face through the gravel, just to prove what big, smart men they were. But I got away."

"Thank God for that," I said, standing. "As for now, Perry Talbot, I have fifty people downstairs, probably all wondering where I'm at. More importantly, Celeste Davenport Reynolds is here. Now, you can stay in this room and rest. As a matter of fact, I insist on it. However, I want nothing to happen which enables Mrs. Reynolds to know you are here. Understood?"

"I agree with you on that score," Perry sighed. "Oh, Verity—you must tell me—Is Miss Eldredge here?"

"No," I replied carefully. "No, she is not here."

"Now that's funny," he went on. "She said she would be. You see, Lorena wrote me, and told me that she was going to break things off with the Captain, tonight. Now, I can tell by the look on your face, that you don't believe me. But she did, I tell you—she promised me! Of course, her parents are going to be perturbed, to say the least. But we figured that the hostilities with Great Britain would soon be over, with General Washington now running things. Why, I'd wager that this whole mess of a war will be done with by the spring. And then, Lorena and I will be going to Charleston."

"Are you sure?" I practically whispered, my heart pounding. It was too good to be true.

"Positive, Verity. As I said, Lorena Eldredge promised me that all would be resolved this very night. And when we are happily settled in South Carolina, I want you to come and visit us."

"I should like to," I replied, a wicked image of Landon and myself walking arm in arm up their front steps dashing happily through my brain. "Now I wish to extract a promise from you, Perry. Promise me you will always let me know where you are, and that you are safe and well. You see, I believe this war may go on a little longer than you expected. However, rest assured, it cannot last forever. And when it is done, you will have your truly perfect woman at your side."

"Of course, Verity. I promise you," Perry grinned. "But just one more thing—if you don't mind my saying so—that gown you have on just doesn't suit you. Why, I would even go so far as to say, begging your pardon, of course, that it makes you look cheap."

I turned. Adele's face was horrorstricken, sweet old woman that she was. However, Perry's words had not bothered me. Indeed, all I could think of, as I looked into his sweet and gentle face, is that I might lose a very good friend because of this horrid thing we called "hostilities." How sad a sentiment to have on what was, for the most part, a very pleasant evening. I thought of what Landon had said earlier—the notion of him facing the precipice of his future. Well, this young man was confronting the same, but the valley below him was riddled with war. I had to put it out of my mind for the moment, if only for Perry's sake. So instead, I glanced down at my unseasonable dress, and smiled.

"And I agree with you, Perry Talbot. Why, after tonight, I will most likely never wear it again."

With that, I left, quietly closing the door behind me.

⚭⚭⚭⚭

"Oh, Mrs. Lynford! This is a truly charming party!"

"Perhaps, Mrs. Lynford, you and your husband would dine with us at our Officers' Mess on Tuesday next?"

"In addition, my dear lady, there is a special soiree to be held at the Lyttletons' on the thirty-first, in order to usher in the new year."

Surrounded by a dashing array of soldiers, I leaned against the baluster of the foyer stairs, and smiled like a tenderhearted angel.

"Why, that all sounds so lovely!" I ventured, turning my gaze towards the music room, where Diana's forcibly robust voice could be heard in song:

> *Mortals who Fancies and Troubles perplex,*
> *Whom Folly misguides and Infirmities vex,*

Whose lives hardly know what it is to be blest,
Who rise without Joy and lie down without Rest . . .

"That sounds familiar," opined one officer.

"It should," I replied evenly. "Miss Kirby warbles it at every party."

The men threw back their heads and laughed wildly. It was sly, and stupid of me, I suppose. However, I did not care. Well, I did not think to care, that is, until I noticed that it was Landon Diana was singing to. My goodness, but was I to lose all the men I had interest in to brashly untalented hoydens?

"Madam," interrupted Beals, as he made his way slowly towards me. "There is a Mister . . . mm . . . There is a certain Reuben Cady, in the pantry, to see Master Timothy Gorman."

"In the pantry?" I repeated disapprovingly. "Why? Whatever for? Please have the gentleman brought to the front of the house at once."

"Mm . . . it is a rather delicate situation, Madam, you see—"

Before Beals could venture an explanation, the door to the pantry flew open, and a burly man with a gruff, unshaven face strode into the hall, smelling distinctly of fish and various other unsavoury exhalations of the docks.

"Sir," I began coolly, grateful that half a dozen or so British officers were conveniently at my side. "What might we do for you?"

"I want to speak with Timothy Gorman," he responded in a voice that rasped like gravel. "And I know he be here."

"And what might I tell him is the purpose of your visit?"

With a swift jerk of his arm, the disgruntled man reached out beyond the door, and dragged to his side a young girl, no older than fifteen, whose tear-swept face was barely visible beneath the disheveled tangle of her pitch black hair.

"This be my purpose. This be my daughter, Debra Cady. She and Master Gorman have something very important to discuss. And if that jackanapes won't come out and talk to my girl, I have three of my boys waiting in the street, who will help him make up his mind. So, what will it be?"

Immediately, Landon was at my side. He glanced at me questioningly, and I nodded. At once, Sergeant Stone was sent to locate Tim. And in the few moments the Sergeant was away, I sadly studied the poor girl who was twisting and writhing under the painful contact of her father's strong hold on her wrist. But for the grace of God, I could be like that. Yes, there were so many girls like this one in Boston, with no education, no money, and certainly no future.

Sergeant Stone returned with a terribly reluctant Tim, and no sooner had they appeared did the incensed Reuben Cady raise his abrasive voice once again.

"Mr. Gorman," he spewed, his breath reeking badly of cheap whiskey. "I'd like you to meet your future wife—my daughter—Debra Cady."

"I—I do not understand," Timothy managed with lofty indifference.

"Then I'll spell it out for you, Mister High and Mighty Gorman. I won't have me only daughter nurturing a bastard—a bastard that be yours."

"I would say that would be rather difficult to prove," Tim retorted, as I winced in sympathy for the pitiful girl, whose tears now flowed free as rain. What shame she must be feeling. And in front of all these people, too.

Then Landon's voice was heard, direct and commanding, yet elegantly gentle all the same.

"Are you saying, Mr. Gorman, that you have never had any association with this distressed young woman?"

A hush fell upon the house, as heads turned towards the Captain. He was indeed awe-inspiring.

"No," Timothy answered slowly. "No, I do not deny knowing this girl."

"And do you now deny that this unborn child might possibly be your own?" Landon asked with quiet severity.

A crowd had gathered at each available doorway, as Timothy paused before making his most difficult response.

"No, sir."

Landon addressed the churlish old man with the same formal politeness he would have offered a true gentleman.

"There you have it, Mr. Cady. Now, if you will permit me to do so, I shall make certain that Mr. Gorman is brought round to your home in the morning."

Before anyone could speak, Timothy stepped forward.

"No, Captain Vale; Mr. Cady. I will go now."

Our guests watched in horrified silence, as Timothy Gorman walked out into the cavernous darkness of night.

"Oh, Timothy!" sighed Lucy, adding to the awkward gloom. "You've traded in your utopia for a dunghill piled high with rotted oyster shells."

Charles Davenport waved his hand at the musicians, demanding song, as the foyer emptied out amidst frenzied whispers. I glanced up sadly at the Captain. I feared his birthday celebration was not at all what he could have hoped. From the parlour beyond, there came a merry burst of laughter as Diana related some comical fancy from her days on the London stage. Apparently, Tim's misfortune had rapidly become nothing more than an untimely memory.

"Verity, let us go someplace quiet and talk," the Captain said decisively. His face was troubled. I nodded and took his hand; leading him towards the dimly lit sitting room across the hall. However, this attempt for privacy proved futile, for a select few of the merchants had gathered in this somewhat secluded spot in order to continue bemoaning their uncertain futures.

We found the dining room congested with the more gluttonous members of the party who did not wish to see the highly polished chafing dishes returned to the kitchen unemptied. The merchant Blackwell, and the rum-sodden Roscoe Bennett, were indulging in an endless palaver over the remains of a goose dripping in rich, thick gravy. Then, over in the breakfast room, the merchants' ladies had gathered to gossip about the "loose women" who surrounded them this evening; quickly changing the subject to calash bonnets and polonaise gowns, whenever it appeared that an unwanted person was listening.

"There you are, there you are!" we heard Charles Davenport saying, as he turned the corner and discovered us. "I have been looking all over for you. It is time to gather in the parlour for a toast to our celebrated Captain. Quickly, before midnight strikes, and the birthday has passed!"

So it was that we all joined together with glasses raised on high to Captain Landon Vale. Although I cannot recall his exact words at this time, Charles Davenport delivered the toast in his typically well-versed way. However, it was when everyone had their glasses to their lips that you, Jeffrey, spoke out from the hall.

"Oh, yes—rather," you said flatly; each word stinging with insult. You were so despicably drunk. You were forced to grasp the stair rail in order to avoid stumbling. I was thoroughly ashamed.

Charles deftly raised his glass again; this time to a new toast, and the guests looked on with great curiosity. But I was watching you, Jeffrey. And you were too much the coward to hold my glance. Instead, you motioned Valentine Hale to your side, and you leaned on her, whispering something in her ear that made her laugh. How could you behave so?

"To my new son-in-law, Marlon, and my beautiful daughter, Celeste, who will honour me with the title of grandfather, sometime this coming June."

I turned and looked at Charles, as the room erupted in polite murmurings and applause. What was this? Then I heard one of the merchants' wives saying something about a baby. A baby? Oh, dear God. Marlon's face was flushed with pride—although I think it was an act for the benefit of his audience. As for Celeste, her downcast face was ghostly pale; but her eyes burned with an intensity that frightened me.

I glanced once more in your direction, Jeffrey, but you were gone. I heard the front door closing quietly. And I knew, or I guessed—in any case, I practically ran to the front door. Perhaps I should not have, but I did. I opened the door with near violence. Yes, there you were, staggering down the walk; Valentine Hale in an equal state of intoxication by your side. And I know it seems cruel to say, Jeffrey, but if I had a pistol, I would have shot you both dead in your tracks, and taken pure satisfaction in it.

"That bitch," I suddenly heard Lucy saying under her breath, and I was shocked, for I did not know how long she had been standing there next to me. "That bitch has broken the vow! It's broken; broken! And I shall never forgive her!"

"It does not matter, Lucy," I said quietly.

"But it does! Can you not see? We, all of us, take our pleasures where we find it. But never with our friends' husbands! Never, never, never!"

I reached out and placed my hand on her arm. I had never known Lucy Wellman to possess such heart.

"Perhaps Valentine Hale does not consider me a friend," I said slowly, my voice void of emotion. My eyes turned wearily again towards the walk. Perhaps I had hoped to see you returning, Jeffrey. Someone was walking towards us—no, it was two figures, moving towards our house in the fog. They were speaking to one another, until they saw me standing there.

It was Warren and Mary Eldredge. I do not believe I even tried to smile.

"Good evening, Mrs. Lynford," Warren Eldredge said with false brightness. "I trust Captain Vale is still here."

I nodded, and ushered them both into the house. How rude of them to arrive without invitation. However, I reminded myself, it was ill-mannered of me not to have invited them. I sighed, and now attempted to smile at Mary Eldredge, who hovered at my side. Her husband had disappeared into the crowd, in search of Landon.

"Such a lovely and eventful day," Mary murmured, her eyes fixed peacefully on the celebration before her.

"Yes," I said evenly. However, should the truth be known, the events of this particular day did not seem to me to be so very lovely.

"Perhaps not the weather, of course. But when such great occasions as a birthday, and so on, are commemorated, what is a little rain?" Mrs. Eldredge went on quite cheerfully.

"Yes."

"My daughter, Lorena, is so very, very delighted. She is back at the house now, overseeing the last details for the Captain's midnight birthday celebration."

"How nice," I managed. Indeed, it was not. So this was how the Eldredges repaid my wishes to honour Landon's birthday without them. However, in light of my actions, what else could I expect? Yes, I had been catty and selfish. And now I was to pay dearly for such unpleasant behaviour.

Warren Eldredge returned with the Captain at his side. Landon looked so very tired. He took my hands, and gently pulled me aside in order to speak to me alone.

"The Eldredges have created a quiet little fete for me this evening. Believe me, Mrs. Lynford, I was not aware of such arrangements; otherwise, I would have told you."

"Yes," I said dumbly. I was so very unhappy; and so very close to tears.

Landon lowered his voice and went on, his tone sorrowful and sweet, "In light of the present circumstances, Verity, I think it almost best that I do go."

"Yes," I said. There was nothing left to say.

Warren and Mary Eldredge mentioned something about the Varneys join-ing them. Warren was sent at once to locate them, while Landon walked out the opened door slowly.

I watched as he left. His figure was godlike in the wavering shadows of the night, and the silver of his laced coat and fringed epaulette sparkled with the intensity of stars in the shallow light of the moon.

"We are all so very excited," Mary Eldredge went on, smiling at me as if I cared. "There is so much to do, what with packing the house and all—"

"Where are you going?" I asked, the faintest glimmer of hope burning at the back of my brain.

"Why, Edgecombe Castle, of course. That's the Vale estate, in England. Whether the marriage is to take place in the late summer, or early fall, we have not as yet determined."

"Marriage?" I echoed, not quite sure what had been said, for my mind was rather busy painting a blissful image of the Eldredges moving far, far away.

"Why, the Captain and Lorena, of course," Mary said, and something in my face must have shown surprise, for she laughed in a little, insincere way, and went on, quite confident that she was indeed ruining my life; my dreams.

"Surely you must have known! Why, it has been understood that the Cap-tain would marry our dearest daughter, Lorena, for years now. The marriage is planned to take place at Edgecombe Castle, however, our Lorena opts for London. She is young, you understand, and society excites her."

Mr. Eldredge returned with the Varneys in tow. Then, fortunately for my sanity, they left without assaulting my ears with any more useless and unnec-essary conversation. I closed the front door, and then turned and walked up the stairs like a sleepwalker. There was no need to excuse myself to anyone. No one would care.

I pushed at the door of my room, mechanically. It was as heavy as lead. Once inside, I leaned against the door with a sigh, which was all that stood between saneness and a tumult of tears.

Throwing the bolt on my door, I ventured slowly towards the window. I pulled the cool veil of the drapery aside, and rested my troubled forehead against a chilled pane of glass, seeing nothing; grateful for the cover of darkness. My mind was an empty chasm, and the pain was still so unbearably tight in my throat.

Confused by time, I could have been standing there a brief minute, or all of an endless hour, when Perry Talbot came up behind me and slid his muscular arms about my waist. I did not flinch, or turn, or even so much as utter a sound as he laid his head against my neck and sighed, his warm breath rustling the loose tendrils of hair that played about my cold skin.

Still, we did not speak. And after what seemed to be a long, empty, cavernous void, my mind commenced to react again. But I did not think of you, Jeffrey, or Landon and Lorena—no, only of the young man pressing against me through the slight, flimsy barrier of my dress.

The view from my window began to make an impression on me. Somewhere out there, candles were lit, furnishing a faint beacon against the unknown of the night. I saw the vague outline of rooftops, jutting into the murky darkness of the sky, and I followed with my eyes, the occasional, vaporous billows of smoke which floated upwards like whispers soon forgotten. If I closed my eyes, I could hear the tender exclamations of the night—the slow lap of the ocean as it surged over the virgin sand. Then I did close my tired eyes, drawing myself closer to the boy, lured by the steady rise and fall of his breathing, and finally lulled by the rhythm of his being.

Perry spoke. I opened my eyes.

"I saw you," he said slowly, quietly. "I saw you, downstairs, in the hall when—when Mr. Lynford left—and then again, with the Eldredges. I heard them. I heard it all."

I replied nothing. The torment in my brain raged at me once more, and I closed my eyes, praying desperately to shut out even the tiniest hint of the truth.

"I know it's over," he whispered. "It's over for the both of us."

Still, I did not venture a single word, as my mind tortured me with lightning-like glimpses: My white party dress—The warm glow of the chandeliers overhead and the sweet allure of bayberry—Landon's face as he drew me near to whisper something—Catches of music—Peals of merry laughter—A perfume of pine branches, against the savoury and tantalizing scents of goose and plover drowning in gravy—The clink of silver and glass—The lines of a certain poem: *Me thinks like mine, your pulses beat; and labour with unequall heat*—The seductive warmth of Landon's smile, and the fervent thought of what it would be like to be kissed by him.

"Undo my gown, please, " I said after a long pause. I tried to concentrate on the night outside my window, as I felt his trembling fingers reach round to the tiny hooks of my bodice. I glanced up, desperate to see the stars. They had to be there, hidden and struggling behind the fog-bound clouds. I shivered, but I was not sure whether it was from pleasure, or from the pain that was still so fresh in my heart.

Ever so gently, he removed the robe of my dress, the material of which sent a shudder down my bared arms. Perry's hands, less fearful now, worked at the silken ties of my paniers. I searched in vain for the lone beacon of light. It had vanished. The slight glimmer had yielded to the stronger veil of omnipresent darkness. However, somewhere far above, I believe I finally found the stars.

One solitary tear cascaded down my cheek—a tear, I am sure, that had come from my heart. There were no more to follow. Not yet.

I turned to Perry without a word. But my eyes spoke to him, and he comforted me.

We gave ourselves to each other that night. It was, perhaps, the true death of my innocence. We clung to one another and wept in passion, as outside, the molten stars began to cool and fade away.

Gather ye rose-buds while ye may,

Old Time is still aflying,

And this same flower that smiles today,

Tomorrow will be dying.

Herrick—*Hesperides*

DECEMBER, 1775
THROUGH JANUARY, 1776

I LAY AWAKE in my bed, listening to the mocking call of the chime clock on the mantle. Two in the morning passed; then three and four. Somewhere thereafter, you returned, Jeffrey. I heard your futile attempts at treading lightly in the hall. Your door closed. And then, I slept.

We managed to avoid each other for the entirety of the next day. I sent word through Adele that I was unwell, and needed rest. No response ever came from you.

On the second day, we did confront one another over breakfast. I was silent. You were contrite. How strange it is that people who are sorry for what they have done, will talk endlessly about absolutely nothing at all. You spoke of future parties Charles Davenport intended to have, and rambled on about the hardships your merchant friends were encountering. Within an hour, however, you were conversing about the weather. The weather! Such a safe and stupid topic for two people who, in truth, have not a single thing of merit left to say to one another.

I remember telling you that I did not desire to go to the Davenports that evening. You agreed that we had been out far too often, and a nice, quiet time at home would be welcomed. I imagined you were only saying such things in order to impress me. You then went off to the Varneys, to discuss business;

promising you'd be back in time to take dinner with me.

Not long after you departed, a letter came from Landon. I expected one, actually. Landon had not returned to this house since the evening of his party. In one sense, I was glad. The memories of that day and night still haunted me with the deepest pain. I opened the folded page carefully, and read his words:

17 December, 1775

My dear Mrs. Lynford,

I have taken up tenancy at the residence of merchant Edmund Platt. Their quartered officer perished in the June battle at Bunker and Breed's Hills, and as Merchant Platt's mother is aged and disabled, they were quite uncomfortable alone in the house.

This I have done with your needs in mind. My presence in your home, although constituting some of the most pleasant recollections of my life, has created substantial discord, I fear. It has always been my belief that newlyweds should be left to their own devices, and this I shall do for you very willingly.

I thank you with all the gratitude my heart has to bear for my lovely party of last evening. As the demands of my post grow with each passing day, I can relish your happy event as the last civilised celebration I had the undeniable pleasure to enjoy.

I am . . .
    Madam,
        Your Humble and Devoted Servant,

Landon Vale

I laughed at the notion of Landon's soiree being "civilised." It was a bitter laugh, but at least I had the power to do it.

You returned for dinner as promised, Jeffrey. In addition, you remained throughout the entire afternoon and evening. I answered you in monosyllables, and then eventually, not at all. Strangely, you never seemed beset by my belligerent mood.

The following days and nights played themselves out in very much the same fashion. You were terribly cordial, Jeffrey, and I attempted a weak imitation of your benign spirits in return. But it was no good. You see, whether you realised it or not, you were trying to take Landon's place in my day to day life. Sadly, your barren attempts only reduced me to tears.

I made it clear that I no longer wished to go out—especially to the Eldredges. You did your best to stay at my side and amuse me, Jeffrey; but within a fortnight, I was begging you to enjoy the society of others. I was not, nor did I wish to be, fit company. Happily, you took up my invitation, and left me alone in the house with my thoughts and my grief. I promised that within a week or so, I would accompany you to Charles', but for now . . .

I was trying, Jeffrey. I was trying very hard to forgive, and forget. However, first, I had to forgive myself.

಄಄಄಄

As the chill days of winter set in, food became more and more scarce, for the provincial army did what they could to prevent fresh supplies from entering Boston.

Loyalist-friendly ships came slowly but surely; carrying hogs, sheep, chickens, and ducks, as well as grain and other needed provisions. But during those lean and hungry days of scanning the horizon for the welcome sight of sails, some desperate measures were taken. The King's soldiers raided Cambridge farms, confiscating what livestock they could procure under fire. Strings of warships plagued coastal towns, threatening bombardment if sheep, cattle, coal, and cloth items were not delivered to the docks at once. Back here in Boston, even the old town bull went before the butcher.

Day after day, and night after night, a constant bellowing of cannon-roar echoed through the air. It was the only thing people talked about at the Davenports' these days, where circumstances had cut Charles' entertainments to—as he himself put it—"meager wine and pleasant conversation."

Frightened by the incessant clamour of cannon and musket, your darling Valentine Hale moved herself immediately into the Davenport home; supposedly making herself available as a companion to the sickly and silent Celeste. Diana was also a constant visitor at the house on Garden Court Street. Her association with Hector was finally at rest, and she was bored and lonely. Or so she claimed. It seemed she spent a great deal of time in private conversation with her consort of old—none other than Marlon Reynolds.

So it was where once Charles' company might have been found discussing new plays and books and George Romney paintings, the topic almost invariably turned to cannons, food, and firewood. Half of Boston had been leveled in order that her inhabitants keep warm. Fences were sawed down, as well as old houses and weakening wharves. The stately row of sycamores behind the Brattle Street Church had been reduced to a sad column of stumps. Even the infamous Liberty Tree was no more, for the soldiery despised seeing it from their cluttered camp on the Common.

"Where will it all end?" asked Charles, lifting his glass of slightly soured wine to his lips. "Dear Lord, where will it all end?"

So absorbed in his thoughts was Charles, that he did not see Celeste's painfully incriminating stare.

∞∞∞∞

Watching through the reflection of the looking glass while Eric dressed my hair, I squirmed about impatiently on my bench.

"Hold still!" Eric whined at me as he deftly tilted my head with his light fingers. "Goodness, but you're jumpier than the last healthy hen in the chicken coop!"

Eric Atwood fashioned hair for the ladies of Boston. He was terribly sought after—not only for his fine abilities as a hairdresser, but for his flair for being just as deceptively cruel and emotionally coy as the canting circle of women he attended to.

I glowered at him in the glass.

"You would be skittish too, if you were to face the kind of evening I am about to."

Eric nodded sympathetically in return, as only men of his overly sensitive nature were wont to do.

"Going to the theatre alone, my friend?" Eric asked, clicking his tongue. "My, my! I never thought I would witness the day when Verity Lynford, the great stage goddess, would be reduced to playing the lone swan."

"My husband is in Concord," I explained, attempting my best to sound casual. "His father is gravely ill. So, my companion for the evening is Vera

Davenport—God help me."

"Bring some rolled-up stockings to stuff in her mouth when she gets to snoring too loudly."

"Thank you for the advice," I grimaced.

"It is such a shame Captain Vale is no longer in the house," he began in that lofty air I knew meant gossip was to follow. "Of course, he had to remove himself after the—well, you know . . ."

"No, I do not."

"Oh, my dear! Do you not know what people are saying?"

I shook my head no, which annoyed him. With a slick readjustment to the stance of my head, Eric went on; delighted, I am sure, to unburden himself of the news he so desperately wanted to impart.

"Well, it has been bantered about town that you and your ever beautiful Captain became—how shall I say it without sounding too, too jealous?—far more than friends. Opinion has it that all was fine and lovely until the night of the Captain's birthday soiree in your own home. The hearsay about that little event is that you announced to Vale that you were carrying his child, and he went flying out of the house faster than a twig in a hurricane."

"You cannot possibly be serious!"

"Oh, but I am," Eric mumbled slyly, cocking one eyebrow. "So, is it true?"

"What! Good heavens. Do I appear to be with child?"

"Not yet," was his even reply.

"Well, I am not. It's all foolishness, I say. Oh, why do people always talk so?"

"Be grateful they still do."

I made a sour face at him in the glass. It did not shake him. In fact, I believe it amused him.

"Then tell me, my lonely friend. What provoked your perfectly handsome Captain to leave your sweet little nest, just to take up with a twitchy, old eunuch, and his ancient hag of a mother?"

"It has nothing to do with me," I mumbled, quite sick of the subject.

"Somehow I doubt that," Eric went on, undaunted. "Of course, now that you're no longer fluffing up your counterpane for the Captain, I'm sure Miss Kirby will make another go at him. Diana can be madly driven, when she senses a good show of gold."

"Good luck to her then, for the Captain is currently engaged to the entirety of the Eldredge family."

"Why, whatever do you mean?"

"Oh, Lorena Eldredge, then," I sighed. "Yes, if you really want to know what happened the night of the Captain's birthday—he became betrothed to Miss Lorena Eldredge. That left precious little time for me to "fluff up my counterpane," as you so nicely put it."

"I had not heard," Eric muttered, placing his hands on his hips. "Heavens, but I hear everything. Are you positively sure?"

I shrugged.

"La! There it is," he responded, and went back to the business of styling my hair. "And now, speaking of talk, would you like to hear the latest tittle-tattle about your friends?"

"Oh, why not?" I ventured nonchalantly, and flipped open a box of chocolates in anticipation of a good laugh.

"Well now—you know how Samuel Loring is housing the ladies Stanwood?"

I merely nodded, my mouth full of sweets.

"It seems the venerable Virginia is claiming to hear wedding bells in her future. But it is Eve who is experiencing the fireworks, for it is whispered that Samuel slyly makes his way 'neath her warm, cozy bedclothes nearly every night."

"No, really? Merchant Loring, and the saintly little Eve? Who would have thought it?"

"Very few, and Virginia least of all. Imagine what she would do if she found out! Why, she would probably spit out her last tooth in anger! And speaking of old, have you heard the latest about William Isn't-My-Hair-Perfect Collamore, and the ancient Priscilla Nuttings?"

I shook my head no, my eyes alight with curiosity.

"They are leaving for Philadelphia in a week. Widow Nuttings claims that the siege is giving her palpitations, poor thing. Oh, William refused to go, at first—said he'd rather starve here than rot amongst the Quakers. But then he realised just how painful starving would be, without Priscilla's money. Ooh! Could I have one of those?"

I nodded once again; holding up the candy box to him.

"Delicious!" he murmured, licking his fingers with glee. "And speaking of delicious, have you heard about Val, and her never-ending pursuit of Charles?"

"Who hasn't?" I moaned.

"Well, my dear lady. The fox has been bagged."

I glanced up sharply in the glass.

"What do you mean?"

"Miss Valentine Hale has finally ensnared her golden ram. Lucy told me all about it, this afternoon. It seems that poor Charles at last relented, and sought solace and comfort in the arms of Celeste's kindhearted and selfless nursemaid—none other than our Val. Can you believe it?"

"I don't even want to picture it," I replied, just as a knock was heard upon the door. It was Vera.

"If you're coming, Verity, we must leave now. The piece starts in half an hour."

"Oh, I really do not wish to go," I said in one breath, stretching my arms out before me. "The whole thing sounds ridiculous."

"But General Burgoyne wrote it," Vera protested innocently.

"Then I rest my case," I replied, feigning boredom. In truth, the thought of being in the same audience with Landon Vale and Lorena Eldredge made me thoroughly ill to my stomach.

"I say, Eric," I exclaimed all at once. "Do come with us!"

"But I have no ticket," he responded, his face pleading to go in spite of his words.

"Bah! That poses no problem. For we know all the right people, don't we, Vera?"

Laughing, I slipped my arm through his, and we all went downstairs and out into the still, dark blanket of night.

⚮⚮⚮⚮

The Blockade of Boston was advertised as a rather humorous piece, in which Burgoyne attempted to—as he phrased it in song—"rest on our Arms, call the Arts to our Aid; And be merry in spite of the Boston Blockade."

Frankly, I thought the entire spectacle was rather exasperating.

General Washington was being portrayed as a bumbling moron in shabby dress and a lopsided wig, complete with a long, rusty sword. The Boston radical leaders were also being parodied as a bevy of idiots, practising dual-sided politics as they sang:

> *Ye tarbarrell'd Lawgivers, yankified Prigs,*
> *Who are Tyrants in Custom, yet call yourself Whigs,*
> *In return for the Favours you've lavish'd on me,*
> *May I see you all hang'd upon Liberty Tree.*

Yes, I found myself somewhat annoyed by it all. However, Burgoyne was no fledgling playwright easily run out of town. Such insults just had to be borne privately. Besides, I was the only one not laughing. Seated next to me on both sides, Vera and Eric were roaring so heartily, they sounded close to bursting.

For the most part, officers were in the piece, for Burgoyne, as author, had desired it so. This meant that although Lucy and Rebecca were having the time of their lives, sharing the stage with "Britain's finest," many of Charles' actors were sadly unemployed. In fact, only Darcy and Roscoe Bennett found parts available for themselves.

I sighed, my eyes wandering stealthily about the house. In the dim luster of the stage lighting, I could see Samuel Loring and his two ladies not very far off to my left. Glancing carefully over my shoulder, I could make out the figures of Charles and Valentine seated in the rear of the house, nearby Landon and the Eldredges. How handsome Landon was, with his eloquent face immersed in shadow. There, at his side, sat Lorena in pale comparison.

"Lorena Eldredge," I scowled under my breath. "Of all the people in the world."

Suddenly, one of the officer-actors, whom I did not know, dashed out onto the stage dressed as a provincial Sergeant, and announced breathlessly that alarm guns had been fired. He went on to report that the Rebels had attacked the town, and were at it tooth and nail over in Charlestown. The audience applauded madly, believing it to be a new bit.

"What the deuce are you all about?" the officer-actor shouted with furrowed brow. "If you won't believe me, by Jesus, you need only to go to the door, and there you will see and hear it all for yourselves!"

In a flash, the King's officers stampeded towards the exits. Those who were on stage called out for water with which to wash the theatrical paint from their faces. Voices were heatedly raised against one another, and ladies swooned in the desperate confusion.

"Oh, my!" Vera quavered, her small pig-like eyes quelling up with frightened tears. "I believe I shall faint!"

"Don't you dare!" I snapped, grabbing her arm and nearly wrenching it in the process.

"But the Rebels are such filthy creatures, Verity. Why, I'll be raped—I know it!"

"Oh, dear God!" exclaimed Eric, slapping his hands to his face. "I feel faint, too!"

"Stop it!" I hollered at them both, glancing about nervously as soldiers clambered over chairs, trampling the musicians and crushing their instruments in their wake. The entire hall was in a state of madness, and here I was saddled with a ridiculous old woman and a fidgety fop.

"Land of Goshen!" I exclaimed loudly, just for something to say. And then, I saw Landon Vale.

He claimed to have been waving, and calling out my name, but in the chaos and pandemonium, I failed to notice. What I had noticed, however, was that he had made his way over to us by crossing over the very theatre seats themselves.

"Captain!" I muttered in confusion.

"Good evening, Mrs. Lynford," he returned, arriving at the floor by my feet, and finishing with an elegant little bow. "Such a lovely evening for a battle, do you not agree?"

"Oh, please do not jest with me now."

"Precisely what I was about to say, my dear lady," he went on, looking about over his shoulder:

"Ah! Mr. Loring—might I be so bold as to inquire if you would kindly escort these—" he glanced curiously at Eric, "ladies home? I am afraid I have a little business to attend to across the bay."

"Why certainly, Captain. It would be an honour."

"Good, good. And speaking of business, Mrs. Lynford—perhaps I could check in on you, later—that is, if all outside is the trifle it appears to be. You see, my dear lady, you and I have something very important to discuss."

"We do?" I asked cautiously.

"Yes, we do," he answered with a knowing stare. "Now, if you will all excuse me."

I kept my eyes to the floor until he was gone.

⌒⌒⌒

I was waiting in the front parlour when the Captain arrived at our little house on Charter Street, sometime after midnight.

"What has happened?" I asked quietly when he appeared in the doorway, his shadow swallowing up the dimly lit room.

"The Rebels set fire to roughly a dozen houses across the bay, killing seventeen people."

I said nothing. My guarded expression was unchanged at the news.

"That is precisely why, my dear Mrs. Lynford, you are going home to Concord before the month is out."

"Oh, no!" I objected, finally reacting. This was not what I wanted to hear from Landon—no, not in the least. "Please, Landon—please do not send me home!"

"I cannot, in good conscience, have you stay here," he replied, putting up his hands in protest. "Every day brings us closer to war on Boston soil. And with Mr. Lynford continually absent, you will not be safe."

"I do not care, Landon. Please believe that I do not care!"

"Oh, but you will care. What would happen to you if the town came under fire, and you were in this house alone? Do you think the Rebels would let you be? And I will not be able to hold your hand through it."

"And what makes you think I would ask?" I retorted angrily, hot tears welling in my eyes.

"Verity," he said quietly, kneeling before me where I sat, sullenly turning my head away. "Do not make this difficult. After all, it is you I am thinking of."

I paused a moment, struggling against a great desire to sob out loud. Strangely, all I could think of was the evening of Landon's birthday. He was kneeling before me then, just as he was now. Only then, it was a poem we were discussing, not war. And yes, back then I was near certain he was going to kiss me. But not now. Not ever.

I stood at once, walking away from Landon and from the tender memories that burned in my brain. It was all so bitterly pointless, now.

"This is my house. And siege or no siege, I do not intend to abandon it," I said stubbornly.

"For what cause, my dear? To be blown to bits?"

"What if I convinced Jeffrey to come back into Boston and stay with me?" I mumbled in a defeated tone.

"That would obviously permit me to leave your fair town without fear or compunction as to your well-being. For certainly, Mr. Lynford could get you to move from this place."

"Leave?" I stammered, the gnarled look of hatred vanishing from my face. "I do not understand."

"The King's troops cannot stay here forever, you know. General Howe is already considering his options."

"But where will you go?"

"New York, I believe. We have encountered marvelous support from the Loyalists of that town. Merchant Loring is currently planning his relocation there, as is Charles Davenport."

"I see," I snapped, my ill humour returning. "And when was I to be told about all of this? Did you plan on shouting your farewells from the bay? So much for me, then. I imagine it will be: 'Good-bye, Verity, and good luck!' Bah! I have known better friends, to be sure."

"You are tired and distraught. Otherwise, you would not talk this way; I know it. Seriously, my dearest friend, I would take you with me in a minute. However, I have duties of my rank, and of family, to consider. And there is nothing I can do to change that."

The truth of his words was like a slap in the face to me. Yes, the others would be off to New York, where there would be lavish balls and suppers. Charles Davenport would start up his theatre company again, in one of those elegant little playhouses he was always talking about on Nassau Street, or at Cruger's Wharf. Then, Lucy, Rebecca, and all the rest, would become the cream of society, while I, Verity Lynford, sat alone in my father's taproom, back in boring, old Concord, waiting endlessly for you, Jeffrey, to come home from that vile Gore woman's house. But worst of all was the image of Landon and Lorena kneeling against each other on a cozy little porch, kissing each other with all the passion two hearts had to give, while the rain ran torrents around them.

"It isn't fair!" I sighed, the tears coming at last. "You led me on. Yes, you did; you did! Oh, it just isn't fair."

I did not mean to say what I did, hinting that Landon owed me, a married woman, an explanation as to why our imagined romance went nowhere. Indeed, it was perhaps only my own foolish expectations that believed such an outrageous thing was ever possible.

"Verity—Verity, my dearest, what are you trying to say to me?"

I glanced at him through choking tears. Yes, I was a complete and utter fool to ever manufacture a hope that this exceptional man would ever be in love with me. And now, perhaps, even our friendship had been put to fire.

"Oh, go away!" I managed through strangled tears. "Leave now, Landon Vale. And may I never see you again!"

He did as I asked—but not before pausing at the door and leaving me with one of the most grievous looks I ever saw a grown man give.

In the midst of life we are in death.

Book of Common Prayer

☙

THE INCIDENTS OF 5 MARCH, 1776
AND BEYOND . . .

ORD came from you, Jeffrey, that your father had passed away during the second week of February. I would have left Boston directly to be at your side, but you thought it best that I should not. After all, Stephen Lynford had never approved of our marriage, and there seemed no need to mock him now with my presence. I did feel sympathy for the man, however. It disturbed him, at the end, to be leaving a world which had been agitated by such tremendous turmoil.

At last, you returned to me on the first day of March. To be certain, I was overjoyed to see you. Alone in the house with Celeste's maiden aunt and two ancient servants, my ability to remain calm during indications of full-blown war was ebbing like the tide.

The very next day, on the second of March to be precise, the bombardment of Boston officially began.

The provincials' General George Washington had raised fortifications at Cobble Hill, Lechmere's Point, and Lamb's Dam; thus covering a solid line of territory from Cambridge to Roxbury. Only a few hundred yards away, across the river, the King's men were also constructing new artillery works. It was said that both sides were experiencing the same problem—frozen ground.

The provincials were guessing at a British retreat. Word had come to them from Boston of vessels being prepared for long, hard service; and that a large quantity of biscuits were being baked. It was a likely presumption, for as with the weather, all signs were ripe for the picking.

And so, the cannonading which had begun on Saturday, March the second, continued for three solid days. Like a caged animal, I ran about the house, covering my ears every time a cannonball exploded somewhere in town, rattling the very foundation beneath us. By nightfall, we would join the others from our neighbouring streets, gathering in frightened clusters outside to watch in speechless horror, as the shots streamed overhead like wayward shooting stars spiraling down from the heavens. It was also during these dreadful days of excruciating apprehension that we decided once and for all that a move back to Concord was most definitely in order.

Come Tuesday morning, the dawn revealed that the provincial army had put up two forts on the Dorchester Heights. It was easily shown to the King's baffled Generals that the three days of bombing had been staged only as a diversion to front the true purpose of the Patriots. The sobering sight of these fully manned fortresses with their heavy cannon left the British army somewhat dumbfounded.

General Howe was advised that the King's fleet would never withstand the fire from those batteries atop Dorchester Heights. Indeed, the General was shocked and amazed that such a feat could be accomplished within so short a time. It was said around town that Howe guessed that the work had been rendered by at least fourteen thousand of the Rebel army.

The day of reckoning had come.

⬭⬭⬭⬭

Somewhere around half past four, on that fateful Tuesday, Beals came to me with a hastily scribbled message from Celeste Davenport Reynolds. I thanked him before reading it, and bade him to go to the pantry at once and find something to eat. I had not seen Beals in three whole days, mind you. I believe he was evading bombardment by submerging himself in the root cellar.

Once Beals tottered off, his fingers clenching and unclenching with every nervous step, I walked to the window. Outside, a torrential rain had begun to fall. I held the crisp paper up against the meager light, and read:

Mrs. Lynford,

I am at a most dangerous point. I am overcome with a sense of anxiety, remorse, dread, and anticipation, all at the same time.
There is no one in this house that I can trust. I must speak with you, at once. Please do not fail me, or I shall be forced to take a recourse, the likes of which would astound even my "dearest" father . . .

She had signed it, "Celeste Davenport Talbot."

Without hesitation, I ordered the carriage brought round, and I found my old hooded cape I wore during my days back in Concord. It was homespun; completely worn, and somewhat shabby, but it was far more protective from the perils of a driving rain than the more fashionable ones I had since acquired.

The coach was prepared. I opened our front door against a thrusting wind, and holding up my hand before my face, I ran to the carriage, boarded it, and instructed the driver to take me at once to Garden Court Street.

The wind whistled about the coach, low and mournful and sadly matching my mood. I closed my eyes, not wishing to behold the devastation which had so quickly conquered the town of Boston. Ah, dear Boston. I was a fickle friend. I did not like you when we first made our acquaintance, now nearly two years past. I was a bride then, and I believed my beauty should outshine yours. How silly of me. You, dear Boston, have survived fires, floods, and plagues, only to come back stronger and wiser. It matters not that your churches have been pulled down to make room for drilling troops, or for the Queen's Light Dragoons' horses to strut about in a ring. In so brief a time, new temples will adorn your bright face, and you shall be whole again. And men shall come to worship you as never before.

As for me, my friend—ah, I have not fared half so well. I came to you, in love with one man, and soon shall leave, loving another. My heart, like your houses of worship, has been pulled down and trampled—by my own doing, yes. And were I to have the gift of God's chance to live it all over again, I would cherish every moment I had been blessed with. In this, and only this, would I have the remotest hope of becoming stronger, wiser, like you, Lady Boston. So, please forgive me for ever having shunned you.

The coach suddenly lurched and stopped. Startled, I opened my eyes. Within a minute, the coachman was at the door. One of the horses, it seems, was struck by a roof tile, loosened by the gale. He bade me to wait inside the coach until another conveyance could be sought. But I shook my head no. Garden Court Street was, at present, not so very far away. Therefore, I decided to forge the weather on foot. Time was of the essence, and I did not wish to waste it on waiting for another coach. I directed the coachman to stay with the poor horse until he could be brought to his feet and back to the stables. Then, into a whirl of whipping wind, I took my leave.

It was within moments of my departure, however, that I realised what a fool I was to leave the comfort and safety of my carriage. All around me, debris flew about in the raging wind, and the rain assailed my face like an attack of small nails. Turning about in circles to avoid being hit, I lost my sense of direction altogether. Defeat was something I never wished to admit to, but at this moment, I was going to toss aside all pretenses and seek shelter from this violent storm; if only for a few minutes. Celeste, and her imperial demands, would have to wait.

Most of the houses and storefronts were dark, their inhabitants long since departed for safer soil. Fortunately, just a few doors away, a glimmer of a light beckoned to me through my rain-swept eyes. It was a chandler's shop. A wooden sign above, depicting a brightly lit candle, swung precariously in the grey fury of the wind.

The door was unlocked, and I entered silently. The warmth from the lit candles reached out in welcome to my rain-stung face. The shop was so still. I was afraid to utter a word at first, for it appeared that no one was around. I then shook the rain from the hood of my cape, and as I did so, I heard a faint mumbling of voices. It came from a back room, and it confused me for a moment, for my ears were still ringing with the echo of the storm outside.

I ventured a rather timid "hallo," which went unanswered. Stealthily moving across the wide-board floor, I went towards the voices. The door to the back room was half open, and through it, I could see the shopkeeper and several soldiers moving cordage and baskets of candles to a rear door, where a wagon was being loaded. I was about to announce my presence, when I felt a hand press gently on my shoulder. I swung around in a flash to face my opponent from the shadows, and my eyes widened in shock.

It was Landon.

"Verity—" he exclaimed, and he might have said more, except that my entire being went weak at the sight of him, and he had to come forward at once to my aid.

"Verity, are you all right? Madam, you are ashen."

With overwhelming strength, Landon practically carried me to a corner of the shop where a collection of crates was piled up by a stalwart beam. I leaned against the beam, and loosened my cape, placing it atop the stacked boxes beside me. I found it terribly difficult to catch my breath, and I felt so terribly odd inside. A million thoughts and phrases were running through my head, but I could not grasp a solitary hint of them.

"I never thought to see you again," I said softly.

With the grace of a dancer, Landon removed his regimental coat, and wrapped it around my shoulders, his arms staying close about me. The warmth of his body remained within the coat—yet I shivered, not certain whether it was from the pain that still lingered fresh in my heart, or for the simple fact that the close contact with his coat tantalized me with the image of taking Landon Vale to my bed.

"Mrs. Lynford," he began, and his voice was casual and efficient. Nothing like the tone I adored listening to on the afternoon of his birthday party. Nothing like that at all. "Why are you out on such a violent day as this? And why are you still here? Has not even your own husband the power to convince you that to stay here in Boston means unavoidable peril? I cannot find it in me to understand your folly."

"Oh, Landon," I managed, my eyes welling with tears. "I said so many horrid things to you the last time we were together. I have thought of those moments, over and over, and I have despised myself for the unkind way in which I had treated you. But now I can see, it does not matter. You do not care."

He caught my arms, which forced me to look within his eyes. How searching they were; yet guarded. My head and my heart were reeling with confusion.

"Forgive me," he said, and his voice was low and gentle. "I have been giving orders all day. For certain, Verity, I did not mean to sound officious with you. However, I am concerned as to why you are out in this storm."

"Mrs. Reynolds asked to see me. She is . . . despondent, otherwise, I would not have risked travel in such weather. Indeed, my carriage was disabled, and I walked here. It was not far."

Landon called out to Sergeant Stone. He appeared at once, his face brightening at the sight of me. The Sergeant was then ordered to secure me a coach, and have it waiting outside. Then Landon paused until the Sergeant was truly beyond the chandler's office door, before turning to me once more.

"You must heed what I say," he went on, cautiously. "Tomorrow, we are staging an attack on the Dorchester Heights. If we are successful, we shall prevail in this unsavoury business, and the rebellion will be over. If we fail, then we shall have to evacuate Boston by sea. Now, my dearest friend, I must know, if that should happen—is there anyone who can protect you when I am forced to leave? Please, Verity, I must know."

I wanted to throw my arms about him and whisper that only he could ever protect me. But I did not. So much was lost already. Landon was betrothed to Lorena Eldredge, and I—yes, Jeffrey, I was committed to you.

"Yes, Landon," I said calmly. "Jeffrey will protect me."

"You must be prepared for one thing, Verity. Your husband, Jeffrey, may be accused of aiding us. In that case, is there anyone on the provincial side—anyone at all—who could stand up for you?"

My face coloured hotly as I thought of Perry Talbot.

"Yes, Landon. Please do not fear for that. And let us not waste time on formalities, when really, we should be saying good-bye."

Another soldier came forward from the depths of the shop and reported that the men had finished loading the wagon. Landon instructed him to go on to the docks with the men. He would soon follow. One quick bow to me, and a salute to the Captain, and the soldier was gone—the door to the storeroom closing behind him, and blotting out the light and the noises beyond.

I began to cry.

"Oh, Landon. Why has it come to this? I cannot bear to have you leave me. My heart has come to hold the image of your face, and the sound of your voice as its greatest treasures. And now—oh, Dearest God—"

I wanted to tell Landon that I loved him. But I could not. Why, I could not so much as look into his eyes. All was indeed lost. There was nothing left. Nothing would ever matter any more.

"I cannot relieve your pain," Landon said gently, as he reached into his waistcoat and removed his watch, pulling off the fob and pressing it into my hand. "However, you must be brave, my dearest. And I—I pledge to you my undying friendship and devotion, forever."

Without a moment's hesitation, I reached for the painted miniature of my mother, which I wore always. Removing it, I placed it gently into Landon's hand.

"And I am yours—forever," I vowed, choking back the tears.

Landon put his hand to my chin, and gently lifted my face to his. His eyes were a haven to me; the only true haven I had ever known. Mere moments from now, I would never see them again.

"Landon," I whispered. "Kiss me good-bye."

He wavered for a moment, and his face was troubled. I knew what I had asked was wrong, and I closed my eyes, afraid of the truth; afraid of losing him; afraid of almost everything.

And then I felt the tenderness of his lips against my forehead. It was, perhaps, the kiss he would give a sister, but I did not care. His caress then moved to the bridge of my nose, and then to my temples; lower and lower, until I could not control myself a moment longer. With a sudden boldness I did not know I possessed, I took his face within my hands and kissed his beautiful mouth.

His resistance was momentary. He pulled me closer, and in doing so, his regimental coat dropped from my shoulders to the floor. The strength of his muscular arms and thighs pressing against me nearly drove me to delirium, and I melted at the smooth, velvet taste of his tongue. Yes, Jeffrey. I kissed him. And I was aching to take in all of him, and never once think of you.

However, Landon pulled away. He was right, of course. He was engaged to marry Lorena Eldredge. And I was married to a man who loved another woman, and fornicated with whores besides. Of course, by this particular point in my rather turbulent life, how far different was I? Yes, Jeffrey, be proud. You taught me damnably well.

He picked up his coat from the floor, and slowly walked away. However, before leaving, Landon turned to me, his eyes pleading, I believe, to the message of mine, and he said, "I will never marry Lorena. For I could never make her you."

He paused for a moment, and then left. Like a sleepwalker, I donned my cape and walked out into the storm, and then to my waiting carriage. Strangely, I remember thinking nothing.

⚭⚭⚭⚭

I arrived at Garden Court Street to find Celeste being attended to by Valentine Hale in the sitting room by a sparsely lit fire.

"Leave us," Celeste snapped at Valentine in a tone I would not have previously dreamt possible from her lips. Valentine did leave, but not before giving me one of those snide looks which indicated she had triumphed in seducing my husband away from me. Frankly, I felt like laughing. You were more than entitled to each other, as far as I was concerned.

Celeste was now in her sixth month of pregnancy. For the sake of politeness, I asked her how she was feeling. Celeste merely shrugged and made it known that she would have destroyed the child, had she the means. But now, Perry would just have to learn to love it, for it would be half hers at least.

I glanced at her wearily. Celeste then thanked me for coming in such distressful weather, and asked if I would take tea. She was almost the delightful young lady I once knew. But that image was temporary.

Celeste wasted no time in reporting to me the true meaning of her message. Over tea and cake, Celeste confessed that she had been confiscating funds from her father—funds that she was going to use to enable her and Perry to run off to Charleston in the spring. She had sold some of her mother's jewelry to "discreet" dealers, and had traded off her father's vintage port for cash.

And then she laughed.

"It was the same port I sent over to the Eldredges, the night of Landon Vale's birthday," she conceded. "I thought it would be fitting if I acknowledged Lorena's engagement to the Captain, from both Perry and me."

"You didn't," I said, horrified. "But how did you know?"

"Oh, I visited Miss Eldredge, you see, a few days before your party. We talked. I convinced her that Perry really loved me, and I pointed out the advantages of securing her name to that of the Captain's as soon as humanly possible. The Eldredge family, you see, is fearful of any spoken slights aimed at their rather precarious reputations. Oh, what an empty-headed fool Lorena is! However, I praise her idiocy all the same. For don't you know, her quick and dirty engagement to the Captain only left Perry hurting, and in his pain, he has turned to me!"

"Have you heard from Perry? Has he spoken of his feelings for you?" This I asked with supreme caution. There was much to fear from this girl.

"His feelings have merely been implied. This, I understand completely. The post, you know, is constantly intercepted at Boston Neck. Obviously, my darling is mindful of our personal, and ever perilous, situation. Therefore, he has sent only one letter; the words of which are seemingly those from a friend. He dares not intimate more. However, he does love me. Of this, my heart is certain."

Silently, I could not agree with her. You see, I had received two letters from Perry; private missives really, which I shall share with no one.

"Now, this is where you come in, Mrs. Lynford. Once this war is over—and my dear friend, Captain Edmund Ferrol, insists that it shall be very soon—you must have Perry Talbot to your home. You see, I know Perry has been there before. And I shall meet him there, baggage, and money, and all. Then, he will know with all the power my love has to give that we have no other choice but to be together. It shall be glorious."

Aha, I thought. Captain Edmund Ferrol. Oh yes, Celeste, only a conniving young woman such as yourself, could see Captain Ferrol as a fine friend indeed.

"My only ploy in this perfectly happy plan is this blasted child," Celeste went on, casually. "But alas, it cannot be helped."

"I see," I said. However, I was no longer truly listening. My mind was going back to a night nearly one and a half years before. It was the night I met Perry Talbot at the Salutation. Only, it was not Perry I was thinking of. It was Lucy Wellman. Yes, on that memorable evening, little Lucy Wellman was talking about the ridiculousness of women who never let on to the men they were secretly in love with. And it struck me all at once, like the fiery tip of a lightening bolt. I had to abandon all rules of decorum, and find Landon this very afternoon, and tell him from my heart that I loved him. It was that simple.

But dare I? Dare I risk all that was supposedly sacred, merely to apprise a man who is betrothed to marry another, that I wanted him to throw all of that aside for me? What of honour? What of duty? Such things were of vast importance to a gentleman. Then I remembered the words Landon spoke to me in the chandler's shop, just one scant hour before—he would never marry Lorena. Yes, he said he would never marry Lorena Eldredge because he could not make her into me.

I stood at once. I believe Celeste was startled by the intensity so plainly written on my face. It was then that I thought quickly. In Celeste's purely selfish state of mind, she would easily believe any promise I made in her favour. So, I did. I stood there in Charles Davenport's parlour, and vowed to this arrogant little girl that I would assist her in her plan to steal away with Perry Talbot. Of course, I was lying to her. And I lied to her without a single shred of remorse. After all, I was making a pledge against a tomorrow that for many of us could be quickly altered in the twinkling of an eye.

It was then that I saw that tomorrow. When Landon heard from my own lips that I loved him, everything would change. There would be problems, of course; but we would be together. And what of you, Jeffrey? Fear not. With your father's money now firmly in your possession, Avella Gore could easily be bought. Like the oldest and most sour apple on the tree, Avella Gore would fall into your hands with avid enthusiasm; just as long as your wallet was always plainly in sight. Such cozy solutions for us all, really.

I left, my entire being trembling with a vehemence I had never known. The storm was still raging, but it was nothing compared to the raging of my heart. I searched the docks, and the streets, and finally, I bade the driver to pause while I went to the officers' headquarters. However, Landon Vale was nowhere to be found. I could have pushed on, but I knew I could not detain the driver any longer. Thoroughly dispirited, I was forced to give up, directing the coachman at last to take me home.

You were waiting for me, Jeffrey. You were remarkably distressed about my being out in such rough weather. I thought perhaps that once you knew I was safely home, you would leave, but sadly, you did not. I wished you would. You see, I was going to go out again, on my own. I was ready at that moment, to walk out of this house and never see you again.

It did not happen that way. You stayed at my side constantly. It was as if you knew. And when I started to cry, you did not ask me the reason. I believe that if you had, I would have told you everything. Instead, we sat silently together in our fussy little parlour, while from the dark recesses of the hall, the clock haunted me with its inevitable portent of passing time. Like a mocking enemy, the rhythm of its pendulum took over my mind chanting: "all is lost, all is lost, all is lost."

∞∞∞∞

There was a hint of battle that very day. The British answered the taunts of General Washington by dispatching five regiments out to Castle William, while six more were called upon to parade at seven in the evening, and then prepare to embark at Long Wharf. From the other side of the bay, the provincials cheered them on, ready for a fight.

However, the tide had turned late in the afternoon, and the wind was picking up steadily. Flat-bottomed transport vessels were being tossed back against the wharves, and an attack seemed all but hopeless. While the night seethed with storm, General Howe and his commanding officers opted for a complete evacuation of the town.

Come Wednesday morning, General Washington and his troops watched in bewilderment as the British sailed away from Castle William and back to the safety of Boston. Washington could only assume that the sight of the formidable fortresses had frighten them off completely.

The King's troops did not evacuate on the eleventh of March, as rumoured, but nearly one full week later; taking with them a little more than one thousand Tories.

In the ten days that General Howe gave these civilians to pack up their things, these fine families of Boston had been thrown into utter turmoil. Space on board the transport ships was extremely limited. Already, such items as household furniture and bits of luggage were floating about in the bay, having been hurled overboard at Howe's orders.

Despite the General's issued warnings against damage and fire, plundering and destruction flared on uncontrollably. His soldiers were ordered confined to their barracks early each evening, hoping to keep drunkenness and disorder to a safe minimum. However, with all the uproar and confusion, these wayward soldiers managed to wreak havoc just the same. Even the stately portraits of the King and Queen, which hung in the Town House, had been ripped and grossly defaced.

So it was that on the seventeenth of March, they were gone. Or so we thought. It was not until four days later that we learned a detail of the King's men was sent upon Castle William, in order to destroy the island fortress. And then, a great mishap occurred. A mine exploded prematurely, taking the lives of seven men. Captain Landon Vale was one of them.

And now I am here, in Lorena Eldredge's home, surrounded by costumed mourners who cannot possibly conceive what it was like to know, and to love, this very wonderful man.

Yes, now I am here, alone. And all is terribly lost.

One is easily fooled by that which one loves.

Moliere—*Tartuffe*

⚭

21 MARCH, 1776 . . . AS THE NIGHT
CLOSES IN

"VERITY, my dear—Verity, are you all right?"

I looked up and focused on your face, Jeffrey. Slowly, the hushed whispers of mourners returned to my ears. I glanced about, blinking. By all indications of the quarter chime clock, I had been lost in my memories for nearly two hours.

"Verity, dearest wife. Are you ill?"

"No," I managed to say, my voice nearly all but gone. "I—"

I did not finish my thoughts.

"Come, wife. We are going home. It is nearly eleven."

I nodded. You patted my shoulder gently, and left with the purpose of calling for our coach and getting our things. I looked down at my right hand. It was clenched, and terribly cramped. I tried to open it, but my hand was void of its typical senses. Slowly, I worked the fingers until a release was reached. Within my hand was Landon's watch fob. I had been holding fast to it, the entire evening. The impression of it seemed to be permanently etched in my hand.

I stood slowly, and looked about. Many of the visitors had departed. Lorena had moved closer to the fire. Next to her sat a young man I did not recognise. He was whispering something in her ear, which made her laugh ever so lightly. Who was this untoward gentleman? Then, I watched in mystification as Lorena placed her hand within his, and leaned her weary head against his shoulder. It reminded me of a day—oh, nearly a year gone by now—when I sadly observed Landon and Lorena, speaking softly together on a bench by my father's flower garden. How fortunate for Lorena that she could continue her polished performance when her typical leading man has, without warning, been suddenly replaced.

We bid our quiet farewells to Warren and Mary Eldredge. Side by side, they appeared to be completely benumbed. Despite the hollow vacancy in her eyes, Mary Eldredge regarded me with a gaze which told me at once she knew of my attachment to Captain Vale, and that it was stronger than any bond her daughter may have thought she enjoyed with him. However, what did it matter now? Nothing mattered now.

We went home in silence, Jeffrey. You held my hand. We went inside our dowdy little house on Charter Street—soon to be no more the haven of my remembrances, and you lit the fire in the parlour. Then you bade me to sit.

"Verity, we must speak," you said. "Perhaps you feel that now is the least opportune time. However, I feel it is best. You will understand, I know."

I said nothing. I did not even nod. I sat in the wing-back chair closest to the fire and accepted the glass of port you handed me. I took a sip. Its nectar offered me no particular sensation—pleasant, or otherwise.

"When I first met you, Verity, you made an impression on me which, at the time, I did not quite comprehend. Oh, I knew you were taken with me. It was written in every action you made, and every word you spoke. Perhaps you could characterise me as an egotist, to say such things. But it was true, was it not? And I was, I will admit, rather flattered by your attentions. You see, women of my class never made very much of me.

"However, at the same time, I was deeply infatuated with Avella. You knew all of this. Why, I had so much as told you directly. And there is no sensible reason to expound upon it now. Suffice it to say that this grandly foolish affection continued to possess my heart until as late as last Autumn. I will say no more, as the entire, distasteful subject should now mean nothing to you. We are free of her, at last, for I have seen the woman for what she was, and what she is. And I will brook no further association with this creature. Her image is now blackened on my heart."

You looked into my face, anticipating some sort of approval, I am sure. However, I merely shrugged. I always knew what kind of a woman Avella Gore was. Why, more than half the town of Concord knew as well. So for you to make such a simple discovery this late in time, gave me no noticeable sense of satisfaction.

"I must, if you will permit it, go back to our earlier days, when I frequented your father's tavern. I am a man, Verity, who all too often finds his refuge in drink. I have been aware of this ignoble side of my nature for quite some time now. And I have, on numerous occasions, made an effort to put a end to this inexcusable pattern. However, I have so often found myself powerless before the lure of a bottle. I do not know how to explain it really. Perhaps it is just that drink has the ability to enhance my expectations. And when they are not met, drink has the mastery to excuse them. Does that sound so very strange?"

I shook my head no, and then stared into the flames of the fireplace. I was grateful that you did not require too much of my opinion. Thus far, I had little to give.

"That is why I was forever drawn to your father's taproom. To be quite frank—at first, your continual need to converse with me was somewhat annoying. But I will say, that was only at first. Over time, I found myself coming to seek out your company. Your humour and wise advice worked on me like a tonic. I can see, only now, how very happy you made me then.

"I—I was not attracted to your appearance, my dear. How laughable to say, really—for when I gaze upon you now, I can so readily see the grace and beauty most men would go to war for. Ah, how damnably funny that I should say that just now."

I looked up sharply at you. Thank heavens you were pouring yourself another glass of port, or you would have for certain recognised the pain your words had so callously flung at my heart. I downed my port quickly, a slight glimmer of feeling racing through my veins. Oh, Landon, I thought. And then I thought no more. You poured me another glass, and went on:

"Indeed, my dear, I admired your mind. Is that so profane a compliment? Are women so very vain, that it is worthless to be admired for vast wit and intelligence alone?"

"No," I managed to say. Why, only a few short months ago, Landon told me he admired my brain. Of course, he was laughing when he said it. Yes, Landon said he adored the powers of my mind, when I was not being foolish. That is what he said. I had not thought less of it through his words.

"So, when I married you—no, perhaps I should say, when I asked you to be my wife—it was something else altogether that prompted me. Oh, Verity, please do not be wounded when I confess this to you—but on the evening I asked you to marry me, my mind was in a complete mix as to why I had even ventured such a proposal in the first place. I did not love you—not in the unbounded and whole way a man should love a woman he is to spend the rest of his life with. However, I will say this, my sweetest friend—at least my heart knew then what I have come to realise myself, now. You, and you alone, are the only woman I ever truly loved."

You paused. I said nothing. I believe you were momentarily disheartened that I did not fling myself at your feet in gratitude. Oh, I might have—a year, or so, ago—but time has a way of making one older and wiser.

"When we first moved here to Boston, I was admittedly apprehensive. I did not believe you would fit in with a society such as the likes of Charles—or in completely reverse circles, the Eldredges, or the Varneys, or the Kings. Forgive me, but I saw you as an unsophisticated woman from the country unable to do, and to say, the proper things in front of proper people. Oh, how very wrong I was! You not only fit into these groups, but with your charm, and grace, and endlessly amusing wit, you compelled them all to crawl to you. I could not believe it. I should have, though. You see, Charles Davenport himself once hinted at the very power you hold behind those magnificent eyes."

I glanced at you, but still I said nothing. Of course, I remembered it all. I was eavesdropping around the corner in my father's taproom; listening to Mr. Davenport praising me up and down like an alluring statue roped off at arm's length in some private gallery. My only hopes were that his words would make any sort of a favorable impression on you. Well, at last they have. I was, strangely enough, at this very moment experiencing a wee mite of compensation at your praise. Perhaps indeed my senses were returning to me.

"Such a confusing time, those early days of our marriage. It is difficult for me to explain, even now. I was—so very happy—in the beginning. Marriage was as new to me as it was to you. Would you consider me boastful to concede that I adored the attentions you lavished on me? But then, you became intensely infatuated with Charles, and Lucy, and all the others. The point I am trying to make is that they took you away from me. I did not like that."

The fire required another log. You tossed one on, paused to pat my hand, and then continued:

"That is when I began writing to Avella. How foolish of me. And my admission of my actions to you only drove us further apart, Verity. I then believe, in your hurt and confusion, you set out to challenge me by being, and doing, all the things I disliked the most. And I was left to watch what little fiber we possessed, get ripped and torn carelessly, day after day after day."

Ah, yes. I remember that conversation, too. You had told me you were in love with Avella still, and you were even so preposterous enough as to make it my concern to correct the path of your heart. What a laugh! You timidly demanded that I begin to look, and behave, differently. Yes, I remember it all. And now, you intimate that I *challenged* you by doing exactly what you asked me not to. You, Jeffrey, of all people, should be thoroughly aware that when you scold a true drunkard for drinking, he shall only curse you by drinking more.

"What did you expect?" I asked softly. My voice neither incriminated nor excused. It was far too late for judgments now.

"I was completely and utterly wrong," you answered with quiet and calm sincerity. And then you knelt before me, your eyes wholly expectant.

"So, what are we to do now?" I sighed, and put down my port. I did not wish to have any more.

"But, Verity, my heart's darling, that is the beauty of it. We need not do anything. I love you. That is what I am trying to say. I love you with all the power and depth my heart has to give."

I peered deeply into your eyes. How pleasant they were—fawn-brown, and innocent, like a child's. The colouring of your skin was so very noble— you looked like a Roman god on a shiny coin. Yes, you were still very hand- some to me, Jeffrey. However, I was then to remember that face, and how it turned all its romantic attentions towards yet another.

"And when did you decide you loved me, Jeffrey? Was it after your infatu- ation with Avella Gore—or during your affair with Valentine Hale? Or have I, perchance, factored your timings ill?"

I watched the change in your face. It was easy to see that you did not wish me to mention that horrid woman's name. Well, I have, Jeffrey. And I doubted that any explanation you could give me on this score would prove satisfactory.

You stood and went to the side table, pouring surely your tenth port of the evening. It was just as well. I did not wish to look into your face any longer. My feelings for you were becoming terribly confused. Like the wings of a bird, they soared high and happily one moment, yet crashed down with disap- pointment to the coldest murk of the earth, the next.

"Of that subject, I am thoroughly ashamed," you were saying as you stared plainly at the wall before you. "Oh, Miss Hale flattered me well. She told me how wonderful I was; how smart, and how very wise. She tried, I believe, to take your place."

"You seemed willing to let her," I observed dryly.

"I could not help what I felt," you said, turning on your heel all at once. "You see, I did not know how to deal with Captain Vale being in love with you."

My face paled. I reconsidered my need for a drink, and reached for my glass.

"You do not deny it then?" you asked with icy suspicion.

"The Captain's feelings are—were—never mine to confirm or deny."

I believe my sense of calm alarmed you, Jeffrey, for you returned to my side, taking my hand and holding it to the side of your face.

"Verity, please understand how completely destroyed I was made to feel. It took months, perhaps, I know, but the day did finally dawn when I realised you were the true object of my heart's desire. But I was too late, wasn't I? When at last I opened my eyes, it was Landon Vale who brought you your coffee at breakfast, and it was Landon Vale who walked with you on quaint and rustic afternoons. At supper parties, it was always Landon Vale who sat at your side, and who whispered private thoughts in your ear. There was never a corner of our lives together, Verity, that I did not turn and see Captain Landon Vale there, beside you.

"You cannot tell me you never came to feel the same way about him. It showed in your face, your words, and your manner. You were in love with him, too. Yes, I heard from practically everyone present about your behaviour the night of Vale's birthday, before I arrived from Charles'. Was he in on it, too? Was Charles Davenport conspiring against me? Oh, he is exactly the sort to unite his favorite stage decoration with a celebrated soldier, just to spite me. Davenport has a way of doing such things, just to keep his so-called friends constantly in awe of his twisted talents. That is why he was forever putting the two of you together at his drunken social parties. That is why he sent me out for champagne on the evening of your Captain's birthday. How pleased everyone was, to tell me of your happy conquest. And how amused they were, to see me played for a fool."

"So you demonstrated your newfound title by abandoning the party with Miss Hale in tow?" I asked directly. I did my best to lessen the venom in my voice. After all, my "conquest" of the evening—although not with the man you believed it to be—was still somewhat equal to your pathetic transgressions.

"My evening with Miss Hale was not at all what you might expect. You see, she made it quite clear to me that her tender affections were valued at a rather high price. I realised, all too late, just why she had praised me so. I imagine she believed my fortune to be greater than it was. That settled things; I left her little hovel somewhere after midnight, and walked the streets, dazed and disillusioned. However, I made a vow during those silent, agonizing hours that I would win you back. Understand, dearest wife, that you are worth it to me. Somewhere around four in the morning, a rather peevish sentry advised me to take myself and my pitiful mood home to bed."

I ducked my head. Was I really to believe you? If all this were true, then I was the Judas of this union. It was neither funny, or ironic. No, I told myself—if I was the only one to wander outside the bonds of our marriage, I was nothing short of damnably despicable.

My face heated with colour, and I wanted to cry. Oh, Jeffrey, how could these hateful things have ever happened to our love? Perhaps the true fault was that our individual devotions were never equally matched. Our love never walked hand in hand; indeed, my feelings ran hard and fast before yours, once upon a time. However, now, you admit a need to maintain my heart's pace. What was I to say? Would you want me now, if you were to hear exactly what I have done?

"You are angry with me because I have condemned your beloved Captain," you went on, and your voice was gentle. "Forgive me, darling. You see, I had vowed to myself I would not even so much as mention his name tonight. Up until the very moment these indignant words flowed from my lips, I swore not to thrash out the hurt I endured because of him. The true purpose of my talking to you this evening is that I love you, Verity. I need not try. I love you with every ounce of my being, and I shall never stray from the sweetest gift of your affection—that is, if I am indeed auspicious enough to be rewarded with your trust once again."

"Oh, Jeffrey—" I managed sadly. Beyond that, I did not know what else to say.

"I do wish to tell you one very important story about your Captain Vale. He came to see me, during the cannonade—oh, perhaps the third or fourth of this month. Regardless, my dear, the point to all this, is that Vale made me an offer of a post in New York, provided of course, that the King's regiments settled there. He mentioned a position as a mediator, of sorts, for any provincial prisoners taken there. Captain Vale was not at leave to furnish me with all the details of the offer. However, if I had further interest, I was to see a certain Lieutenant Colonel Dane. This I have done."

I looked up at you, somewhat bewildered.

"My heart's darling, there is so much for us to think over, and discuss. And I wish, most of all, for you to consider the vast importance of our future together. For apart, we are nothing—and I am worse still. So please, think about us first. And when that puzzle is solved, you may determine whether we go back to Concord, and live in my family's home, or, go to New York, and renew our love, and our lives, to the happiest degree."

I smiled, my eyes brimming with tears. I then took your hands, and kissed them.

"Yes, Jeffrey. Let us talk more, tomorrow. For I am so very tired."

"Then I will leave you. Will you be all right?"

"Yes, Jeffrey. I wish to stay here by the fire for awhile to finish my port, and think."

"Then goodnight, my love," you said, going to the stairs. However, you paused and turned to me and said, "Verity, I have but one question, which will finally settle the soul of my heart once and for all. And your answer should be only the truth, for I believe I can bear it either way. Did you truly love him?"

Had I the strength and courage of a fool, I could have related all to you, Jeffrey. Yes, I could have begun with the recollections that swept through my mind just a scant few hours ago, at the Eldredges' home. But I failed you, Jeffrey. "To thine own self be true," Shakespeare once said. And now, coward though I may be, I knew that my heart's memories would remain locked within my silent heart forever and evermore.

"Captain Vale was my friend," I replied quietly. "You see, he reminded me of everything that is important in life."

"I accept," you said softly, and then disappeared up the stairs.

I sit, staring at the fire, and I envision the pleasant life we now could have, Jeffrey; New York will be our choice for the future, for I see nothing of good in our returning to Concord. There, we will associate with Charles Davenport, to a certain degree. More importantly, we shall have children. First, a darling little girl who will be very much like you in looks, Jeffrey. Then perhaps, a second girl, who will come to be a terror like myself. Lastly, your son. We shall be content. You, Jeffrey, will happily have the wife that you asked for. Yes, I believe I could now look and behave as you wish. It does not seem so very difficult a request. In return, I shall not only have your devotion, but best of all, the most tender remembrances of a secret passion that once ruled my heart.

My heart. Yes, suddenly, the messages of my heart are swiftly overtaking the calm instructions of my head. I am not in love with you, Jeffrey. It is Landon I am in love with. It is Landon I want to be with.

I stand. My knees are shaking, but a force within me, which I do not comprehend, practically propels me towards the hall. I take my cloak from the bench, and stride outside our door. Yes, my entire being is trembling, and a tense knot has coiled itself tightly inside my chest, but I am not afraid. I pause—only long enough to breathe in the heavy fog-bound air of the night—and then whatever it is that leads me, entices me to continue on.

I hasten down Charter Street; my every step determined, and my mind an empty chasm. I never see another soul. Yes, I walk, unafraid, all the way to the beach at Hudson's Point. And there, before me, lies the sea—those vast and treacherous waters which have taken my Captain away from me.

Something remaining of the woman I once was, cautions me not to venture another step. However, a small, gentle voice in my heart bids me to come closer, closer—closer, still. Yes, even the faint, yet omnipresent horizon is whispering my name, and below my feet, I believe I hear the sounds of happy laughter calling out from the rippling tide, as it rushes headlong against the sand.

I face this spiteful ocean. But it does not frighten me. No, indeed, it now lulls and soothes me with its rhythmic beckoning. Atop the endless waves, golden shimmers of light dance before my eyes. It is like the light from Landon's eyes, when he smiles at me. And then I know, without fear or trepidation, that with a mere few steps, I will be with my Landon once more. The coil of pain, which had wrapped itself so tightly about my heart, begins to lessen, and a sense of serene peace overwhelms me. Yes, in only moments, we shall be together for eternity, Landon and I. I am content, at last. I am not afraid to go.

I walk into the shallow waves. I do not even feel the cold. How could it be cold, when Landon is somewhere out there, waiting for me? The weight of my drenched gown begins to hinder my steps, but it does not matter. Soon, such things shall never matter again . . .

"Mrs. Lynford! Oh, dear God—Mrs. Lynford—stop!"

Startled, I turn. A man, whose face is partially disguised by a black, unlaced hat, is running towards me. Something of reality cracks through the calm resolution of my brain, for I immediately scream, and attempt to break away from my unwelcome assailant.

"Mrs. Lynford—please! It's me, Sergeant Stone. Oh, please, Mrs. Lynford, for the love of God—"

"Sergeant Stone?" I question, my voice barely audible. "But why—how—"

He pulls me from the churning waves. I do not fight him. Indeed, at this terribly confused and unearthly moment, I cannot be altogether sure just what I had been doing by striding recklessly into the tide.

"Sergeant Stone," I manage again. This time, I look at him with some sense of comprehension. Strangely, he is not in uniform. He is wearing a cloak of blanket wool, and his clothes are worn and ill-fitting.

"What—what has happened?" I ask, as if slowly coming out of a trance. "Why are you here? I believed you to be dead, too."

He leads me towards the shore, his grasp firm, but gentle, upon my arms.

"I'faith, Mrs. Lynford, I should have been in a boat, pulling for the frigate in King's Road. However, when I heard the news of the death of Captain Vale, I had to come straight to you."

"I—I don't understand."

"I was outside your house, trying to think of some way to get your attention without knocking at the door, when you came out. Your face was so strange, I could not bring myself to disturb you just then. So, I followed you here—and thank God, Mrs. Lynford. Whatever were you thinking of, walking into the ocean like that?"

"I'm not sure," I reply, my teeth chattering in the cold. The Sergeant then puts his woolen cloak about my shoulders, and continues to speak:

"Oh, Madam, I must tell you about the Captain. After what I had done to you, following the battle on the Charlestown hills—and then—this. Yes, you have to know. They all think the Captain blown to pieces, but I know better. He went back into the fortress, looking for me. We were just about through the north gate when the mines went up. Captain Vale and I were blown clear into the water. I saw a Navy jolly boat pick him up, but I was too weak to holler to him. A fisherman pulled me in, just as I was about to surrender all to God. He was kind enough not to turn me over to the Rebels, but he bade me not to stay in his house any longer than necessary. He gave me these clothes—

they belonged to his brother who was killed on Breed's Hill.

"I have told no one about Captain Vale. However, have faith, dear woman, for he is alive. But only you and I know. And it must remain our news, and our news alone—for it can be no other way. Now, can you accept this burden, Mrs. Lynford? I must know."

I nod dumbly. The Sergeant still holds me awkwardly by the arms. But I cannot mind—no, indeed, he has saved my life.

"I cannot stay, Mrs. Lynford. If caught, I will be put to trial, and face certain death. Now, come away from this place, Mrs. Lynford. I will see you home."

"No, Sergeant. Please take care of yourself. I am fine. You were so good to come to me, but now, you must run away. I will not do anything foolish—not now—not when I know—"

I cannot finish my words. I almost cannot bring myself to believe that my Landon is truly alive. Perhaps this is all a vicious dream. But it couldn't be. I feel so very cold.

"Go, Sergeant!" I say, releasing myself from his grasp. "Go, and God be with you, my friend."

"Until we meet again, Mrs. Lynford, I give you good night. God save you, Madam. And God save the King!"

I watch as he leaves. And when he is gone, I turn towards the sea. It is at this moment that my heart leaps from my chest to my throat, and I begin to tremble. But it is not just from the cold. I try to think, to comprehend all that has happened; however, I am completely powerless.

Instead, I gaze out towards the dark and dismal horizon. I am reminded instantly of the night of Landon's birthday—that sorrowful night when I saw him leave me—his figure godlike in the wavering light of the sullen moon. And then, later—later that evening, as I gazed out my bedroom window, so desperate to see the stars. I looked above my head now. The fog had cleared, and yes, the stars were there, etched like rays of hope against an uncertain sky. And I am comforted.

The sea begins to call to me once more. However, this time, it is not with hidden malice. No, indeed, it is a most wondrous sound. And then, an image comes swirling out of the mist; dancing before my eyes.

It was the very night Captain Landon Vale was introduced to me at Charles Davenport's supper party, which had been given in his honour. I saw myself standing in greeting to him. Previously, I had not been able to recall the words that passed between us. And that fact had troubled me deeply. However, by some sweet miracle of fate, the sounds of our voices reached out to me from the mystical waves, and I was to hear it all again, as if it were for the first time.

Landon—oh, that is a lovely name. May I assume it is your mother's?

Why, yes, dear Lady. You are correct. However did you know?

Because, sir, we are two special people in a very lonely world, who hold a fond devotion for their dear mothers.

Then divine intervention has played its part, Madam, and brought us here, together.

Yes, Landon. I am here. And I am waiting for you.